TINDR

BOOK FIVE

THE CIRCLE OF
CERIDWEN SAGA

TINDR

OCTAVIA RANDOLPH

PYEWACKET PRESS

Tindr is the Fifth Book in
The Circle of Ceridwen Saga by Octavia Randolph

Copyright © 2016 Octavia Randolph

Pyewacket Press

ISBN 978-1-942044-21-5 (Hardback)
ISBN: 978-1-942044-04-8 (Paperback)

Book design by DesignForBooks.com

Front cover photo: Landscape image by Michael Rohani. Deer image
© photographer Spe/Dollar Photo Club. Textures, graphics, photo
manipulation, and map by Michael Rohani.

The Circle of Ceridwen Saga employs British spellings, alternate spellings,
archaic words, and oftentimes unusual verb to subject placement. This is
intentional. A Glossary of Terms will be found at the end of the novel.

LIST OF CHARACTERS

Dagr, a fisherman of Gotland

Thorkel, a prosperous farmer on the island of Öland

Ladja, a woman of the Rus

Rannveig, a skilled brewer of ale

Tindr, son of Rannveig and Dagr

Ragnfast, Tindr's cousin

Estrid, the daughter of Ragnfast's neighbour

Assur, a newly arrived Svear boy

Ceridwen, a Welsh-Saxon woman, formerly of Kilton

Sidroc, a Danish warrior, formerly Jarl of South Lindisse

Sigvor, a young woman of Gotland

Ceric, Ceridwen's son

Hrald, Sidroc's son

Sparrow, a freed Frankish slave, formerly of Tyrsborg

Eirik, a wastrel

The family of Osku, a Sámi chieftain and trader

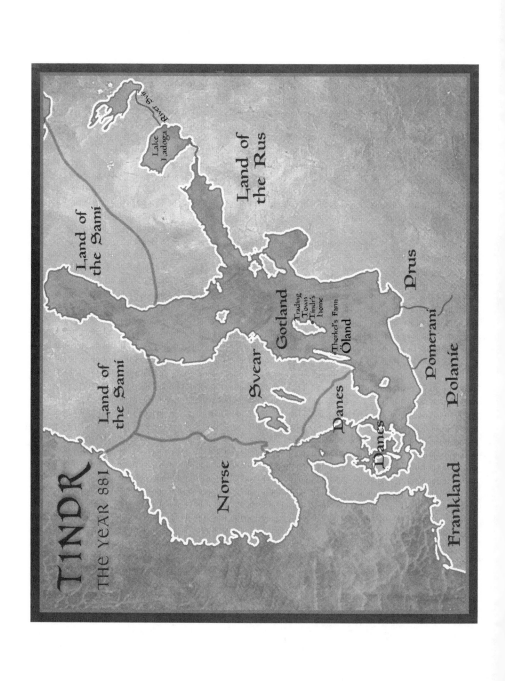

TINDR

THE YEAR 881

Land of the Sami

Land of the Sami

Norse

Svear

Gotland

Trading Town
Tindr's home
Thorkel's Farm
Öland

Danes

Danes

Danes

Land of the Rus

Lake Ladoga

River Svir

Prus

Pomerani

Polanie

Frankland

CONTENTS

TINDR

PREFACE

The island of Gotland lies near the middle of the sea known as Baltic. Of old it was an enchanted land, rising out of the sea each morning, only to be drowned by salt waters every night. Not until man brought fire to Gotland did it stand firm against the sea that embraced it. Njord the sea-God relented then, pulling back his watery cloak. After this great forests arose on the island, and the Gods Freyr and Freyja learnt to love it as their own.

The Baltic lapped also the amber-rich shores of the lands of the Danes and that of the Svear. Their young men became fierce warriors, the Danes sailing far West and the Svear East to win silver, gold, and slaves. It was the Danes that caused such grief during the reign of the famed King, Ælfred of Wessex; but the greatness of the young King was such that he halted their ravening and shared out land to these Danes. Many settled there in Angle-land. A warrior named Sidroc was one.

The lands of the Svear and Danes were wracked too with fighting, as war-chiefs arose and called themselves Kings.

But the island of Gotland knew unusual peace. It had no King, and no large settlements to plunder. Its coasts were ringed with mighty limestone rauks, the twisted bodies of giant trolls which had petrified when the Sun caught them in their night-wanderings. Its forests *sheltered the noble red deer, which ran leaping from fen to glade.*

A young man would roam these forests. His parents called him Tindr.

DAGR
ISLAND OF GOTLAND

The Year 845

DAGR had not yet seventeen years when he went with his father to the Thing up in the middle of the island. The folk of Gotland regarded the island as having three parts, for the very first Saga of the Gutes tells how the founding man on Gotland, Tjelvar, had three grandsons, and each of them held sway over one third of the island.

Each third had their own Thing, or Summer lawgathering, and Dagr's people were of the South. Yet Dagr's father had received a summons from an angry farmer further north, and go he must. The prior Spring he had sold a ram to this farmer, a good animal and a proven sire of hearty, long-fleeced twins. In due time word had come back that the farmer wanted the four ewes back that he had traded for; the beast had acted randy enough but had thrown no lambs. The aggrieved party had the right to be heard in their own third, so Gunne resigned himself to the trip. They would make it by ox-drawn waggon; Gunne was of an age at which his bones hurt if he walked too long, and he thought it best to take the four ewes along with him, should he lose in the dispute. If he won he could sell them at the Thing for another ram, or carry them back with him if a bargain could not be struck, and at any rate he wanted them in good condition so that his trouble over them was not doubled. He would welcome the comfort the waggon could provide, for the journey would take two days, with all the kit that entailed, and then at his age he could not expect to rest easy on the ground as he had when he was younger. So he and Dagr packed the waggon. The ewes were easy to pick out from the rest of his flock, as they bore the same notches in their ears they had come with, along with that nick he had added. As Dagr drove them up the ramp into the waggon bed Gunne reflected on the ewes' fineness; he was even then regretting their loss.

Dagr was his youngest son and eager for the adventure, and the farm was already in the hands of Gunne's eldest boy, who had himself four children. Dagr was one of eight offspring, all of whom had lived, and for this Gunne was known as a most fortunate man. But Dagr's mother had died not long after his birth, and he had been raised by his father and sisters. Now most of these sisters were wed, only the younger two remaining. As the farm always went to the eldest son, Dagr and his brothers knew from an early age that their Fate was to go as fare-men; to make their way in life through fishing, trade, or if they were fortunate, through the wedding of a maid who had a farm to her name. Indeed, his brothers had already left home to seek their way. But Dagr was thinking of none of this as they set off, the ewes firmly penned behind the rails of the waggon, his father perched on the narrow plank seat at its head, and he walking alongside the big spotted oxen.

Besides his eldest brother and his family, Dagr walked away that day from his father's brother, Ake. He was well into his sixth decade, bent of back, bandy of leg, and nearly blind, and a great favourite with Dagr, as Dagr was with him. Ake had had no sons, only daughters, long gone now to the farms of their husbands, and his brother's youngest had become a kind of son to him. All of Gunne's stock were hard-workers, but Ake had besides the soul of a skald, and could recite long passages of Saga tales to liven the slow-passing nights of Winter. From Ake, Dagr had heard at length of the wonders of Asgard, realm of the heavens which held the halls of the Gods, and of the strange ways in which the Gods lived and moved in their midst here in Midgard, this middle-place where men trod. Ake too, as eldest, made sacrifice on behalf of the whole farmstead at every Blót, that blood-time of Offering.

As his sight dimmed from the milky film in his eyes, Ake became a man who saw in his dreams. He had once told Dagr his Fate was held in water. They were by the well when the old man told him this, and Dagr's brother, hurrying by, had chortled and reminded Dagr not to take all day about hauling up the bucket wanted in the kitchen yard. Now, bidding fare-well to his brother and his son as they left for the distant Thing, Ake squeezed his bleary eyes shut a moment. "You will lose something," he warned. "Take care."

The Thing for the middle third was held in a broad meadow at the crossing of the two main tracks heading East and North. There was a fast-running brook, and the wood at the edge of the meadow was generous in giving up kindling. The Thing was always called when the first Moon of Summer was at its fullest, to give light with which to travel should it be a long day on the road, and also to make gathering around the many camp-fires the more cheerful for the assembled. The work of the Thing, though, was always done by daylight, as was only right when dealing with matters of justice. The Law-Speaker, the man who knew and remembered the laws, sat and listened as each case was presented in turn, and made his decisions, which were always binding. The rest of the Thing was a three-day festival of eating, drinking, gossiping, and trading, looked forward to by all who could afford the time and travel. It was also a chance for young folk who had not mingled for a while, or who had never before met, to eye each other from their respective family campsites, and for their elders to make discreet inquiry about the character and fortunes of prospective sons – and daughters-in-law.

Dagr and his father arrived at the Thing late in the day. They had been on the move for two full days and most of a third; the rains had been heavy that Spring and there was still much mud to slow the big cart-wheels in the ooze-filled ruts that had formed. They had missed the best campsites and so needed to set up across the track from where the Law-Speaker's circle was. Outside this were the stalls of traders who made it a point to attend each of the three Things in turn in a three-year cycle. These had with them some of the finer goods that came ashore at the various trading posts on Gotland – furs and seal-skins from far North, heavy bars of Frankish or Svear iron, cast bronze shield-bosses, box-locks, and ornaments, even gleaming silks from the furthest reaches of the East. One or two might even have the priceless beads of pepper-corn, curling sticks of red cinnamon, or the hard and fragrant nuts called all-spice.

Beyond the stalls were the camp-sites of the families who had made the journey; some seeking justice, others fleece, wool-wax, grain, tallow, beeswax, or honey to sell or trade. As Gunne had the ewes with him, and they needed grass, they rolled the waggon to the outermost margin of the Thing-place, not far from where the horses of the well-to-do were paddocked, and turned their oxen into the common ground with the beasts of the others. The sheep they entrusted to a farmer who had brought his dogs with him.

Gunne was weary, and aching too, from the jostling of the long journey, and as soon as they had supped he crawled into the waggon, beat up a mass of straw, and pulled a tarpaulin over his head. Dagr sat up a while on the hard ground outside, arms looped over his drawn-up knees, until their slight cook-fire sputtered and died. He could hear the blowing of the oxen not far away, and see them too, for the long Summer nights have a lingering dusk. As the day finally died, the campfires across the meadow winked the brighter. Snatches of song could be heard, a few drifting words, some distant laughter. He would know no one here, but he thought he might go out and walk about and see what he could see.

The darkening meadow was marked with the peaks of small pitched tents, and the larger forms of the wains and waggons that had been driven there. The cooking-fires of many were nearly burnt out, but around a few of them folk still sat talking, glad to poke another handful of sticks into the coals and visit with friends they had not seen for several seasons. Near the margin of the woods burnt a larger fire, and Dagr could hear from the raucous laughter that a group of young men sat around it. There would be ale there, and perchance he might be invited to join in a cup.

The talk and laughter had an ebb and flow to it, and as he drew nearer he saw why. Several women, all young, had paused not far from the fire, and the men were calling to them. Dagr thought them all to be maidens, both from their youth and the way they had stopped to listen. They each held a bucket or crock in their arms, and he reckoned that they had been to the spring for water, and were heading back to their families' camps.

"Our ale is good, and would only be better if you would share it with us," tempted one of the men, addressing the maids from across the fire ring. The fire was a large one, and Dagr was able to see the maidens he spoke to better than the men themselves, most of whom had their backs to him.

"This water is sweeter, and knows no lies," returned one of the maids, which Dagr thought a clever retort. She stood in the middle and in front of the other girls, and he gauged her to be perhaps the eldest, and certainly their leader.

"To taste our ale would take you but a moment," coaxed another of the men, holding a cup out to them. In answer the maidens only laughed, then whispered amongst themselves.

Dagr looked at the men about the fire. There were six or seven youths, some long-haired and with finely trimmed beards, others beardless, ranged about on stools and scattered benches. From a few sparkled the glint of silver jewellery, a wrist cuff, a neck ring. And all were arrayed in their best; even in the low light Dagr could see a few of their tunics were embellished with coloured thread-work. The cups they held were of the sort taken on travel, wood; for they were light in weight and unlikely to break. At one side sat a small, tapped cask. From the way the drinkers' speech sounded Dagr knew the cups had gone round quite a few times.

"If your ale be as sharp as your voice, 'twould make my lips pucker," answered the maid who had spoken before. It was said in a tone of light mockery, and though she half turned her back on the men as if to lead the rest of the maids away, she did not move off. Two of the youths hooted at the double meaning of her words, and Dagr stepped further from the shadows to make the speaker out.

She was of mid-height, with a white, broad brow, small nose, and a mouth that had returned to a smile. Her hair was so long it touched the sash tied at her neat waist, and Dagr did not think it was only the fire's glow that made it look red. The paired brooches pinning her gown at her shoulders were deeply embossed, and from them hung a row of polished amber beads of no little size. Something about the way she stood her ground with these youths made Dagr think she had been raised to have a high opinion of herself, and looking at her, and listening to her banter, he admitted that she deserved it.

The jesting and coaxing went on. "Our ale, I admit, is not as good as that which you might brew," tried one, a husky fellow with dark hair and a full beard.

"I brew no ale," sauced back the red-haired maid, "and if I did you would be unlikely to be offered a drop from my hands." The drinkers groaned, and laughingly shook their heads.

"If you will not drink with us, at least tell us your names so that we may speak to your fathers in the morning," one of youths called out, which drew loud hoots from the rest of the drinkers.

At this the girls looked ready to move on, and the one in front shifted the crock she held.

"You shall never know my name," she said with a smile.

As she turned to leave she caught sight of Dagr, standing behind the fire. Their shared look lasted but a moment, but it was enough to make three or four of the drinkers turn and notice him.

Dagr, for his part, did not move his eyes from her face. He took a step closer to the fire and addressed her with a few lines he recalled from his Uncle Ake.

"Red is her hair, like fire, like the sunset beam which crowns the peaks of Asgard, where Frigg the Queen awaits."

At first there was silence. Then, "Whose pup are you?" sputtered one of the drinkers, who looked to be no older than Dagr himself.

Dagr was not yet grown to his full height, but was even then well-knit, and as he took a stride forward he cocked his fisted hand on the leather of his belt. His broad shoulders thus looked even broader, and of the brawn of his arm he thought none could find fault.

"I am Dagr, son of Gunne, of Öja," he told them. "Here to settle a dispute about a ram," he added, as if both ram and the settling of the dispute were strictly up to him.

One of the long-haired youths stood up. "Öja?" he repeated, with a ready smile. He was a bit unsteady on his feet, but the silver bracelet on his wrist and the shine of his knife's hilt marked him of a rich family. "A Southerner, then, and deserving of our hospitality. Also a poet, and worthy of our ale. Welcome, Dagr."

Dagr grinned back to his host and moved into the circle. The girls took this chance to make their escape, though one of the youths slurred out, "Stay, O lovely Frigg" in a feeble attempt to keep them longer. But indeed no light remained in the sky, and behind them all had heard questioning voices calling out, no doubt seeking the needed water and the daughters who bore it.

Once in her tent, lying between her sleeping parents, Rannveig considered the Southerner who had looked at her and compared her to Frigg, Odin's wife, the Queen of the heavens. His name was Dagr. She had never seen him before and very likely would never do so again, unless their paths somehow crossed over the next two days; the Thing was a crowded place. He was not bad-looking, and there was a decided steadiness about him. He was not tall, and he certainly looked young. Yet there was boldness in his manner, and surely in his words, that made him stand out from the jesting crowd of idle drinkers. And the fact that his first words to her were akin to the things trained skalds spouted in the great halls of the rich further marked him. She wished he would have stepped a little closer to the fire's light so she could have seen his face better. She wished she had not had, at last, to turn away, not goaded by the distant calling of her mother which she had twice already ignored, but by the heat which she felt in her own cheek at looking into the stranger's eyes while he compared her hair to a sunset.

When she had finally fled the fire circle the other maids had chaffed her about him, repeating his name, wondering about his people and prospects, and most of all teasing her for the way he had proclaimed himself an admirer upon first glance. She fell asleep at last, straining to recall his exact words to her, and cursing herself for not having remembered it all.

An hour after sunrise Rannveig was walking back from the latrines dug out beyond the first line of trees. Her back was stiff from the thinness of the lone feather-bed she had shared with her parents, and the fact that stuffed between them she had been unable to move much. In the new light she saw the front of her over-gown was smudged with charcoal ash, and she had but one other with her. She should have carried the crock with her for more water, and had left it back at her parent's camp. She was walking, head down, brooding on these things and not noticing the man walking before her, crossing also from the line of trees and headed back to the morning camp-fires.

He paused for a moment, perhaps scanning the camps to find his own, and she ran into him. It was Dagr. Her booted foot caught his instep, and he staggered a moment, but quickly straightened up. He blinked his eyes and looked at her, sweeping his hand across his brow, and she saw his eyes were blue-green, and slightly bleared from a night's drinking. His hair was light brown and fell unevenly to his shoulders, and he tossed his head to send it away from his face.

His mouth opened, and broke into a smile. She saw that they were just the same height, and the raking morning light showed the scant stubble upon his chin, which looked as if it had never yet been shaved. He was little more than a boy.

Her cheek flamed again, but it was her own doing, not his. Rannveig was a maid of over twenty Summers, and had found no man to please her. She had lain awake last night thinking of this one, who turned out to be a lad.

"Hej," he said. He was watching her face and hoping his greeting did not sound as uncertain to her ears as it did to his own.

"Hej," she returned. She felt a fool, standing in the harsh light before this boy. She wondered if now, looking into her face a mere hand-span or two away, he thought her old.

"I am Dagr," he said. His eyes were still fastened on her.

"Já," she returned, and glanced down to her soiled hem. "Something about a ram."

He laughed then. "Já. My father sold a ram to a man from near here, and he wants his ewes back."

She nodded her head in a short motion, and made as if to leave. He lifted his arm, a small gesture of supplication.

"Will you not tell me your name?"

She was silent. She was standing out in an open field, on the pathway back from the latrines, talking to a boy who made her feel a fool.

But Dagr would not give up. "I know only that you brew no ale, and will not drink with strange men, as befits a maiden of good birth." He took a breath. "And that you are of rare loveliness." This last line he had also learnt from the tales told by his uncle.

She tossed her head, a short, impatient jerk. "Who fills your head with such stuff?"

She watched his own head move, a little jolt as if he had been slapped. She could not stop herself.

"You are a boy. Go and play a boy's games, and leave me in peace."

She made a movement with her shoulders, a little shiver, almost as if she were shaking him off, an unwanted wrap. Then she moved from him, towards the waking campsites.

Dagr stood speechless in her wake. He did not expect a rebuke, and did not welcome being called a boy. He had known last night she was the elder of them, just as he knew Frigg was a Goddess. One did not expect beauty to be always attainable. It did not keep him from admiring her, and wishing to tell her so. He stood there, watching her retreat, seeing the slight sway of her blue gown and the long, light red hair trailing down her back from beneath her white head-wrap. He shook his head, but as he did, a realization was born within him, and steadily grew until he could name it: She had actually considered him a potential mate, at least last night. That was why she was angry this morning.

This knowledge flared up like an oil torch, warming him from the inside out with an unaccustomed heat. It then died out just as quickly, quenched by the simple facts of their lives. She was a few years older, strong-headed, and well-to-do. The skillfully-cast bronze brooches on her gown, the deep yellow amber beads resting on her breast between those brooches – her folk could and did take care to give her the finest, and the fancy-work on her sash and hem showed she had time enough to do such things with her needle. And she was pretty, very much so; the small nose and rounded cheeks dusted with light freckles, the skin beneath those freckles as white as new-drawn milk. Her eyes were pale blue, not wide, rather a bit narrow, and flashing beneath the bow of reddish brows. Those eyes had looked at him carefully for one moment, and then dismissed him.

He had nothing. His wrist bore no cuff of silver, his neck no twisted chain, and the knife at his side was of the plainest. Unlike most gathered here at the Thing, he wore an ordinary tunic and leggings, not those on which some loving mother or sister had lavished care in decorating; his brother's wife was a big, good-hearted woman, and kind, but had her hands full enough with her children; she kept Dagr and Gunne decently clothed but nothing more. When he left to make his way his portion would be a small one; it was all his father, with many daughters to dower and other sons to provide for, could give. He knew of farming and animals just what any other youth his age did, nothing more. He was an indifferent hunter, and had fished but little, but he liked the sea none the less.

No wonder she spurned him. And – he was younger. Maids did not wed men younger than they, at least not often. He might grow prosperous if the Gods smiled on his efforts, but that one thing he could never mend of. He let go a sigh, then continued on his way back to his father's waggon.

By mid-day Gunne was ready to leave the crowded meadow. He had found the farmer with whom he had swapped the ram, and convinced him to take back the ewes. He had no wish to wait until late afternoon, when he had been told the Law-Speaker would address the case, nor to stand before so many strangers and plead that the ram had always done his duty in the past by his ewes. No, he had slept poorly in the waggon-bed, with so much boisterous talk and song going on about him; and he wanted to go home. The farmer had led the ram in question to the pen where Gunne's ewes awaited, and Gunne, a peace-loving man, had expressed his regret to the man. Dagr stood by, watching it all and saying little; they had scarcely arrived and now would be off again.

They had already hitched the oxen up, and Gunne pulled the tethered ram back to their waggon. "You are destined for the pot," he muttered to the old ram, who glared balefully back at him. The four ewes he had given up would all bear lambs next Spring, by another of Gunne's rams, so that his loss was doubled, perhaps three-times as great, should they all throw twins.

"Já, the pot for you," he reminded the beast, as it lowered its horns and tried to butt him. Together they pushed the ram up the plank ramp and into the waggon bed.

But before they left Dagr and his father walked the line of trader's stalls, looking for a good pair of shears. Gunne was as able as any farmer to forge simple tools, but a well-aligned pair of shears, one that would take and keep a sharp edge, and that had good spring to them, was a craft beyond his skill. There were two black-smiths there, and Gunne spent some little time looking over the wares of each, and after a decent amount of chatter he settled on a pair forged by the first, who Gunne had known from the start he would buy from, but for the sake of an improved price had made show of with the second.

As his father was closing the bargain, and drawing out silver from the small pouch hidden in his belt, Dagr glanced up and down the teeming way. Nearly opposite the iron-worker was the stall of a silver-smith. Dagr and Gunne had walked past the display of braided necklaces, thick coiled armlets, and hammered wrist cuffs. Arrayed on a makeshift trestle of planks lay bowls of silver beads and other baubles, such as women covet. Two women approached, stopped, and now bent over the table, and Dagr saw from the blue gown and long red hair that one of them was his maiden. The other, he guessed, was her mother, for she was older, but too had red hair, now fading with age. But she was as well dressed as her daughter, and Dagr did not wonder that they had stopped to look at silver. He drew closer and peered over their shoulders. It was not silver beads that had caught the maid's attention, but a bowl of something even brighter – round glass beads. They were red, blue, and green, with tiny specks and swirls of other colours mixed in, and some were spheres and others short cylinders. The trader was offering them loose so that women could string, upon twisted linen thread, a combination most pleasing to them.

At that moment his father, having lost sight of his son in the crowd, called out, "Dagr." The red-haired maiden straightened up and turned and found herself looking into his face. Colour bloomed across her white cheek.

Rannveig ducked her head as soon as she saw the lad's face. What sort of a hussy was she become, turning like that at a man's name, looking for him as if he mattered? She busied herself with the beads her mother was still counting out, and did not stand upright again until Dagr had left.

Back home Ake greeted Dagr with an embrace. "What did you lose?" he wanted to know. Dagr had returned with every meagre possession he had travelled with. But thinking back on the red-haired maiden, he knew there was in fact something he had lost to her.

⬡⬡⬡⬡⬡⬡⬡⬡⬡⬡⬡⬡

Dagr left home the following Spring. He went first to the farm of Gulli, his middling brother, nearly a day's walk away. Dagr's brother shared the farm with his wife's brother, and his wife, and it was made lively by the children of both couples and by the yet un-wed sisters of Dagr's brother's wife. Gulli raised sheep, grew barley, rye, oats and vegetables as all farmers did, and was beginning to be skilled in iron-working. He had, like every farmer, some skill in forging or mending tools, for the nearest iron-smith was more than a day's travel away from the farm, and in deep-snow time impossible to reach. Gulli was not content with hammering up a useable substitute for a broken pick-head, but wanted to provide through his own handiwork the tools he and his brother in law needed. So Gulli took to the trade of Weland, the smith of the Gods, and had learnt to draw credible nails, fashion iron clasps and hinges, and hammer out smooth and level strapping-bars to embrace the wooden chests that held bronze or silver goods.

Though Dagr mainly earned his keep in the fields, Gulli was glad to show his young brother a few of the things he was mastering, so that Dagr's time with him was well spent, and he learnt enough of forge-work to make a passable file. Then too, Gulli's wife had her two sisters living with them, the older of whom was not averse to allowing Dagr to steal an occasional kiss. She was an attractive enough maiden, and was besides quite handy about the household; for being dedicated to the gaggle of geese who ran to greet her every morning, had increased their number to the extent that boiled or roast goose was no rarity at the farm. But she would allow little more than a kiss to Dagr, for despite the family connection she had in mind a man with more prospects than the youngest son of large family could offer, a youth who had as yet no property, riches, nor home of his own to bring her to. Still, they were the first kisses Dagr had known, and he said goodbye to her with a grateful warmth not solely arising from the half of boiled goose she had packed into his leathern food-bag.

For it happened that the next Spring Dagr set out West, to the sea-side home of his eldest brother but one. Dagr had rarely seen any of the western coast of Gotland, and to reach his brother's he walked for a full day. Tufi had taken to the sea, and was a fisherman with his own boat. Dagr had always liked looking at the sea on those occasions when he had found himself within sight of it, and now he had the chance to feel the heave and swell of the Baltic beneath tarred planks of straked oak, to smell the salt-brine and taste it upon his lips, and to hoist the sturdy mast and struggle with the damp and flapping sail. Together he and Tufi would heave the heavy net over the ship-rail and tease it out as it spread and dropped, and together they hauled it back in, thrashing and glistening with fat herring and cod if the day were good.

To begin Dagr had to grow his sea-legs, for the first times out he felt himself as wretched as a hound who had drunk soured milk. As the Summer progressed he found himself more and more at ease on water, and even began to complain a bit if the winds were so light that there was no pitch nor roll to the trim little boat. At this Tufi would grin and remind him that they had not yet been caught in a squall; came the day they did Dagr would change his tune soon enough. They did not set sail every day, only those dawns that foretold the smoothest weather. On off-days they had the task of drying the net upon upright pikes struck into the stubbly grass just above the beach. There they could try every knot, look for weaknesses, and mend up any holes through which their precious catch might escape. There was also the endless work of gutting, flaying, salting, and drying the fish, for the settlement where Tufi lived was so small that only a few could be sold fresh.

Some years back Tufi had taken to wife a young widow, and they were raising her two children and the three they had brought forth together. Her first husband had also been a fisherman, one whose boat had last been seen beating against the rapidly growing waves of a late-Summer storm, and she welcomed the fact that Dagr was now here to help Tufi. Her eldest boy was not quite big nor strong enough to fish, but all the young helped in the salting and drying, and one of her girls, with the nimble fingers typical of the young, was a true help to her father in the twisting of the hempen strands used to stay the fish-net knots.

Dagr spent three years with them, by which time the elder boys had joined Tufi on his forays. It was then that Dagr's older brother suggested that Dagr cross the Baltic westwards to the land of Svear with a hull full of last Summer's dried and salted herring. Last year he had gotten a second boat for his young brother's use, which Dagr had been paying off to him in labour, in Summer through fishing and in Winter through the bits of useful iron-work that Dagr could forge before the small fire-shed. Dagr would sail with another man on board, Halle, a neighbour of Tufi's, and like his older brother, a seasoned fisherman.

Halle had often made the crossing and knew which bays to put into, and where their fish would be most welcome. It was but a long day's sail, straight West, and even should they need to beat against the wind the entire trip should take no longer than four or five days, including that spent unloading and selling the stock-fish.

Dagr, Halle, Tufi, and the older boys rolled the casks holding the salted fish up the treaded gangway and aboard, lashing them well. They had Dagr's share of what he had caught, and a number of casks of Halle's as well. There was a cask of water, and one of ale, and food for two men for many days, also fish hooks and a small net, for Tufi knew well that in a misadventure at sea such things had often been the saving of a crew. As the journey would take him away from his own box bed, Tufi's wife insisted Dagr carry as well his featherbed, a thick one she had stuffed and sewn for him when he had first come to live with them, the ticking made of linen well-oiled and then waxed, as proof against fleas. Halle laughed at this, shaking his head and pointing out that if any man should be able to sleep well on a wadmal blanket on the hard deck it should be a young one; but that night, trying to settle himself into sleep wrapped only in his own blanket, he secretly began to regret that his wife had never pressed him into enjoying any such comfort himself.

They set off just before dawn, when winds are always light, and sailed due West, the rising Sun behind them lighting their watery path and making the grey-green water shimmer. As the Sun rose in the sky, so did the wind, forcing them to tack to reach their goal. The greener mass of Gotland receded from view as they ploughed on, and in time a dark smudge on the water's edge proclaimed land ahead. They took turns at the steering oar, even though the waves were not demanding of a man's strength, and Dagr reflected that the boat, small as she was, was a good one, and he lucky to be sailing her.

Dagr had never before been out of sight of his homeland, and knowing that soon he would be landing in Svear-land added to the thrill of anticipation he felt at the potential profit his cargo would yield. Halle knew ready buyers aplenty, and if they arrived before other Gotlanders or stock-fish traders from the Baltic rim, they could sell at a premium. He could finish paying Tufi for the boat, and perhaps invest in a new sail as well. On top of this was the gladness any young man feels when approaching a new land, even one as similar to his own as that of the Svear.

Dagr was at this point in the prow, leaning into the wind and gazing at the slowly growing landmass ahead, and thinking on all this. He heard Halle, standing at the steering oar, cry out. He turned.

Coming across the water towards them was a ship: long, low, and serpent-slender. The large single sail billowed against the wind, but this was not the only cause of its speed. Twenty-five or more pair of oars rose and fell into the Baltic, the blades dripping with sparkling beads of salt water before swiftly dipping back into the dark sea.

Without knowing how he got there Dagr was now at Halle's side, watching with an open mouth the ship bear down on them. The men on board it were silent; there was no whooping nor war-cries, but Dagr's fishing boat was their unmistakable target.

"Svear? Are they Svear?" asked Dagr.

"I hope they are not Danes," Halle answered, without taking his eyes from the ship. "May Freyr protect us," he added, under his breath.

The ship had now turned slightly, and they could see the carved figure of a clawed animal atop the raked prow. The sail had once been dyed red, but was now the colour of a faded rose, and blotched with newer patches of undyed linen. A weather-vane of gilded silver swung above the rowers. The ship was packed with men, those rowing who they could scarcely see, and many who stood, their faces set and eyes fastened upon them.

Dagr turned to look at Halle. They had no weapons with them, naught but their knives at their belts. There was a sea-axe which Dagr always carried in his tool-chest, and a few pikes to help with snaring nets. Nothing to defend themselves with against these warriors.

"What – " he began to ask, but before he could finish a voice cried out from the crowded deck.

"Your ship is ours," it said.

Dagr recoiled; it would seem a bad dream, were not his insides churning.

He could not make out which man had spoken; most held spears and now he saw grappling-hooks in the hands of two or three. The warriors had not troubled themselves to put on ring-shirts or helmets, such show would not be needed against two fishermen.

"Your ship is ours," repeated the man, who Dagr saw wore a padded red tunic and a cap trimmed with fur. "Drop your sail." Another voice rang out, with words neither Dagr nor Halle could understand.

Halle straightened himself and bellowed out, "We are men of Gotland, and free born."

This proclamation was ignored, and the war-ship dropped its own sail in preparation to come alongside.

The man who had spoken did so with the accents of the Svear. Halle tried again, "We are free-born Gotlanders."

"Drop your sail," was the only answer, and Dagr and Halle did, letting it lie as it fell along the keel.

"We sail to Asnen in Smáland, then to Lister and Kivik, with our herring," insisted Halle, naming those ports of the Svear.

One hook was thrown, and then another, and the small boat strained at the force of being pulled, then gave a shudder at the glancing impact as the two hulls met. As soon as they did, men began leaping aboard, whooping and calling as if they were about to swing their swords. In fact few even had bothered to strap them on, and only three of the invaders had leapt over with spears in their fists. Some of the men were dressed as Gotlanders or Svear, in woollen or linen tunics and leggings, but fully half sported the full and gathered bagged trousers of the Rus, worn under the longer tunics favoured by them. The Rus were Svear who had long ago sailed to the eastern most limits of the Baltic, and thence down the great river Volga to the land of the packs of timber-wolves. The Rus were canny traders but came rarely to Gotland, and Dagr had heard they were feared warriors as well.

The man in the red tunic now climbed aboard. He was a few years older than Dagr, and looked like a Svear, with long yellow hair, but wore the gathered trousers of the Rus. At his side was a man about the same age, or perhaps younger, who wore a dark and sleeveless leather tunic trimmed with fur over a blue under-tunic. He wore his sword, one of some length, and Dagr's eye fell for a moment on the garnets glowing redly in the pommel and guard.

Some of the warriors who had leapt aboard first were now ranging over the small boat, pawing over anything not lashed down. One of them snatched up Dagr's new brown mantle which he had taken off in the afternoon's warmth, and he watched the man swing it over his own shoulders. Another grabbed his blanket. Anything they did not want was flung into the sea. Out of the tail of his eye he saw the small pot of pitch be thrown overboard, and then his featherbed be tossed over the rail as well.

"I am Dagr, son of Gunne, and this is my boat," he told the two men who looked to be the chieftains. Despite his fear his voice was strong, for he felt anger rise within him.

The one in the red tunic answered.

"Well. Your name may be Dagr, but the boat is ours." His furred head was turning right and left, following the actions of his men who were rifling through Dagr's things. He turned back to Dagr and Halle. "Give me your silver," he ended with, gesturing to their belts. Dagr and Halle emptied their pouches of the few coins and bits of hack-silver they carried.

"We are Gotlanders, and free-born," Halle protested once again, but the one who wore the sword raised his hand. He said something in a tongue Dagr could not understand to the other.

"You Gotlanders always have gold," said the red-tunic.

"We have stock-fish, salted and dried, to be sold in Smáland," answered Halle, raising his own hand to the distant coast of the Svear.

"Are you not Svear?" Dagr hazarded to ask. He knew that traders on land could readily become raiders at sea, yet he hoped that his ship would be spared by reminding them of past bonds. Just a few days ago these very men may have landed peacefully at any trading post on Gotland, bartered, bought, and sold goods, and left his brethren at home nodding their heads in satisfaction. Once at sea they became ravening pirates again.

The red-tunic looked at him. "I am Svear," he admitted. "But now I am with the Rus, and serve a Rus warchief." The one with the sword now spoke to some of the men, who began prying open the stock-fish casks, one after the other. The chieftain did not seem too crestfallen at the truth of Halle's words; though the casks revealed no hidden gold, the fish could be sold at a profit, and also used to feed themselves as well.

The red-tunic turned to Halle. "You know the coast of the Svear?"

"From Birka to Skania," Halle answered.

"Good," returned the man. "You will be useful, and be our pilot. I am from inland, and these parts are not well known to me." He lifted his head and spoke to some of those who had opened the casks. "Take him to the steering oar."

Before Halle could speak he was propelled by a body of men through the crowded boat and up over the side into the war-ship. Dagr did not like to see him go, and was aware that when he swallowed he could feel the growing lump in his throat. Another command was given, and Dagr watched while strange hands hoisted his boat's square sail and secured the lines.

The chief now looked at him, and spoke, with a flick of his wrist at the ship-rail and the water lying beyond.

"Get off," said the Svear in the red-tunic, though it was all too clear to Dagr what the chief's meaning was.

Dagr froze. The Rus chief drew himself up, and placed his hand on his sword hilt.

"Get off," repeated the Svear. "Either your live body or your dead body is going over."

He would not live long in the cold water, and they were three or more hours' sail from land-fall; no man could swim that far. He was being told to end his life.

Of a sudden he recalled his boyhood self, and standing by his Uncle Ake by the well on his father's farm. Ake had closed his blurred eyes and told Dagr that his Fate lay in water.

He shifted his eyes down at the deck, noticing a nail which needing pounding down, and stared at it as a precious thing.

The Rus chief spoke once more. Dagr looked again at the men, and then the Rus chief began to draw his sword. Dagr placed one hand upon the ship-rail and hopped over it as if it were a sheep-pen fence.

The shock of the water stung him, and he surfaced tossing his wet hair off his face. Both ships were already moving away from him. The oars of the war-ship dipped and rose. For one desperate moment he hoped to find a dragging line to cling to, some way to stay hidden under the curve of the hulls and be towed along. But even if he were not seen and a spear not sent through him, the cold of the water would kill him. He thrashed about, unable to see the edge of the coast. The war-ship moved further away, trailed by his boat. He could see a few of the warriors aboard her. He propelled himself up out of the water for a moment, hoping to see where Svear-land was, so that he could turn away from it and die swimming back to Gotland.

Then he saw the billow of white upon the water, like a great swan's wing. It was his featherbed. One corner was stuck up in the air. It floated upon the water a few strokes away. He reached it, closed his hand around one edge of the waxed linen. He heaved himself as gently as he could upon it, fearful every moment that his weight would send it under. But it did not. If he clutched the edges with his fists he could pull his head and chest out of the water. The mass of down billowed round him, captured in its casing of tightly woven cloth. He coughed and spat to free some of the water he had swallowed, pressed his face into the bed, and kicked his legs to warm them.

"Njord," he choked out, calling upon the God of the sea. "If I live I will give myself to you."

ANOTHER ISLAND

IN the morning Dagr still lived. He had at times during the long night felt he had gone mad, or was already dead, and must somehow awaken either in his own alcove at his brother's house, or amongst all lost seamen in Ran's watery hall. As the Sun rose he was trembling with cold, but he knew he lived.

His legs, trailing in the water, were so stung with cold that he could not feel them. He tried to turn himself upon his back, but feared losing grip on the featherbed that had saved him. It was become his whole island, and he clung to it with clenched fists.

A sea-bird flew over his head, squawking, and then a second. Once he lifted his chin enough to see a few sitting on the water, preening their feathers with arched necks in the lifting light. They lived on water, but were meant to do so. He lowered his face, wondering what the odds of a ship finding him might be.

After a while the waves picked up, and began washing over his lower back. Each onrush of water felt like a lash against his chilled skin. If the weather was to turn he could not survive another night. But the Sun was lifting higher over his head, and the sky was that clear sharp blue of late

Summer. The growing waves meant something else. He grunted and pushed himself up. His hands were covered by cold sea water as he did, but he could raise his chest enough to really see.

His heart leapt in his breast. There, beyond the billowing white margins of the featherbed, was land. It was not more than a hundred paces away, if he could walk it. That is why the waves washed over him; they were curling up from hitting the sea-bottom. He craned his neck and looked down over the edge of the featherbed. The water was clear, and he could not see the bottom. He was caught in a gentle current, floating offshore, heading South.

He looked again at the land. There were spruce and pine trees above a thin line of sand. Some boulders. No houses nor fishing huts, no sign of folk. But if he were to live he must reach it.

He tried to calm himself, gauge if in fact the current was bringing him nearer to shore. But he watched the shoreline slipping by, growing no closer. There was a promontory further down, and he feared that if he passed it he might be truly swept away from land again. So he began kicking his legs, or trying to, and throwing his body cross-wise across the featherbed so that he could angle towards the beach.

He kicked and kicked. He had so little strength left that he scarcely could hear the splashing they made. The waves retreating from the shore pulled him back, and he struck out at an angle. He wondered if he could still swim; clutching to the bed he could use only his legs, yet he feared giving it up.

My Fate may be in water, but it has not killed me yet, he told himself.

He unclenched his fists and pushed himself off the featherbed. He drew his hands to his chest and pushed them back out again through the cold water, and kicked with every bit of strength he could summon. He thrashed his way, almost clawing through the water, but he drew closer. Suddenly one foot hit bottom. He stumbled and went under for a moment, then stood, and with halting steps staggered out upon the sand, water streaming from his shivering body.

He fell upon the sand just beyond the reach of the water. He lay gasping, then turned himself on his back. The bile rose in his throat and he rolled over, retching up sea water. His belly heaved with racking spasms. His hands were still clenched in talon-like fists from gripping the bed all night, and as his belly roiled he rose on his knees and pounded them into the dry sand.

A few tears escaped his eyes. He had nearly died. His ship was gone. The Rus had taken Halle away. These few facts rolled about in his brain, first one, then the next, then the last.

He turned again to his back and sat up. He saw his boots were gone; he had not known that. He still had his knife and his belt. His lips were cracked and his neck and hands were badly sun-burnt. His throat ached from thirst.

He pushed himself up to stand, and then fell down again. When he awoke the Sun was high overhead. His head ached and his thirst was such he could not wet his lips with his tongue.

"Hej," said a small voice behind him.

He turned to see three children, two girls and a boy, standing on the edge of the sand.

"Hej," he told them. His tongue felt swollen and he thought his speech was slurred. He struggled to his feet, which made the children step back.

"I am a Gotlander. My boat was taken by pirates, and they cast me overboard. I need help." He could just form the words. He did not try to move nearer them, for fear of frightening them away. He lifted his hands in supplication.

The elder girl nodded, and spoke to the others, words Dagr could not make out. Then all three turned and vanished into the trees.

He slumped down on the sand once more, his back to the sea, looking at the spruces. After a while the children returned, flanked by two men, one young and one old, holding spears. Dagr remembered them asking, "Can you walk?" but little else they said on the trip to the farmhouse.

There was a track through the trees they went along, and then an open meadow filled with sheep. A cluster of steep-roofed buildings stood beyond these, and as they grew nearer he heard the barking of dogs. A pack of hounds, some snarling, ran out to greet them.

A large number of folk milled about, and he was led inside the largest of the houses. There he was given ale to drink, and then hot meat broth. His damp and sandy clothes were taken from him and he was wrapped in a blanket. He sat by the fire, blinking up at his hosts as he ate and drank and told of what had befallen him. Then he was shown to an alcove, where he slept for how long he knew not.

The noise of the hall awoke him. The doors were opened to a bright and blue day. His clothes had been rinsed and dried by the fire, and the leather of his belt and knife sheath oiled to draw the salt out.

He had washed ashore on the island of Öland, a long slender spit which lay just off the East coast of Svear-land.

His hosts were sheep and goat herders, prosperous ones. The older man, Thorkel, had also traded as a youth, and his sons too had crossed the Baltic, South to the posts of the Prus, and many times to the West coast of Gotland. Now they were content to stay on their island home, for as Thorkel told him, "Hot-head young Svear range about the sea, and even Danes have sniffed about, snatching at what they can." He was not surprised at Dagr's tale of the Rus; they had been spotted around Öland and the mainland before, both pirating at sea and landing to trade at well-guarded posts. He questioned Dagr rather closely about the Rus chieftain, when Dagr was strong enough to recount the story in detail; and seemed disappointed Dagr had not found out the man's name or lineage, "For I went twice up the Volga in the land of the Rus, and each time found it a profitable adventure."

When Dagr told of how he had at last neared land and abandoned the featherbed which had saved his life, Thorkel listened thoughtfully. "It is a good thing you struck for shore just there," he remarked. "Past the spit the current quickens. You would be half way to Frankland by now." The old man was grinning as he said this, but Dagr stifled a shiver just the same.

Thorkel had two wives and many children, the eldest son of whom lived in the smaller house across the yard with his own family. Thorkel had a barrel-chest, short legs, long grey hair and a wispy beard that made him resemble one of his he-goats. The older wife was also grey, plump and sedentary, and marked by a ringing voice as she ordered her household about. The younger wife was not uncomely, but so modest and quiet that she was easily overlooked in any gathering. Thorkel's married son was a gawky, raw-boned sort, weak-chinned and with colour-less pale hair; and his wife young, pretty, and querulous. They had four young ones, adding to the large number of Thorkel's own brood. There were as well a raft of serving folk, bonds-men and perhaps slaves, Dagr could not be certain; and also a number of youngsters attached to these folk. There were ten or more women of every estate work-ing at spinning or standing at the tall looms beating up the woof; and maids and youths at work in the fields cutting hay, hoeing late weeds out of the rows of turnips, or toil-ing in the large kitchen yard.

The first full day Dagr did little but eat and drink. The older serving women clucked over him, giving him a hot drink of boiled sage-leaf broth, and smearing his chest with beaver fat to help soothe the cough he hacked with; his lungs burned as if sand had gotten in them. Towards the end of the day a serving man brought him a pair of boots he had made, cut from goat-hide they had tanned themselves on the farm, and Dagr thought he had never had a better pair.

Now that he was shod he asked Thorkel if he might have a rooster to sacrifice in thanks to Njord, which the old man readily provided. "Njord spat you back out, and is owed his due," Thorkel agreed. He rubbed his face and added, "And I forget if he has had even so much as a hen's egg from me this season." Thorkel's wavering voice was more like a bleat than Dagr had ever heard outside of a goat. They went together to the fowl-yard, and Thorkel pointed out a few likely subjects from amongst the young roosters that danced and hopped as they approached.

Dagr looked at them in turn and made, as one making the sacrifice must, the final choice. He snatched the bird by the feet, and carried it, red wings flapping, past the sheep meadow and down the forest track to the beach. There he wrung its neck. He laid the rooster on a rock and pierced its breast with his knife, then pricked his left thumb with his knife tip. He pressed the bead of blood that had welled on his thumb into the wound on the bird's chest. He raised his eyes to the rippling water before him. The Sun was going down, paling the sea to a soft grey.

"Njord! I, Dagr, son of Gunne, come to make Offering to you. You did not swallow me. I give you this bird, and I give you myself. Ever will I follow you, knowing that of all Gods, Njord has favoured me. Accept this Offering, and my thanks."

He walked to the edge of the water, and hurled the rooster out upon its silvered surface.

"And keep Thorkel and his folk also in your favour," he did not fail to add, remembering his host. The feathered body began to drift atop the water. Dagr watched it, remembering the feathers that had saved his life.

By the next morning he was feeling almost himself, and bethought him how he might begin to repay his host for all he had done. Thorkel did not think it likely that Dagr would be able to find a ship to take him back to Gotland until Spring; the trading season on Öland was over, and now that word had spread about the Rus pirates it would be hard to hire a man to take him, regardless of how much silver he was promised. And Dagr could promise none. He owned little but his boat, and now not even that.

"My brother will think me dead," Dagr reflected aloud at table that night. With so many goats, the women made fine soft cheeses from the abundant milk, and he was savouring this, spread upon a freshly baked loaf. It recalled his sister-in-law, and the good butter and cheeses she drew from her cows.

"Já," agreed Thorkel, spooning up his browis of shredded goat-meat and barley, "and you almost were. But as you live and eat, Spring will come, and with it traders who can carry you back to Gotland."

A serving woman who was bringing a platter of oatcakes to the table placed it just before him, and gave a sly smile. The amount this youthful stranger could eat was remarked on by all in the kitchen yard, but when you had nearly lost your life there was no limit to what one could enjoy; and besides, he was yet young and not come to his full size, as one of the older women pointed out.

He went to his alcove that night troubled about many things, how to get back being the chiefest. He lay awake a long while, hearing the soft snoring of others, the low whistling of the wind as it blew in through the smoke holes at the gable ends, and from outside, the occasional bark of one of the hounds. He sighed and turned. His box bed was laid with a thick layer of straw, which had sheep-skins upon it, and the blanket too was of squared sheepskins laced together, warm and soft. He had already seen that each day the women of the hall carried the skins outside and gave them a good shake to restore their loft. But as he settled in once more, hoping that sleep would come, the image of his featherbed came to him, and he seemed to see himself upon it, clinging to life, and recalled Thorkel's words about being swept into the open sea on the way to Frankland.

He slept, but in the dark of night awakened with a start. His alcove curtain was being drawn back, and he felt a small hand – a woman's – upon his shoulder. She slid in next him, and he felt her sit up, and the action of her pulling her gown off from over her head. He gave a quick intake of breath, but was too startled to speak. Her hand reached out and found his face, and caressed his cheek. She made a low murmuring sound, almost like a dove.

He could see next to nothing, and feared for a moment it was a mistake; she must have meant another man's bed; but as soon as she turned to him Dagr could do naught but accept the warm pressure of her body against his. He could barely breathe in his excitement. He let his hands lift and slide over her form. He traced the curve of her shoulder, the softness of her skin, the small yet rounded breasts, which felt beneath his fingertips like the choicest fruit. She shifted her narrow hips and moved onto her back, and pulled him atop her.

When he awoke she was still there. It was not yet dawn. She lay on her belly next him, and he let his fingers find her brow and stroke back the hair which covered it. She rose a little, and put her hand on his chest.

"Who are you?" he whispered.

"Ladja is my name," she whispered back. "One of the women of the household." Both the name and the way she spoke told him Norse was not her first tongue.

"Why . . . . ?" he began, not knowing how to ask why he had been so favoured.

"I am of the Rus. I want you to know that we can give, as well as take."

"Of the Rus?" he repeated.

"Já. The old man stole me from my home on the banks of the river Svir, by Lake Ladoga, six Summers past."

"Are you a slave?" he asked next.

"Já, and nai. More than a slave, less than a free-woman. The old man meant me for his son, thinking I would make a good second wife for him. But when we got here his first wife would have none of it."

"But you must stay?"

"What else can I do? And I have a child, as well, a boy." She was pulling on her gown. "I must go now." She leant forward and kissed his face, then slipped out of the alcove into the dimness of the still hall.

When the household gathered to break its fast Dagr looked about him. There were several women who could, by their forms, be that named Ladja. Then he saw the woman who had placed the platter of oat cakes before him last night. This morning she held a tray of eggs which had been seethed in butter. She had brown hair, and as she neared him again, he saw that her eyes were a warm but light brown. She looked at him, but this time did not smile.

He saw her again, later in the day, in the grassy side yard near the barn. She was carrying out an armful of sheepskins, and shook each one with a snapping motion of her wrists. Tiny curls of wool fluff, freed to the air, showed in the sharp sunlight as she did. She looked up and saw Dagr watching her. It was then she smiled, and Dagr wondered if these were the very sheepskins from his own alcove on which she had given her warm softness to him.

She came again that night. He had lain awake, waiting, and had at last dozed off. Then came her hand, reaching

for him, and the gentle pressure of her slight weight settling in near him. He once again felt her motion as she
drew off her gown.

"Ladja," he whispered, putting out his hand. It touched
her face, and he felt her nod.

She lay down. "Was last night your first time with a
woman?" she wanted to know.

He nodded his head in the dark, too abashed to speak.

"I thought so," she said, but with no unkindness.
"Tonight we will take our time." Her soft voice took on a
playful note. "You are not a bull in a field, jumping on and
off the back of a cow, for fear of being gored."

It was in this way Dagr learnt the art of love. Ladja
did not come into his alcove every night, and he never
knew beforehand when she would, which made their
times together that much sweeter. She had made it clear
he should not speak to her during the day, no more so
than he might speak to any of the serving women, and as
hard as this was he adhered to this request. He saw her
going about her daily chores, and saw too the boy which
must be her own, for though all the women cared together
for the children of the farm, this one sought her out. Like
her he was brown-haired, but his eyes were blue.

"Is Thorkel the father of your son?" he asked her
one night, after they had given themselves. He hoped it
would not pain her to answer, but he wished to know. She
snorted.

"That old goat. Nai. Not him. And I never let his
coward of a son near me. I would have screamed for his
wife if he had so much as looked at me." She paused a
moment. "I am not certain who is. After I found out I
was not to be the son's wife, it was hard for me. I had no

standing, could be sold away . . . Some of the serving men raise crops on their own, on strips of land the old goat has granted them, and which they have cleared. I thought perhaps . . . " she did not finish, only shook her head.

"Why must I not speak to you in the daylight?" he asked now.

"Because Thorkel likes you," she almost hissed. "He would give me to you if you asked. And this I do not want." She moved as if impatient with him, and was in fact searching for her gown. But before she left she gave him a kiss, nonetheless.

Dagr became one of the household. The dogs learnt to accept him, coming up in packs of three or four and sniffing his outstretched hands, and then beating their thick tails against his legs in consent as they milled about him. He always had a smile for the little girl who had found him and brought him help; she was one of Thorkel's daughters. He played dice and got good at it, taking small sums of silver off of Thorkel's bewildered eldest son, and the old man himself. And now that his strength was fully returned, he set about making himself useful. He worked alongside Thorkel's sons and field men as they cut and threshed, and joined with them in building a new Winter shelter for the sheep, stacking up and fastening the horizontal planks to form the pitched walls, and twisting and securing the stiff handfuls of dried sedge which made up its shaggy roof. In short, he worked as hard, or harder, as any of the men, be they sons or slaves, and this was not lost on old Thorkel, who insisted Dagr sit with the near members of his own family each night at table.

Thorkel had an anvil of flat stone, with an iron hammer and tongs, and Dagr made good use of them. He forged a variety of punches and augers, and even a well-balanced cauldron frame, and made a credible job of it. But the Fall days quickly dwindled into darkness, with Winter coming on; and Dagr felt the distance between himself and Gotland all the sharper. Still, he reminded himself that every day that passed was one day closer to Spring and the hope of returning home.

Then he would think of his lost boat, and of Halle, perhaps dead or even further away than he, and his sadness would return. Sometimes he would walk through the trees to the beach on which he landed, and stand gazing over the water at a land he could not see.

"When I am home," he told Ladja one night, as they nestled in his alcove, "I shall never seek another land. I will get a new boat, and fish; but always within sight of Gotland."

She nodded, resting in the crook of his arm.

He spoke to her with sudden earnestness. "Ladja," he told her. "When I go, come with me."

He felt her response before she spoke, for she stiffened in his arm.

"Do not grow to care for me that way," she warned, but there was naught but tenderness in her voice. "There is a man at home I think of every day. He will be wed by now, but when I return he will send away his wife, whoever she is, and wed me."

He had half expected her rebuff, but it hurt him still. He was silent, and after a moment she went on.

"When they took me from my home I wore golden ear-rings, and finger-rings also of gold," she said, and Dagr had before noticed the tiny holes in her small ear lobes. "They hang now from Thorkel's wife's brooches. Before I go I will take them with me, and step ashore the banks of the Svir again wearing Rus gold."

"But . . . how will you reach there?" he finally asked.

"In Spring you will go with Thorkel and many of his people to the trading post at the southern tip of Öland. One day when I am there to help carry back his goods I will find a trader, heading to the land of the Rus. I will be his woman aboard ship in return for his ferrying me there."

He took a long breath. "And your son?"

"He is half Svear," she answered. "If he wishes to come with me, he will, but it is his to decide. I was taken from my home-land, and will not do the same to my son."

"You are so . . . sensible," Dagr said.

"We women have need to be sensible. If we were not we could never survive all the foolishness you men put us through."

The days of Fall dwindled, and hard Winter arrived. Dagr felt the days were shorter and the nights colder than on Gotland. Thorkel laughed at a young man's fancy, but admitted that home-sickness could drain the savour even from the feasting of Blót, that chill month of sacrifice and slaughter, and the revelry of the Winter's Nights festivals, when one could take heart that the Wheel of the Year had turned and the Sun would begin its steady ascent in the heavens.

Farm work in Winter is mainly the tending of beasts and the fixing and making of tools, and while Thorkel's sons and serving men fashioned new wooden handles for shovels and picks, Dagr busied himself at the forge fire-ring he had made. He made iron strappings to hold together the staves of newly-made wood buckets, and drew forth nails and spikes. The short days passed.

When the snows were deep the younger folk pushed themselves about on wooden skis, poling their way over drifts. A few times Dagr went thus down to the shore of the Baltic. The forest which had been closed with leafy shrubs and tangled undergrowth now lay open to his kick and thrust. There at the edge of the beach he would look over the slush of frozen sea water. The sky itself seemed frozen, a pale swirl of milky blue and silver grey, melded to the chunks of thrusting ice which floated slowly with the current. He would gaze towards home until the blasts of icy air drove him back to Thorkel's warm hall.

And there was Ladja. He did not ask her again to come with him back to Gotland; now that the year had turned he felt that if the Gods smiled he would find a ship to take him before Mid-Summer, and as restless as he felt, he need be content with that hope. And she was, he knew, treading her own path. Her resolve was such that he did not doubt that one day she would in fact step ashore on the banks of the Svir. She had told him their first night that she had come to him to show that the Rus could give as well as take. Dagr must content himself with that.

After the Spring thaw the fields dried out under the ever-higher Sun. The air was still chill, but the meadows sprung a riot of fresh green grasses beginning to be dotted with yellow, blue, and white wild flowers. Lambs and kids were born, in abundance, and Thorkel's son's wife brought forth a new daughter. Shearing days began, and thick raw wool was pushed into cauldrons of boiling water until globs of wool-wax rose to the surface.

Dagr, missing any form of fishing, had a mind to make
a weir in one of the deeper pools of a stream in the woods.
He might come up with eels, or even bream. He recalled
seeing a few sea-berry shrubs growing near a beach a cove
away from the one he had washed up on, and set out to
find a few and dig out their roots, good for weaving into
fish weir nets. He went with an axe and a pike, made his
way through the burgeoning woods, and thence to the
narrow beach in which grew the shrubs. He pushed his
way through the undergrowth and onto the pebbled sand.
He straightened up, and stared. There, hauled up on the
beach, were two fishing boats. One of them was his.

His surprise was so great he dropped the pike he
was holding. It had been many months since he had seen
her, and he felt as a man would if a prized horse had run
way, and then trotted back home. When he could tear his
eye from her he scanned the beach. There was no sign of
folk, and from his vantage point he could not be sure if
foot-tracks lay in the sand. He had his knife at his belt,
but decided the axe to be the better weapon, and walked
as quietly as he could to the boat. If any Rus be sleeping
within he wanted to be ready to meet him.

His boat was not the nearest to him, and he cau-
tiously approached the first and peered over the side. It
was empty. He walked the few strides to his own, crossing
in front of the bow so he could look in the side she listed
to. Again empty.

His hand went to her straked side, and he lowered
the axe. His tool chest was gone, but the mast was there,
lying against the keel, with the linen sail furled next to it.
The steering oar looked as it always had. There was a new,
and larger anchor stone, with a quantity of hempen line

attached. He climbed over the rail. He picked up the sail and unrolled it, letting it pool at his feet. It was sound, and he re-furled it. Coils of line lay near the end of the mast. He stood there a moment longer, and then he saw the head of a nail, sticking up slightly from the deck. It was the last thing he had been looking at before he had leapt over the side to his seeming death.

He jumped down to the sand. It was hard-packed and gave little proof of his having been there, but he crouched down and backed away, brushing it gently with one hand until he reached the tree line. Then he ran for the farm.

Thorkel was sitting on a stool in the kitchen yard having his hair cut by one of his daughters when Dagr ran up to him, panting, to tell of his find. The old man sputtered in his amaze, and the daughter brought Dagr a dipperful of water to slow his words and give them both time to absorb this news.

"I will take her, now, if you allow a man or two to help me push her into the water," Dagr was saying. "She is up high on the beach, but I will only need them for this, nothing more."

There was still a month until the trading post in the South would open; this was not what Thorkel had planned. His head was thrumming. No one should have landed in that cove, and yet there was not one but two strange boats, one of them stolen. And the thought that pirates might be near was none too comforting. Yet as Dagr talked, the old man regained some of his wits, and began nodding as he thought aloud. "Já, it is only right and just for a man to recover his own property," he agreed, "and even if I am questioned I can truly say I saw no one steal a boat."

A small throng of folk had gathered around them at this point, and Thorkel began gesticulating and giving orders, though the two cooks, who had doted on Dagr's zeal for their efforts, had already begun filling a food bag for his journey. Several of Thorkel's younger sons were eager to be those who would help push the boat into the sea, but Dagr, looking over them, insisted the two strongest of the farm hands be allowed to serve, and that his safety in getting away cleanly was dependent on the quickest and fastest exit, with the fewest spectators.

Thorkel would not be left out of the witnessing of this act of justice, and went for his mantle, the hair on one side of his head a hand's length shorter than the other. Dagr stood about, looking at the line of faces, and saw Ladja. He wished to speak to her, and time was short. He was trying to think of a way to be alone with her when Thorkel returned, cloaked and ready to leave. First he pressed a small purse of silver in Dagr's hand, insisting he take a share-man's wage for the work he had done over the Winter, "For the smithing would have come out of my own purse, if you had not done it."

This benison was unexpected, and Dagr placed his hand over his heart as he took the silver. He went then to the old man's wife, and thanked her for her hospitality, and for the wool mantle she had had woven for him, and which he wore now. As he dipped his head to her he saw again the slender hoops of Rus gold, two large and two small, strung on a necklace of silver chain links and hanging from the brooches over her heavy breasts. One day Ladja will find a way to slip those rings from your chain, just as I am about to take back my boat, he thought.

Then Ladja was crossing to him. She had taken the food bag out of the hands of the cook and came to his side to deliver it; he was already walking, Thorkel in tow, towards his goal.

"Take this silver," he hissed, trying to push the purse into her hand.

"Nai, you will need it yourself," she answered. "I will have gold," she reminded him, with the faintest of smiles.

"Share it with me, then. For the sake of what you have been to me." He had poked his fingers into the bag and extracted what he hoped was half of the coins and hack-silver within. As he took the food bag he pressed the silver into her palm. Her lips pursed, but she nodded.

"I thank you, Ladja. I hope you are on the banks of the river Svir this Summer."

After a final wave to the household he did not look back. Thorkel surprised him by breaking into a little jog, and the four men were quickly at the cove.

"There is danger sailing so early in the Spring," Thorkel reminded him as Dagr lay the food bag and water-skin in the prow. Dagr did not bother to answer that danger had caught him in late Summer, when sailing is thought to be the safest.

Together Dagr and the two men pushed the boat down the beach. The tide had gone out a bit, but once the stern was in water their pushing was eased. Then Dagr took hold of the rail and pulled himself up and over. The men gave a final push, and the boat was free.

He wasted no time lifting the mast. As he busied himself he saw the men retreat into the trees, Thorkel last.

He sailed north up the Öland coast for a while. It was past mid-day and he could never reach Gotland before dark, not this early in the season, and not beating against the wind as he must do. He dropped anchor in a cove at the northern tip of Öland, ate some of the roast lamb and bread from his food-bag, and as the sky darkened, wrapped himself in his mantle to sleep. He felt the gentle heave and swell of the sea, and looked up at a sky swimming with stars. When he got home he would make Offering to Njord. He thought on this, lying safe and dry within his own boat, lulled by hearing its creak and the lapping of the water against her sturdy sides.

At dawn he was underway, sailing due east. He saw one small fishing boat, no more than that. The wind was fresh and his sail billowed in catching it. He skimmed over the silvery water, his hand firm on the steering oar, his face fixed on the place Gotland would appear. The Sun was not yet overhead and he sailed into its growing warmth.

When his island home emerged, dark, low, and long, on the edge of the water, he began to laugh. As soon as he could make out a landmark he steered north up the coast. He saw a few boats, specks on the horizon, and wondered if one of them was Tufi's. He hoped he would be home when he drove the boat up into their cove.

As he neared the place, Dagr knew there was water in his eyes. He could see the snug house, the fish-hut, the long row of still-empty drying racks. Tufi's boat was not there. He ran his boat up until she caught in the sand, and threw over his new anchor-stone to keep her there. He leapt out.

One of Tufi's youngest ran across the grass and up to him, calling joyously, then darted towards the kitchen yard. Dagr strode there, coming almost face to face with

Tufi's wife as she stood at the work table, pounding a slab of salt fish with a mallet.

Her mouth opened.

"The featherbed you made me saved my life," Dagr told her. Then she burst into tears.

NJORD AND SKAÐI

WHEN Tufi sailed in later he saw Dagr's boat, and leapt from his own to embrace his younger brother. The household was up late that night, eating and drinking, and the little glazed crock of mead was opened to salute the return of he thought lost.

Halle was alive; he had returned just before the onset of Winter. The Rus had attacked a farm on the coast of Smáland, and Halle, who had been ordered to stay with the ship, had found opportunity to slip over the side and run into the trees. After a fitful night in the woods he met a goatherd driving his herd from their Summer pastures. In a few days he found a fur-trader to take him to Gotland, where he made his way home. But he had had to stop at the house of Tufi and tell them Dagr had been thrown overboard. Halle's shock seeing Dagr alive was perhaps even the greater than his own brother's, and he needed many cups of ale before the colour returned to his cheek.

"I will have my wife make me a second featherbed, one for my boat," he resolved, "so I may become a seaduck, as you did, and live, should I find my way into the sea."

Dagr worked hard all Summer. He had lost the entire value of all the stock-fish his boat had been taken with, and still owed Tufi silver for the boat. The weather was fair and fishing was good that year, and soon the drying racks were strung with pale slabs of salted cod and herring.

But he was restless. The year had changed him in many ways, some which he could name and others he could not.

"Dagr, you should wed," his sister-in-law would prompt him. He nodded, but with no real conviction. Then he would remember the comfort of a warm body pressed against his.

There were families with likely daughters nearby, a few of whom, Tufi's wife privately suspected, were being sent rather too often for the families' true wants to buy fish, for if the maidens arrived and saw Dagr's boat was out they appeared crestfallen. But she could interest Dagr in none of them. Just to the north of them was Fiskehamn, one of the largest trading posts on Gotland, and well known for its fish, as its name belied. It was another place in which a man looking for a wife might profit by spending time at, for inland farmers came, families in tow, to trade grain or wool for stock-fish. No woman caught his eye.

Yet the harder he worked the more restless he became. Tufi no longer needed him, for even with his bigger boat he now had his sons to aid with hauling, which is why he had helped Dagr buy his own boat in the first place.

Toward the end of Summer Halle, who ranged broadly up and down the coast, stopped by with news: there was a trader on the East coast of Gotland, almost directly over-land from where they now stood, paying good prices for stock-fish. Tufi's fish were nearly all spoken for, but Dagr, due to his long days hauling full nets, had a surplus. He determined to hazard a trip down the coast and round the island's sharp point to reach this eager trader. It took two days of easy sailing to reach there, dropping anchor at night in a barren cove just around the wind-driven southern tip.

Dagr sailed into the trading town just at mid-day. It lay in the crook of a sheltered bay, near a jutting spit of rock, and had a shallow shingle beach of white limestone pebbles and coarse sand. A wooden pier, newly built, proclaimed the town's intent to grow as a trading centre; it had as yet a single line of stalls and small warehouses lining the short road that ran along the water's edge. A few men upon the road watched Dagr's approach, and after he had dropped the sail and steered the boat near the pier, stood ready to catch his thrown line. After exchanging greetings with the men he tied up his steering oar, and they pointed him to the stall of the stock-fish trader he sought.

After prying open the casks and inspecting their contents the trader offered Dagr a half-mark more of silver per cask than he had expected. On top of this, they sealed their business over a deep cup of ale at the trader's stall, where the man's wife brought forth steaming bowls of dried fish stew, and hot loaves of bread.

"Lucky are my fish, if this be the Fate of those I have sold you," Dagr praised, lifting the wooden spoon to his mouth, which made the woman dip her head to him. He oft times had a nice turn of phrase ready when needed, a continuing gift from paying heed to his old Uncle Ake. The trader grinned and nodded his head in agreement.

Back out on the trading road Dagr looked about him in satisfaction. His belly was full, the pouch at his belt heavy with silver, and his boat was empty. He had received courteous welcome and made a profitable sale; this place was a good one. He spent a long moment standing on the edge of the pounded road. He looked out over the Baltic, knowing that the first land-fall was far to the East. The light looked the same on this side of the island, but he felt different. He looked out towards shores more distant, the great trading routes that followed faraway rivers and traced into the lands of the Rus and its white-furred foxes, and deeper still to the South, to those lands of glimmering silk and fragrant spice. He did not care to think of the Rus pirates, but for a moment he let Ladja's face and form rise in his mind.

The wind picked up and ruffled the water he gazed at. The Sun was warm on his back but he saw from the length of his falling shadow that it was heading down. If he left now he could sail until dusk, make landfall and spend the night on the boat, and be back at Tufi's before night tomorrow. He would not be back this way, not until next Fall when he had more fish to sell; and even if he had racks full of them at Tufi's the winds would soon make the sail perilous. He must leave now.

He turned and began walking towards his waiting boat. He had a full cask of water and had eaten little of the food he had aboard; nothing need stay him. Then a woman came out of the stall he was passing.

She was of mid-height, and wore a blue gown with a long-sleeved shift of yellow beneath it. A white linen head-wrap was knotted at her nape, and her red hair streamed out from underneath and fell over her shoulders to her waist. She had a basket over her wrist, which to judge from how lightly she bore it, must be empty. He knew her at once. It was the red-haired maiden he had met at the Thing.

He stood without moving, looking at her, knowing he was smiling. She looked at him and paused.

"Hej," he said.

He was not sure she knew him; the look on her face was shifting.

"I am Dagr. We met at the Thing, several Summers past. You were carrying water and would not stop to try the fellows' ale."

Some light flickered in her face, her red brows lifted. His face was sun-browned, his hair sun-streaked and wind-blown, and at this moment his clothing was none too clean. He was taller than her, now.

"You wore a blue gown, lighter in colour than that which you wear today," he prompted.

"Já," she finally said. "The sunset on the peaks of Asgard. Your father's ram." The lips began to bow in a smile beneath the small nose. "But we did not meet. You are wrong there. You spoke to me; that is all." There was no hint of smile now.

"That is true," Dagr admitted.

He could not stop looking at her, and knew he should stop; she must be wed, and her husband might step out of the doorway and collar him for staring so. Still, he looked. She had changed but little, her cheeks perhaps less rounded beneath their pale freckles, her light blue eyes a bit sharper. The mouth too, a little more defined, as befit a woman who freely spoke her mind.

"You would never tell your name. Will you tell it now?" he asked.

She paused long enough to make him speak again, for fear of having offended her.

"That is my boat. I fish on the western coast. I landed this morning and sold my stock-fish to the trader there" – he lifted his hand to the stall with the red awning.

She nodded. "I saw you both roll the casks to his place." Then she added, "I did not know it was – you."

He nodded. "Já, Dagr. He who finds you lovely as Frigg." He was smiling again, and chose to disregard the little wince she made. "Will you not tell me your name?"

"I will tell you now. It is Rannveig," she answered. He took heart at once; she would have warned him not to speak thus if she were wed.

"Rannveig," he repeated. "A fine name. And do you still brew no ale?"

Here she laughed a moment. "You have sharp ears to recall every word I uttered so many years ago."

"Only five Summers," he corrected, as if it had been five weeks. "And of your ale?" he asked again, almost teasing her. He hoped to see her smile again.

"If you must know, I now brew very good ale," she returned.

"So the God has spat in it?" he asked.

She laughed aloud. "My father said that! When I made my first batch of good ale, he told me the tale of the queen who despaired of her brewing. She prayed to Odin and he flew by and spat in her big crock, and the ale foamed and was the best in the land."

"Old Ake, my father's brother, told me of that," Dagr said. He did not find it hard to believe that her father had compared her to a queen, or her ale, at least.

"I should like to taste it," he said, after a pause. Of a sudden she cast her eyes down, and he went on, "To raise a cup with your father."

"He is dead," she answered.

He nodded, then went ahead and asked what he must know.

"And you Rannveig, are you wed?"

Her lips pursed a moment. "Not wed," she said. Her voice was quiet as she said it, but after it was out she lifted her eyes and stared him full in the face.

She began to walk, and he fell in next her. "Do you live here?" he wanted to know.

"Not here, but at our upland farm. We have a hall at the end of that road" – she pointed up a short but steep hill, to a wooden hall with a stone front – "but I let it as a store-house for grain and hay for the folk here on the trading road."

"We?" he wanted to know.

"I mean, it was my mother's. She has joined my father. I have a brother Rapp, much older. Years ago he wed a girl whose folk raised horses. They live at her farm. My parent's hall and farm are mine."

Dagr had never heard of even the smallest farm being held by a lone woman; it was far too much work. "Who farms it with you?" he asked.

"I grow apples," she explained. "An old couple and their son come to help with the haying and vegetables, and pick and dry apples with me every year. My grain I trade for. I keep only one cow, and a few hens; nothing I cannot care for myself."

He had a hard time accepting this. "So you are alone? You farm it alone?"

She gave a slight shrug. "Apples need little care. Before Mid-Summer I pick off the smallest so that those which remain grow the larger. I have a skep full of bees, and the trees flower well. Before my mother died we planted many apple-seedlings, so I have young trees coming up too."

He said nothing, taking this in, and saw her eyes flick to his boat, waiting there at the pier.

"It is a different life from yours, that is all," she finished.

He too looked at his boat, and the life it represented. His eyes then moved along the broad swath of limestone shingle to the line of the gently lapping Baltic.

"It is a fine bay," he told her. "Good shelter, and a pier too. You should live here."

"Do not tell me where I should live. I love the farm, my apples, the land." She was almost snapping at him.

"But here there are folk, and goods, and . . . the sea," he tried.

She gave her head a little shake, but her mouth had softened.

"The sea-air – " he began.

"Sea-damp," she corrected.

He began to laugh a bit despite her. She looked at him, her head cocking on her white neck.

"We are like the tale of Njord and Skaði, one arguing for the sea, the other, the hills," he said.

The God of the sea had wed a beautiful giantess who cared only for the hills and woods. Njord hated the hills and snow, and she hated the waves and damp, so they parted.

She looked quickly away, and he thought he should not have spoken of such things; to jest of any marriage, even an unhappy one, with a maid was to open a chest which might be difficult to close.

The silence that followed was broken by her. "It is late in the season for trading," she noted. She had inclined her head to the trees that ringed the trading road. He looked with her, saw their leaves already beginning to rust, standing out more sharply against the green of the pine needles.

"Já," he answered. "But I had heard it could be to my profit to come."

"And was it?"

"Já, it was," he said, but he was smiling at her as he said it. "And also I have a full half-mark of silver more for each of my four casks."

She shook this off. "Well. If you have made your profit, you should be off."

"The wind is picking up, and the water is roughening," he said, raising his hand to the sea, though there were no more white tips on its surface than before.

She pressed her lips together in a tight smile. "Then leave your boat here, and walk home. Overland it cannot take you more than one or two days."

"But early snow can overtake a man, this time of year," he returned, willing to say something as improbable as this to buy more time with her.

For answer she gave a toss of her head.

They had reached the mouth of the pier. A bench made from a slab of wood sat off to one side of it. He slowed, hoping she might stop and sit. When she did he settled down next her. She placed her basket at her feet.

"What did you buy?" he asked, trying to return to a lighter mood.

Her eyes followed his down to the basket, then back. "Nothing. I took tapers to the grain-merchant."

"Bees' wax tapers?" She had said she kept bees for the sake of her apples; they must do well if she could also dip tapers.

For answer she gave a short nod. The Sun was dropping, casting all about them in a warm yellow light. He glanced at his boat, waiting. If he did not speak again he feared that she would rise and bid him fare-well. He made a small sound in his throat.

"Tell me of your life, Rannveig," he invited. The Sun striking her hair made the tips of it golden.

Her lips parted, and she spent a long moment looking at him, but she spoke.

"My father had the apple farm, and my mother's parents gave her the hall; she had no brother. As I said, my brother Rapp had married well, and moved upland to raise horses. We had serving folk here at the hall, and at the farm men who helped with the heaviest work. My father did some trading across the sea, sending apples from our farm, and sheep-skins he would trade for to the Prus and Pomerani; one ship a year only. We had enough; plenty. I was born in the hall" – here she turned her head over her shoulder to the timber and stone building at the top of the hill – "but I liked the farm best. One year my father bought a half-share in a herring-ship, a ship that sailed from here, and never returned. It was a great loss, as my father had borrowed silver with which to buy the share."

Her eyes went to Dagr's fishing boat as she spoke, as if seeing it made the loss fresh again.

"He died not long after that, in Winter. My mother knew he had buried silver and we spent much of Spring trying to find it. We dug and dug, beneath the floorboards at the farm, by big rocks, everywhere we could think of. We knew he needed it in Odin's hall, and wanted only enough to keep the farm up. We never found it.

"So we let the hall, and she and I worked the farm. We sold many of the beasts, planted seedlings so we could grow more apples.

"Last Spring she died. Their ashes are there, at the place of burial." She lifted her chin across the beach to a spot at the far end of the trading road.

He considered all this. She had been cherished by her parents, spoilt, even. Her life had been an easy one; it was likely her sharp tongue and high expectations that had kept her from being wed. Then the comfort she had known was lost with the herring-boat, and her father died. A picture flashed in his mind of her and her aged mother bending over the soil, planting young trees.

When she turned her head back to him his eyes fell upon the necklace about her throat. "The last time I saw you, you were choosing such beads," he recalled aloud.

Her fingers went to the glass beads of red, blue, and yellow. "Já," she said, with a slight smile. "I have always liked them." After a pause she went on. "And that is the last time I saw you." She looked steadily upon him. "It is fair, now, that you should tell me how the years have passed for you."

He nodded. "And so I shall. The following Spring I went to one of my brother's farms. I spent the year with him, then thought I would try fishing. I have always liked the sea, and have an older brother, Tufi, who has made a good way for himself fishing on the western coast, near Fiskehamn. I spent three years with him, learning boats, handling nets, dressing and drying the catch. As Tufi's own sons grew and could join him on his boat, he got me this smaller one – " here he nodded towards his boat – "and I worked steadily to pay him back."

His words slowed. "The first time he sent me to Svearland with a load of fish to sell, pirates caught me. They seized the ship, took the man I had sailed with as their pilot for their war-ship, and forced me overboard."

He heard her small gasp, but he was looking down as he recounted this.

"I was saved by clinging to a featherbed – my own – which had been thrown over as well. I washed ashore on the coast of Öland. I stayed with a rich farmer for the Winter, and then saw my boat in a cove not far away. I took it back, sailed to Gotland and my brother's family. That was last year." He gave a slow and steady exhale. "And now I am here."

"Sailing is full of danger," she murmured. She herself was looking down, as if she could not look upon the water after hearing this.

He wished to turn the talk back to her.

"So you are alone, Rannveig. And have not yet wed."

She jerked her head. "I know what you are thinking: Here is a woman with a farm, and a hall, to be had for the asking. You are wrong!"

"You do not know what I am thinking," he corrected. His voice was low and firm, for he had not forgotten that once she had considered him a potential mate. The rush of recognition of this fact he had felt years ago returned in shadow form to him now.

"I see a woman as lovely as Frigg, but as angry as a crow."

She gave a little exhale at this, almost a snort. He went on, with new earnestness.

"We have spoken of the last time we saw each other. Now I will speak of the first. That first time I saw you, by the fire-light, it was clear you held yourself in high regard. I spoke courteously to you, when the others were jesting and calling. Next morning you chided me for being a boy.

"Despite what you think, today I am asking you for nothing. I need ask for nothing," he stressed, warming to his words. "I have my own boat. If I wanted to wed for the sake of silver, I could do that. There have been women enough who would take me."

At once he regretted it. It sounded a boast, and was not quite true, besides. And it made him sound as if he had a woman in every port. Well, let her think that if she would.

Even so he was not prepared for the tartness of her response.

"I am sure that when you wed you will win silver as well as the woman of your desiring," she said, jumping up.

"Then I hope you have silver," he said.

She was in the act of turning from him as he said this. She stopped, and faced him where he still sat upon the bench.

"You, my tart-tongued beauty," he said.

He stood. He leaned towards her, his face as grave as was his tone. He gazed at her long enough that she was forced to speak.

She was shaking her head. "Stop. I . . . I am . . . old." She let her eyes meet his as she frowned. "I will wrinkle and grey before you."

"How old?" he asked.

"Five-and-twenty, six-and-twenty . . . " She looked down. "I try to forget."

"At Blót I will be twenty-two. Is that so great a gap between us?"

She still wore a frown.

"There is a wrinkle, already," he smiled, leaning forward to kiss her forehead.

When he pulled back he saw tears gleaming in her eyes.

"How far to your farm?" he asked now.

So his jest was over, she thought. He must be worried about her making it back before nightfall. Let him go his way; she would go hers.

She let her eyes lift and scan the sky for a moment. The skies were paling above the tired trees. Fall was coming, and soon.

"There is time to reach there before dark," she answered.

But Dagr had made his decision.

"Then let us begin now," he told her, and stooped to pick up the basket at her feet. He straightened up and fastened his blue-green eyes upon her. "If you wish it, I will leave in the morning, and never see you again."

She swallowed. "And if I do not wish that . . . ?"

"Then we will hand-fast, tomorrow. And I will send word to Tufi and his wife to join us for our wedding feast, at Blót."

APPLES

DAGR went to his boat. He took the small leathern pouch of tinder and striker from his toolkit, for he was woodsman enough not to enter woods near dusk without it. His food bag he left behind; if he need sail in the morning it would be there for him. He glanced about his boat, then checked the line holding her to the pier. Rannveig stood by the bench they had been sitting on, not quite watching him. She felt a tightness in her chest, and in the waves lapping before her almost heard the blood pulsing in her ears.

He jumped down on the wooden planks of the pier. He knew he was grinning, and tried not to; her head was lowered as if she wished, by not seeing, not to be seen.

He took her basket from her once more, and laid his fire-striking kit inside it. She wished he had not taken it from her; without it she had nothing to hold, nowhere to put her hands. She clutched her light shawl with them instead, hugging herself as if she were cold. The wind had picked up slightly, sending a few early-downed leaves skittering. She led him up the steep hill, at the end of which sat her hall.

When they reached the top he turned a moment to look back. There was the sea, stretching away in an endless wash of blue-grey water, deepening at the horizon where the sky was already beginning to darken. And there was his boat, lashed safely, riding gently at the pier's end. He could see the whole trading road from here, and down the length of the coast to the far close of the shallow bay.

He said aloud what he had said to himself earlier. "This place is a good one."

She had paused when he had, and had turned with him, looking back. For answer she gave a nod of her head. The lips were pressed together but the slightest of smiles hung there.

Her hall was small but sturdy; like, he thought, his boat. He could see why folk would wish to store their grain there. The fact that the two narrow ends were of stone marked it as having been built by a rich man, and one who took care that what he touched might last. There was a well near the front door, and as they passed the long wooden side of the hall he saw a stable, of almost the same size as the hall. She led him past this, where a wall of spruce trees fronted the woods behind. He saw the narrow track, and Rannveig stepped onto it.

They barely spoke as they walked. It was awkward, walking in a woods unknown to him, following the blue gown and trailing red hair of this woman who kept her face resolutely forward, never stopping to look back. He need watch his feet, they both did, and if the trees had not already shed some of their leaves the way would have been dark indeed. The Sun gleamed dully in the West before them. They passed a fork, in which the track widened to the right, but they stayed on the narrower left path. It was full dusk when the trees thinned.

There was a meadow, and beyond that rows of neatly planted trees. Dagr could see that apples hung there; he could make out clusters of dark spheres against the sky. To one side grew a great tree, an oak, he thought, and then sat the house. It was small, far smaller than the barn behind it. He saw a cow move, walking across a small paddock towards them, and heard her low.

So they were here. Rannveig's step had slowed just a little. When the cow lowed, she turned to him.

"I must milk; and the hens need penning," she said. She sounded a bit breathless; they had been moving quickly through the forest.

"I will do it," he offered, looking to the cow.

"Nai," she said. "Not – not her; she fears men, and will kick. I must do it."

He nodded; some cows were moody and resented a stranger's touch. "The hens, then," he agreed. Some were already in the barn, awaiting the handfuls of grain they could count on. He called the rest with a click of his teeth, and scattered their reward as they strutted in, a few dancing with outstretched wings.

The cow had followed Rannveig, and he swung the door closed behind them as she pulled at the full udder. A window high in the wall sent a shaft of light onto the straw covered floor. He watched Rannveig as she filled the basin. She seemed intent on her task, eyes lowered, hands working steadily. The cow was making little grunts of contentment as she moved her jaws side to side. The fresh-milk smell added to that of the fowl and the cow herself, filling the space with the warm aroma of animals at their feed.

When she was done Rannveig poured the milk into a thick-walled crock. She bent to pick it up, but Dagr reached down and took it from her. A little colour arose in her cheek, visible even in the low light they stood in. Again she nodded, wordlessly, and led him to one of the out buildings. He lowered the crock into the stone-lined trench waiting there. She shut the door and shot the bar across it.

It was dim enough that the coals of the kitchen yard cooking-ring shown a black-frosted red. Rannveig picked up a poker and opened the coals, then laid three more pieces of wood upon them.

"You will be hungry," she said, looking at the fire, and not him. Her voice was so quiet that he had need to move his head closer to make her out.

"It is your ale I am eager for," he answered.

She looked at him then, and he thought she swallowed as she nodded.

The house stood before them. He had taken up her basket, but now she reached to him and took it into her own hand. She paused to light a short length of twisted rush at the fire's edge.

She did not lock her door. She pushed it open, and went swiftly from place to place, lighting cressets with the flaming rush. When she was done she tossed it in the cold fire-pit; there was still warmth enough not to need an indoor fire.

There was a small table and two short benches before the pit. There were four sleeping alcoves, two on each wall, one of which was without curtains, and she laid the basket there. The other three had curtains, all drawn open. It was clear which was her alcove, for the others had no featherbeds within. Dagr saw the whiteness of linen on her bed, and the dark coverlet of curly fleeces sewn together. Rannveig saw him looking at it, and moved to a chest set against an outside wall. She lowered a dipper and filled a pottery cup, and set it on the table, then filled a second and did the same.

He wished she would speak, but he himself was at a loss of what to say. He stood there at her table-side, and picked up the cup. The cressets flickered and jumped, filling the space with their darting light; the breeze must be coming from the smoke holes at the gables. He looked into the darkness of his cup. The smell of her ale met his nose as he lifted it to his face. It was herbal, and deep, and strong. He took a draught.

Without putting his cup down he spoke. "The ale, like the woman, is a fine one," he told her.

She had not taken up her cup, but now she met his eyes. "I thank you, Dagr," she whispered.

Now he put his cup next hers, and closed the slight distance between them. He again kissed her brow, letting his lips press against the cool skin there. Then he reached his arms about her, gathered her into him. He lowered his head, let his mouth touch hers. She tasted her ale upon his lip, then tasted him as with his tongue he traced the line of her lips. He slowed himself, kissed her again, gently. He felt her shoulders were tensed but she offered her mouth readily enough.

His tongue was pressing at her teeth, and his arm around her waist was arching her neck and head back the slightest bit. Her own arms had lifted and now reached to him, touching the sides of his face as their lips clung. He kept on with his kiss until she was gasping and breathless.

When he moved his hips to hers so that the hardness of his prick pressed against her gown she gave the smallest movement, almost a shudder. But she did not let go.

One of his hands still held her at the small of her back, but he let the other move along the wool of her gown to her breast. He cupped the roundness of it, warm and full beneath the fabric, and with reaching fingers felt the nipple beneath harden.

"You, who are as lovely as Frigg," he murmured, "take me into your bed."

For answer she moved her hands from his neck, began untying her sash. He let her free for a moment as he worked at his belt and the toggle of his leggings. His lips returned to hers, and he reached down and began to pull up the skirts of her gown. She stayed his hands with a little sound, and he watched her own fingers at her shoulder brooches. Once free of them the straps of her overgown fell. He picked up hem of both gown and shift and in one movement pulled them over her head. Her head-wrap came with them. He stopped kissing her just long enough to yank off his boots and leggings.

She wore naught but her shoes and stockings now, and the single strand of coloured beads about her neck; and he stood before her naked. The hardness of his body was pointing at her, leaning towards her in its yearning.

She kept her eyes on his face, and he wondered if she was fearful; she seemed almost to sway, as if she might faint. He had backed her up against her box bed now, and he placed his hands on her shoulders and lowered her to sit. He dropped to his knees, untied the linen bindings of her stockings, and stripped both them and the low shoes off.

With one arm about her shoulders and the other under her knees he laid her down before him.

He had not expected her to be a maid, not at her age; yet maid she was. Later he bethought him that she would be none other; her pride was such that she would not give herself carelessly, regardless of how lonely she might be. But as he began to stroke her body, feeling her tremble beneath his hand, Ladja's words came back to him, Tonight we will take our time.

That is what he did. Despite the heat of his own desire, once she was naked and in his arms he did not give way to his need. He kept kissing her mouth, her throat, the curve of her shoulders. He rolled the beads of her necklace in his fingers, saw how they nestled in the hollow of her collarbone. He stroked up from her breast to her armpit, and swept his fingers down the length of her arm, teasing the inside of her wrist, to end in the palm of her hand, where his finger traced slow circles. He kissed her again. He let his hand knead and caress the softness of her breasts. She was panting, and his own breath came fast. His hand travelled down to her waist, rested a moment at the fullness of her hip, then slid down her leg. His fingers played against the back of her knee as they had in her palm. Then he drew his hand up, slipping it inside her thigh, stroking upward to where her thighs met in a tangle of red curls. His hand rested upon the crispness of those curls. His fingers pressed over the mound there, gently, gently.

"Rannveig," he murmured. She answered only in the quickness of her breath. He brought his body closer alongside hers; he could wait no longer. He drew his prick up her leg, hot and iron-hard, the tight flesh of its rounded knob soft, even yielding as it pressed against her thigh. He slid his arm beneath her, flattening her into the feather-bed, and with his knee pressed open her own.

He hung above her a moment. The light from the cressets played about her, lighting her face and breasts. Her eyes were closed.

"Look at me," he breathed. "This is Dagr, who saw you once and never forgot."

The eyes fluttered open. He saw the tears welled at their corners. Her lips parted in a smile.

He brought his hips to hers. He went as slowly as he could, feeling his way into the richness of her hollow, pausing as she gasped, drawing backwards for a moment, pushing deeper into that sacred warmth until his prick was buried. Even then he waited, his strokes small, his weight held by his arms on either side of her. Her arms came slowly up around him, her hands holding his neck. His movement grew, as gently as he could make it. She began to lift her hips in small echo of his, two seals joined and buoyed by water. Her hands had moved down to his ribcage. Now they slid to rest in the small of his back, and she pressed him into her. At her pressure he quickened his movement, and after a few more strokes he came off, shuddering. He tilted his head back, eyes to the roof of her little house, and breathed out a sigh. He dropped his face to hers, kissed her brow a final time, and then her lips.

He stayed there, hanging over her, looking down upon her face. She had closed her eyes again, and the hands in the small of his back that had held him there had relaxed. He withdrew, slowly, and settled himself at her side once more.

She drew her legs together. She felt the dribble of his seed upon her inner thigh, and wondered if some blood from her broken maidenhead be mixed there. The muscles of her groin twitched from having been pressed open by his weight. The pain she had felt when he entered her had been sudden and sharp, but had dulled with his movement. She was left with a low burning ache there in her deepest part. She turned on her belly, then on her side, face away from him.

Dagr dropped his arm about her and pulled close to her. His body wrapped hers, his knees resting in the hollow of her knees, his belly against her back. His hand went to the face he could not see and traced the outline of her cheek, and her lips.

There were many things he wanted to say. He wished to praise her beauty, the softness of her skin, the generous curves of her body. He wished to thank her for years ago thinking him a mate for her, and somehow thank her for the pride that had kept her a maid. He wished to tell her that next time would be better, easier and with less pain, and that there were many ways in which he wanted to caress her; and that he wished to do so, right now. But her seeming discomfiture was such that he could say none of them.

He could not tell her of how he wished to tease and thrill her, for he could not know if there would be a second time. He had left it up to her, and her silence and her turned back made him feel there would not. He pulled the long hair away from the nape of her neck and pressed his lips there. She said nothing, moved almost not at all, yet she had a short time ago looked at him with tears in her eyes and pressed his body deeper into her. That was something, that and lying here in her bed. Even if she sent him away in the morning, he had been first with her; it was not a gift she could give again.

The room was growing dimmer; she could hear the hiss as one of the cressets guttered and went out. She was turned away from the room, but her eyes were open and faint flickers of the oil lamps were cast upon the wall she faced. He still held her, his hand gliding past her breasts and resting on her belly. A man's hand touching her anywhere like this was new enough to make her heart pound.

This was a man she had seen once as a mere lad, years past, and had nearly forgotten. Then here he was in her home, pulling off her shift and pinning her to her bed. She knew almost nothing about him, and it would be her choice whether or not they spent their lives together. She tried to still her breathing, and reflected that as little as she knew him, he seemed to know her. It was Dagr who had said that he would be her husband if she wanted him; he had already made his choice, and it was her.

She could either take him now, or go on alone. She did not flatter herself that she would have more chances to wed. Yet her life was her own, and following the death of her parents it had been more and more one of her own making. She need account to no man, consider no one in her choices, and she had relished the freedom this allowed even as she accepted the bitterness of growing old alone. Now was Dagr come over the sea to challenge her in this.

Her breathing slowed enough that he thought she slept. Dagr reached to the foot of the box bed, found the sheepskin coverlet, and pulled it over her. They lay upon the sheet of heavy linen and he let it be. He swung his legs onto the floor and stood. He went the short space to her table and took up his cup, the cup from which he had taken a single swallow of her ale. He drained it now, and took up hers as well and drank it down. It was indeed fine ale, and the corners of his mouth rose as he recalled her laughing when he had asked if Odin had spat in it.

The second of the three cressets now flicked out. He looked around the farmhouse, noting things in the dim light he had not seen before in his arousal. The roof beam just before him was badly scorched; there had once been a house fire. Next to the cresset that still burned was an iron rush holder, empty. The piece was crude; he could work a better. There were two stout old chests of iron-strapped wood, the smaller upon the greater, near the door. He wondered what she kept locked therein, bronze cups or perhaps one or two of silver.

Still naked he went to the door, pulled it open to the night. The air was mild, more so than he would have expected. With a half-Moon lighting his way before him he went to the base of the oak, braced his legs and watered its roots. He half-laughed at himself, marking, like a hound, her property.

He returned to her house just as the final cresset died. He pulled the door shut as noiselessly as he could, and groped his way to her bed. As he sat down, feeling the mass of feathers give way beneath him, he thought of Ladja's slight weight as she sunk into the fleece-covered straw in Thorkel's house; then of the featherbed on which his life had been saved.

He draped his arm around Rannveig, closed his eyes, and listened to her quiet breathing. He wondered if he should wake her now; tell her the things he had wanted to say. But no, she slept, and old Ake had told him answers came in dreams. He would let her find hers there.

Rannveig did not sleep. She lay awake all night next the man she had given herself to. When she was certain he slept, she turned on her side, raised herself on her elbow, and fastened her eyes on his face. The Moon was setting and enough of its pearly light fell through the smoke hole to see him. The face was still, the brow smooth, the lips just slightly parted. At last she lay down again, and just before dawn herself slept.

Waking that first morning Dagr moved his arm, felt a woman's form there. He opened his eyes and turned towards her. She was facing him now, and deeply asleep. He wished to kiss her forehead once more but did not. If this was the last hour in her bed he did not want to wake her and bring it to an end.

When she opened her eyes she swept the red hair from her cheek.

"Yesterday I baked bread, in the morning. It will still be fresh," she told him in a low voice.

He hung on each word, trying to make out her meaning. She wished to feed him, and herself. It was not the request to dress and leave that he had feared. He lifted himself on his elbow.

"Is this your way of telling me that I am your husband?" he asked.

"There is butter, and honey too," she went on, her voice even softer. A slight smile played on her mouth. "And apples."

He sat more fully up. "Am I then your husband?" he demanded.

Now she answered.

"Já. You are my husband, Dagr. And I, Rannveig, am your wife."

Now he kissed her, forehead first, and then her lips. Her hair was spilling over her shoulders and breast. In the new light it was wonderfully red, just as her narrow eyes were the blue of the noon sky.

He turned from her, spotted his belt on the floor, swung his hand at it. He pulled from the pouch all the silver that he carried. The six marks of silver he had earned yesterday fell out, along with a small quantity of plain coiled hack-silver.

"I have more, at Tufi's," he told her. "Eight full marks. And I have the boat."

He swept his hand over the jumbled silver, spreading it across the linen they had slept upon.

"This is my bride-price to you, Rannveig. All my silver, that here, and that Tufi will bring to me."

She closed her eyes at this. All his silver he offered her, leaving himself nothing but his boat. And his boat was his first real possession, that with which he had earned this silver, and would earn more. Dagr needed nothing more than her brown hull to make his way.

She could not offer him this farm in return. She had lost it already; had known in the night she must give up living here, so that he could be with his boat.

"Your brother, Rapp – is he far?" he asked. "He is your kin and must witness for us."

"He is not far," she answered. "The next farm over, the broader track you saw in the woods." She was smiling fully now. "Watching his face when we tell him will be worth the walk. He despaired of me ever accepting a man."

"I give thanks to Frigg that you did," he returned. He too was smiling, but above that smile his blue-green eyes were serious. "Even the Goddess herself wed. I am glad that Rannveig could too."

THE BOY

Spring 860

THE boy awoke in his own bed. All was still; only the yellow light cracking through the woolly red curtains told him it was day. He had been hot, and his small hand reached now and plucked at the linen tunic lying damp and cold upon his chest. He pushed back the sheepskins which had covered him and sat up.

His sisters Hedinfrid and Holmfrid always woke him, laughing as they pulled back the curtains to his alcove. The three of them had been playing – yesterday? – on the floor of their father's fishing shed, Hedinfrid lifting him into a big basket and then placing another on top to make a tiny house for him. He laughed back at them as he sat crossed-legged on the rough bottom, watching them move jerkily between the slits of the woven reeds, here-gone-here-gone. He wanted to see them now. He poked through the wool curtains. He had just learned to jump down from his box bed without falling.

His sisters' alcove was across from his. Their curtains were blue, and were still drawn shut. He would surprise them this time.

The boy pushed through the heavy wool. One panel clung to his back as he climbed up into their box bed, flooding the alcove with a shaft of sunlight. Hedinfrid and Holmfrid were not there. Nothing was there. The red and green striped wool blanket they slept under was gone. The curly sheepskins to warm them, gray and cream and black, these too were gone. The featherbed alone remained, stripped and barren as if it were washing-day.

So they were hiding. He would jump down and find them. This time he fell, catching his bare foot on the smooth wooden edge of the bed, but only swept back the light brown hair from his moist face as he stood up. His back was to the rest of the room. He thought maybe Hedinfrid and Holmfrid might be under the featherbed. He lifted one corner. Not there.

He felt hot again, and his legs did not move as he wanted them to. He would find Hedinfrid and Holmfrid. The room grew brighter, and he did not know why. He turned and saw his Nenna walk through the door from the kitchen yard. One hand was clutching her looped up over-gown, and he knew she had been to the hen house. He saw his mother smile at him, her mouth moving.

"Tindr," she said. But he heard nothing.

Rannveig was crossing over to him. "You should not be out of bed so soon, my little one," she told him. She knew her face was again wet with tears, though she had mopped it with her apron twice as she stole the eggs from the hens.

The boy stood looking up at her with his blue-white eyes, seeing her smile, seeing her tears. Hearing nothing.

"Tindr," she said again, her voice rising.

He cocked his head at her. She called him again, face strained with effort. It frightened him to watch her. Her mouth formed his name again. He could not hear her. He started to quiver. Her hand loosened about the eggs she clutched, and Tindr watched with widened eyes as they rolled and dropped from the gathered wool of her gown to the wooden floor boards. One did not break.

His mother must be yelling; he could see the cords in her throat tighten and stand out. The house brightened again, and by the tail of his eye he caught a movement from the main door. His Dadda stood there, hands extended towards him, mouth open. His face grew red, calling. His Nenna looked back at Da, her empty hands limp at her sides.

She came to Tindr now, turning her back on the ruined eggs, scooping him up in her arms, kissing his face and sobbing. He felt the warmth of her arms and tasted the hot salt tears that dropped from her face onto his own. He felt the heave of her chest as she clung to him. But he could not hear her. Then Dadda was there, arms about them both, mouth open, cupping his large rough hands gently upon his tiny ears.

"Nai," Dagr was saying. "Nai, nai . . . " He could not go on, and let his tears choke his words as he shook his head. They could not have lost both girls to the fever, only to find their son left deaf as well.

The boy was almost smothered in their embrace, and only when he began to bawl in fear did they release him. His Nenna took a gasping breath and smiled at him, her eyes scrunching over her wet cheeks and reddened nose. Tindr patted her hot face and then closed his fingers around a strand of her hair.

They laid him down in his own box bed again, and stayed there, he thought, a long time, each with a hand upon him. He knew they spoke, he watched their lips and saw the movement of their throats.

Tindr heard none of it. He fell asleep with nothing more than the rushing of waves or the soughing of leaves in his ears, that and the sound of his own small beating heart.

THE SONG

Summer 864

TINDR and the other children had been down at the sea's edge; his boots were wet from the shallow wavelets slapping at the shore, and the hems of the girls' gowns were ringed with dark sand. His house was almost at the water's edge, and close to the wooden pier where trading ships docked. But the slope of the stony beach was gentle enough that his father could haul right up on it in his small broad-hulled fishing boat. Now, thirsty in the warm afternoon, Tindr trooped across the white rocks to home, the rest of them in his wake.

His mother Rannveig was at her brewing, as she nearly always was at this time of day. Her husband Dagr had built her a special shed last Fall, just for her own use, and together she and he had fashioned the little malting-oven she used to toast her barley. It had all taken half a season's fishing profits to equip, for she needed copper pans too; and a little more silver, which Dagr did not know about, from her own treasure-pot, to pay the potter for the large glazed crocks and a store of thick-rimmed serving cups. Many on the trading road had admired her ale, had jestingly told her at Winter feasts they would pay for it, and she had thought to try these promises and create enough so that she could sell it to those less skilled in the brewing-arts. This first year had gone well, though she was still at times uneasy with brewing in such quantities. The larger the crock, the greater the loss when any soured.

She heard the children as they came into the garden, the three girls singing some little nonsense song, the two other boys trying to drown them out with a rhythmic chant, and her own Tindr grunting his low *uh, uh uh*. She rose from the stone quern at which she was grinding her sprouted barley and turned and smiled at her boy.

My pretty Nenna, Tindr thought. She always smiles at me, more than to Dadda or anyone else. He grinned, blue-white eyes twinkling, and lifted his fist to his face, thumb pointed into his mouth: thirst. She had honey-water, cool in a thick brown crock, to draw off for them, ladling the light golden liquid into wooden bowls for each before shooing them off to the shade of the trees.

They took their bowls and downed the sweet drink. Then they sprawled on the ground not far from where the brown cow lay, her jaws working under flicking furry ears. Along the wooden barn wall the geese combed their strong beaks through the grasses, parting the roots and tossing back the grubs they found curled there. Speckled hens scratched in and out of the open barn doors, shaking the dust from their red and white feathers as they flapped their wings, but the sheep were all at their upland farm, where their barley and oats and vegetables came from, and apples too.

The other children were neighbours, both from the steep road which rose up after Tindr's home, and from the side roads that shot off from the main trading road. One of the girls rose and pulled a handful of small yellow wild-flowers from the longer grasses, and plopping down again began weaving the lengths into a chain. As they passed it from hand to hand, each girl adding a new green and yellow link, they began to sing once more.

Tindr liked singing. He knew it was different from speech, for a singing mouth was opened and full, and often people sang together, which they almost never did in speech; then it was one at a time. And people sang when they were happy. He watched the girls' faces as they sang, happy himself just to look at them. The two other boys were off bothering the geese. One of the girls smiled at him as he watched her mouth round and stretch, the small knob at her white throat bobbing. She smelled good. There was something of mint about her, and Tindr knew her hand had brushed some as she picked her flower. He rocked forward from where he sat and knelt before her, and laid the tips of the three long fingers of his right hand on her throat. She flinched just a little, but smiled at him as she went on in her song. He felt the fluttering of her throat, the small knob shifting up and down, the tremor of her song. He opened his mouth, and sang too.

She stopped, the pink mouth freezing shut, and he pulled his hand back quickly and ended his singing. She lifted her head and began to laugh. The other two were laughing as well, laughing and pointing. He had seen such laughter before, and knew it was towards him. He pitched himself back and away from the girls. The boys now had joined them, and one of them thrust out his arms like wings and stretched his neck skyward. He saw the mouth round, the energy from the chest as some sort of sound came forth. Tindr leapt up to stand with them, reaching his arms out as well. If the girls would laugh at him he would play with the boys. He picked up his song again. But the leading boy turned on him and pointed at the geese, then at Tindr. He too was laughing. Tindr's singing sounded like the honking of geese to them.

He stepped back, stung, and snapped his mouth closed. His cheeks were hot and he feared he might cry. All of them were before him now with arms outstretched, boys standing, the girls still sitting, prompting him, teasing him to sing again. The girls rose and flapped their arms, began to circle him. The flower crown they had made was torn by their feet. He felt unable to move, and knew tears had crept their way down his face. Then his father Dagr came, walking slowly but with fastened eyes out of his fishing shed, twining tool still in hand, glowering at the laughing children.

⁂

He could not call his parents when he needed them.

He could let out a bawl, or a piercing shriek, if he had hurt himself. But if he wanted his mother or father, he would resort to a honking bray. Tindr remembered their names, Nenna and Dadda, how these words felt in his mouth when he had called them when he was very little. But though he felt the force of his own lungs, his tongue moving, throat quavering, he could not hear himself try to form "Nenna" or "Dadda". He saw by their faces how awful it sounded when he tried; his Da would drop his eyes to the ground, and the smile on Nenna's face shifted, as if she were hurt.

So Da made him a little whistle, carved from the leg bone of a sheep. It had two holes drilled in it, and Da showed him how to blow through it, and how to vary the sound that came from it by closing one or the other hole with his finger. Tindr blew once with both holes open to mean his Da. And because he remembered the word Nenna so well, he blew twice for her: Nen-na.

He wore the whistle around his neck, at the end of a hempen cord. It was the first of many, for he would lose them climbing in the trees or break them tumbling in the grasses. But the bone whistle gave him a voice to call with.

⚜

Tindr spent part of every day, Winter or Summer, in the forest. Dagr took him hunting in Fall, taught him how to weave snares and handle a bow. His cousin Ragnfast, a few years older and bigger than he, sometimes walked down from his upland farm and joined them, spending a night or two as well. Tindr saw they looked almost like brothers, but Ragnfast's eyes were not the strange blue-white of his own. They were a milder blue, and were often lit with his smile. He could make Tindr smile too, and did not care how his laugh sounded. Ragnfast was strong and good with horses, which his parents bred, and he taught Tindr how to ride. Ragnfast had sisters but no brothers, and with Tindr he could roughhouse and ride and hunt. He had been a part of Tindr's life as long as both boys could remember; there at every Blót, every Winter's Feast, every Summer Gathering.

Ragnfast recalled Tindr's sister Hedinfrid well. They had both six Summers the last time he saw her; Tindr was no more than a toddling boy, and the other sister, Holmfrid, just a little older. It was Hedinfrid that Ragnfast sometimes saw in his dreams. Hedinfrid had straight pale yellow hair that curled at the tips where it fell over her shoulders and back. Her eyes were the blue of the brightest Spring flower, the blue-star. Her right cheek crimped into one deep dimple when she smiled. She liked to slip her small cool hand into that of Ragnfast when he came down with his folk from his upland farm to play. Ragnfast told her once that he would wed her, and Hedinfrid had smiled and nodded. Then she was dead.

Many young died that Spring, taken by the fever that had reddened the cheeks of Hedinfrid and her little sister. Ragnfast had been sick too, but unlike Tindr, had lost nothing to the heat burning inside him.

As Tindr grew Ragnfast came more often, to the pleasure of all at the sea-side house. Ragnfast was with them the first time they visited a snare that Tindr had set. It was laid at a well-known hare-run, where Dagr had snagged hares before. But this snare had been woven by Tindr, and set by him too. He had braided the sheep's sinew himself, and tied the small loop that the larger one would hang from. He had struck down a long pine seedling with his axe, and bent it over the slight trail where the hares ran, and drove in the sticks to direct the hare to the waiting loop dangling a hand's length above. That morning the three of them walked slowly through the leaf litter and fallen pine needles, past the browning and curled fern fronds to the bottom of the small ravine. There, nearly at the end of the run, where Tindr had set it, lay the caught hare.

It was still alive, panting in the flattened grass, one powerful thumper turned up to show the short fine dark hairs. The wedge-shaped head lolled out upon the dry grass. Tindr took it all in. Its eye looked like one of the glass beads his mother wore about her neck, a near-black bead with a spark of fire in its darkness. His father gestured him forward. A rabbit's heart can be stilled by pressing it with the fingers and so quickly ending its sojourn here on Earth, but a hare with its broader chest and forceful thumpers is best killed by the blade. Tindr drew his knife; he had seen his father kill hares many times, and knew he had to grasp the hind legs firmly and cut quickly at the throat.

The spilt lip of the hare trembled. Tindr had never taken any life before. The hare's strong digging claws were sharp, and the long teeth pointed like one of his father's chisels. Those teeth just showed now, as the hare turned its head as he neared it. Tindr wondered how long it had lain there, if it had in fact been caught just after dusk when they had left the snare. He thought of the savoury pot of browis his mother would make from it, and how she would praise him for carrying home fresh meat, her hand touching her heart in thanks. He thought of the soft blue-grey pelt that would be his to line his boots with. He thought that it was alive now, and would soon be dead, and by his own young hand.

In his line of sight he saw his father step forward and draw his own knife. Tindr awoke and stretched out his hand to his father's arm. Dagr stopped, re-sheathed his knife.

You came from somewhere, Tindr said within himself as he closed his hand over the hare's thumper. He pressed the leg to the second hind leg, and brought his knife forward. *The Lady sent you, the Lady and the Lord, they that rule this forest.*

He brought the fist that gripped his knife to his breast a moment. *I give thanks for your life*, he said, and plunged the knife tip into the soft hollow of the furred neck, wetting the dried grasses with its blood. *I will remember you. You will run the forest again.*

⁂

Tindr grew tall and lean, even as a boy. He was happy and good-natured, and after a few terrible weeks stopped looking for his lost sisters, pulling back their alcove curtains in hopes of finding them there. His lost hearing too he seemed to take in stride. He made himself known to Rannveig and Dagr by making signs with his hands. He was their teacher, and as he grew they made up signs together. Yet nothing had prepared them for his deafness; when he was little it was constant vigilance. He could not heed their shouted warnings that he had backed too close to the fire, the pan that held the bread was still hot, the knife sharp, the wood pile he clambered upon unstable and likely to roll. Tindr burnt himself, cut himself, fell from trees. He cried. He learned.

He tried too, to speak, not just the low *uh, uh uh* that he uttered when in play, but fully-voiced calls and cries. His desire to be understood was great, and if he could not make his needs known by his fluttering hands he would respond with the braying calls that were difficult for listeners to bear. It was just this that the other children scorned him for, mocking his sounds by miming animal movements. A few of them would try to gesture back to Tindr, learning to understand him, but others jeered and would not. Rannveig and Dagr knew that some folk along the trading road shunned Tindr and thought him an Idiot, though they knew he was bright.

Rannveig could scarcely bear the pain she saw in her son's eyes, and helped him to say less, for that was the only way to still the taunts. But his laughter she welcomed, for she thought no one should have that stifled in their breast, and if it sounded like the geese the others claimed it did, they would have to bear with it, for it was Tindr's own good heart and humour coming out.

She knew he sang in secret, too, to the household kine and hens, had watched him lay his long-fingered hands about the cow's neck, and thus feel her bellow and low; and Rannveig had listened as he sang back to her, varying his call in pitch and volume without being able to hear it himself. He felt it, she knew; felt the trembling in his own throat and chest, just as he did in the throat and chest of beasts or folk when he touched them.

As he grew it was the beasts that Tindr gave his time and care to. He fed the pigs, drew eggs from the hens, milked the cow, penned the geese each night. The goslings followed him about and the hens ran to him. The fat pig lifted her spotted snout and looked at him when he neared, and not only when he brought her the cabbage stalks. At milking time Rannveig thought he got more from the cow than she did. These were his chores, but he did them with an active pleasure and curiosity in the animals them-selves. There were always thick-furred skogkatts, the half-wild forest cats, about his mother's brew-house and its grain store, and he tamed these so that they dropped their half-eaten mice by the bowls of milk he set out for them each morning. Once he watched one worrying something in the under-leaves of the mugwort his mother grew, and lifted a spiked ball that was a frightened young hedgehog to safety. He kept close watch on it until its spines hardened and lengthened, and the skogkatts knew to leave it alone. This spiny, sharp-nosed creature became a favourite of Tindr, by owl-light waddling towards him for bits of cooked fowl.

No beast was too small to catch his eye and prod his interest. He followed trails of ants through the Summer grasslands and lay inches from their scurrying columns, breathing shallowly so as not to disturb their relentless advance and retreat. His mother kept a beehive at the edge of her herb garden, and from the time he was able to lift the straw skep himself he showed no fear of the buzzing creatures as they landed upon his hands or circled about his head. He sometimes would wrap his arms about the domed skep, feeling the activity of the hive through the woven plaited coils, the pulsing of so many minute bodies crawling and hanging and fanning their shimmering wings about the dim waxen cells. Tindr did well cutting out the dark yellow comb and drawing the thick honey, and the hive flourished. Soon his mother could brew mead from the comb-washings, and melt and dip precious beeswax tapers. His movements were quiet and calm, the way he ever acted when with animals, and in a few years the single hive had grown to eight, both about the sea-side house, and up in the woods behind Rannveig's empty girlhood home at the end of the road. Rannveig and Dagr would look at their solitary child and see his true friends in the animals that surrounded him.

RAGNFAST

DAGR saw his son was good with the bow, had watched him pierce a hare from five-and-twenty paces, and thought the boy, who spent so much of his spare time in the forest, had the makings of a true hunter in him. The boy's blue-white eyes were keen as a falcon's, and he could hold his narrow frame from all movement, and stand riveted in a glade with no flinching or restlessness. So Dagr built an archer's target for Tindr out beyond the limits of the kitchen garden. He dug a narrow ditch, and set five broad wooden boards on end within it, then tamped the soil well to hold them upright. Tindr helped him do this, and when they were done Dagr sent his boy to fetch some cold charcoal from the kitchen yard.

The tops of the boards were almost as tall as Dagr, and far over the head of Tindr. They had set them as snug to the next as they could, yielding an almost unbroken surface, adze-smooth, and seasoned to a soft brown. Tindr ran back with his hands clutching two pieces of charred pine. Dagr stood back from the target wall, and taking up a piece of charcoal, looped a small oval at one end, joined by two nearly vertical downward lines. He then drew a big oval, describing the body of a deer. He stood back and looked at what he had drawn.

Tindr stood back too. Then he started to laugh, a light, snorting bray, his face bright with glee. His father dropped the charcoal and dusted off his hands by slapping them together. He put his hands on his hips in mock anger and stared first at Tindr, and then at his drawing. Dagr could not help but laugh as well. His deer looked like one small sack linked to a large one by two short lines. He waved his hand at the waiting wood, then touched his ear: Tindr do it.

Tindr set his tunic sleeve to the few lines his father had made and rubbed them out with his forearm. He knelt in the grass, and taking his knife from his belt, sliced quickly away at one of the pieces of charred pine. He took it up and stood before the upright wooden boards.

He too began with the head, but it was angled as a deer's truly is, a chiseled muzzle, protruding eye, and flat cheek. A muscled neck swept down from this, the sinew drawn in to show the line of brawn a stag in rut carries there. He went on to the wither knob, then dropped to the breast and the rest of the body; powerful haunches, hocks bent as they should, slender legs, one of them raised, ending in cloven hooves. It took him some little time, and he paused to rub out some of his lines before he picked up again. Before he stopped he returned to the head, and there scribed a rack of antlers branching out above the ears. Then he turned back to his waiting father.

Dagr grinned in acknowledgment, and clapped his hands together a single time: Good. He knew the boy could draw; he did so in the dry dust with the end of a stick, or in the smoothed ash of the cold cook fire. There was a

woman, Álfhildr, upcountry, famed at scribing runes, and
Dagr thought Tindr could one day do as well, and was
teaching them him one by one, at least the ones he knew
to draw himself. But this fine deer surprised him. It could
only have been drawn by one who had spent much time
looking, one who had truly seen a hart as it raised its head
in a clearing, one who had noted the sharp planes of the
head, the sweep of a neck taut with muscle, the ripples of
flesh along the haunch, the impossible fineness of the ten-
dons. One who had watched and studied deer, and begun
to understand the truth of the beast.

Tindr's round cheek coloured at his Da's praise. The
charcoal had crumbed to dust between his fingers, and
his right hand was black with it. Heedless of his mother's laundry chores, he wiped it on his legging. His father
picked up a sliver of charcoal, and drew two crosses on
the deer.

"Here, at the heart," he told his son, crossing strokes
over a point of the barrel just behind the front legs, "and
here, the lungs." The second cross lay further behind the
shoulder. Tindr nodded gravely. He had seen the deer his
Uncle Rapp, Ragnfast's Da, had downed with one arrow
at just these points. His own Da was not a bowman.
Dagr found it hard to spend half the morning crouching
beneath shrubby growth, or standing stock-still behind a
tree, waiting for prey to wander into view. On his boat
all he need do was follow the currents and swooping sea
birds to see where he could drop his nets with profit.

But they both took up bows now, with a dozen arrows
sitting upright in a wooden bucket between them, and
Dagr let fly a few. When all twelve stood bristling from the
new target, he tousled Tindr's light brown hair with his

calloused hand and waved him forward, gesturing that he not forget the afternoon milking of the cow. Tindr nodded and grinned, then strode to reclaim the arrows. Not all had hit the charcoal deer, but one of his had come closer to hitting the marks his Da had drawn than even Da's had.

※※※※※※※※※

Not long after this Ragnfast came for the day, riding his new horse, a gift from his father Rapp. The horse was a roan gelding, and man-sized, not the small mare he had ridden since he was Tindr's age, and he wanted to show him off to his cousin. It was high Summer, and after the two boys worked together to finish Tindr's chores there were still many hours of daylight left. Ragnfast re-saddled his horse, which he had staked in the tall grasses behind the house to graze, and after he climbed up Tindr swung up behind him. The older boy felt almost grown-up as he touched the gelding's barrel with his heels and started down along the pounded soil of the trading road. The roan was well-built, full of spirit, yet with none of the female moodiness that made Ragnfast's mare, small as she was, sometimes a challenge to handle.

Tindr had one arm about Ragnfast's waist, but the gelding's gait was steady and Tindr already had a good seat upon a horse. Many of the stalls along the road had closed for the day, but the few people they passed nodded their heads or called out cheerily to the boys in greeting. The sea to their left looked as blue as the late afternoon sky, with only the slightest of cream-coloured foam ripples, and the slanting sun cast a towering four-legged shadow trailing behind them. Tindr grunted once and made his cousin turn in the saddle to see it, and chortled with Ragnfast when he felt his cousin's laugh with his arm.

They rode to the end, past the last stall, that of an old woman who sold braided linen wicking for oil cressets and tapers. She drowsed on a bench before her rolled up awnings, but snapped awake when the gelding snorted. Her brown face creased into a hundred lines as she grinned at the boys, and they grinned back. Everyone bought from her, and she knew the boys and their families well. Above her head they could see into the dimness of her tiny space, spot the bound coils of white wick which faintly gleamed in the dusk within.

Then they went a short distance beyond, to where the mighty carved image of Freyr stood staring out at the endless-seeming sea. He had just been repainted at Mid-Summer's Day, his green cap and tunic, brown face, and yellow braided beard still shiny from it. On a horse Tindr's eyes were almost level with the God's, and he found himself dipping his head after looking into the painted orbs of Freyr. This was the God of horses, of all running beasts, and he and his sister Freyja ruled the forests and marshes of the island. His Nenna and Da had told him much of these wild siblings. Freyr was a skilled sailor too, and Tindr had come here Spring and Fall with Da to leave an Offering at the start and end of each fishing season.

Ragnfast looked at the painted face too, and had an idea. They got down now, and Ragnfast had Tindr hold his horse while he went up to the bulk of the carving's torso. He laid his hands upon it for a moment, then came back to Tindr, and taking the reins, led the gelding nine times around Freyr's all-seeing eyes.

"Long life, good health to you," Ragnfast said aloud. "Never lame, never elf-shot, never with croup," he asked. "No whistling sickness befall you," he added. "Let no rabbit hole find your hoof," he went on, as he circled. "Peace-maker in the herd." Running out of asked-for blessings he finished with, "And never to throw me."

He realised then he had no Offering to leave the God. Behind the carving stood three sturdy poles, fixed at their tops with shallow iron baskets holding recent kills of fowl and piglet. He knew the leathern pouch at his belt was empty of any silver, just as it usually was. Ragnfast had asked many blessings from Freyr upon his new horse, and had nothing to give in return.

He looked at Tindr, and plucked at the bottom of his silver-pouch to show it was void. Tindr went to his own belt. Nothing but the whitened skull of a little bird he had found in the morning under the bean plants. Nothing suitable for a God. Then his hands went to his neck, and the cord there. He pulled the bone whistle over his head, held it dangling to Ragnfast. Tindr knew the Gods danced, and that men danced to such sounds as his whistle made. Give this, he signed to Ragnfast.

So Ragnfast did, looping the cord around the out-thrusting arc of the God's yellow beard, where he might find it easy to play. Before they mounted he touched his heart a moment and turned his hand to Tindr, using his cousin's way of saying Thank you.

Riding back they saw, across from the closed amber-worker's shop, a group of girls settling themselves on flat stones on the beach. There were five or six of them, the eldest with spindles in hand, or with little ones in tow. Ragnfast could hear their shrill laughter before he could

make out who they were. As they neared them they saw
their friend Estrid, who lived at the farm closest to Ragnfast; Gyda, a girl of about the same age who lived on a
farm not far from the fish-drying racks beyond Freyr; two
small girls, the sisters Ása and younger Astrid; and lastly
Sigrid, who had her baby sister Sigvor with her. Sigrid's
mother kept a stall on the trading road, stocked with bolts
of the thick boiled wool fabric, wadmal, that all used for
blankets and heavy mantles.

Sigrid was one of the comeliest maids on Gotland, or
so Ragnfast had heard said. She was also a little older and
taller than he was, and he was glad he could rein up before
the group on such a fine horse. As they neared Estrid got
up and ran to them in greeting, calling out to Ragnfast on
what a handsome horse he had got, and stopping before
Tindr to touch her ear, point to her eye, and smile, and so
tell him it was good to see him.

Little Ása and Astrid were afraid to come close to the
horse, and Sigrid glanced up for just a moment at the boys.
The baby Sigvor was at her feet, her chubby self propped up
by the smooth side of the rock Sigrid sat upon. She waved
her hands, one of which clutched a stick of bleached drift-
wood. Sigrid, after her glance up, turned her attention
back to her dropping spindle. She sat perched on the rock
so that the whirling wooden shaft had a longer drop down
the sea-shelf, and Ragnfast found himself also looking at
it as it spun down. Then he lifted his eyes back to Sigrid.
For a moment Ragnfast wished that Sigrid were alone,
and that Tindr was not behind him, his thin legs dangling
down along the gelding's barrel. But then he would have
to speak to Sigrid, and he did not know what he would say.
He thought he should have called out to her as soon as he

recognized her, some easy word of greeting as he reined the horse closer so she might admire him. As it was they were stopped at the edge of the road, and even Estrid, who had waved goodbye, had turned her back and was sitting down with the others on the beach.

Tindr, balanced behind Ragnfast on the saddle, began to wonder why they did not go. The girls were friends, but they were doing nothing interesting, and they had little ones with them too. He wanted to swim while the Sun was still strong. He saw Ragnfast looking at the girls, especially the big one, but did not know why. When girls got big they did nothing interesting, except make good things to eat. He jiggled his legs a bit and the gelding started forward a step. Ragnfast pulled back on the rein as he turned his head to his cousin. Tindr made a low grunt, and raised his hand in question. Ragnfast gave a final glance at Sigrid's lowered profile, then nodded and touched his heels to his horse's flank.

Back at Tindr's the two went down to the sea edge, stripped off their clothing, and paddled about in the chilly Baltic, the hot dryness of the air making it feel all the colder. They stumbled out, skin tingling, shaking themselves like dogs in the yellow sunlight, and rubbed themselves warm and dry with their tunics. Then they dressed, and searched a while amongst the piles of white limestone that formed the shore line. Some of the stone was shrouded with dark, almost charcoal-coloured lichen. Patches of bright yellow-green lichen shone on others. The wind was steady, and it ruffled their hair and made their tunics flap against their legs as they walked, chins upon chests, looking down.

Ragnfast heard the whistling of the wind. The chirping of the birds picking over Rannveig's crab-apple tree carried down to him, and a few sea-birds dipping and wheeling above their heads mewed out harshly as they walked. Ragnfast raised his head to their noise, as Tindr did to their motion. But their eyes soon dropped again to their feet. All sorts of treasure lay there, stones that looked like the blooms of flowers, or the furling fronds of plants, or smooth cones like peaked caps for a mouse, and white pebbles that looked like shells but were really solid stone.

Tindr picked these up, and turned them over in his hand; the best ones he would slip into the pouch at his belt. He wondered how they could be plants, or shells, and yet be made of stone. Trolls, those night-faring giants who lived deep in the forest, would be turned to stone if daylight caught them. That was why the island was ringed with the mighty rauks, the huge limestone stacks. Trolls had come down to the sea to frolic at night and the Sun had surprised them. As they writhed in agony their horny bodies were transformed into twisted stacks of limestone. Trolls howled, Nenna and Da had told him. But once they were become rauks they were as silent as the stones he held in his palm today.

After a while they headed back up the rocky beach to Tindr's home. There were no ships at the wooden pier, and the trading road was almost empty of folk. They passed through the open-walled building that housed the brew-house, and waved to Rannveig as she stood at one of her big brown crocks, stirring with a long paddle the brew within. Soon they would have to come and carry out shelves of pottery cups for her, stacking them onto the long table at the back of the brew-house. But they still had time before the Sun dropped low enough to signal that.

They slipped into the dim house for a moment. Ragnfast had brought his bow, and Tindr took his down from
where it hung on the wall by his sleeping alcove. They
went out through the kitchen garden to near where the
trees began, passing Ragnfast's horse where he was staked.
Tindr's archery target stood back there, pocked over with
holes. He had redrawn the deer many times, sometimes
facing left, other times right, drawing it higher or lower
upon the wooden boards so he would have to shoot up or
down. Both boys had quivers at their hips, and they stood
side by side, one arm outstretched, the other lifted and
bent at the elbow, sighting down the length of the iron-
tipped birchwood arrows they held nocked and ready.

They did not shoot for long. Ragnfast was as good as
Tindr, better really, and as he was older and taller his bow
was the larger and stronger. Tindr liked to gesture to his
cousin to let fly his arrow, and then try himself to come as
close to its tip as he could with his own. He nicked many
an arrow shaft this way, and was kept busy shaping new
ones to make up for those which he had rendered useless,
but the challenge of training his eye and hand to hit so fine
a mark was worth it.

But the length of the day, the swim in the cold sea, and
then the shooting at the deer-target took their toll. Ragnfast sprawled out upon the grass, his bow lying beside
him, and after a final draw Tindr too dropped down.
Tindr rolled on his stomach. The grass was sweetly ripe
but scratchy upon his face, and he lifted his head up and
supported himself on his elbows. Small flowers of white
and yellow dotted the grasses, but Tindr was thinking of
the flowers that were stone, and the shells that were stone,
down on the beach. They were once something, but now

they were something different. Just like the trolls who stood captive forever on the shore.

He rolled to Ragnfast, lying on his back next him, and sat up. Tindr touched his ear.

"You," said his cousin, nodding. "Tindr."

Tindr looked ahead and past him. He touched his ear again, then held his hand out before him but a hand-span above the grass. He lifted his eyes to make sure Ragnfast followed, then moved his hand higher, then higher still.

"Growing," guessed Ragnfast. "Growing up." He sat up too, and made the gesture Tindr used for his Da. "A man."

Tindr shook his head, touched his own ear, lifted his hand to the ground three times, at three different heights. He rocked forward up to his knees, and with his hands smoothed the skirt of an imaginary gown.

Ragnfast paused. He looked Tindr in the eye, then nodded again. "You. And your sisters." He could not know if Tindr understood, so he mimed pulling long plaits over his own shoulders. He touched his own ear and pointed again at his cousin, then held his hand, as Tindr had done, at staggered heights.

Tindr nodded his head, hard. Já, his sisters.

He did not know how to ask the rest.

Tindr pointed at his cousin, then to the space before them where they had both indicated the sisters. He paused a moment, drew breath. Then he raised his hand to shield his eyes, as if he looked for something. His cousin watched a long moment.

"Do I look for them," Ragnfast whispered.

How could he look for them; he had been there at the burning place when the small bodies of Hedinfrid and Holmfrid had been laid upon the pyre. They lay side by side on a narrow pallet, their round faces pale, their yellow hair combed so it fell over their snowy gowns. He recalled a linen sheet billowing down over them, and that sheet beginning to curl and brown as the fire rose. He knew he stood between his own mother and father as he watched, and that a great number of folk were there, and men and women cried aloud. He remembered not believing Hedinfrid was dead. He remembered turning to see many fresh graves. He did not remember more.

Tindr was searching his face. Ragnfast drew a sharp breath and looked back at him.

Now Tindr touched his own temple. This meant What or Why, but his cousin saw that now it meant something more, something deeper: Remember.

Do I remember them, Tindr was asking him.

Ragnfast began to nod his head. "Já. I remember them." He tapped the side of his own head. "Holmfrid was not much bigger than you," he told Tindr. He signed with his hand the lower height. "She was yet a babe," he went on, and drew his fists to his eyes and wailed mock tears.

Tindr began to smile at this, and nodded his own head. His own fists rose to his eyes to mimic a howling child. They laughed together for a single moment.

"Hedinfrid . . ." began Ragnfast. He could scarce form the name. He swallowed.

Tindr rocked forward, staring at him. He could recall almost nothing of them, nothing except the laughter he could no longer hear. The memory of their last day together was all he had, sitting cross-legged inside the recess of the basket and glimpsing the two laughing forms of his sisters between the woven interstices: here-gone-here-gone.

"Hedinfrid . . ." said Ragnfast once again. He brought his finger to his face, drilled its point into his right cheek. "She had a dimple . . . here." He swallowed again, and closed his eyes a moment. When he opened them Tindr was still staring at him.

Tindr recalled that dimple, now. With her face at rest it barely showed on Hedinfrid's cheek. When she smiled or laughed it was deep enough for him to put his finger into it, and he recalled doing so, and Hedinfrid laughing the more.

Ragnfast jumped up. His face was wet, and he dragged his sleeve across his running nose.

Tindr rose too. He blinked away the water in his eyes. The girls had been here, and now they were gone. Ragnfast had brought them back to him, if only for a moment.

ASSUR

ASSUR was the youngest son of a family which raised sheep and grain. Their small farm was on one of the side tracks that led off the main trading road. They were not Gotlanders, but had recently come from the land of the Svear. They kept much to themselves; a story had got around that Assur's father had fled the mainland to avoid being outlawed. His crime was unknown, but those who had watched him whip his oxen saw he was a man of high temper. Apart from a few small trading disputes they were peace-abiding here, though not likely to put themselves forward in any way. The children were a rag-tag group, raw boned, with a sloping gait and shoulders scrunched up high, as if to ward off blows.

Assur had a purple birth-mark on the right side of his neck, one that began just above the jaw and crept down onto his throat to his collarbone. He was the same age as Tindr, more heavily built, with a big head that ended in a shock of yellow hair. His eyebrows were so light as to be hard to see, so that his round eyes wore a look of constant surprise.

It was the start of warm weather when Assur first showed up. Tindr and Ragnfast were on the pebbly beach not far from Tindr's house, setting up balanced stacks of small flat stones, and then seeing how far they could stand away from them and still knock them down with a thrown rock. Estrid was with them, having come with Ragnfast and his parents to the trading road for the day. She was at the water's edge, plucking shells from the darker rocks the sea lapped at.

Tindr looked up from where he squatted on the pebbles, setting up another target, and saw the new boy appear along the edge of the road. Assur put his hands on his hips and looked down at him. Ragnfast, building his own stone stack, noticed too. Both boys stood.

Ragnfast began to turn to Tindr, but his cousin had already raised his arm, waving the stranger down. Assur took the long way to reach them, jumping from rock to rock. Estrid too was watching, and came up from the water to stand with her friends Ragnfast and Tindr. The new boy stood on a chunk of rock before them, looking down on the small cairns the boys had been building.

"I am Estrid. I found these," she told Assur, opening her hand to show the round white shells within.

He glanced at her hand, then looked back at her face.

"My name is Ragnfast," said Tindr's cousin.

Assur turned his head to look now at Tindr. It was then his birth-mark showed.

"What is wrong with your neck," Estrid asked.

Assur glared at her.

"Does it hurt?" She was already reaching her hand towards his jaw.

He jumped backwards off the rock, away from her.

"Nai. It is a mark, nothing more."

Tindr was squatting again, and waved Assur to kneel next him and build a cairn of flat stones. Assur did not move. Tindr began building his pile.

None of them had ever seen the round-headed boy before. "What are you called?" Ragnfast wanted to know.

"Assur."

The new boy looked down at Tindr, at work piling the warm white stones. "What is your name?" he said, to the top of Tindr's head. Tindr kept looking down, intent on his stacking.

Assur's boot came forward, nudged Tindr on the shoulder. Tindr looked up, squinting against the sun at the boy.

"What is your name," he repeated. "Tell me."

Tindr saw the demand in the boy's face. He grunted.

"What is wrong with him?" Assur asked, still looking down at Tindr.

"Nothing," answered Ragnfast. "He is deaf. His name is Tindr."

"Deaf?"

Assur squinted his round eyes shut. Old people were deaf. Not boys. Assur looked back to where Tindr knelt, looking up. "You deaf?"

Tindr saw the scowl, turned his head down to his work.

Assur kept staring at Tindr's bent head.

"He cannot talk," Ragnfast told him, squatting back down himself.

The new boy shook his head. At least deaf old men could talk, even if they did yell, just as you had to yell at them to be understood.

Assur looked around, then rubbed his toe against a stone. "We could run," he said. He was already moving down the beach, away from them.

Ragnfast followed, waving with his arm that Tindr should too. Estrid put down her shells and ran after.

They raced along the water-darkened edge of the beach. Ragnfast was oldest and tallest, and did not think it would be much of a race, but he knew Tindr was also fast. Even with the start the new boy had taken, the two cousins found it easy to catch up to him. Ragnfast over-took the boy well before they had reached the wooden pier. Assur had turned his head to look over his shoulder, once at Ragnfast, and then at the gaining Tindr. Ragnfast passed Assur, but as Tindr too passed, Assur gave him a shove. Tindr stumbled and fell. He leapt up again, his left side wet from the sea water, and sprang after and then caught up to Assur. Tindr swung around to face the boy.

Assur was red-faced and panting; he had almost fallen himself from the force of the push he had given Tindr. Ragnfast had seen it all, and hauled up before them. Estrid had caught up, and gave a little cry when she saw Tindr's torn tunic sleeve, and the small beads of red welling on the underside of his forearm. Tindr's other hand lifted and brushed the sand and tiny pebbles from his skin, smearing the blood as he did so.

"Tindr!" Estrid pulled off her linen head-wrap and went to his side with it.

"Why did you do that?" demanded Ragnfast.

"What?" asked Assur, looking not at him, but at Estrid.

"Pushed him. You wanted to run. I beat you. He was beating you. You pushed him."

Tindr looked back and forth between the boys. Estrid began to tie her head-wrap around his arm. The scrape stung, but he did not look at it.

"Nai. He ran into me," Assur answered.

Ragnfast caught his breath, looked to Tindr, then to Assur.

"So ask him," Assur challenged. "See what he says."

Ragnfast lifted his hand. He first tapped his temple. He pointed to Assur, made a shoving motion, then pointed at Tindr.

Assur snickered. "Is that how you talk to him?" He gave a laugh, and waved his hands meaninglessly in front of Tindr.

Tindr looked at him, at the sneer on his lips, and the plump hands flailing in air. His look lasted a moment longer, then Tindr turned on his heel and walked away. Estrid trailed after him, and it was she Assur was staring at as they went.

<hr/>

Dagr had need to stop up a few slow leaks in his boat, and now he and Tindr knelt within the hull, smearing tar and a mass of brushed-out cow-hair and dried moss between a few strakes which had lately shrunk. They had gone together to the tar-sellers on the trading road, Dagr carrying back the small but heavy pot of thick pitch, Tindr already holding the basket of cow-hair and the moss he had collected from the forest floor over the past few days. A day earlier two men had helped Dagr haul the heavy boat high up upon the shingle, and Dagr and his son climbed aboard the tilted hull and began their work.

Tindr liked the smoked aroma of the tar; it was to him the smell of every soggy marsh and every rotting tree stump and every cold fire he had ever sniffed, but darker, richer, and warmer than all of these. Dagr used a tapered wooden spoon and a scrap of oiled hide to pack the mixture in, but Tindr still found himself with tar-splotched hands by the time his father gestured he could go clean them in the sand.

Tindr squatted on the stony beach near the second set of upright supports for the pier. He scrubbed his hands with wet sand and tiny pebbles until his palms were pink and only a finger and thumb nail showed the black line of tar lodged there. As he stood he saw a knot of children moving along the beach towards him. He squinted to make them out. He did not know them. Perhaps they had come from some far upland farm; now was the time that many would make their final trip to the trading road before the shorter days of Fall made it a two day journey and not one.

The children slowed, and the youngest of them began picking up stones and flinging them into the water. He would not go to them. He could not make himself known to them; they would not understand his signs, know he was deaf, nor even his name and people. And the more folk there were the harder it was for him, trying to watch their faces, guess what they meant. As he watched them one of the older, a girl, turned and looked at him. Her arm shot into the air, and Tindr saw the smile on her face. It was Estrid. She took a few steps nearer him, touched her ear, pointed to her eye, then waved him to come closer. She was happy to see him and wanted him.

Tindr took a step, then recalled his Da working back in the hull. He lifted his bone whistle to his lips and let out a long shrill call. Dagr's head appeared from over the ship rail. Tindr pointed to the children, and grunted his *uh, uh uh*. Dagr glanced down the beach, nodded Já, and held his hands out flat and straight in front of him, the sign for assent. Tindr grinned at his Da and went to the children.

Estrid was the only one he knew. There were a couple of boys about her age, and one younger, and a small girl. The taller of the boys was in a tunic too big for him, so that it reached well past his knees. The other boy's leggings had been patched front and back, and one of the patches was half ripped off, showing his pale kneecap when he walked. Estrid was now sitting on a rock next to the little girl, and was combing her fingers through the child's hair. Tindr was close enough now to see they all had round eyes and light yellow hair. He nodded to each as they looked to him, and saw that the bigger boy's lips moved. Tindr looked down and watched Estrid.

She had taken off the little girl's head wrap, and it lay, a limp and yellowed rag of linen, on the far whiter lime-stone of the sea edge. The little girl was fussy and squirm-ing, and Estrid was picking at something in the child's hair, above her ear. Tindr got close and saw it was a burr. It had gotten caught in the child's hair and had worked itself up, as burrs will do, close to the skin.

The little girl tried to turn her head to look at Tindr, and as she did began to cry against the pulling of her hair. Tindr saw the pink mouth round and the face scrunch, and saw as well that the small face was dirty. Estrid was trying to calm the girl, and pulled her on her lap so she could pick out the burr.

Another boy, a bigger one, appeared at the edge of
the beach, having come from the trading road. Tindr recognized him at once: Purple Neck. That was why these
yellow-haired, round-eyed children were here; they must
be his brothers and sister. Purple Neck stepped up upon
a flat topped rock, and looked down at them. Tindr did
not know whether to stay or go. He sat down on the rocks
near to his friend and the squirming little one and waited.

Assur jumped from rock to rock to reach them, as
he had when Tindr had first met him. The last leap was
a long one, and he almost lost his balance as he landed
before Estrid. She looked up at him and said something,
then turned her attention back to the burr trapped in the
little girl's yellow hair. Tindr saw Assur glance his way,
then turn his eyes back to watch Estrid. He saw Assur say
something to Estrid, and Estrid say something back, without stopping in her work.

Then Assur was pulling his knife from his belt. He
leaned over Estrid to the little girl, and put one hand on
his sister's head, and with his knife in the other sliced
through the tangle in her hair. The other boys were looking open-mouthed at their brother. The child shrieked.
Estrid jumped up, the child wailing at her knees. Assur
stood with his knife in one hand and the yellow clump of
hair in the other. Tindr looked at the frightened girl and
saw the patch of nearly bare pink scalp where her brother
had sawn through the fine hair. The girl was too big for
Estrid to pick up, but she knelt down at the child's side to
try and soothe her. As she did she turned her head back
at Assur and said something in anger to him; Tindr saw
her twisted lip. Assur dropped the hank of hair. He was

re-sheathing his knife when Tindr saw Assur's head turn towards the road.

A man stood there. Tindr and Estrid saw Assur stiffen as he looked up at the figure gesturing to him. One of the boys picked up the sobbing little girl and went to the waiting man. Assur made his way to him, and when he reached him the man extended his arm and struck Assur backhand against the side of his head. The little girl was red-faced, screaming all the more, and the man looked again at the bare patch on her head and cuffed Assur a second time.

Tindr sat watching from his rock. His Da had never struck him thus. He knew other boys got birched, and some girls too, but he had not seen a grown man hit a boy in the head like that.

He could only recall his Da hitting him once, a long time ago, when he had the idea to try to lower himself down the well while sitting on the edge of the big wooden bucket. His Da had caught him before he could swing himself over the hole, and had swatted his backside. He remembered how white his Da's face had been.

"I almost had it picked out," Estrid was saying, aloud, but to herself. She mimed to Tindr the action of her small fingers, working their way through the silky hair. She looked up at the retreating group, sharp against the skyline. She could still hear the wailing girl. "He would not wait!" she went on, angry for the child's sake. "Said he would help me. Oaf! Troll!"

OF THE HUNT

AFTER his morning chores were done Tindr would walk into the woods. He did so nearly every day, rain or Sun, and only if the snow was beyond his knees was he forbidden to go. But first there were the beasts to care for. Before the sky was fully light he would make his way to the small barn, to find the cow waiting outside the barred door for him. He would let the flock of gabbling grey geese out, and as they streamed, wings flapping into the day, she would follow him into the dim stall where the deep copper basin awaited. Bending into the cow's warmth, Tindr would sometimes turn his head and press his ear against the short stiff hair of her flank. He could feel, rather than hear, the rumble of the workings of her gut, and the bellows-like action of her soft inhalation. If she lifted her head to low he felt the tremor in her bulk, and he would low back to her, feeling in his own chest the vibration which he hoped sounded like hers. She did not mind his singing, just as the skogkatts did not, and as he poured out their dish of warm milk he might place his hand on their furry chests and feel the thrill of their heavy purring in his palm.

A woman had now come to live with them, Gudfrid by name, for Rannveig was grown so busy with her brewing she needed help. Gudfrid had taken over the kitchen yard, and Tindr would carry the milk basin to her, and return to the barn to gather whatever eggs the speckled hens had left him.

If Dagr was fishing that day he might already be gone, but if he were not the family would sit together with Gudfrid and break their fast, out by the cooking-ring if it were Summer and dry, and in at the small wood table when it was cold or wet. Gudfrid was a fine cook, better, Tindr realized, than his own Nenna, and there were crisply toasted loaves of bread which dripped with butter, tangy bowls of thickened milk skyr, eggs boiled or fried, and steaming crockery dishes of boiled oats which Tindr drizzled with big spoonfuls of his golden honey.

Then Tindr would leave. When he was small it was not easy for Rannveig to watch him slip into the trees and out of sight. He knew to be home by midday; when the Sun was over his head he must return. He would be needed to weed the gardens, carry and stack kindling, and help his father with the nets and catch when he came home. Until then he was in the marshes and forest, alone. Except he was not alone.

Over his head birds flew, and perched in branches. Tindr could not hear their song nor chirps, but from the tail of his eye would catch a small movement and he would stop and watch. By seeing if they startled or not he learnt to slip his booted feet gently under the fallen leaves, or to tread upon the green and arching ferns which made no noise. His sharp blue-white eyes would trace the paths of small moths and butterflies as they lit upon the wildflowers which ringed the open glades, and with those eyes he would follow the movements of clouds of gnats as they rose and fell above still-wet grasses. Tiny creatures such as mice and shrews scurried before him, and the spiny hedgehogs which made him smile would waddle off when he discovered them in the act of digging up grubs. Red foxes would flash into view, turn their pointed muzzles his way, then trot on. The big blue-grey hares would sit up on fallen logs at the edges of clearings and look at him before bounding away, dark thumpers hindmost.

The first time he saw a boar he stood, stock-still, as the beast turned in his direction. He had seen a clump of bushes shuddering, and waited to see why. The four yellowed tusks, up-flaring and down-hanging, with one broken off short, he saw first, followed by the moist and dark leather of its snout. Then came the bristled sloping head, arching from the thick neck. He saw the boar snort, could make out the movement of the thrusting lower lip, and the beady eye met his for one long moment. Then it turned and ambled off.

But the red deer that ran the woods of Gotland were his favourites, those young stags and does, and larger harts and hinds that filled him with pleasure. He marvelled at their speed and grace as they darted and leapt through the grasslands and through the stands of birches and hazels. The delicate slenderness of their strong legs, the chiselled planes of their faces, the lustre of their dark eyes beneath tufted and ever-moving ears – they had to Tindr a wild beauty that the finest horse could not match. And they could appear and disappear in a moment. A deer would emerge before him, firm and solid and with chest expanding with its breath. In one beat of his heart it would be gone, his mind recalling a ruddy flash of colour where it had stood.

Several times in late Spring he came upon their fawns, finding them curled up in tall grasses. He would wonder at their red and spotted coats, their tiny cloven hooves at the ends of folded legs. One day he did nothing but await the return of the hind, hiding himself behind the cover of trees until she arrived to nuzzle her young. The fawn stretched its neck to meet its mother's nose, then sprang up on its spindle legs to stand at her side. The small angled face ducked under the slender flank of the hind, and grasped onto the teat waiting there. After the briefest space the two were off, bounding into the forest undergrowth.

He had beheld the source of those fawns, seen in Fall the antlered stags come sniffing, lips curled, after young does that trotted coyly just out of reach. Then the doe would stop, and sometimes look behind her. Tindr would watch with breath held as the stag extended his neck, tongue reaching and nostrils flaring, as it sucked in the scent of the ready doe. He saw the long and red male member of the stag swell, as the stag reared up behind her and embraced her as he stood. Their bodies met, and after a few thrusts the stag would drop, head lowered, away from her. After a short while the stag would again return to the doe.

At rut the stags were at their most majestic, muscled bodies thick from Summer's good feed, antlers at their greatest span, and coats almost shimmering. This act of creation called forth their best selves, made them even more impressive than they were at any other season.

Tindr had ever witnessed the mating of animals, from the roosters of the kitchen yard who fluttered and danced on the backs of the hens, to the skogkatts, crouched low with swishing tails, to mighty bulls who seemed to call open-mouthed to their cows. He saw the urgent need of male animals to join their bodies with that of their female kind, and guessed too that many females shared this desire, for he saw how mares swished their tails and stretched their necks to the stallion. He knew his own prick was the same tool that ram or bull or stallion bore, and knew too that after some while, long or short, young would come forth from ewe or cow or mare after she had been touched and held that way. All of these things were good. Increase in fowl and beasts meant life-giving food, and wool and hides for protection. Without beasts no folk could survive, and Tindr had been taught to give thanks to the Gods who created and protected them.

But in the greenwood this act took on a new significance. Part of it was the wild setting, one far from other folk, which he had become a part of, almost akin to the forest animals themselves. Part was the glory of the stags themselves. No other male beast was transformed by their rut as were they, and the lustre of their coats as they pursued the does made them magnificent to behold. And part was the knowledge that the Lady of the Forest, Freyja, the Goddess of all woodland beasts, appeared here on Midgard as a hind. So great was her love for her deer that she herself came in their guise. She came, he was told, as a white hind. None had ever seen her; but if she permitted man but a glance, that is what they would see.

It was with this feeling of reverence, even awe, that Tindr began to hunt deer. It was his Uncle Rapp who first took him, with his cousin Ragnfast, out at dawn and into the forest beyond Rapp's farm lands. Ragnfast had come to fetch him on his big roan horse, and Tindr spent several days at their farm. Tindr had already proved his sharp eye and steady hands at home by shooting hares and squirrels, and had so filled the target boards his Da had made him with arrow pecks that he and Dagr had dug them up and reversed them to give him a new surface on which to draw his deer. Now Rapp took his son and nephew into the dawn woods. He had wanted to wait another year with Tindr, thinking the boy young enough to tire easily, but when Tindr learnt Ragnfast would go he begged that he might join them, cupping his two hands together in a bowl shape, and bouncing on the tips of his toes in his eagerness.

Tindr, already at home in the forest, well knew how to walk without snapping twigs or unduly moving brush. He knew too that if he were upwind of a deer his scent would betray him. He could spot and follow scat, and judge the age of cloven hoof prints in soft soil. These things he had learnt himself; or rather, the deer themselves had taught him. It was left to Rapp to show him how to select a spot neither too near nor far from a deer track, choose a tree to hide his presence, and wait. It was Rapp who taught him to draw a deep but quiet breath as he lifted his nocked bow; and Rapp who showed a clean kill, the deer dropping after a little start in a heap after the arrow shattered the ribs and lodged in the heart, and a failed kill, in which they trailed the bleeding hart a long way before Rapp could end its torment.

"The Lady will be angry, and the meat not as good," he told his son, as he shook his head at himself. Tindr could not know what words he spoke, but his meaning was clear. Together, and at Rapp's hands, Ragnfast and Tindr learnt how to gut the animal, how to make the drag sling to make it easier to pull the carcass through the woods and to the kitchen yard where it must hang and grow tender. And it was Rapp who showed Tindr the rituals which must be attended to; the washing of the hands and face before entering the woods, the small Offering of a pour of milk, a hen's or goose egg, a silver trinket which the generous Goddess would be glad to accept in return for releasing a deer marked for them to take.

Ragnfast had been out with his father before, but had taken no deer himself. Each time he took too long to ready and lift his bow, let fly an errant arrow, or stepped on a noisy twig and alerted the deer before he could do either. But this time out with Tindr, both boys made their kill. Ragnfast shot a young stag on the first day. He hit the shoulder, but his father Rapp was there to take the second shot and drop the beast. Gladdened by this take, the three headed back to Ragnfast's, where his mother and sisters welcomed them. The second day, one of steady drizzle, yielded naught. Now it was their third morning out, sharply chill and with a damp and grey mist rising from the leaf-littered ground. The mist did not give Rapp heart; it would only deepen in the glades in which they would be most likely to come upon deer, and shooting at shadows was the best way to lose the arrows they had spent much time forming.

Tindr could not know that red stags in rut roar, bellowing through the forest to call a ready hind. He had sometimes seen them stretch their necks, open-mouthed, but could not imagine the sound. Hunters would harken to the call and begin their tracking. On that third and foggy morning, no stag sounded. But Tindr saw one, moving with lifted head through the hazels on the far border of the glade. The antlers that crowned that head were massive, many-pronged and reaching. Tindr reached out and touched his uncle's arm. Rapp turned his head, saw the prize stag, a true hart, one of five or more years of age. Tindr tore his own eyes away from it long enough to look at Rapp's face. Ragnfast stood at his father's elbow, eyes wide as well at the mighty deer. Tindr allowed himself one small gesture, his hand to his own ear. Rapp wondered if an arrow pulled by that slight frame could bear power enough to kill the beast. But he could not deny him; Tindr had seen him first. He nodded.

Tindr set arrow to his bow and raised it. The hart had moved a few paces further off, lowered its head, again lifted it. It turned its chiselled head toward where Tindr stood with his uncle and cousin. The muscled neck, ruffed at the throat with a mane, turned in profile to him, the chest and barrel open to his arrow, as if the hart were his own drawing on his target boards come to life. *Lady, give me him*, Tindr prayed. He had held his breath as he drew back his elbow, and heard the low humming, a kind of soughing, in his ears, a sound he heard at still-times, falling to sleep, or standing in snow. *Lady, give me him.*

His draw-hand reached his cheek; he let fly the arrow. Tindr could not hear it whistle, nor the low thwack of impact as it pierced the chest just behind the front leg. He saw the upward jolt the hart made, the mighty rack of horn lift a final time, the front legs crumple.

He swung his bow on his back and ran to the hart. When Tindr shot a hare or squirrel he always ran to the downed beast, ready to pull his knife should the animal be still alive, and suffering. He did the same with this first stag he had downed. Luckily Rapp and Ragnfast were just behind him. It was on its side, hooves facing where Tindr approached, his arrow lodged deep in the chest and standing out at an angle. The rack of antler kept the hart's head from the ground; its eyes were open. Tindr made a move to draw his knife and go to it. But Rapp wrapped his arm about his nephew's shoulders, holding him back. Tindr turned and looked up at him. His uncle was shaking his head, then made the sign for Do not do: clenched fists, crossed at the wrist.

"Those legs can break a man's arm or jaw," he said to Ragnfast. The hart had fallen atop a tangle of low shrubby growth, its leaves withered and worn brown; only at the very tips could any green be seen, that late foliage that soon would be killed by Winter's frost. Tindr stood there, gazing down upon the dying beast. This close to it, it was even larger than he had thought. Its smell filled his nostrils, the scent of greenwood and fur and male musk. Tindr had always wondered at the beauty of the red deer. Now, standing just before a great male, he felt he had scarce beheld such beauty. All stags in rut had a special lustre to their fur, but this close he saw a shimmer in the red coat that looked as if the coloured lights of Winter played upon it; subtle tints of gold, green, and blue that could be glimpsed along the neck, flank, and haunch.

The front legs kicked out, and Tindr, startled, saw the deep chest heave a final breath. The head lolled back, caught, face upwards, where one of the antler prongs rested in the vines. As Tindr watched he saw the colours of the coat begin to drain. The shimmering subsided, just as the golden specks in the sea were lost as the Sun rose higher. The coat was thick and reddish-brown now; nothing more.

Tindr gave a little yelp, not meant for his uncle or Ragnfast, but for the hart, for the loss of beauty, for the loss of its life. He looked to Rapp, who nodded at him, letting him know he might pull his arrow now. Tindr went to the beast's head, and dropped on his knees. He stretched forth both hands, and laid them upon the great neck. He felt the warmth there. His lids were lowered as he knelt there, palms flat upon the cooling beast.

I will remember you, Tindr was saying within his breast. It was for me, and by me, you run no more; Lady Freyja chose you for me. Now you will feed me, and Nenna and Da, and we will be part of you. He looked up at the interlacing of barren branches over his head. The mist was burning off, leaving the sky a soft and silvered grey. Lady, he said now, I thank you. Let him run again.

Tindr rode back to his home flanked by Rapp and Ragnfast, leading a horse which bore the great hart he had taken. He watched his uncle tell of the hunt to his parents, and saw their pride at what he had done in their faces before they ever signed it to them. Dagr skinned the carcass and the pelt was Tindr's to have upon his box bed. His father sawed the great antlers from the skull so that Tindr might keep them as well, and each time Tindr stroked the fur of the pelt or closed his hand about the spine of antler he knew a trace of the great animal's life-force. They smoked the haunches for Winter use, but Gudfrid made pies of the organs and neck-meat, and they had slabs of meat fried, from the loin. The first time Tindr tasted of the deer he had killed, water welled in his eyes. He was in the deer, the deer was in him.

This was the first of many harts and stags that Tindr would bring to feed himself and his parents. Their flesh filled the cooking cauldron, and their hides warmed their beds and plank floors, and became Winter tunics, gloves and shoes. His Da showed Tindr how to make toggles to fasten clothing from the small joints of the bones, and how to carve spoons, pleasant to the mouth for their smoothness, from the antlers and larger bones. The stripped sinews made the strongest thread imaginable. Gudfrid even boiled down the hooves to a sticky liquid, good to adhere pieces of leather together to make thick soles for rocky ground. Every part of the deer went to good use; nothing was wasted.

His Da built a bigger smokehouse, and Tindr helped him set the oak planks tightly together to hold in the thick smoke that would issue from the little fired-clay oven set into the soil at its side. From the peaked roof of the tiny building Dagr fastened iron hooks to hold the haunches as they steeped in the drying smoke of the low apple-wood fire burning inside the oven. A handful of green apple-wood chips added each morning slowed the burning, sending billows of aromatic smoke into the small repository of Tindr's forest gain. The meat they smoked there would last the whole Winter without spoilage, and bore the mellow richness of both orchard and forest.

In late Fall and Winter, when Dagr could not launch his boat for heavy winds and ice upon the Baltic, Tindr could yet be depended upon to bring fresh meat home. They had of course a ready store of salt fish, and those vegetables that could be buried in the cold ground: cabbages, parsnips, carrots, skirrets, turnips; but of fresh flesh there would be none without Tindr's bow. Soon he would awaken knowing if this was a day he should hunt, or not. It was as if a voice spoke to him, not through his closed ears, but within his breast. He thought it a woman's voice, the Lady's, beckoning him to come, or bidding him stay.

Tindr began making small wooden deer. The first one found him, not long after this first kill. He was out walking the woods and in his path lay a twigged tree branch. Lying as it did it looked deer-like. A curved twig led to a small ascending piece for the head and neck. From the body dropped two straight twigs, like legs. He took it home, shaped it a bit more, peeled off the bark. With his knife tip he tipped in two eyes. It was smooth and white in his hand, and he held it a while. Then he took it back into the woods where he had found it, and left it resting against the roots of a tree.

After this he made a wooden deer after every kill. He used the ends of smoothed planks saved from the building of houses, boats, and furniture; the man up the hill had many such scraps he was glad to let Tindr have. Of an evening, by fire-side in Winter or by Summer's long twilight, Tindr might be found carving the figure of a deer, no larger than his own hand. It was right that the hands that pulled the bow string should then pay tribute to the life thus reaped. Rannveig and Dagr watched him at his work, and though Tindr never signed to them what he was doing, saw him walk into the woods with them. These he carried to the base of trees and left, as Offering.

THE TRADING ROAD

A merchant knorr had just landed at the wooden pier. It was late morning, with the brisk snap of Fall in the air, and the sky above the Baltic wore a paler shade of blue than it had in Summer's heat. Folk were already gathering to meet it; a ship coming this late in the season was sure to hold the hides of seals, or even perhaps furs, things which needed time to have been dressed.

From the trading road two young men, brothers, Ketil and Botair, rose from opposing work benches to join the others. They were in the rope and line business, ever a good one for a sea-faring people. They wove stout hempen rope from the hackled woody stems of plants they grew themselves, and those grown by others who sold to them; and when they could, cut leathern line from the massive hides of walrus. Such line was the most highly prized of any, for walrus skin had greater strength than any other hide. A skillful hand could begin at the outer edge of the prepared hide and trace a spiral with his shears, heading ever inwards, to end with one perfect length of line many ells long. A walrus hide line so made and conditioned was worth many times that of even the finest rope of hemp, and on the rare occasions when Ketil and Botair had made one, they had pocketed a handsome profit from ship owners.

The knorr was broad-beamed, not large, and from the look of the few chests and casks lashed upon the deck, was on its way home, with perhaps not much to offer to the Gotlanders. A barrel-chested man of middle years was tying up the steering oar, and three younger men, likely his sons as they all shared a brighter version of the older man's reddish hair, were making all fast. The weapon-smith, whose forge sat a distance off the trading road, but who had happened to be returning from Rannveig's with a small wain so that he could carry away several crocks of ale for his new son's birthing-party, called out in greeting to the steersman. It was returned readily enough; the knorr was, as several had assumed, of the Svear, and now headed back home after trading around the southern Baltic rim.

"And have you iron, either good ore or bars?" asked Berse, the worker of metal.

"I have no iron," answered the Svear, finishing with his tying up.

"Then fair sailing home-ward to you," returned Berse, turning back to his ale and his wain.

"Furs?" called out another man, who had caught the thrown line one of the red-haired sons had tossed him.

But the Svear shook his head, as if in real regret. "Sold. All gone to the Prus."

The line-catcher shrugged his shoulders. The Prus were a tribe of traders on the southern coast of the sea; they would be closing their Baltic trading posts now and heading to their homes in advance of Winter and its deep snows.

A group of boys had now seen the knorr, and the men who gathered before it, and came clattering across the wooden planks of the pier. One of them was Botair's younger son, Ring; his brother Runulv had grown too old for boys' games. He was joined by Tindr and two round-headed boys that Botair remembered seeing but whose names he did not know; he recalled hearing the family were recently arrived from Svear-land and had already made trouble. Botair's son spotted his father but did not approach him; when he found him with a strange trader he knew he must be left in peace.

"What then do you carry?" posed a third man. This was Botair. He hoped one day to have a ship himself, and had been looking at this Svear and his crew and imagining a day when he and his sons had the same.

"Treasure," answered the Svear. He seemed a dour sort, for he spoke this word without a note of triumph.

The men were silent, but all pressed a little closer to the knorr's side. The Svear scanned their faces.

"Have you a gold-worker?" he asked them, letting his eyes lift uncertainly to the few buildings lining the trading road.

"I, Tume, work in silver," answered one man, "and Holmgeir here works in amber." The Svear captain looked at the two men, both of his age, and both prosperous-looking, as befits workers in precious goods.

"My treasure is greater than gold," returned the Svear. He did not keep the crowd waiting longer, but bent over and unlashed a small chest from near the keel. He lifted it into the arms of one of his sons, who moved to the ship rail so all might see. The Svear lifted the domed lid of the chest. Those nearest got a glimpse of whiteness.

"Walrus tusks," he explained. He reached in and held up one each in his hands. "Six of them."

It was some of the best ivory that the Gotlanders had seen in years, free of cracks, smoothly tapering, the warm white of thickened cream. The Svear took all six out, four of which were nearly as long as a man's fore-arm, and the third pair only a bit shorter. Only those who dealt in costly goods could hope to buy them, and only the most skilled of carvers would be entrusted in their cutting.

The boys pushed forward with the rest of them to eye the tusks, and one gave a little yelp of astonishment as the gleaming wealth was held up before them. Tindr knew the tusks of boar, but had never seen any as long and thick as these; boar they could not be. He tapped his temple to ask Ring, What? Ring touched his own teeth in answer, but could not describe a walrus, which he had never seen himself. Tindr was left to goggle at the notion of any beast with teeth as great as this. A troll, perhaps.

Ketil and Botair looked at each other. If the Svear had tusks, he might have the hides that bore those tusks. But they would bide their time, let Tume the silver-smith bargain for the two tusks he could afford, and then, knowing the Svear had fattened his purse already, ask after that they sought.

Several in the crowd, content at the glimpse of such richness, began to drift back to their waiting work benches or homes. The boys, satisfied, wandered further down the pier. Tume himself walked, with hastened step, to his silver-working stall, and after unlocking a series of chests locked within chests, returned to the waiting Svear with a fat purse bulging with silver ingots.

"It is a poor time, when Gotlanders, the richest men in all the Baltic, can buy only two tusks," complained the Svear to the brothers. The captain was still on board his knorr, and his sons had returned the treasure chest to its keel-side holding. They had all turned to watch the back of the departing Tume, holding his prizes clutched to his breast.

"We are but a small trading town," apologized Ketil. A few Gotlanders were still with them, waiting, as Ketil and Botair were, to find out what more the ship might offer. Ketil glanced around and saw his nephew Ring at the very end of the pier, with Tindr.

"If you have tusks, perhaps you have hides," suggested Botair.

The Svear trader looked at the brothers in turn, as if doubting their ability to buy. They had none of the usual signs of prosperity about them. Still, the wealth of the Gotlanders was well known. He should not be hasty to judge whether these two could provide a home for the second portion of the goods he still sailed with.

"Come aboard," invited the Svear, and the brothers climbed over the rail, one of the sons helping.

By the stern, and again lashed near the keel, lay a lumpy bundle shrouded in an oiled tarpaulin. Two of the red haired men untied it, and then unrolled it before Ketil and Botair.

They looked at what lay before them, and then lifted their eyes to the other. Two walrus hides stretched upon the deck, of so great a diameter to nearly span the breadth of the ship. Ketil knelt down before them. The hides were thick, yet so supple in the hand that they turned gracefully over his rotated wrist. With the aid of one of the sons, he lifted each and reversed them upon the deck, needing to slow his breath to hide his growing interest. They had been expertly scraped, not with a steel blade nor flint, but with the gentler, sharpened bone-scraper used by the folk of the far North. The inside surface was kid-smooth and free of gouges, scraped little by little to free it from the thick and precious fat the walrus grew to shield it from the icy waters. The women of the Skridfinn, the Striding Finns or Sámi, scraped thus.

"They are the best I could find of the Sámi," the Svear was telling them. "I went myself, as soon as the ice had cleared, in early Summer. The third hide I sold also to the Prus."

All Gotlanders knew of the Sámi, but few had gone to their lands. They ranged far north of the eastern shores of the Svear, where the Baltic froze over hard in the deep bay. They wore only skins, had their own Gods, and it was said they owned deer which they had trained to harness.

"You yourself went?" asked Ketil, looking up at the Svear. The older man nodded. "Já, and my sons with me." Ketil looked with new respect to the red-haired men.

Here Botair cleared his throat. Ketil arose and squared his shoulders. They had between them about nine marks of silver, most buried under the floorboards of their respective houses. They could not hope to buy both, but Ketil folded half of the larger over, and then pointed to it.

"This one," he asked, "how much silver for this one."

The Svear stroked his upper lip. "Silver I have plenty of," he answered.

Again Ketil and Botair looked at each other. They had not a scrap of gold, if that was what the red-haired Svear sought.

But it was not. "You Gotlanders, it is said, have the finest sheep of any land. I want sheep-hides, twenty of your best; and shorn and washed wool. Also a small cask of wool-wax, of which yours is agreed to be more than of passing quality."

Botair let out his held breath. Ketil nodded, and tried to keep the smile from his lips. One of the men still upon the pier whistled softly. Good sheepskins and wool were as common amongst them as trees. The wool-wax boiled from out of that wool, once cleaned and strained through linen, became a valued liniment for rough or burnt skin. The brothers should have little trouble fulfilling this Svear's demands.

"I will go and fetch some hides, so you may see them," Ketil said. "My brother will stay to make sure no others offer twenty-one in our stead."

He clambered over the side, and took off at a trot to their workshop on the trading road. He passed through the fronting stall and out to the side yard. His wife Tola stood there, at work with some hempen rope, braiding and twining six lengths of it into an open basket-weave. She had each end tethered round a rounded post as she worked her knots, and looked up and smiled as Ketil hurried by.

"A Svear trader. A walrus hide," Ketil explained, as he vanished into the doorway of their small house. He snatched at a few thick-fleeced sheep-skins, two from their bed, one from the floorboards, and gave each skin a shake. He hustled back to the pier with his arms full of them.

Once aboard he showed the sheep-skins to the Svear, one by one. One had been lightly sheared to be curly, the other two left in the sheep's longest wool.

"We can give twenty, of this quality, shorn, or long," he told the man.

"As large as these, or larger," added Botair, who had only grown more attached to the walrus hide during the little time he had stood over it awaiting his brother.

"And the wool?" asked the Svear. He had handled the fleeces in turn, and stroked them in a way that the brothers knew he valued their softness.

"By the evening you will have all, twenty fleeces of this fineness, a cask of wool-wax, and a sack of wool, shorn and washed. They are ready and waiting. We have only to go to our farm to fetch them."

The man nodded. "That is good. But there must be two sacks, and they must be of white wool."

Ketil opened his mouth. The three fleeces he had carried from his house were all grey, one light grey, the other charcoal, and handsome too they were. White sheep were but a third of their flocks, and hard to increase, for even a white ewe could, and often did, bring forth grey lambs.

"White . . . " repeated Ketil.

Both bothers looked down, and the Svear was forced to speak again.

"I have a hall full of women, and they will give me no peace if I return with no white wool," he admitted.

They looked at him and reflected. He was a wealthy man, would have at least two wives, and at his age, plenty of daughters too. Grey wool could not be dyed, save to make the lightest of it dark blue or black. The white could take on any colour, yellow, green, red, blues of all ranges, all shades a rich trader's wives and daughters would covet.

The Svear's red-haired sons were nodding their heads solemnly behind their father.

Ketil wracked his brains. They could trade with neighbours for enough white. It would be costly, but the single walrus hide would bring them more profit than they had seen in any two years. He nodded to his brother.

"Two sacks of white," they agreed, and the Svear nodded and smiled. "The woman Rannveig, there," ended Botair, pointing to the newly-built brew-house not far away, "is a fine brewster. Let us seal our business over a cup of her ale."

At the pier end the boys watched the men move off and make the turn to Tindr's. They had been jumping from plank to plank, and now went back to their game. One had a soft piece of limestone with him, and with it had drawn rough squares on the knotty surface. These they must jump in order, and then try jumping to only every other square. Tindr was long of leg and did well. Good-natured Ring was sturdy and strong, and would stagger, laughing, as he fell short. The other two boys were Assur and his younger brother. This last was too small to make any of the longer jumps well, and soon dropped out, but Assur played with intent, hurling his bulky body forward from square to square. He took the chalky limestone from Ring and drew two squares even further away, then gestured to Tindr that he go first. Tindr bit his lower lip as he gauged the distance, then made the jump, landing in the centre of the square with a loud *uh*.

"Uh," repeated Assur. "Uh, uh."

Tindr had turned and was grinning back at them, not knowing what Assur had said.

"You grunt like a pig," Assur said, looking full at Tindr.

"Go and make your jump," Ring said.

"You go first," Assur challenged.

"It is your square, you drew it. Go and jump it." It was clear from Ring's crossed arms that he did not think Assur could do so.

Assur crouched and swung his arms, then made the leap. He fell short, both feet striking the drawn line.

Ring hooted, and Tindr laughed his short braying laugh. Assur turned on them. He scanned their faces; even his brother had laughed. His cheeks flamed red, so that the purple mark on his neck stood out less sharply.

"You grunt!" he repeated, fixing on Tindr. "You grunt like a pig." Tindr was looking, unknowing, at him, and now Assur lowered his head and swung it from side to side, as a sow does ploughing up the soil for grubs and roots.

Tindr's eyebrows lifted, and his blue-white eyes narrowed under them. He charged at Assur, arms swinging.

The heavier boy overpowered him, and with a wild swing knocked Tindr in the head, sending him face-down, sprawling onto the planking. He would have rolled off and into the water if Ring had not grabbed at him and reached his arm.

"He began it," Assur was saying. His little brother was hanging around his leg, stopping him from moving towards Tindr, who lay on his back at the edge of the planking.

Ring heard a man yell, and looked towards Tindr's house. His father Botair, along with Tindr's father, Dagr, were already at the pier mouth, and striding to them.

Tindr was sitting up now. Blood was running from his nose, and his eyes were dazed, as if he could not focus them.

Assur's small brother looked as if he wanted to run, but there was nowhere to go. He began shuffling his feet from side to side, and began to sniffle. Assur put his hands on his hips and faced the coming men, but as they grew closer he dropped them at his sides.

Dagr took it in as he approached. There was so much Tindr did not know. Things which other boys learnt by hearing were lost to him. What he knew of folk and their ways must be read through his eyes. He missed so much through not hearing.

And he knew that he did not punish Tindr enough; that good as he was, he was, in his way, spoilt. "I will not let one birch twig fall on him," Rannveig had warned Dagr the year earlier, when Tindr had set a hay rick alight at the farm by shooting with flaming arrows. "We must make him understand, but he will never be whipped."

"Who did this," Dagr asked, looking to his son's bloody face. He saw the small bone whistle Tindr wore about his neck was broken in half.

There was silence for a moment, and then Ring answered. "Assur hit Tindr with his fist; he was making fun of him."

"He began it," Assur retorted. "He came at me first."

Dagr had before seen this boy whose neck bore the ugly birth-mark which marred him, and seen his people, the mother a faded and worn shell, and the father loud-mouthed and untrusting. That the boy was marked had made Dagr wonder if he would become friends with Tindr, as if the two shared some kinship. But each time they were together there was trouble.

"Let this be the end of it," Dagr ordered.

ESTRID

I T had been a snowy Winter, and Tindr had not seen Estrid during all of it. He had only seen Ragnfast once, when his cousin had fastened on his wooden skis and kicked and poled his way across the ridged drifts of his family's farm land. Ragnfast had made his way to Tindr's, stroking through the forest which then lay open to the eye under its blanket of snow, and spent two mirthful days with them. They skied long distances together across fields and meadows, tracking rabbits and watching kites and goshawks soar over their heads. But Estrid he had not seen since before Blót.

She came to the trading road with her parents and her older sister, walking alongside the ox cart they had driven. It was packed with bundles of wadmal, and would return with pottery cups, an iron basin, new lengths of hempen rope, a small tub of beeswax, and sacks of grain to last them until their own oats and barley could be harvested. Estrid was already a good spinner, as was her sister, and both her sister and mother had worked hard at their upright looms over the Winter, beating up the woof of the thick fabric. As Estrid helped carry the bolts out and lay them in the waggon bed she had felt a thrill of pride in knowing that some of what she held in her hands had been teased and spun by her. Their flock was not a large one, but her father was jealous of their care, guarding them from straying and from theft, insisting they be covered by the best rams he could find, and shearing each himself; he would allow no hired man to help.

Once at the trading road Estrid was free to roam and see what friends might be about. Her parents and sister would be busy at the stalls and warehouses. It was midway in Spring and not all of the trades-folk had opened, but the rope-making brothers Ketil and Botair were always there, and Botair's boys, Runulv and Ring might be about. The brothers, though, were now of an age where they no longer played, and Estrid, when she saw them again after the absence of so many months, was aware that they were become almost men. She came across them on the beach. Botair had bought a boat, with hopes of both trading and fishing from it, and the boys were working within as it lay hauled up on the pebbles not far from Botair's stall. They barely glanced at her, gave her a wave and a smile, and turned back to their task of enlarging the opening for a bigger steering oar. So she kept walking, towards Tindr's and the brew-house that his mother kept.

The day was cool and the skies filled with scudding clouds, and the wind blowing made it feel as if Winter was come again. She was glad to walk past the empty brew-house and into the kitchen yard, where Rannveig was standing near the warm little malting-oven where she toasted the grain for her ale. Gudfrid was there, too, turning from the smokehouse door. There was already something in a cauldron over the fire. Both women waved her over.

"And how pretty you have grown!" was the first thing the cook said to her, which made Estrid's cheek colour.

Rannveig nodded her head in agreement. Her mouth was smiling at Estrid, but it was not without a twinge that she looked upon her; her youngest girl would now have been about Estrid's age.

"A cup of broth," she offered instead, and dipped into a thick pottery cup a ladle of the fragrant broth in which a capon was simmering.

"Tindr is about, he will be glad to see you," she added, when Estrid had finished the broth. Rannveig stood up from the work-table where they were sitting and scanned her small garden. She thought he was out checking on his woodland bees; best keep the girl here until he returned.

He did so not long after, a sack tied to his waist which held a few tools he had taken with him, lest the forest hives needed to be better secured to the stands he had built. Later in the season the bees' wax itself would fix the skep to the platforms, but now with the bees still sleepy they might be upset in a strong Spring gust.

He greeted Estrid with a grin, touching his ear, touching his eye, pointing to her: I am happy to see you. Tindr did not see how much Estrid had changed. He saw she was taller but little else; he knew he was taller too, his legs longer than last's years leggings. He was glad she was back, glad that soon with longer days they might wander the beaches and choose the best of the shell-shaped rocks to take home with them.

First he took her to one of the garden hives. Estrid had no fear of Tindr's bees. He moved slowly and calmly about them, and if he was ever stung she never knew it. Certainly they had never stung her. They walked together now to one at the edge of the herb garden. The domed skep perched on an old tree stump there. The straw plaits Tindr had woven and twined together were bleached and worn; he would shape another to replace it this year. The skep seemed still. Tindr placed his hands at the base, and tried to lift. It stuck in one place, and he drew his knife's point along a part of the yellow-stained rim, breaking a waxy seal. He took the skep in both hands and slowly lifted it. Estrid had seen inside before, but each time she did her grey eyes opened wide. Pale yellow, golden brown, dark brown, smoothness and lumpiness, a mass of slow moving tiny bodies. A smell like the sweet tapers Rannveig made, and the smell of a spoon of honey being brought to the lips, and a smell of warm soil. As Tindr peered inside, a few bees crawled out upon his hands, resting there, wings motionless. Estrid watched him smile as he looked, and then his hands slowly rotated the skep down to its base. He placed his hands on the outside until the bees that had rested there flew off.

One of them landed on Estrid's face. She flinched, and her eyes crossed as they turned towards the tiny creature on her cheek. Tindr smiled, stretched out his hand, and laid it upon her cheek. He kept smiling at her until the bee crawled onto his thumb. He slowly lifted it away, brought it to his mouth, and breathed upon it. The slow wings began to beat, and off it flew. Estrid raised her hand to her cheek where the tiny legs had tickled her, and smiled back at Tindr. He treated her as gently as he did his honey bees.

After this they walked to the side of the garden that fronted the beach. Dagr had built a low plank fence here, just tall enough to keep the salt spray from Rannveig's brewing herbs. In its sheltered lee a cluster of wild flowers had begun to bloom. Estrid bent and picked one of the yellow ones; they were not out yet at her parents' farm. She plucked off the petals, one by one, and began to sing a song that all children knew. Tindr had watched her and other girls sing this, many times, and smiled as Estrid's mouth opened. As she sang she nodded her head once to the left, then to the right, then looked up into the sky, pulling each petal in turn. It was a game, and after she had finished with one flower, she picked another to begin again. Tindr lifted his hand and laid it on her white throat, just where the small knob was moving as the shape of her mouth changed. She smiled at him, and Tindr began to sing too. He watched her mouth, and felt with his fingers. She let off pulling the petals, and helped him by beating time with the hand that held the flower. He tried to move his lips as she did, make the same shapes hers did. His song was a honking bray, but he was happy with it. She lifted her other hand and placed it on Tindr's throat, wanting to feel what he felt as he touched her there. The knob on his throat was larger and moved more. She could feel it ripple up and down as his bray grew louder or less shrill. They were both laughing as they sang.

They were standing face-to-face, Estrid with her back to the garden, Tindr with his to the sea. Of a sudden Estrid stopped. She was looking past Tindr's shoulder, and he turned to see what she looked at. The boy Purple Neck was there. He had been walking on the beach and saw them there.

Both Tindr and Estrid dropped their hands, but Assur had seen them at their play. He moved to the low plank fence and stepped over, unbidden, into Tindr's garden.

Tindr did not want him there. He watched Assur say something to Estrid, saw the slight nod of the boy's yellow head in his direction. Assur was smiling at Estrid. She was still holding a flower in her hand, one that bore but two petals, but that hand was now down at her side. She smiled briefly at Assur, then looked at Tindr. But Assur was speaking again. He lifted his hand, put it on Estrid's throat. The flinch she gave was greater than that with which she had greeted the bee. Assur was talking at her, moving his other hand, but she remained still. He reached down and took her hand, began lifting it to his own throat. The purple birth-mark almost touched the knob there which moved as he spoke to her.

The year she had first met Assur she had wanted to touch that purple mark. Today she did not.

Tindr saw her brow scrunch. She bit her lower lip, then gave her head the smallest of shakes, which only grew when Assur pressed her hand on his neck.

"Nai," she said.

Tindr remembered the word Nai, knew what it meant; remembered it just as he had Nenna and Da and his own name, Tindr. He often knew when it was spoken; saw the upper lip lifting and rounding. Sometimes the head would shake from side to side just as Estrid's was now. It meant the same as his sign, Do not do, fists clenched, wrists crossed.

"Nai," she said again, but Assur did not release her. She pulled her hand from Assur's neck and pushed him away, her narrow shoulders turning, her face twisting as she did. Assur caught her hand and tried to pull it back to him.

Tindr bared his teeth at Assur, and lunged at him.

Assur jumped back. The deaf boy was howling at him, a horrible shrill cry that he thought only ogres could make.

Tindr did not come at him again, just stood his ground. Assur was scared of him, scared of being like him, but it was the deaf boy Estrid liked.

Assur saw Estrid's face was pink with anger, and he thought, disgust. It was aimed at him. The deaf boy could touch her, and she welcomed his touch. But not his. She was looking at the ground now. The flower she still held had lost its final petals. He did not mean to do this, and he did not know how to tell her. Everything he did around her angered her, or made her run away. Everything he did when she was near him was wrong. He did not know how to tell her this, and made a little movement towards her, lifting his hand.

Estrid stared back at him. She read in Assur's face that he was sorry, could see it in his slumped shoulders too, but he had frightened her. And he had worried Tindr so that he had become something else, like a wild animal. When Tindr screamed like that, it frightened her as well. She knew she should be kind to everyone, but she did not like Assur, and it was all his own fault.

She looked to Tindr, who met her eyes. They knew Assur's father beat him; they had seen him strike Assur hard on the trading road. Sometimes Assur had black eyes or red welts on his wrists. But neither wanted him here now.

Tindr jerked his head in the direction of the fence. A low whine, almost a growl, came from under his gritted teeth.

Assur took a step back, shifted his eyes, saw that the deaf boy's kin had moved from the kitchen yard to the foot of the garden. It was not the sight of Rannveig and Gudfrid that drove Assur away. It was the faces of Tindr and Estrid.

GROWTH

WHEN the snow retreated each Spring, Tindr once again spent hours walking the woods. There was growth everywhere. Each day the forest was different. Reaching twigs with unfurling buds, ferns springing and uncoiling from moist and dark soil, mosses brightening into their vivid green. Even at the height of Summer, when all had reached its greatest form, there was change. The smells of Spring were of growth, of strain and expansion, the sweet dustings of nectar and pollen hanging like tiny yellow lanterns on every tree blossom and flowering shrub. His bees were covered with it, golden robes they earned by forcing their way into the secret folds of flowers.

Summer's warm air bore the fragrance of meadows dotted with spiked wildflowers, each scent subtle but different to his nose, the clean grassy smell of hay, the pungency of steaming piles of animal dung. Even the dust smelled different in Summer, drier, powdery. The grey and white limestone rocks he walked or sat upon grew warm. If he touched his tongue to them he tasted a chalky mineral brine, a remembrance of those salts of the sea, and of the soil.

He was growing too. From Summer to Summer he always noticed what things he could do this year that he could not do last. He could go up the ladder to the hay loft two treads at a time, if he wanted; he could not do that last year. But he could no longer fit comfortably into the smaller grain chest when it was empty and hide there; he was too big. His knees knocked against the marred wooded walls and he had to twist his shoulders and bow his head. Last year he had fit just fine, and could recall years when the chest had seemed big to him.

It was not just his arms and legs. Other parts were changing. Sometimes his leggings would tighten at the crotch, and he would get hard there. He did not know why it happened or when it might happen, it just did. Sometimes he and Ragnfast would have pissing contests in the woods, aiming their pricks to see who could wet the furthest on a tree or boulder, and that was fun. But this was different. His prick would swell, and almost ache for him to touch it. He would wake up at dawn with tingling heat growing there, and at the base of his stones. The pleasure it gave him to hold himself made him gasp. Sometimes he woke up, already sticky with the fluid that had pumped out, the pleasure a warm memory, like a good dream.

Tindr did not like to go to the Thing each Summer. It was crowded with folk he did not know, and even when he found his friends there, they would want to rove around with other boys as well. Then they would have to tell the new boys that Tindr was deaf, and that he could not talk. He would have to watch the strangers as they squinted

and tried yelling at him. He knew he slowed his friends
down when they stopped to gesture to him to include him
in some game; he saw it in their faces, even Runulv and
Ring, even his cousin Ragnfast. There was sport he could
not partake in without hearing, and he had often to stand
by and watch as the others played. And the Thing, in all
its busy-ness, held danger too, with many waggons, wains,
and herds of cattle being driven along, with no roadway to
keep to. He could not hear them coming up behind him
or to the sides, nor hear the shouted warnings of drov-
ers. Once a man with a barrow nearly ran him over, and
turned back and twisted his face at him. Tindr knew he
was cursing.

Dagr and Rannveig saw all this, and when in his thir-
teenth Summer Tindr gestured to his parents that he
did not want to go, they let him stay home. Gudfrid was
away herself, up to her sister's upland farm for a visit, so
Tindr would be alone. They would be gone three nights,
but home at dusk on the fourth, the heavy ox-cart they
had borrowed to carry crocks of Rannveig's ale consider-
ably lightened by the draining of its contents. The Thing
was always good business for any brewster or brewer, and
Rannveig took special delight in the long lines that formed
before her, cups and pots at the ready, to buy her ale.

Tindr had the care of the cow, geese, and hens under
his keeping, just as he always had, and they had begun as
well to keep a black and white splotched pig. She had just
farrowed and had nine tiny versions of herself scampering
about after her heavy teats. Other than caring for these
beasts morning and evening, and making sure the weeds
did not invade the rows of growing carrots and turnips,
his days would be his own.

The first day he spent many hours in his own forest, or so he thought of it; that expanse of woods that began behind his mother's empty hall at the top of the hill. It was the place he set his rabbit snares, shot squirrels, watched and waited for his deer and rare boar, and the place too where he had now three bee skeps. A track ran through it, branching off to the apple farm to the left and Ragnfast's farm to the right. The track to Ragnfast's had been enlarged and widened to be a true path, large enough for horsemen single file, while that to the apple farm grew narrower each year.

In his forest were great stands of dark fir and spruce trees, reaching ash trees standing, as is their wont, alone, delicate clumps of white barked birches, tangles of small leafed hazels, marshy places that oozed rich mud, and two rilling streams, one with a shallow pool that he had often splashed in. With no promise to return when the Sun was overhead he took his time in his ramble, turning over rocks to see what worms were about, sitting on the edge of a sun-warmed glade while birds darted and flicked their wings, retreating back into the woods to study a rotting and fallen tree trunk made host to swarms of beetles. Only his hunger drove him back home, and after sitting up late and sleeping out by the cooking ring, he left the next morning with a leathern bag with bread and cheese stuffed within.

This day he ranged South, behind the trading road as it were, skirting flocks of sheep and catching glimpses of the sea as he did. There were places here of scraped ground, dazzling white to the eye, flat pockets of limestone bearing the same rock-hard seashells and flower buds and plant stalks he found at the sea's edge. The limestone cliffs were full of slabs of them, which looked like small furling blooms and even crawling things, stilled forever, changed to stone. The air above his head rang with unheard bird-song, but he watched warblers dart and skip on the steady breeze. The brilliant light of the Sun in the clear and cloud-less blue sky reached overhead and spanned the horizon.

He searched a long time, and at his leisure, steadily fill-ing his bag with the best of the special rocks as he chewed on the bread and cheese he had drawn out of it. When the Sun was lowering his bag was heavy, and he realised how thirsty he was. His water-skin was empty. He looked about him. He was not far from the farm where Runulv and Ring lived. They would be gone to the Thing, but he could stop and drink from their well before he turned and made his way home.

Botair, the brothers' father, kept sheep and pigs, a cow, and hens, of course. Botair, like Tindr's father, fished, so he kept no cattle. But he grew fine purple grapes, and Tindr walked along a long row of them, just beginning to colour from a frosty green to pink, as he approached the house. A yellow, slanting light fell on all, and the sedge-thatched out buildings fairly glowed golden in the slowly dropping Sun. No one was about, in either the fields or the kitchen yard he passed, and Tindr did not blow his bone whistle to announce his coming. He went to the well, pulled back the cover, and dropped the little cup in, hauling it back out by its hempen string. He drank all the cup held, then dropped it again and refilled his water-skin.

He replaced the cover and was turning to leave when from the tail of his eye he saw someone come around the narrow side of the house. It was Runulv. Tindr was about to step forward and go to him when he saw that Runulv led someone by the wrist: a woman. The way Runulv held her wrist and then pulled her to him, they must know each other well. Tindr thought she was the daughter of the woman who cooked for Runulv's family; he could not be sure. Runulv's back was to him, but he could see the girl was laughing. Tindr stepped behind the shelter of some berry bushes. Runulv held the woman against his body, and Tindr saw he was kissing her; his hands went up under her head-wrap into her amber-coloured hair. They moved closer to the wall of the house. They kissed a long while, and Tindr felt his breath growing short as he watched. Runulv let her go, but then extended his arms before him and pressed his hands into the wood planks of the house on either side of her, prisoning her in. She was still smiling, and they kissed again.

Tindr watched Runulv's hand drop down her gown, reach for her skirts, and gather a handful of fabric. He pulled, and Tindr glimpsed the top of her low brown shoes, her grey woollen stockings, and then their dark bindings. Runulv kept pulling, gathering the green wool and white linen shift in his hand, and Tindr saw a flash of knee cap, then the white roundness of her naked thigh. Runulv moved his hand now, dipping it under her skirts, lifting higher. Tindr could see Runulv's hand move under the gown, just beneath her shoulder brooch, but what caught his eye and held it was that white roundness of her thigh, which now ended in a patch of light brown fur between her legs.

Tindr had been holding his breath to keep himself from crying out in his excitement. He let it out as slowly as he could. His heart was racing and his leggings tight at the crotch where he had swelled against them. He watched

Runulv lean towards the girl, saw him touch his hips to hers, and for that moment the furred patch between her legs was lost to him. Then Runulv dropped her gown, and led her around the corner from whence they came. They were gone from view. Tindr would have cried aloud in dismay if not his breath be stifled in his throat. He had dropped to his knees. His eyes burned from having held them, unblinking, on Runulv and the woman. Crouched there behind the bushes he choked out a little cry, knowing the hardness of his own body, knowing somehow that touching himself would be different from what Runulv and the woman must be doing.

OF THE LADY

TINDR delighted at skiing, and Dagr had made him his first pair when the boy was yet small. The long ski was rubbed with softened bees' wax to help it glide over wet snow, while the short ski was wrapped round with animal skin to help it grip with every kick. He and Dagr would set out in the short Winter light, leathern packs at their sides, to see if Tindr might find some rabbit or hare to bring home to flavour the pot; or sometimes just to stroke their way through the woods that lay open and dazzling white. When Tindr grew older, he made his own skis, and chose a straight sapling of whitebeam or ash to fashion as his pole. With the pole in both hands and stroking steadily with his back foot, he could move over the whitened fields and billowing drifts faster than he could run on the beach.

In heavy snow Tindr relearned every year woods he knew intimately when they were clothed in green. Vast distances lay open to the eye, but familiar landmarks were obscured, just as the pathways vanished under a mantle of snow. Boulders could collect drifts at their base that would cover them entirely. Animals forged new tracks in Winter, shortening distances from the safety of their dens to other cover. He knew when snow was coming, not only by the look of the clouded sky, but by the scent in the air. The smell of snow was to his nose like that of the air just before a lightning-storm, with a kind of bright sharpness to it, but less harsh. That smell, and feeling the soft flakes compact under his boots, were some of his favourite parts of the long and cold Winter.

Winter held time for the mending of nets, and for the making of tools. Dagr stoked up his forge-fire on the other side of the little smokehouse, and with Tindr blinking in the welcome heat hammered out two score of iron arrow-heads for the boy each year. It was work, and each arrow costly too in terms of the making and smoothing of the birch shaft and the feathering of the butt end. Tindr made the shafts himself from an early age. As he grew older Dagr put the hammer and tongs in his son's hands, and Tindr learned how to heat the iron rod to glowing red, how to hammer and pinch and shape the small mass into an arrowhead's sharp and hard point.

This was the time to make new bow strings, for Tindr always carried at least two with him when he was at the hunt. The strings he made from tightly braiding long hempen fibres which he got from Ketil and Tola, the rope-making couple. He ran the coarse fibres over a piece of his beeswax to smooth them, working the wax in with his fingers before he began his plaiting.

Yet Winter was not all work. When there had been a heavy snowfall, the first task of the day was the clearing of it from around the house and kitchen yard. After the fire-wood and stores of charcoal had been replenished, and the animals seen to, there were still a few hours left in the short day for fun. There was a lake not far from

Ragnfast's, and every year when it froze over the cousins would strap the long lower leg bones of deer to the bottoms of their boots and skate over as much of the ice as they had swept clean of snow. Sometimes high winds did this task for them, and nearly all the lake lay shimmering darkly under their blades. The ice looked black, but the lake-world was there beneath them, waiting. Rapp and Estrid's father would saw holes, and with the boys lower lines for the hungry fish below. They would roast these on a stick over a small fire they had built on the banks, and eat them sizzling hot with nothing more than a sprinkle of salt. They were so good, Tindr and Ragnfast would laugh with pleasure.

Life was lived out of doors, and once he had slept and done his chores only the harshest of weathers drove Tindr in. At night, Summer and Winter, there were endless stars streaming across the heavens, a river of light on a black landscape that if he lay back and watched, he would see flow. They were gone in day, but at dawn he sometimes set his eye on one, and watched until it faded away into the blue mantle cast out by the Sun's mighty beam. Fix it as he might with his sharp eyes, he would lose it in the gathering light. Yet the star was still there, he knew.

When the Moon was bright it was harder to see the stars. Tindr liked the way the Moon felt on his skin, and he often turned his face to it. It was not warm, like the Sun. But he could feel it nonetheless, a light like a flow of molten silver he had once seen at the silver-smith's workshop, but with no heat to it, a light with a different call on his skin than the heat of the Sun. He had his own stories about the Moon and Sun and stars, and stories too of the green and pink Northern Lights that glowed above them. These last were strong magic to Tindr, spirits dancing for joy. They gave gladness to all who beheld them, for all who looked upon the writhing sheets of light smiled back, open-mouthed, in awe.

In Fall the forest's secrets were revealed, this short time when it had dropped its leafy clothing and before the generous snow shrouded it again. Everything crisped and began to yellow. Forked branches and twigs danced and twisted in the wind. Fall's last blow of leaves lay all bare. The mouths to animal dens appeared, vulnerable to all passers. Rivulets dried up, sending frogs off for deeper water and the safety of muddy bottoms. Birds flashed through open tree branches where they never could dart in full-leafed Summer. And there were deer. In Spring he saw the hinds, their white-spotted red fawns at their flanks. In Summer he might see a group of yearling deer browsing together. It was Fall in which the stags appeared, come down from the deeper reaches of the woods, to find the waiting hinds. Young or old, single pronged or many, they came, driven by their need to mate. Some would be led by the Lady to a place he would wait.

Before dawn he would awaken and sometimes know, even then, if he should hunt that day. He would dress in the dark, take his bow and quiver from where it hung outside his alcove, get his deer-sling, ready-wrapped and waiting, from the barn. He would go to the well and splash his face and hands, for the Goddess would not bring quarry to an unwashed man. He would move to the kitchen yard cook-fire, take a piece of cold charcoal, and mark his palms, and then the back of his hands, with the sacred runes invoking Her, and calling for increase. *Lady, let loose a deer for me to take. Feed me in this way.*

Then he was off. He might feel from the start where he should head, which track to take, which clump of hazels to shelter behind. Other times he came to a stop, hardly knowing how he had got there; this was not a glade he knew, nor an oak he had seen before. When this happened he felt a buzzing in his stilled ears, as if his heart's blood swirled and washed there, and he knew to nock his arrow and be ready.

Then it came. A stag, or even a many-pronged hart, would step into his view. It might be pacing slowly, neck extended, sniffing the air, or come almost at a prance. But he would know it was his. He raised his bow. *Lady, one arrow. Clean. Little pain.*

As he let fly he no longer saw the broad flank of the stag before him. All he saw was the butt of his arrow, feathers moving away from him at infinite speed, and yet so slowly he saw the shaft part the air.

He would lower his bow and come to the animal. He stood over it as its life ebbed, with his now-empty hands outstretched, palms opened above it as it lay dying. The charcoal marks he had made at dawn by the cook-fire would be smeared. *Lady, I thank you*, he would praise. He would gaze upon the deer. *I will remember you. You will run the forest again. You are one with Her.*

One Fall, early in the season, he saw something he had never seen. He had risen knowing he would hunt. When he felt this way, it was a rare day when he returned empty-handed. Yet the morning wore on, dawn growing into day, a dull Sun climbing through the trees, many of which still bore their leaves, though tired and worn. His bow was in his hand. He stopped and looked about him. He had left the track that he had been following. He rarely felt concern at this; all he need do was lift his head, look at the trees, the quality of light, and somehow know which way to turn to find again a path he knew, a glade he had frequented, an ash tree he had once left a carved deer at the roots of.

This time, lifting his head, he saw Her. A hind of purest white walked before him from out of the birches, not ten paces away. She was large, perfectly formed, her white coat almost shimmering. She flicked her white-tipped ears and looked his way, the nose-leather twitch-ing. The eyes were liquid, a brown as deep and dark as the rest of her was the white of unsullied snow.

He knew he gasped. He knew that doing so at so close a distance would tell a deer he was there. She did not move.

He could scarce draw breath. He felt this hind, knew her somehow, to be the Lady, come as a deer. Come to him.

His eyes were fixed on her. She moved not, look-ing on him. From the tail of his eye he saw the trembling from the thicket of brambles not far from her. He turned his head the smallest notch. She sprang away, gone in an instant. There, emerging from the thicket, came the white, up-flaring tusks and lowered head of a boar.

It stepped forward slowly, its side to him, the dark bristled neck swaying above the broad chest.

A tightening behind his breast bone impelled him to act, as if an unheard voice was speaking. The voice was hers. *Take it.* He reached for the quiver at his hip.

He had never killed a boar before. This too was a beast sacred to Freyja; she was said to take the form of a golden-bristled sow. And now She had led this one to him.

It took two arrows, both in the mid-point of the chest, behind the front leg. Even so, the beast died quickly; he was that close to it, and the arrows drove deep at such little distance.

He knelt over it, wondering at the brawn of the shoulders and neck, the rows of quill-like bristles crowning the spine, the formidable tusks protruding from powerful jaws. The smell of its hide, mingled of male musk and forest undergrowth, filled his nose. He placed his hands upon the beast's neck, making real the life, and the loss of it, giving thanks to it. Hands still upon it, he looked about him. She had been there, the Lady. He had not dreamt it.

When Tindr emerged from the woods to his house he passed rows of near-empty vegetables, where a few late turnips and cabbages still grew. His father was standing in the door of his fish hut, unpicking a knot that had formed in the line above a fish hook. Dagr knew Tindr was hunting, and seeing the boy realized how late in the morning it was; the Sun was nearly overhead in its lowered transit, sitting in a grey sky. Yet Tindr had met success after all. His deer-sling was strapped to his waist and he was leaning forward as he pulled the heavy body behind him. His father put down his work and went to meet him. Closing the distance he noted the odd shape of what Tindr dragged; he could not see the deer's long legs, yet his son was bent almost double by the effort of his pulling.

Gudfrid was at the kitchen yard work table, and looked up and grinned at Tindr as he made his final steps with his burden. The boy's father was just behind him. There were two deer haunches smoking in the apple-wood-scented haze of the smokehouse, and one, killed a few days past, still hanging. They would start the Winter with a full larder, thanks to Tindr; there would be meat enough for her to add to their browis, to make pies, and dry some of it into leather-like wands that would keep all year without going green. There would be hides for her and Rannveig to stitch into gloves and mittens for all of them and keep their hands warm. She was always happy for the work Tindr brought her, and she smiled at him now.

Tindr unbuckled the sling from his waist. He turned and pulled back the edge holding what was within.

There was the boar. He uncovered it and turned to his father. Tindr saw Gudfrid clap her hands together, saw her face wreath in a delighted smile. Dagr spent a moment just looking.

Boar were hunted by men who went out in twos and threes with dogs to run down and worry the beasts. They were killed by spears, and often times not before a dog had been killed by the sharp and slashing tusks. Here was his lad before him, bringing a full grown male which he had downed with his bow.

Dagr saw the two wounds in the animal's side, where Tindr had dug out his arrows. He saw up close for the first time the armor-like thickness of the hide just above the place where Tindr had stilled its heart.

Tindr saw his Da staring, and the look of wonder in his face. He went to the quiver at his waist and pulled out the two arrows he had used. Both shafts had cracked on impact, but it was the heads he showed his Da. The tip of one was badly blunted from that hide, and the bone just beneath it.

Dagr held each point in turn, looking at them, looking at the boar. With one hand still grasping the arrows he rested his hands on his son's shoulders, and looked into the blue-white eyes.

Tindr saw his Da smiling at him. He did not sign his praise to him; he did not need to. He saw it in Da's eyes, shining back at him.

Rannveig was at work in her brewing shed, and Dagr now mimed the act of the raising of Tindr's whistle. His father's fingers went to his waist, and made a short movement as if sorting keys, Tindr's sign for his mother and the cluster of jingling keys, growing more by the year, she wore there.

Tindr grinned back at his father, pulled the leathern cord from out his tunic and set the little piece of bone to his lips. He blew twice: Nen-na.

Rannveig's head popped out from the broad doorway, her hands already buried in her apron, wiping off whatever mess of mashed grain she had been mixing. When she joined them at the cook-fire edge and saw what the forest had yielded to Tindr's bow her hands went to her mouth.

Men were killed boar hunting. Here was Tindr, having taken one. She was proud and frightened all at once. She looked at her boy as if to make certain he was whole and unharmed, then took him in her arms for a hug.

Tindr watched as they spoke amongst them, saw their smiles as they looked to him, and to the boar. Then Nenna was telling him to go fetch Runulv and Ring and their folks, tell them to come at dusk for the feast Gudfrid would make.

That night all the near neighbours crowded round the kitchen yard. Gudfrid had made the richest browis Tindr had ever eaten, thick with shredded boar's meat. She had roasted one of the big leg bones, and stirred the marrow into the stew. It was like partaking directly of the beast's strength. All were eager for it, and had been drinking ale and marvelling aloud at the head of the boar, which sat apart on the butchery bench, waiting for Gudfrid to roast it whole next day. But when they brought their spoons to their lips Tindr saw all fell quiet. Runulv and Ring were seated either side of him, and had been poking him and chaffing him with praise, making him show and show again the two arrows with their split wood and blunted tips. They knew enough not to ask Tindr if they could join him on his next hunt; other than the first hart he had taken with Rapp and Ragnfast, he always went alone. But his friends took such pride in what he had done that it made his face warm. Even Runulv, who was almost a man, looked awed; and those who were men were the most awed of all.

After the guests had left Tindr sat alone at the kitchen yard table with Rannveig and Dagr and Gudfrid. The wreckage of their meal was still before them. Besides the browis Gudfrid had served up a great rack of the boar's ribs, and the cracked and chewed bones were the only reminder of how they had been relished. The fire which Dagr had kept feeding was still high, and gave plenty of warmth to combat the night chill.

Tindr was full, and after the big meal and long day should be ready for sleep. But he need tell his parents something, and did so now.

He made a little *uh* so all would look at him. In the fire's light he could see half of their faces as they turned to him, smiles still upon their mouths. He tapped his eye.

"You saw," Rannveig repeated.

Tindr's hands, fingers splayed, rose to his head, his sign for deer. Then he made a quick milking gesture.

"You saw a doe, a hind," Dagr said.

Tindr looked about him. His hunting tunic was dull brown, like the leaves this time of year. He plucked at it with one hand, while shaking his head Nai.

"Not . . ." puzzled Rannveig.

Tindr repeated the antler sign for deer, the udder for female, then plucked again at his brown tunic. He shook his head and touched the white linen of his mother's head wrap, and nodded his head, Já.

"Not brown? – but white," she said.

"You saw a white hind," Dagr summed in a low voice. As soon as it was out of his mouth both he and Rannveig had caught their breath. Tindr's hands were busy once more. He closed his fingers, flicked them open. This meant, Suddenly, or Then.

Tindr pointed to the boar's head. He nodded, gravely, and almost to himself.

It was Dagr who spoke. "You saw a white hind, and then the boar appeared before you."

Tindr saw his parents turn to face each other. They were not speaking, but their eyes met in a way that he knew they thought the same.

"The skogsrå," Rannveig said. "The Lady of the Forest came to him, and led him to the boar." Her face had paled, even in the ruddy glow of the fire.

Dagr took a breath. White animals were rare, very much so. Without colouring to protect them they could not live long against predators or men who hunted. Still, he had found a white hedgehog when a boy, and reminded his wife of that now.

"It was the Lady," Rannveig repeated.

The Goddess Freyja ruled all beasts of the field. When it was her wont she came to Midgard and walked amongst them, taking the form of a white hind. In this guise she was the skogsrå, Lady of the Forest. But she could take another guise. It was She who let loose game for men to hunt, and if a hunter had found particular favour with her, she could choose him as her bed-mate. She would come then as a beautiful woman, and in this form give her chosen the exquisite pleasure of her body. But it was said the skogsrå exacted a cruel price. Men who had lain with her could never lie with mortal women, and often would sicken and die.

Now the Lady had come to Tindr, at least to show herself.

"We must make a charm for him to wear, to drive away the skogsrå," Gudfrid was saying. She looked stricken. Her thoughts had moved from how she would butcher and cook the rest of the boar to the need to protect this young boy from the wiles of the Goddess renowned for her lust.

Rannveig was still looking at Dagr. "She is marking him for her own," she said, a tremor in her voice.

Dagr had thought of this, long ago. Tindr was a gifted hunter, all knew that. The greenwood was his second home, and Dagr had walked enough with him through the trees to watch how the boy moved there. His eyes caught every movement of the birds or beasts he neared, and he gauged from their actions if he should stop or go on. His sense of smell was acute. His Uncle Rapp had said to Dagr, and not entirely in jest, that perhaps Tindr smelled the deer, just as deer could smell an incautious hunter. The boy knew every animal's tracks, whether in dry dust or deep snow. And he was a skilled bowman. His young wrists were steady, his shoulders strong, and he could hold himself still as a rock. Winter and Summer Tindr honed his skill by aiming at the deer he drew on his target boards. He spent time nearly every day standing before his drawing of a stag, slicing the air with arrow after arrow.

But this, his bringing them a boar, seemed to his father a sure sign of Tindr's favour with the Goddess. The Lady was watching him.

"Whether he knows it or not, he has given himself to Her already," Dagr said.

Rannveig looked at her son. He was young, just fourteen, but so beautiful. His skin was smooth and unblemished, his lips gently curved under a straight nose. His eyebrows were perfectly shaped, and a slightly darker shade of the golden-streaked honey brown of his hair. And his eyes. No one had such eyes as Tindr. They were the blue-white of ice, but there was warmth there, not chill.

Rannveig looked from her boy back to Dagr and Gudfrid. "How can we warn him?" she asked. She answered herself a moment later. "There is no guard against the desires of a Goddess."

Tindr saw the worry in all their faces, and knew he was the cause of it. He had seen it before. Their delight and pride at his bringing them the boar had given way to fear when he told of the beautiful hind. And She was the reason he had taken such rich game; the boar was a gift from Her.

When others felt sad and he did not understand he sometimes would put his fingers at the corners of his mouth, bidding them to smile. Looking at the worry on his mother's face he did not do so now. He tried to smile himself at them. He felt tired now, truly weary.

They could not help but smile back. Tindr had been called, that seemed certain. Perhaps he had been called during that long fevered night when his hearing had been burnt out of his tiny ears. He stood now, signed his good night.

"He must live his own life," Dagr reminded, as he walked to the house. The fire was at last dying down; they would soon follow him.

Before he left Tindr took another look at the bones that littered the table, and at the great head grinning at him from the butchery bench. In the morning he would slip into the forest and go to his remembrance stone. With a sharpened point in his hand he would etch the likeness of this boar in the smooth face of the tall slab, to join the many deer he had engraved there. He did it in gratitude, for Her.

THE WRECK

A full month had passed since Mid-Summer, the days still long and warm. Ragnfast had ridden down to Tindr's for the day. He rode a new colt, one he was training, and led his roan gelding so that Tindr might ride as well. He thought they might ride out to where Runulv and Ring were helping build a new boat with their father Botair. But stopping at Tindr's he learnt of the shipwreck, a way up the coast above Tindr's house.

Dagr and another fisherman had seen it yesterday from their boats, a mast-less trading knorr, drifting along the coast just north of the trading road. They had followed it until it got too close to shore, then landed themselves at their accustomed places; they had nets to empty. By then townsfolk had seen it too. Men paddled out in a flat-bottom boat to where the knorr had caught itself on the sharp rocks. There was nothing left within, save the anchor stone and its tangled line. The mast was gone, not even lying alongside the keel. Ripped and frayed fragments of once-stout netting told where the cargo had been heaved out in high waves; the men could see too the chafe-marks of the absent steering oar, which looked to have shattered. The hull near the prow, caught in a wedge of limestone, had punctured, and the ship lay foundered on its side where it had caught.

Dagr did not go out to see it himself. Though he had been amongst the first to sight it, he let others go and confirm what he already knew.

"Such things happen," he told Ragnfast. Fishing or trading could be a good living, very good; but the fees exacted were the lives of a certain number of the men who relied on it. For his own part, Dagr was less afraid of the sea than of the men who sailed upon it.

But Ragnfast was keen to see it. Wrecks did not happen every year, at least not where you could see one, and even though no treasure had been found aboard or washed up, it was something new. He and Tindr would ride to it, not up the coast for the sake of his horses' hooves, but by a woodland track that would take them close.

He did not know how to tell Tindr of the wreck, but he did not need to. When Tindr saw his cousin arrive with two horses he knew one was meant for him to ride, and he sped through what remained of his morning chores. They had scarcely passed the brew-house and waved goodbye to Rannveig when they saw Estrid on the trading road. With her was her friend Gyda, who lived on a farm past the last of the stalls and workshops. Estrid was there with her father, who had dealings with the iron-smith down one of the side roads, and he allowed that his daughter might go with the cousins, if they did not tarry.

Ragnfast considered. The chestnut colt he was riding was too green to be trusted with a second rider on his back. Tindr could ride his roan gelding with Estrid behind him, and he put Gyda on his colt, and lead him on foot at the colt's head. Gyda was a little older than Estrid, but timid. One glance at the uneasy way she looked at the horse when he suggested this made up his mind. They would all walk; going up the shore-line would be shorter anyway. He and Tindr staked the horses back by the barn.

They set out, the sea to their right, the brilliant green of a sea-meadow to their left. A few times Estrid ran up to the tree-line when she spotted the tiny dots of red that meant wild strawberries grew there, and each time ran back, small hands cupped full of their sweetness.

Tindr wondered where they were headed. He would have liked to be on the big gelding, but his cousin had gestured to him that they would ride later. Once or twice folk passed them, headed in the opposite direction, and he watched Ragnfast speak to them. One gestured with his hands the way men do when something was big. Some of them shook their heads and shrugged at Ragnfast when they answered him.

The shore line dipped in and out as they followed it, with ever larger outcroppings of pitted white limestone. Skirting one of the larger mounds they saw it. It was in the middle of a small bay flanked by tall limestone rauks, sea-stacks of weathered rock.

Tindr had seen wrecks before, but nothing of this size. Sometimes storms washed up the hulks of lost fishing boats. There were times, in still water, where he had looked over the side of Da's boat and seen the ruins of a boat lying on the bottom.

He looked at his friends. The wind was blowing steadily, as it ever did on the beach, tousling their hair, moving the skirts of the girls, making his own tunic flap against his hips. The line where sea met sky was as sharp as if he had drawn it with whittled charcoal, with only the brown hulk of the ship breaking it. That blue sky held not a cloud, and the yellow Sun beat down upon all.

He could tell from Ragnfast's face, and those of the girls too, they had not seen such a large wreck either, and one so close to shore. A few people were on the beach, looking at it, boys mainly, and two figures were out in the water, wading back to land.

He looked a while at it, his blue-white eyes narrowing. It was a dead thing, Tindr felt, as he let his eyes trace its foundered outline. His Da's boat under sail, bucking against the wind and skimming over the furrow of the waves was like something living, something that the wind and the sea and Da's hand at the sail-line and steering oar brought to life. This ship before them, caught on its side, stripped of the mast that was its strong wind-catching spine, its prow stove in, looked a dead and bloated animal.

Estrid's always smiling face wore an uncertain look, and she was clutching her blue shawl about her thin shoulders as if she was chilled. Gyda was squinting at the wreck, then letting her eyes drop to the sunlight on the ripples being pushed towards them. Her brow was furrowed. Even Ragnfast looked grave. He had grinned broadly when they first spotted it, but then had stood with them, making no move to approach closer as the boys now walking towards them had.

They might as well head back, Ragnfast thought. The wreck was just that – something ruined. Hung up as it was on the rocks it might be there a long time, unless someone tried to patch her from the inside and refloat her. A shipwright could try that. For now, there was not much to see, and he had told Estrid's father he would not keep her long. He and Tindr could then ride down to see Runulv and Ring, which was what he wanted to do anyway.

The two figures coming from the water got closer. Ragnfast saw that the taller of them was Assur.

Assur came straight to them. He was with one of his younger brothers, and their leggings were wet from having waded out to get closer to the knörr. Both were barefoot, their shoes up on the dry pebbles of the beach.

"Hej," said Assur.

He had grown a lot in the past year; Ragnfast saw he was almost as big as he was. His neck was longer, making the purple birth-mark look larger. There was some down on Assur's upper lip, not as much as Ragnfast had, but Assur's was hard to see as it was so light. As Assur neared the stones grew sharper, and the way he was walking showed his feet hurt. His younger brother went to where his shoes waited, and put them on.

"Hej," said Ragnfast in return. For want of something better to say he tilted his head at the wreck and asked, "See anything?"

"Nai," said Assur. "The rocks are too sharp."

Ragnfast nodded, began to turn to lead the others away.

Assur looked at Estrid and Gyda and nodded his round head at both of them. Tindr, off to one side, he did not look at.

It was the second time Estrid had seen Assur this Summer. A month ago he and his older brothers and father had come to her farm, looking to trade lambs for grain. Her father did not like the look of the animals and refused them. Assur had jolted in surprise when he saw her come from around the kitchen yard; he must not have known it was her family's farm. His round blue eyes had rounded further, looking at her, but he was nice to her that time and did not try to take her hand and force her to touch him. She remembered how the group of them had moved off at a shuffle, driving the small flock of ewes and lambs before them. Her father had been short with them and she had felt badly. Assur had turned and looked back at her.

Now Estrid gave him a little smile. Assur locked onto her eyes.

"I bet I could see inside, from up there," he said of a sudden. Assur pointed to the ragged limestone bluff that rose at the water's edge on the other side of the small bay. About half way up the face a small ledge projected out over the water.

"Ever climb that?" he asked Ragnfast.

"Sure," said Ragnfast, looking at the bluff. "From the side. No one climbs the front face. It is too steep."

He knew even moving up the spine of the bluff held danger. There were two crevices that had to be leapt over, and you had to catch yourself as you landed so that you didn't fall forward and over the edge. Ragnfast had done it a couple times, including last year with Tindr.

Assur was squinting at the small ledge. The limestone beneath it was greyish-white, and nearly vertical. Above the ledge it raked back a bit, beneath the top of the bluff.

He looked back at Estrid. "I will climb it," he said.

"Do not be stupid," answered Ragnfast quickly. "It is too sheer." If Assur was issuing a challenge, it was one he would not take.

"For you maybe. Not for me," said Assur.

Tindr was watching it all. He knew they were talking about the bluff from the way they pointed at it. He had climbed it last Summer with Ragnfast, following him up. If they were going to climb it again he wanted to go first this time. He knew he was steadier on the rocks than Purple Neck, who was big and clumsy.

Tindr made a sound, a kind of snorting squeal, and all turned to him. He grinned back, then bolted for the base of the bluff.

"Nai, come back!" complained Assur. The deaf boy would climb it first, reach the ledge, have the first peek across the water into the wreck's hull. And Estrid would be watching.

He flung himself down on a rock and pulled his shoes on, then started after Tindr.

"Stupid," muttered Ragnfast, loud enough for Assur to hear. Assur barely turned his head.

"Assur, do not try that," Gyda said, stepping forward herself. She gestured to his younger brother, as if urging him to speak, but the boy said nothing, just bit his lip. Gyda shook her head. She did not know Assur well but felt she must stop him. Ragnfast was right; it looked stupid even to attempt. The ledge hung over a drop of many feet, where shallow water covered the white rocks below. Assur ignored her, intent on catching Tindr.

Tindr had neared the base of the bluff. Assur could not hope to do more than clamber in his wake, but if he caught the deaf boy he would give him a good yank back.

To Assur's surprise Tindr did not head for the sheer face that was Assur's target. He watched the deaf boy skirt the base of the bluff to the left, then begin his climb up the spine towards the top. Assur gave a small hoot of satisfaction. By going straight up he could not only gain the ledge, but continue up and reach the peak before the deaf boy.

To begin he had to himself start slightly to the left, on dry rock, and step his way around to the sheer face and the ledge above it.

"Nai!" he heard Ragnfast call, but he did not turn to look at him this time. He had worked his way a few feet up over the water now, and was staring over his head at where his hands could grip and feet could push from.

The girls had moved closer to Ragnfast, watching both Tindr outlined against the sky as he scrambled and jumped his way across the bluff, and Assur, flattened against the rock face with outstretched arms. They saw Tindr leap across the first of the crevices, and both girls gave a little shriek as he staggered from the impact of his landing. He just went on, intent on what he was doing.

"Tindr, Tindr," called Estrid, breaking from her friends and picking her way as fast as she could over the sharp rocks. "Come back, Tindr," she pleaded.

Assur heard her and craned his neck over his shoulder. He gritted his teeth and moved upward. He pushed off with his shoe, reaching to find another foothold, patting his hand over the rock face for a hand-grip. The limestone was sharp and he wished he had gloves. When he pushed with his feet to move up the face he felt it even through his leather soles.

Ragnfast had joined Estrid. It was no good calling to Tindr, he would have to see if he could catch his eye. If Tindr stopped and came down maybe Assur would give up trying to reach the ledge.

He was about to call out to Assur, urge him to back down, when he saw how much the boy was struggling. Ragnfast had climbed enough rauks and limestone cliffs to know that going up was one thing, coming down another.

Ascending, one could see the hand-hold one reached for. Coming down it was often impossible to turn one's head enough to see the next place where hand or foot could fall. Assur was heavy, and he did not look like he had the strength to grip and swing his legs from side to side to catch the small knobs of rock and continue up to the ledge.

Ragnfast waved his arms, never as frustrated as he was this moment with his cousin's deafness. Tindr was focused on reaching the top; he was nearing the second crevice. Assur's brother had joined them below, and Ragnfast saw how the boy's eyes went from Tindr, leaping and scrambling upon the bent back of the rauk, to Assur, who was nearing the projecting ledge. Ragnfast moved in closer. He could not see how Assur would be able to pull his way atop the ledge; there looked to be few or no real hand-holds.

Tindr leapt across the second gap in the rock. He was steadier on his landing this time, and kept on, nearing the pinnacle. From the tail of his right eye he could glimpse the water swirling far beneath him, and a little further off, the wrecked hull of the knorr, but he looked at nothing but the next crag his feet would touch.

Assur had gotten himself in a place where he could no longer go up. His left cheek was jammed against the rock face. He could see the ledge just above, but it was out of reach. His splayed fingers ached from gripping the rock, and his left leg, on which he bore most of his weight, trembled on the small jutting rock he had braced it on. He swung his right leg out, trying to catch it on something. His foot met rock loose enough to give way in a small shower of pebbles, pinging down the rock face and pelting into the water below.

Both girls cried out in fear, and Assur's brother bawled out his name.

Tindr reached the top, proud to have made it so quickly. He took a moment then to look down. Estrid was jigging up and down, her face knotted in fear, her eyes darting from Tindr to Assur. Ragnfast shot his hands up in the air, fists clenched, wrists crossed: Do not do. He gestured violently that Tindr come down. As Tindr watched them, reading the fear in their faces, he saw their eyes shift from him to something out of his range. He looked behind him along the spine of bluff he had just climbed. Purple Neck was not there.

Assur was at that point trying to edge his way sideways, looking for any foothold he could. His palms were raw and two of his fingertips bleeding. He found a good foothold, moved left, but then his searching hand could find nothing to grip. A small knob crumbled to stone dust in his fist, and his left arm swung wildly out.

The girls and Assur's brother were screaming, but Ragnfast scarcely heard them; he was on his way up the rock face, tracing the same route Assur had taken. Tindr saw the horror in the girls' faces, and saw Ragnfast as he moved at the base of the bluff. He crouched down at the very edge of the pinnacle. He leaned over and spotted Assur, half way up the steep rock face, just below and to one side of the ledge.

Assur's face was so red, and so covered with stone dust, that the purple mark on his neck hardly stood out. His yellow hair, which always looked like a shock of wheat, was plastered to his round head. He looked up and saw Tindr peering down at him. Tindr saw the fear in the boy's eyes, saw the mouth open as he looked up at him. He began to clamber down to him. If he could reach the ledge he might be able to pull him up, or somehow guide his movements.

Tindr had just gained the ledge when Assur fell. Ragnfast was almost half-way to him, and heard Assur's scream. Ragnfast was showered with crumbled stone that came away with Assur's loosened grasp. He saw Assur's dropping body, saw him hit a small outcropping not far from him, heard the dull impact as he splashed through the shallow water below to the white rock bed beneath it. Then all he heard was the shrieking of the girls.

Tindr, from the ledge, saw it all, and saw Assur's eyes widen as he fell backwards through the air. He looked about him, scanned the rock face beneath his feet. He could not go down. He turned and pulled himself up to the bluff's pinnacle once more, and came, leaping and running down its spine.

Ragnfast half-climbed, half-jumped down, landing in the ankle-deep water not far from where Assur lay, face up. Estrid and Gyda and Assur's brother had run there, splashing through the lapping water, as had two men who had just arrived on the beach and had seen Assur fall.

Ragnfast was there first, and then Estrid, her gown soaked to her knees. She was sobbing in little hiccoughing gasps. Assur's brother's face was white, and his fists were clenched at his sides as he looked down at the water. Gyda reached them and placed an arm around both. Tindr ran, panting, from behind them, and jerked himself to a stop at Ragnfast's side.

Assur lay motionless, the water gently washing over his body. A thin filament of blood moved like red smoke through the water under his head, which lay at an odd angle to his neck. His blue eyes were opened, never rounder, never more surprised.

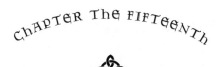

CHAPTER The FIFTEENTH

THE ACCOUNTING

THE two men pushed their way through the young people. With one at his feet and one at his shoulders they lifted Assur from the sheet of rock which formed his final bed.

Another boy who had been on the beach was sent at a run back to the trading road. Gyda and Estrid sat, clinging to each other and crying, on a low rock, their backs to the shipwreck and the body that now lay on the white shingle of the beach. Ragnfast stood, Tindr at his side, with the men who had retrieved Assur from the water.

Ragnfast felt light-headed, as if his body had somehow been stretched to twice its length, and had not enough blood in it. Everything looked too bright; the sky dazzled him. Tindr kept cocking his head, looking at the base of the bluff from whence he had begun his climb, then at the top where he had paused and seen the fear in the faces of his friends, then the narrow ledge which had been Purple Neck's goal, and from which he could not help him. He felt cold and was aware his teeth were chattering.

Assur's young brother was sitting on the stones next his brother's body. One of the men had closed the wide blue eyes. A thin trail of blood from the crack in Assur's skull had followed his passage up the beach, thickening under where his head lay. The small pool of red had grown no larger. His brother sat mutely by, shoulders quivering and tears running down his cheeks.

Tindr looked at him, at the crying girls, at Assur's big and clumsy body. His hand went to Ragnfast's forearm. His cousin turned to him.

Tindr touched his own ear, pointed to Assur, tapped his own chest.

"Nai," answered Ragnfast aloud. He found it hard just then to form words. Tindr feared he was to blame. "It is not on you."

He pointed to Assur, crossed his clenched fists, tapped his own chest. "I told him, nai. He would not listen." Ragnfast raised his hands hopelessly in the air.

Everything had moved so fast during Assur's climb that it seemed time itself was now slowed. The Sun beat down on those waiting on the white beach, living and dead. A sea bird, angry that they were too close her hidden chick, swooped nearby, scolding. A lone cloud passed in front of the burning Sun, making their shadows vanish for a moment.

Then the boy who had been sent broke from the line of trees, running still, with a knot of men hurrying behind him. Dagr was in the lead. Ketil the rope-maker was there, with his brother Botair, and his sons, Runulv and Ring. Alrik, who lived up the hill from Dagr and Rannveig, was a sawyer, and he had brought a broad plank, which he and another man carried between them. The last man with them was Estrid's father.

The girls looked up from where they sat and Estrid ran, with a shriek, to her approaching father. He caught her up in his arms and cradled her to his chest, carrying her as if she were still a small child. His face bent over her. A child had died, but it had not been his.

Tindr waited until Dagr and the rest of them were nearly at the body, then he bounded towards his father and wrapped his arms about him. He made a strangled sound, but kept his face buried in Dagr's tunic and would not lift his head.

Ragnfast was just behind him.

"He did nothing, Uncle," he reassured him.

Dagr was looking over his son's head at Assur's body. His dripping clothes had begun to dry in the warmth of the strong breeze. A fly landed on the dead boy's upturned cheek and crawled there a moment. You again, thought Dagr.

"Assur tried to climb the sheer face," Ragnfast was saying. "We all told him not to."

Dagr looked at Ragnfast's drained face. "You will tell of this later," Dagr said, placing his arm on his nephew's shoulder. The breached hulk of the merchant knorr lay in the water before them, one more reminder of death. Dagr let his eyes settle on it for only a moment. Ring and Runulv had now come to stand with their friends, their gaze moving from Assur to Ragnfast and Tindr, and back again.

Alrik had set the plank down on the uneven white stones of the beach, and now was the body of Assur lifted and placed upon it. His hands would not stay on his body, and kept dropping off the sides of the board. Alrik, seeing this, loosened the dead boy's belt and drew his hands through it, holding them to his sides. The flesh was already cool to the touch.

Assur was carried back on the shoulders of four men. Dagr led them, but by common and unspoken assent they stopped when they reached Rannveig's brew-house. Inside was Assur's mother and as many of his siblings as could be found; others were looking for his father. Rannveig and Gudfrid had already begun to carry in ale from her brewing-yard before Assur's mother arrived; a tale such as this would need ale, both to recite, and to hear. Assur's parents had never before come to the brew-house, though Rannveig had seen his father wheeling drunkenly on the trading road. Now Rannveig sat next Assur's mother, a woman she did not know and had scarcely ever spoken to, and waited.

As soon as the party could be sighted at the end of Rannveig's herb garden the woman began to cry. She saw from the distance her son being born shoulder-high, and knew him to be dead. She was not loud in her weeping. She folded into herself as she covered her face with her hands. She rocked forward and back on the bench, almost as if she were soothing a babe.

They placed his body on a table there in the brew-house. He came through first, with the men who bore him, and then Dagr and Tindr and Ragnfast, and all the others. Rannveig saw her son whole, and her nephew too. She yearned to catch them both up in her arms, but could not do such before a woman lamenting her dead son. She turned her narrow blue eyes, now glistening with tears, upon them, and nodded to each.

Assur's mother rose and came to her son's side. His head was crooked over his left shoulder in a way it never could be in life, leaving the angry birth-mark fully exposed. She untied the knot that held her shawl about her, and began to drape it over Assur's chest. Rannveig had a woollen blanket ready, and offered it instead; one could not wear any garment which had lain upon the dead, and this woman looked like she had nothing to spare. She shook her head with a whimper and laid her shawl down upon him.

Folk from the trading road now crowded in. Amongst the last to come was Assur's father. He had been tracking a lost ewe and he and the son who had found him were both breathless from their haste in coming. He pushed his way into the brew-house. Those nearest touched others in front of them, and space was yielded silently until he stood before the table that held Assur. He set his legs and stood unmoving. His clothing was ragged and his yellow hair a paler version of his dead son's. The flesh between his eyes was pinched together, and he looked at what the table held as if he did not recognize his son.

His wife was already seated at the boy's head, her lowered brow held in her hand, and several of Assur's brothers and sisters ranged about on either side. Estrid saw the little girl who had had the burr tangled in her hair. She was too young to know her still brother was dead, but she kept quiet, her small fingers playing over her own face.

The story was told. Ragnfast, as eldest, went first. He drew breath before he began, and did not waver in his telling, though the odd light-headedness had not passed. Crammed into the brew-house with so many folk, he wondered he was not warmer. A glance at the body of Assur reminded him. Rannveig and Gudfrid had passed cups of ale to all, even the youngest, and that they gave to Ragnfast and Tindr they did not water.

Ragnfast told all, just as it happened. Only one thing did he omit. He did not tell how Assur had looked at Estrid when he had boasted he would climb the cliff face. Just as Tindr had no part in the boy's end, he did not want Estrid to think she bore any of the blame for his actions.

Estrid spoke next, a confused and tearful accounting. Then Gyda spoke, telling once more the same tale they had heard from the lips of Ragnfast and Estrid.

"He was showing off," she ended. Despite the tears still on her cheeks some anger shown in her soft voice.

Her words hung in the air. Heads nodded. Boys did foolish things all the time. This had been one of them.

The two men who had watched Assur fall spoke last. They told how Tindr had tried to reach Assur from the top of the bluff, and how Ragnfast had begun scaling its base to reach him. Either boy could have been killed in doing so.

Through it all Tindr stood at Dagr's side. There was no time for his Da to sign to him what folk were saying, and he knew both Nenna and Da would tell him as much as they could later. Few ever looked his way, a few glances only when his cousin gestured to him, so he knew they were not speaking of him.

When all had been told Dagr asked Assur's father if he wished to question any. The man had been standing at Assur's feet, scarcely lifting his eyes from his son as he listened. Now he looked up at Dagr.

"I have no luck," was all he said. His voice was strained, almost a croak.

Dagr did not take his eyes from the man's face. Dagr knew something of luck. Truly, he thought, you are right. Your hamingja, your luck-spirit, has fled.

THE FIRES
OF MID-SUMMER

IT was Mid-Summer day. Fires to honour the Sun had blazed long and bright all over Gotland. This longest day had worn on. It was now nearly midnight, and on one farm the folk had drifted into distinct camps. The eldest, along with many of the youngest, had headed indoors where they were now asleep. The revelry had begun at noon with circle dances, to the rhythm of pipe, harp, and hand-drum. Dance after dance had trampled the grasses of the meadow, until even the young people, panting and with brows glistening, begged the players to put aside their instruments and leave them rest. This was followed by a feast remarked upon for its richness by all who partook. Ragnfast's parents were known to lay a good table, and those planks set up on trestles under the pear trees were burdened with a whole roasted lamb, fish stew heightened with a green sauce of newly-picked herbs, platters of oaten cakes, and golden-crusted egg puddings. All of Spring's bounty lay there, along with a remembrance of Fall in the form of dried apples and pears made succulent by having been stewed in verjuice. The feast was a harbinger of a good Summer to come, and celebrate they did. Rannveig and Dagr had brought an entire cask of her strongest and best ale, and there was mead as well, carried from the farms of different guests as their contribution to the day.

After feasting and drinking, all returned to the fire, moving in a bit closer as the massive logs had burnt down, and the slightest evening chill could be felt. Stories were told, and songs offered, and laughter, gentle and hearty, rose from the circle. Rapp, Ragnfast's father, was known to have a good voice, and he unspooled every song of the sea, of woodland hunts, and the deeds of the Gods he possessed. The sun finally began to dim. Small children lay over their parents' shoulders, or at their feet, asleep, and these began to be picked up and taken off to the many cots Rapp and his wife had ready and waiting within their house. The oldest too had nodded off, and were awakened by a nudge and sent to bed, often times guided by their grown daughters or sons. These last, with small ones of their own, hovered near the house and its small cook-fire in the kitchen yard. There they sat, sipping broth or ale, talking in hushed tones about the year past, and hopes for that to come. Remaining out by the big Mid-Summer fire were now the several youths and maids.

The day had been a long one, yet with light still in the sky it was impossible to feel sleepy. Tired they were, though, and as their elders left they moved in closer each to each, and their talk grew low. Ragnfast sat with his back to the family farm-stead, as if he wished to forget where he was on this shortest night. As he listened he often times leaned in and shoved another short piece of oak onto the fire, making it so hot that the others jestingly complained he would roast them. None of them moved. They had all been drinking Rannveig's strong ale, and had enjoyed as well a small cup or two of mead, the crock of which had been taken from them by their elders when they quitted the fire. Ragnfast's younger sister was there; his eldest was wed and had a babe, and she and her husband were sitting back by the kitchen yard, already made part of the older folk. The younger sat there at the fire by the young man she would hand-fast at Summer's end.

Runulv and Ring, sons of Botair, were there, as was Gyda, from the farm next them, and Gyda's equally pretty cousin Ása. Sigrid was there, with one of her younger sisters, Steinvor; the youngest, Sigvor, who had but seven years, had been carried to the house in her father's arms. Then there was Estrid, the youngest of the maids about the fire, younger even than Tindr, who she sat closest to. This was her fourteenth Summer, and Tindr now had fifteen.

Ragnfast, their host about the fire, was a little more than three years older than Tindr, and quite a man in form. He was above mid-height, not overly tall, but had a breadth to his chest and shoulders that bespoke the heavy farm work he had grown up doing, and the calm assurance that a man who is good around horses generally bears. All, men and women both, liked him. He had clear blue eyes under strong brows, and a firm chin with a cleft. Such good looks in a man only deepen with age, and Ragnfast was already beginning to be noted for his.

The sky had darkened above them. It was now deeply night, as deep as night can be on the longest day of the year. The day had been a cool one, and sometimes misty, and the night sky wore a thin scrim of cloud. No stars could be seen through it. It was as if a curtain of some heavy woollen stuff blanketed the heavens, removing all points of reference, rendering all limitless. Ragnfast had been gazing into the bright coals of the fire, and now shifted his eyes to the sky overhead. It took some time before he realised that he would see little. There was no Moon nor star light, so effective was the layer of cloud that darkened all about and above him.

He recalled his father telling him that outside, and at night, was the most dangerous time of all. It was not fear of marauding trolls that made his father warn him. It was men themselves. At night, and out from under the cover of a roof and its symbol of home and hospitality, a man could feel there were no limits. A foolish thought could become a reckless deed. A jest could turn on a word into a blood-feud.

As he thought on these things his eyes dropped again, to rest on the glowing coals of the fire. The Sun had died today; each day forward through the long and hot Summer to come would grow shorter. He heard the talk and laughter of his friends, but his thoughts travelled back. He thought of all who sat with him here, and those who were gone, to other fires, or to other realms. He heard the high-pitched chatter of Gyda and Ása and Sigrid and his sister, and saw them, from the tail of his eye, clustered together. Their parents, and Tindr's, and his own, were sitting around the tables at the kitchen yard, or perhaps even asleep on cots in the house and stable. The children were long asleep, and he well recalled being picked up by his own father and being carried away, yawning, from this same Mid-Summer fire when he was small.

He looked more steadily at the girls, comely maidens all, their faces alight in the golden glow of the fire. It was Sigrid his eye returned to. She was the eldest of four sisters, who shared amongst them a pleasing softness to their persons. Sigrid wore the sash about her waist just snug enough to show the rounded line of her hips. He let himself wonder what those hips would feel like pressed against his body.

Ragnfast had known a woman's embrace but once. It happened at last Summer's Thing, nearly a full year ago. He was already working to build up a name for himself in horse-breeding, and had brought with him two young horses he hoped to sell. He was leading one of them, a bay colt of two years, to the trading stall of an iron smith who had expressed interest. It was the second day of the Thing, and his path took him by the campsite of two women, mother and daughter. The daughter was a woman of perhaps six or eight years more than Ragnfast; she had two little ones of her own near her, though there was no man about. The older woman stood spinning, feet planted, eyes lowered, stolid and unmoving. The younger was crouched by her fire-ring. She lifted her head as Ragnfast neared. Their eyes met, and he nodded as he would when one came eye-to-eye with any at the Thing. But her return look was something different. She stared at Ragnfast in a way that made him slow. She finally nodded, without smiling, back at him.

Later that night he was coming back from the fire which had been lit by a group of youths. He had drunk ale; not as much as he would have liked. Walking back to his parents' waggon he passed near to the woman's cook-fire. There she was, still sitting by it. The old woman was gone, in the tent, Ragnfast thought. His feet slowed. She lifted her head. She looked at him for a moment, then her chin

lowered slightly, the smallest of nods. She rose, and Ragnfast stood as she neared him, pulling her mantle closer
about her. She walked to the line of trees beyond the edge
of the field where they were all camped.

Once through the trees she found a small clearing,
and pushed her way past some shrubby growth, he just
behind her. She faced him, and threw back the hood on
her mantle. In the Moonlight he saw the age and care on
her face, and saw that she was comely, too. He wished that
she would speak; he wanted to smile, but her face bore a
stillness that was almost grave.

He knew what she had brought him there for, but
nothing else. Then he bethought him that if she were a
whore, he had but little silver to offer her, for he had sold
neither of the horses he had brought. His hand went to
his belt and the silver pouch tucked there. He began to
speak, for fear of angering her later, should what he could
offer be too little. But she shook her head, and placed her
own hand upon his. He stepped closer and she lifted her
face. He let his lips touch hers. Her arms raised slowly
to encircle his neck, and her mantle, which she had not
pinned, fell from her back.

After the first touch of their lips, they did not kiss
again. But she clung to him with unexpected strength,
burying her face in his neck and gripping his shoulders
with her fingers as they tumbled about upon her fallen
mantle. They did not undress; she merely pulled up her
gown, as he, with one hand, tried to pull off his knife belt
and unhook the toggle which fastened his leggings. He
could not see her body, for her clothing and the dimness
of the glade, and she kept his face close to her own.

When it was over they both lay back, faces lifted to the night sky. She had said almost nothing; a few murmurs, a panting sigh. He began to turn to her.

"Go now," she told him. Her voice sounded as if it came from a long distance.

He opened his mouth, but before he could speak she said again, "Go."

He rolled to his knees, fastened his leggings, found his belt. He stood. She was still lying there, and had turned her face away from him.

He pushed through the trees and out to the field, and went to his parents' waggon. They were both asleep within; he could hear their breathing. His sister slept in the little tent pitched just next it. He unrolled his bedding and stretched down by the fire, glad he need speak to no one. Weary as he was, sleep did not come easily, and he lay there a long time before it did. His last thoughts were flickering images of little Hedinfrid.

The following day he walked by the woman's campsite. He had no need to go that way, and in fact his family was preparing to leave the Thing; he had slipped away for a moment, in hopes of glimpsing her again. As he neared he saw a single figure, a man, seated on an overturned wooden pail. He was of perhaps five-and thirty years, with straggled brown hair and a face that had not been shaved in days. The man held his knife in one hand and a stick in the other, and as he whittled the point the shavings dropped into the guttering fire he sat before.

Ragnfast was so startled he paused. The man looked up, saw Ragnfast, and narrowed his eyes at him. The woman now approached, from the other side of the tent, struggling with the weight of a full bucket of water. She shifted the bail from hand to hand, then glanced up and saw Ragnfast. Her eyes quickly dropped. At that moment the man sharpening the stick called out to her, a short, hoarse cry. Ragnfast went on his way, his heart beating so fast it felt that it had moved up into his throat. He circled around to return to his family.

Now, back at home and surrounded by his friends, he was thinking of none of this; or only of one small part of it, and that was what had changed in his life in the past year, from Mid-Summer to Mid-Summer. The encounter with the woman was perhaps the greatest of these.

Sigrid was sitting next him but one, and her profile was outlined by the firelight, which had grown in brightness as the Sun dimmed. He still thought her one of the comeliest maids on Gotland, and she was still unwed. Her family were sheep-raisers and wool weavers, and she would, he knew, wed none but a man who could boast a large flock of his own. But now, alive to her nearness, he would like to kiss those pink lips which now gathered in a pout as she listened to a story Runulv was telling that was going on too long. He left the fire for a moment and found a palm-sized rock, smoother than most, which he dropped at the edge of the glowing embers.

"The game of hot rock," he announced, standing so all would take heed. The girls laughed, some in protest, and one of the youths whistled. But Ragnfast had left again, gone into the separate little room, used for tools, appended to the steep-roofed winter sheep-shelter, or lamm-gift, not far away. He came back with a pair of iron tongs and an old sheepskin, which he proceeded to tear with his knife into small pieces. He tossed two such pieces to each sitting about the fire.

Hot rock was a game of forfeits, in which a stone is heated and then thrown to the person whose name you call. If they fail to catch it, they must pay a forfeit. When the game was played amongst mixed young folk this was oftentimes a kiss. He who was owed the forfeit could also command the loser to kiss another of his choosing. If the player throwing the rock failed to make a good throw, then he or she could be made to forfeit.

All were busy working a thumb-hole into their squares of sheep-hide to help hold it in place on their palms. Rag-nfast had pride of place in going first. He drew the rock from the fire and held it out in the tongs.

"Sigrid," he said, and threw it to her. But she caught it deftly between the bits of sheep-skin in her hands, and almost without pause called out, "Ring!"

Her throw was not a steady one, and Ring had trouble catching it. I would have made sure to have missed it, and demanded a kiss from her, thought Ragnfast. Instead Ring laughed and said, "Estrid," then threw it to the young maid.

Tindr had seen this game before, but never played with maidens. He had watched Ragnfast and Ring and Runulv play it, the forfeits being arrows or small pieces of hack silver if one dropped the rock. He could not play himself, as he could not call out his target's name. But this night Ragnfast had passed him the sheep-skin hand protectors like everyone else. None had brought out silver or any other goods with which to pay a forfeit, and he scanned about him, wondering what payment might be exacted. He felt without understanding it the anticipation of all, and wore a broad smile on his open face.

Estrid gave a little smiling shriek, but snatched at the rock and jumped up. "Ragnfast," she called out, and almost hurled it at him. He caught it, and almost in one movement threw again to Sigrid, naming her once more. She was caught off guard and the rock dropped into her lap. She leapt to her feet and it rolled to the edge of the fire-ring. Runulv gave out with a low whistle.

A grinning Ragnfast was already at her side. "Your forfeit," he said, leaning in. She raised her chin and with lips pressed duly offered them. He tried to make it linger, but she pulled back.

All were laughing, and it was not the feeling he had hoped. Now it was Sigrid's right to begin the game, and she heated the rock and used the tongs to throw it. "Runulv," she called. He caught it and tossed to Gyda, who threw it to Ring. He again threw to young Estrid. This time she dropped it.

"Ha!" laughed Ring, coming to claim his kiss. He made great show of it, taking her in both arms and bending her back from the waist, then covering his mouth with hers. It was but a jest to Ring, and when he would awaken in the morning with a bad head he would remember none of it.

Estrid had never before been kissed, and when Ring stepped away, still laughing, her cheek was crimson. Most of the others were hooting and laughing, and she herself gave the smallest of smiles, but two there were not smiling.

Tindr, still seated by her side, was one of them. Of course he had seen folk kiss before, beginning with his own Nenna and Da. As he grew older he had seen more than kissing. He had watched Runulv kiss and caress the woman at his farm, and the urgency of Runulv's actions had been conveyed to his own body. Last Summer he had come across a couple at the edge of a hay-field who had put down their rakes in the warm sunshine. They lay upon the mown hay, entangled hip-to-hip, and Tindr, watching with caught breath, knew it to be the same act as a ram and ewe or stallion and mare. But Estrid – she was his friend, and younger even than he. Ring holding her like that and kissing her made her something different. Tindr's face twisted as he watched it, and his own face felt hot, hot as Estrid's looked when Ring released her.

The other who was not smiling was Ragnfast. He was staring at Estrid as if he had never seen her before, this neighbour's daughter he had been raised alongside. His sisters were too old for her to play with, so from child-hood Estrid had played with him, at least until her being a maid got in the way of their fun. Even after that she tagged along when she could, an ever-smiling presence. She was like Tindr in that way, almost always there. Now she sat down again, cheek still reddened, and lowered her eyes, seemingly unaware of Ragnfast's still upon her.

The rock was warmed once more, and the game went on. Runulv and Ring had earlier lifted another small crock of mead from a table near the farmhouse, and were half-way to draining it, but few joined them. Ragnfast's sister Gullaug made a clumsy throw to Gorm, the man she was promised too, and with a laugh they rose and went behind the sheltering wall of the lamm-gift to share their forfeit.

Runulv moved over to where Gyda and her cousin Ása leaned near the fire, hugging themselves against a breeze that had come up. Ring came and flanked them, and pushed another log into the fire.

But Ragnfast crossed over to where Estrid sat, a maid with eyes the colour of smoke. He looked down at her. "Come with me," he said. Her face was puzzled, troubled, almost, but she rose. He led her around the side of the lamm-gift. He could hear a low rustle from the other side, where his sister and Gorm must be. The thatching of the steeply raked roof reached almost to the ground; they would be leaning against it and kissing.

He turned to Estrid where she followed. She looked frightened, and less than her fourteen years. She had been thin as a little child, and still was; willow-thin, but like the willow had a supple grace. Her hair was that yellow of the mead that had swirled in their cups earlier, and it fell in a long and straight line over the paired brooches pinning her gown at the shoulders. He pulled her to him.

He tilted his chin and let his lips near hers. She did not draw back, and he pressed her against his chest. Their mouths met, and before he kissed her his lips played on hers, nibbling at her lower lip, brushing against the upper, then settling firmly upon hers. He brought his hand from the sharpness of her shoulder blade to the round softness of her cheek, and let it rest there as his tongue sought her own. He felt her tremble in his arm, and felt his own excitement coursing in his body, an arousal to a new and higher pitch than he had ever yet known. He lifted his mouth from hers to give them both breath. She tasted of the tang of the ale and the sweetness of the mead they had both drunk, and he knew he tasted thus to her as well.

"Estrid," he murmured, in her ear. It was as if he had never before spoken her name. His hand drifted from her face and found her small breast through the light wool of her gown. Her trembling increased and he almost felt he

held her heart in his hand. As a boy he had caught a fledg-
ing bird by throwing his tunic over it, and had gently taken
up the fluttering thing in his hands. That was how she felt.
He had let the bird escape after holding and looking at it.
Estrid he did not wish to let go.

He pushed against her and they fell slightly backwards upon the angled roof. She gasped, whether from
his weight or the pressure of the hardness of his prick
through his leggings he did not know. Now she made a
small movement, the slightest struggle against him. She
turned her head, moving her mouth away from his.

Tindr had followed them. He was standing at the end
of the lamm-gift. When Estrid moved her face and saw
him, he turned quickly away and vanished around the
corner from whence he came.

Ragnfast saw him too. Estrid broke away from him,
squeezing past his outstretched hand. "Estrid," he called.
But she quickened her pace, almost running.

He followed her. Turning the corner back to where
the fire burned he saw, coming across the field from the
house, Estrid's mother and her married sister. A look of
concern showed on their faces. They reached the fire and
scanned those still sitting around it. Gyda and Ása had
left, but Sigrid was still there, sitting next to Ragnfast's
sister and her betrothed, who had returned from their
stint behind the lamm-gift. Runulv and Ring sat on the
edge of a bench, swaying woozily together. The brothers
blinked across the firelight at Estrid and Ragnfast as they
hurried back to the fire. Ragnfast glanced at all in turn; he
did not see Tindr.

Thorvi, Estrid's mother, spotted her daughter. Estrid's
father had died two years ago; he had been a man of some

temper, and Ragnfast knew he was lucky that he was not striding there towards him.

"Estrid," her mother said. One look betrayed what the girl had been doing. Her cheeks were flushed, her clothes disordered. Her linen head wrap had been pushed off and was dropping down her back, held only by the knot at the nape of her neck. A single stalk of dried sedge dangled from the tip of one lock of her hair. Ragnfast saw that he had managed to unwittingly unfasten one of the shoulder brooches to her gown; the pin had opened and it hung perilously close to falling off.

All were silent. Estrid's sister held her newest babe in her arms, and shifted the child from one arm to the other. Thorvi looked at him.

"Ragnfast," she said, now that he was near enough for her to see him. "I am surprised." Her tone was measured, almost hurt. The families were close, their farms nearest one to the next; their children good friends. She could not tell by looking at her daughter how far things had gone.

She made a small sigh, but with lifted head pulled herself up before Ragnfast. A sterner tone came into her voice. "Estrid is very young," she noted, looking to the girl, who was now re-tying her head-wrap. She had half-turned away from them, trying to hide her flaming cheek. Thorvi's next words were close to an order. "Do not touch her again unless you mean to wed her."

"I do mean to wed her," Ragnfast blurted. It was out of his mouth so quickly that he heard himself speak before he had determined just what to say.

His words jolted all, and at least one gasp was heard. Ragnfast was still looking at Estrid's mother. He knew, of a sudden, the rightness of what he had just said. He slowed himself, took a deep breath, and moved a step closer to Thorvi.

"I, Ragnfast, son of Rapp, wish to take to wife your daughter Estrid, if she will have me."

This was a public declaration, made before witnesses, and must be honoured by he who made it.

Sigrid stood up from where she had been sitting, biting her lower lip as if to keep herself from crying out. This slip of a girl was being pursued by no less than Ragnfast, one of the handsomest men around, who many maids dreamt of. And she, Sigrid, knew five Summers more than Estrid! She would not be left a spinster. She must herself wed, and soon, and to a man with not less than three-score sheep.

Ragnfast's sister Gullaug clapped her hands in joy, and her betrothed, Gorm, gave a hoot of approval.

"A bride-feast! A bride-feast!" called out the drunken Runulv. He had his arm about his brother's shoulder and was trying to rise, as if to make a toast. Thorvi turned to him and he fell silent.

Ragnfast looked at Estrid. Her eyes were cast down, and she was smoothing the skirts of her gown. She finally raised her face. He saw the tears brimming in her eyes, making them glitter. He saw her smile at him.

Her mother saw it too. Yet Estrid was still a child; she had only begun to bleed last year. She would make Ragnfast promise not to touch her until she grew more. Thorvi had seen what befell girls who bore babes at Estrid's age – the loosened teeth, falling hair, births that went on for days.

Thorvi cleared her throat and looked back to Ragnfast. "You and I will speak of this with your parents," she decided. "And she shall not wed until another year has passed," she ended, the firmness in her voice returning.

Ragnfast took heart. "I have four horses. Two are mares I will breed this Summer. In Spring I will have six horses."

Thorvi well knew that a union with Ragnfast would almost assure her daughter a prosperous future; she need fear nothing on that account. Nor did she fear Ragnfast would mistreat her girl; he was a good boy, with a good father. She worried instead that her gifts to the couple would be too slight. With her husband gone she could not dower Estrid as she had her first daughter; the most she might give would be a few piglets and six or eight sheep.

Ragnfast was still pleading his case. "A man with six horses has wealth to build more wealth," he was telling her. He looked again to Estrid, with her wet cheeks and bright smile, and then back to her mother. "She will come to me wearing silver brooches I have given her."

Thorvi nodded her head and repeated, "We will speak of this, you and I, with your parents," but she could not keep a slight smile from raising the corner of her lips.

Estrid went to Thorvi's side, and after a last shy smile for Ragnfast, turned and walked, flanked by her mother and sister, to the farmhouse. Sigrid trailed behind them, hunching her shoulders under a woollen blanket which she wore as a shawl. Runulv and Ring had slipped off their bench and lay sprawling, on their backs, at the edge of the cooling ashes.

Ragnfast stood before the dying Mid-Summer fire. The Sun was beginning to rise, lightening the sky behind the line of birch and more distant fir trees, making their outlines bold against the sky. What had seemed limitless now had limits; he could see landmarks.

He sat down on the bench where Estrid had sat. There was no need to add more wood to the fire; the Sun would light the world soon. He saw a movement and looked up to see Tindr approach. He must have been standing off in the shadows, as he often did when he could not understand what was happening.

Ragnfast raised his hand and touched his own eye, then his ear, telling Tindr he was glad to see him, the surest welcome of all. Tindr nodded, his uncertainty upon his face. He sat down at the end of the bench.

Ragnfast's head was full of what had just happened, and it took him a while to recall that Tindr had watched him kiss Estrid, and had likely been watching when he spoke for her to her mother. He felt of a sudden tired, as if he could sleep for a week. The snores of Runulv and Ring rose from where they lay, and made him smile. He looked over at Tindr. He was staring with fixed eyes into the dying fire, his straight nose outlined by a glimmer of Sun rising over the meadow to their right.

Ragnfast lifted a hand to catch his eye. Tindr turned on the bench. Ragnfast began to laugh.

"There is much to tell," he told him. "I will do my best. I played forfeits as I wanted a kiss – " here he extended his hand out in front of him, and drew it back towards his chest: I want, and then pursed his lips as for a kiss – "and I won a wife." He clasped his two hands together, the sign they used for hand-fast.

Tindr's mouth opened slightly. He raised both hands and touched the corners of his mouth – his sign for Estrid, as from childhood she seemed ever to be smiling.

"Já, Estrid," Ragnfast answered, using the same gesture on his own mouth. He repeated the hand-fast gesture, touching his own chest.

Tindr nodded, but hung his head. A heartbeat passed. Then he grunted, loudly, and angrily, a grunt that rose into a piercing squeal of anger. He leapt up, and with fists clenched beat the air before him as if it were an invisible foe. The noise he made elicited a groan from one of the two snoring brothers, and Ragnfast stood up himself, should any be alarmed back at the house. Sure enough, he turned his head to see Dagr come walking towards them in the grey morning light. Ragnfast feigned a grin and raised his arm to him. Dagr saw his son standing safely by his cousin, slowed, and with a nod turned and walked back.

Ragnfast pressed his finger across his own lips, urging Tindr to silence. Tindr let loose a whine of complaint, but then quieted.

"What?" asked his cousin, tapping his temple. "What is it?"

Tindr gritted his teeth. He could not help his low *uh, uh uh* from escaping his lips as he tried to tell Ragnfast.

He thrust his hand out in front of him, then pulled it rapidly back to his chest.

"You want," Ragnfast repeated.

Tindr's blue-white eyes rolled in his head; at that moment they did indeed look like those of an animal. He snatched at the air, trying to form the right signs. He settled on bringing both hands to his waist, smoothing them down his legs, his gesture for a girl or woman, one who smooths her skirts.

Ragnfast watched as Tindr repeated it, the hand reaching and pulling to his chest, the gesture for a woman or girl.

"You want a woman," Ragnfast breathed.

He nodded his head as he said this. He did not laugh, as he may have if he were not so tired, and had not just asked a maid to be his own wife.

Tindr saw he understood, but with a low whine repeated his message, the reaching hand, the gown being smoothed. Then he gestured holding someone in a hug, and made a kissing motion, his arms wrapped around his own shoulders.

Ragnfast lowered his head, and let out a sigh. He looked back at his younger cousin. Tindr wanted just what he did, and Ragnfast was old enough to know that Tindr might never have it. There was no way he or anyone could help Tindr to the love of a maid.

He thought, for the second time that night, of the woman at the Thing who had led him silently into the woods. This was what Tindr needed, but all it would do was give him a taste of what a woman's flesh felt like. It would not give him a wife to care for, nor the hope of future babes, nor a life lived together.

He could not say any of this, but as he stood, nodding his head at Tindr, he hoped he might realise that he understood. He had no answer for him, and after a long look Tindr seemed to accept this. Ragnfast put his hand on his cousin's shoulder.

There were still hours before most would arise. The young men were all sleeping in one of the barns. Ragnfast gestured that he would go lie down now. Tindr nodded, but shrugged, Nai. Ragnfast watched him walk into the woods, then turned and made his own way across the damp grasses to the barn.

DAGR IS CALLED

WHEN the last of the three Norns, Skuld, took note of Dagr, he was on his boat on the Baltic Sea. Skuld holds the small sharp shears that sever the Thread of Life. She is the eldest of the Norns. Her daughter Verdandi pulls the thread out, teasing it to its appropriate length, and the youngest Norn, Urd, Skuld's granddaughter, does the spinning, as befits a maiden. It is this capricious youngest who chooses whether the thread be of coarse wool, fine linen, or even shining gold; whether a man be born a poor farmer, a tradesman, or a great and mighty warrior.

Skuld is old, and like many old women, needs but little sleep. She is ever watchful, and with a nod and a smile leans down with her shears. "My daughters weary of spinning for you," she whispers, with her gentle, but chill murmur.

She had once before looked at Dagr, but shook her head. Njord liked this young man; leave him be; though one day Skuld would snap the thread for even the God himself. Now however, Dagr caught her attention anew.

It was a clear morning, just at the start of fishing season. The air had been cold and the wind colder when

Dagr had lifted his mast and hauled up his sail in the dark of a new day. Soon fingers of grey streaked the dark, followed by red and yellow beams that coloured also the undulant waves. Dagr never grew tired of watching the Sun rise up out of the sea, just as when, living on the western coast with his brother Tufi, he had not tired of seeing it sink there.

Dagr had good eyes, and they were good even now. They could readily discern by the movement of the water where herring might be gathering. At times the hungry sea birds aided him, but often just by studying the whirling surface he would know the best place to drop his net. He thought he spotted such a disturbance ahead, and set for it. He was heading into the Sun of a cloudless day, and it dazzled him at times, and he had need to shield his eyes with his hand as he fixed on his rippled target.

All was well in his world. The season was starting strongly, and he had his friend Ketil at work braiding him new hempen lines for both sail and steering oar. Rannveig had asked the potter for more heavy crocks; her brewing earned her good silver, and much else in trade. He took almost as much pride in her renown for her ale as she did. And his boy – well, Tindr was Tindr. He had hoped the boy might wish to join him fishing, and Tindr did in fact come with him on days when he thought the haul might be overly large. But Tindr was not cut to be a fisherman.

Tindr had good sea-legs and never had lost a meal over the gunwale, as Dagr had when he first sailed. But he could see that his son had no love for it; the way his eyes fastened on the green of the trees as they left and returned told all. And he knew Rannveig was secretly glad their boy did not wish to take up the way of the sea and its dangers.

Tindr worked willingly enough, on or off the boat, drying nets, gutting and flaying the catch, salting and hanging the whitish slabs of herring and cod. But Dagr knew he wished always to be in the forest. He could not gainsay it, for the amount of game Tindr took in Fall and early Winter had been a true and steady source of sustenance. Tindr's ability at the hunt meant fresh meat to break the tedium of salt fish. It meant smoked haunches of deer that they could trade for needed oil, linen, and grain. When Tindr took a boar it meant a feast for all their friends, so that the blessing of his skill extended throughout the folk of the trading road. His mother feared for Tindr and his future, and Dagr did as well, but none of the fears had to do with hunger or want.

But it was not Tindr that Dagr had thought of that bright morning. Squinting into the Sun, watching the play of gold upon the rippling water, the thought came, unbidden, of Hedinfrid and Holmfrid. His girls had been gone so long. At times, though, there they were, almost before him. A glint of yellow or gold recalled him to their hair. He smiled, without knowing it.

He bent to pick up the net; he was at the edge now of the herring-pool, and could see their silvered bodies tumbling just beneath the surface. As he stooped and took up the net-line a surge of pain shot through his chest. He straightened, gripped the rail. He had before felt this tightness, a burning that spread from his heart, up into his throat, and down into his arm. Rannveig had fussed over him and made him drink boiled dock leaves, as if he had a bad belly. But it was nothing he had eaten, and if he stayed still it would pass. This time it did not. Skuld was there to make certain.

The pain shrank a moment as he clung there, only to re-double; a clenching in his breast that squeezed his heart in a fiery grasp. He gasped for breath, let himself sink down upon the line coiled on the deck, and onto the edge of the net he had planned to drop into the waiting mass of fish that surged about the hull of his boat. On his back the pain eased. His eyes looked up into the brilliant blue of the sky. His sail luffed slightly into view, then swung back out again. The sky was so blue, as blue as the eyes of his lost girls.

⚬⚬⚬⚬⚬⚬⚬⚬⚬⚬⚬

When Dagr did not return that afternoon Rannveig and Tindr sat up all night. At dawn every boat was launched to look for him. His boat was spotted, drifting, at noon that day. The men who boarded her lifted Dagr's cold body to one side of the keel. "Look at these fish," said one, wiping his nose with his hand. The herring still swarmed about the hull of Dagr's boat. "We will drop his net, bring it full back to Rannveig," said the other. This they did.

They carried his body to Rannveig and laid it upon the kitchen work table. She stood at its head – not keening, not crying – as shoulder-to-shoulder they placed Dagr before her. Her narrowed eyes beheld the man she loved.

The end had come, but not in the way she had expected. Soon after their hand-fast she had ridden the night-mare. The dark mare had carried her to the beach, on which she walked. There she found his washed-up body, sea-weed clinging to his face. His handsome form was bloated, his skin silver-green, like the fish he had sought. But here before her was her own Dagr, perfectly dry and whole. The long, always tousled brown hair, now showing strands of grey; the heavy and worn green tunic he liked to fish in, and which she had watched him pull over his back so many times. His strong and calloused hands were gently cupped at his sides, the hands that had built their house here at the water's edge, raised the mast of his boat, hauled in the swarming net, and caressed her own body. Save for the pallor of his skin he could have been asleep.

"He always knew his Fate was held in water," she recalled aloud. Her voice was as dry as her eyes; but the larger light in her had been snuffed out, and this she knew. "He gave himself to Njord, and Njord was kind. He did not claim him after all." She looked at the two who had found his boat. "I am grateful to have his body," she told them.

Tindr had been standing behind her and to one side. He had watched the somber procession make its way up from the beach, and knew from their lack of haste there was no need for hurry. Now his mother turned to him. Tindr stepped forward and looked upon his dead father's face. His blue-white eyes scanned the length of him. They too rested on his hands, then returned to the face. It was his Da, but it was no longer Da. The lump that had closed Tindr's throat was forced down; he swallowed it, and his throat reopened in a howl. No cry had ever come from hound or wolf to match the single howl that sprang from Tindr's chest.

***

It was Tindr who thought to take the sail from his father's boat and use it as his shroud. The next day all on the trading road and from nearby farms met at the place of burial, where Dagr's body was consigned to the flames. The bone and ash were swept up and taken by his widow and her son to Dagr's boyhood home. She had the crockery urn buried in the ground, and great stones rolled into the shape of a ship's hull around it. She made sure that Dagr was at the place the steering oar would be.

When she and Tindr returned from the South, Rannveig sold Dagr's boat. The buyer was a fisherman from down the coast, looking for a second boat for his son. When he came to sail it away Rannveig walked down with him to the pier, where she looked a final time upon the vessel that had been her husband's love and livelihood. She pointed to the small nail head, still raised, by the keel, and told the new owner the story about it. He listened with nodding head. "No hammer shall touch it," he promised.

THE SKOGSRÅ

SPRING had been dry, and Summer long and hot. Tindr moved through the forest, aware that even there the sustained heat was leaving its mark. Leaves drooped limply, curling at their edges. Ferns, spread to their fullest extent, looked dusty and almost brittle. Even the animals were slow. A rabbit sat up on a fallen log, washing its twitching face, and let Tindr come within a few feet before it finally hopped down and away.

One of his hives had swarmed, and he had been walking slowly amongst the trees, looking for the bees. He had found them massed against the trunk of a larch, a living gold and brown cluster of wings, crawling and circling. He had carried a new skep with him, and wedged its base into an outcrop of nearby rock. At the heart of the swirling cluster upon the larch would be the queen. He breathed gently on the mass and with his fingers parted it. The queen lay there, diminished in size, but recognizable. He slowly took her up and placed her in the woven skep, then stepped away to allow the train of bees to follow her in.

He had been out for hours, looking for them, and was glad to have found them. The more honey he could provide to his mother, the more mead she could make, and mead sold for five times the price of ale. Since his father's death such things mattered. Rannveig's hair had faded to grey, but she still worked long and full days. She had expanded her brewing, enlarged the brew-house, and hired women to help her serve each afternoon. Folk were always thirsty in Summer, and she did good business. In Winter's depths it was another story. She began selling her ale by the crock-ful, so that even when it was too cold for folk to gather in her brew-house those who liked it could carry it away and drink before their own firesides. Gudfrid helped her in this, and Tindr cared for their beasts, chopped and piled firewood, did most of their vegetable gardening. Without the silver of his father's stock-fish trade it was what was needful to do. When Tindr took surplus game they traded the excess meat for grain or goods.

He was much alone. He had ever spent part of each day in the forest, but as a boy had always had his friends to play with as well. Now Ragnfast, his best and closest friend, was wed. He and Estrid had a child, a little girl, and another child coming. They had taken over the horse farm, and though they greeted him warmly each time they met, those times were rare, for their own lives were full. He and his mother still came to their farm to sit before the Mid-Summer fire. Estrid was kind as ever, a smile always on her lips, the grey eyes filled with tenderness. Ragnfast would show Tindr the foals that had been born that year and the progress he had made in training the older colts and fillies. There would be a feast beneath the shade of the pear trees, and much drinking too. But now Ragnfast was host, with his father Rapp, and a father himself. When it grew dark and those with young ones retreated to the smaller fire of the kitchen yard, Ragnfast and Estrid went with them. Tindr was left at the big fire with his other friends. Soon, he knew, Runulv would no longer sit with him, for he and Gyda would hand-fast at Summer's end. By next Summer they might show up at Ragnfast's with their firstborn babe.

There was growth and change in everything, Tindr saw that. Whether amongst folk or in the forest, cycles repeated themselves with little change from year to year, season to season. Then someone was gone forever, like a great elm that had commanded the skyline but had withered and died. A sapling, freed from shade, grew rapidly in its stead, just as a new babe was born to take its place amongst those left behind. It was the circle of life.

The young men his age now had wives, or at least sweethearts. Tindr had neither. When he gathered with other young folk they welcomed him, but when they paired off and sat together, or left the group to walk around the side of a barn to kiss, he was not one of them. Maids like Gyda and her cousin were nice to him, and had even learnt a few of his signs. Others ignored him. Last Spring a new family had arrived at the trading town from up North, the brother of the silver-smith. They had a daughter close to his age, a maid with curling brown hair. Shortly after they settled Tindr walked along the road, back from the wick maker. The new girl was working in her uncle's workroom. Tindr had noticed her once before, and seen that she had noticed him. Now she raised her head from her polishing as Tindr passed, and looked at him. He smiled and dipped his chin a moment before he moved on. A day later she came to the brew-house, alone. He was at the edge of the herb garden, and instead of going towards the rolled-down awnings of the brew-house proper, she came to him.

She smiled as she neared him. Her mouth opened and she began to speak to him, gesturing to the small crock she carried.

He felt his heart almost turn behind his breastbone. She said something more, still smiling, the pink lips raising and bowing. In a moment more it would be over, he feared, the smile gone from her lips. It was hard to hasten that moment, but he could not stand for it to go on.

He made a small *uh*, and touched his ear. She cocked her head slightly, looking at him.

He touched his ear again, and pulled his bone whistle from his tunic. He blew out the two notes for his mother.

Rannveig appeared from the back door of her brewhouse. The maid turned to her, her question on her face. He watched his mother explain that he could not hear her, saw the girl's quick look back at him, the pretty lips now pursed. The lovely head gave a short nod, then turned from him. His mother was gesturing the maid to go to the brew-house where she would fill her crock. She walked off, and before she turned as well his mother looked at him. Tindr had seen the look before. His Nenna was smiling, but the hurt in her eyes was for what he was feeling inside.

"A man you cannot talk to," Gyda had once explained to her cousin, "a man who cannot hear what you say, cannot hear his babes cry nor teach them to talk . . . what maid with choice would choose Tindr, handsome as he is, knowing how hard it will be?"

Ása and Gyda had sighed together for his sake, but had no answer. Almost all liked him, but none would have him.

Tindr had stopped by a clump of silver birches. The Sun had reached its highest point overhead and would crest downward. The light it threw turned the small birch leaves over his head into green gems. He felt listless in the heat, and the water-skin at his side was close to empty. He had found his bees; he should head back home. He looked about him. Not far from here ran a swift-running stream, which ended in a small pool. Even now the water should be clear; it was not a stream he had ever seen dry. He would splash his face, have a drink, then turn for home.

He left the track, walking through ferns and under-growth, pushing a few vines from where they draped from trees. The ferns and mosses grew thicker here and looked as bright as if a good rain had watered them; he knew he was nearing the stream for them to look thus. There was a smell in the still air, not the green odour of growth, nor the mineral tang of dry soil, but one almost of flowers, and he let his head turn from side to side to see what grew near to so scent the air. He could not tell, and parted the thin branches of some sapling aspens and kept going.

There was the pool. The stream that fed it lay almost hidden from where he stood, and he paused a moment. Trees rose up from the banks, and rocks large and small crowned with moss rimmed it. A shaft of brilliant Sun struck the water, and he saw rock at its bottom and the waving fronds of green and brown plants swaying in the slight current. The pool was much deeper than he recalled, and had a rare beauty about it. He wondered if he had mistaken the place, yet it seemed familiar; he had come right to it.

He stood looking, watching a dragonfly dart and hover above the water, and became aware of his thirst. He took the final steps to the edge, walking over a bed of moss so thick that it rolled and clumped upon itself.

He knelt. Something moved across the water, on the bank he faced. A white hind stepped forward from the shadow of the trees and stood opposite him.

He had not seen Her for so long, not since the grey day he had taken his first boar. Sometimes, Summer or Winter, he thought he caught a glimpse of moving white as he walked the woods, but it was never more than that, a fleeting glimpse, and he was never sure. Now here she was again, looking at him, the coat a white so pure it almost shimmered. The dark brown eyes took him in, unblinking, but soft. The delicately tufted white ears shifted over those eyes. She lowered her head to drink: an invitation.

He watched the neck stretch and downy muzzle touch the water. He dropped both hands through the rippled surface, pulled them to his face, splashing the heat and dust from it. He drank with cupped hands of the cool and sweet water. He shook his head when he was done, driving the wet tips of his long hair behind his shoulders. She was gone.

He sat back on his heels. He was not hunting now; his bow and quiver were hanging by his alcove. Perhaps she came just to show herself to him.

He stared at the place she had been. An arcing row of ripples spread towards him across the water, marking where the muzzle had touched and drank. His hands dropped to his lap.

A long moment passed. The spark that had been struck in seeing the hind left a candle's glow within him. He looked into the rippled water. He would take off his clothing and bathe in it. He unstrapped his knife belt. His boots were those he made himself, of boar skin. Holding them recalled him to that first boar he had taken. He pulled off leggings and tunic, then stepped into the water.

It was deliciously cool, and so clear he surprised himself with how deep it was once he moved into the centre. If he bent his knees slightly he could drop his whole body under. He fanned his arms out on the surface, plashing so that the ripples washed the wet bottoms of the rocks along the banks. He dunked his head again.

He opened his eyes underwater to see the green world shimmering and dancing above him. Then, still underwater, from the tail of his eye he caught a glimpse of something white-fleshed. He burst from the water, looked about him. He saw nothing in the water, and the banks were empty.

He let himself sink again, up to his shoulders. The Sun found an opening through the dark of the trees and pierced the water with light, striking his face and shoulders with its warmth. Again, a flash of white in the water beside him. He lowered his head toward the water, looking for it, then gasped. Two gentle hands stroked his waist from behind, one on either side of him.

He turned. As he did the hands surrendered their hold on him. Before him in the water stood a naked woman. Her lips were parted in a half-smile. He could not make out the colour of the eyes; they seemed dark, but shifted in hue as he gazed on her. Her wet hair was so light as to look like Moonlight. Locks of it, running with water, lay over her shoulders and arms. None fell on the roundness of her breasts, nor over the rosy nipples.

She lifted one of her hands, laid it over his heart. The hand was cool, yet as she pressed it there upon his chest he felt the warmth in the palm. It was Her, he knew.

He closed his eyes. His heart was pounding under her touch, suddenly too large for his ribs to encase. He felt fearful to raise his hands and try to touch her, and wished to prolong each moment of her nearness, her touch, lest she vanish if he tried.

He sensed her movement towards him, the water pulsing gently from her body to his. Lips touched his. His eyes fluttered open just long enough to see the beautiful face a breath away from his own. Her lips, again, on his. A kiss, his first from a desiring woman.

His arms came up out of the water, raining droplets. They yearned to close around her, but fear and wonder both kept him back. It was she who moved. She caught up his hands in her own and brought them to her face. She kissed the back of his right hand, and then the palm. His fingers curved around the beautiful mouth as she did so. She brought his left hand to her face, kissed the back, then the palm. Bow hand and arrow hand did she bless.

The lips were soft, but cool. Only after she pulled them away did he feel the lingering heat of their impress.

She still held his hands, each in one of her own. She was looking at his face, at his lips, his eyes. She drew his hands towards her, and laid them upon her breasts. His breath had stilled, or he was not aware of his breathing; but he could feel the pumping of his heart. His hands closed about the softness of her breasts. Her nipples rested in his palms, and as he tightened his gentle grasp he felt them harden and rise. Her eyes were half-closed, her lips slightly parted in the smile she gave him. He took a breath, felt he was nearly quaking. Every particle of his body was alive, alert, enraptured.

She moved closer to him. His hands surrendered her breasts. They went to the smooth flesh of her waist, up the curve of her back, and wrapped themselves there. Her lips found his, and he quivered in response as her tongue flicked at his. Her mouth clung to his now, one hand resting on his face, the other clasped about his shoulder. As gentle as her touch was, there was strength behind it, that power of a muscled animal under a coat of softest fur.

She pressed her body fully against his own. He felt the firmness of his naked chest against her, let his loins open where she held her hips to his. His male body coursed and reared in response. The sheath had already tightened and withdrawn as the flesh underneath it hardened. His prick lay upright between them, pressed against the soft curve of her belly, the tingling heat of his own body seeming the greater in contrast to the coolness of her flesh.

She pulled her mouth away from his. He saw the smile on her lips, and in her eyes. She took his hand, leading him to the bank from which he had first seen her. There, on the bower of the thick and green moss, she laid him down. As he dropped down on his back he could not bear to be parted from her touch for even a moment. He kept his reaching hand always upon her, her own hand, her waist, her knee as she knelt next him.

She bent over him, kissed his lips. Her mouth lingered there, and every touch of her lips and tongue was a touch also deep within him. His body thrilled to the sight of her, her lips upon his, her flesh under his hands and pressed against his own. But the water beginning to run from the corner of his eyes came from his heart, from her desiring of him, for the gift she was giving.

She pulled back her face from his, and swung her leg over his hips. Her hand went to the base of his stones, then grasped the hardness of his prick. He was gasping, as if for air, his eyes fastened on the gentle smile on her lips.

She lowered herself over him, slowly and with her eyes closing. Her body took his into her wet warmth.

For his man's body to be embraced in this way was beyond his imagining. He had at times to close his eyes, for the bliss of opening them and seeing her there as she straddled him. He lifted his hips in rhythm with her motion. He moved his hands to stroke her face, to cover her breasts, to hold her at her firm waist as she rode him. Each stroke gave exquisite pleasure. He felt the urgency of every male animal he had ever watched mount a female. He felt the power of the great stags who reared on their strong hind legs to fall upon their does and hold them in that sacred embrace. With this urgency and power was a thrill of pleasure even greater than the need. All this was his, and the very moment he lived in, the Lady come to him and bringing him to manhood.

Each time he felt he could bear it no longer and must come off she slowed, looking down on him with her half-smile. Yearning, he took her by the waist, urging her, but she placed her hands on his chest. It was only when he loosened his grasp on her that she began to move again. He kept his hands lightly upon her waist and she rose and fell over him. Then she turned slightly, twisting her shoulder to reach behind her, one breast now in profile to him. She took his stones in her hand, and as her fingers closed around him his eyes were forced shut by the depth of the sensation. Behind his closed eyes he saw deer, leaping through his forest. Her movement quickened, and as he came with a shower of light behind his closed eyes he bucked up, driving himself deeper into her wet and welcoming depth.

He heaved out a sigh, shuddering still. His hands holding her at the waist felt the expansion and release of her own breath. He opened his eyes to see her leaning forward over him. The soft lips again touched his own. Then her hand rose and touched his eyes, stroking them closed once more. His last glimpse was the half smile on her lips.

When he awoke he looked into a paling blue sky. He lifted himself on his elbows. Across the pool from him the trees had darkened into a mass of deep green and shadow. A glinting shaft of lowering Sun was caught between leafy boughs.

He looked down at himself. Alone as he was, it was real. She had come to him. His body felt different. It knew something it had not known before.

He sat fully up. The pleasure she had given was still fresh, quelling the rising pain of finding himself alone again. He gave himself the time he needed to think on her.

She did not speak. It was like the best of dreams he had dreamt, in which no one spoke. At times he rode the night-mare and all were shouting, faces straining with effort to make themselves understood to him. She had said all by her look and touch.

Her touch. He shook his head, then hung it. Now he understood the mystery, that dance of desire and fulfillment between male and female. Why she had come now, or come at all, he could not know. He only knew his gratefulness, and now his sense of loss.

He struggled to his feet, found his clothes. He walked back through the darkening woods.

When Rannveig saw him enter the foot of the garden he saw, even from afar, the look of relief on her face. It was late; she had already milked the waiting cow. He saw the worry on her face, saw her try to swallow it. She smiled and gestured that he must have found his bees; he did not return with the skep he had taken. He had almost forgotten them.

He ate little, for which Rannveig blamed the heat and Gudfrid her cooking. He had two cups of ale, and then a third, which he rarely did. He watched his mother and Gudfrid at their tidying, then nodded at them as they bid him goodnight. His mother came and gave his hand a squeeze before she went in. He smiled at her, sorry for her worry, and she let him be. He was sitting now on top of the kitchen yard table, his feet on the bench, looking across the dusky garden into the trees that now had faded into the dimness of the forest depths behind them. To one side the sea rippled and shone under a rising crescent Moon. But Tindr's eyes were on the woods.

He pulled off his tunic. He let his hand lift to his chest, and laid his palm against his heart. She had touched him there, and many other places. He would not be the same again.

CHAPTER THE NINETEENTH

STRANGERS

Late Summer 881

TINDR turned from sliding the bolt across the barn door. The fowl were safely penned for the night. He had finished his supper and gone off to complete his evening chores, and this was the last of them. His mother and Gudfrid still sat inside the brew-house, talking over a meal to which they had invited the neighbours. Fall was near, but there was still a lingering dusk which seemed bright after the deep gloom of the barn.

He paused and looked beyond the narrow strip of beach across the waters of the Baltic. His eyes scanned the distant horizon, one made sharp by the piercing rays of the lowering Sun. Sometimes when he looked thus he had a waking dream, in which his father's boat sailed home to them.

As he thought on this, his eye dropped closer, to a small boat approaching the beach not far from the pier. The mast was still up and the sail unfurled. It was driving right for the beach.

It was a very small boat, and Tindr wondered from whence it came. He could see a figure in the stern. The neighbour's children were playing amongst the rocks and they stopped in their play and watched the boat drive in. The sail was dropped and the hull scraped along the limestone shingle until it stopped. A man rose from the stern, and jumped out, went to the bow. Now Tindr saw a second figure, a woman. The man helped her from the boat, and had his arm about her as she walked a few steps to one of the larger rocks, upon which she sat.

The man heaved the boat a little further up the beach, enough so that the tide could not lift her. The man was tall, and Tindr watched him as he slung several packs and rolls over his shoulder. The last things he took from the boat was a round shield, which he hung from its strap over his back, and two spears.

A warrior. Sometimes war-ships landed at the pier, bearing men heavily armed as this one was. They looked for salt and fleece and iron-work and good Gotlandic stone, and had glass beads and silver neck-rings and arm rings to trade in return, sometimes even silk. This was one of them, alone, with a woman. Tindr looked again at the smallness of their craft, the number of packs the tall man carried. The boat they sailed in, the fact that they carried all they owned – these were folk who had come across seas and through danger.

The warrior and the woman stood together now, and Tindr watched the man scan the buildings of the trading road. He looked squarely at the brew-house with its half-rolled awnings, and gestured to the woman at his side. Tindr hung back, watching from the garden.

When the door opened Rannveig was facing it, as befits a good host. Their supper was drawing to a close, and her friends would soon be giving her their thanks and heading home up the hill. She did not expect customers just now; her afternoon trade was over, and it was early for those wishing to come after their own suppers to drink and perhaps throw dice.

A man came through the opened door, heavily laden with a variety of packs. The first thing that struck Rannveig was his height. He was unusually tall, and quite lean. The second was the number of weapons he bore. There was a sword of great length at his side, and not one but two spears in his hand. She could see part of a round wooden shield where it hung from his back, and see also that the metal rim was badly dented from a blow. A warrior.

Just behind him came a woman, carrying a small leathern pack and a lidded basket with a handle of curious make. She took her place next to the warrior. Such men sometimes had slaves with them when they landed on Gotland, but one glance told Rannveig this woman at his side was no slave. She wore a thick necklace of braided silver about her neck, and though her face was wan it held beauty, and, Rannveig felt, told of high birth. She was not overly tall, and was strong-featured for a woman, with eyes a deep and vibrant green. She stood straight, though she looked as if she could scarcely keep her feet for her weariness. Her woollen gown was the colour of oak leaves in Fall, a shade a little lighter than the reddish gold of her hair. The hem of both skirt and sleeves was covered in thread-work, of interlinked russet and brown spirals. She was a good needlewoman, and had had time to become one. She was looking at Rannveig with the ghost of a smile on her pale lips, as if she did not believe where she was, but was glad nonetheless to be there.

Rannveig was aware that her friends had fallen silent, taking in the strangers. She nodded to the man as she approached, inclining her head to give him leave to drop his packs against the wall. He did so with a nod of his own. As he straightened up she had a closer look at him.

His hair was dark brown, and an ugly scar, now old, creased one cheek. His eyes were of a blue so dark that she was not certain of their colour until she neared him, but they were steady. Like those of the woman with him, his clothes were travel-stained and worn, but there was no hiding the fact that they had been finely woven, well-cut, and sewn with care; the clothes of a rich man. And none but a warrior of some renown bore weapons such as this one did. Rannveig had never seen a knife worn this way, not hung straight down from the hip, but sideways, across the belly. Her eye took in the jewels of red and blue that sparkled in the hilt. Garnets, she thought, and some precious blue stones. She saw on his right wrist a bracelet with a silver disk inscribed in flowing lines.

"Welcome," she told them. "I am Rannveig. I can offer ale, and food."

"Both, and I thank you," the warrior said.

This was all he said at first, but it was enough to tell her he was a Dane. The hand that bore the bracelet plucked at his belt and the pouch tucked there. He spread it open and she caught a glimpse of the silver within. No matter; looking as they did, she would have fed them even if they could not pay.

She looked behind him and to the left, saw the new boat on the beach, felt the catch in her throat. Wherever they had sailed from to reach Gotland's eastern coast, they had travelled long miles over open sea. Their boat was so small; they had Njord's favour to survive.

The warrior's eyes followed her, saw she had caught sight of their boat.

"You will be weary," she said, looking again to the woman.

He nodded his head. "And my wife has suffered much from the sea, and is weak," he answered.

"Sit, and I will bring you food."

"I am Sidroc," he said now.

It was an act of trust to share his name, this Rannveig knew. All, upon meeting, spoke their names at once; custom and courtesy demanded it. When a man did not name himself, there was good reason. Trouble might be following him. This Dane had reason for caution.

"Are you trading?" she asked in return. It was unlike Rannveig to ask a direct question of a traveller, but something goaded her on. She had made up her mind to feed them, but if he had reason for caution she might too. And their look, their very presence, stirred her interest.

He paused a moment. "I will be."

"My father fished, also traded for salt," he went on. "Once when I was a boy he came here, to Gotland. He liked it well. He told me of it when he returned."

She smiled. "So you have come to see for yourself," she said, looking at both of them.

He nodded. The pretty wife did not seem to understand their speech. And she looked as if she were about to fall. She had placed her hand on the top of the nearest table to brace herself.

"Sit, sit," Rannveig repeated. "I will bring you ale, and food."

She brought two thick pottery cups and a full ewer of ale. She went out to the kitchen yard. Gudfrid had preceded her, guessing that the couple would want food, and had the browis ladled up and ready. It had the last of Tindr's smoked deer haunch in it, which is why Rannveig had called the party, but in a few weeks he would begin hunting for the season and replenish their larder. Rannveig piled a number of small loaves on a wooden platter around the crockery bowls of browis and took them out to the couple.

"Who are they?" her neighbour Alrik asked in a low tone when Rannveig sat down again.

"I do not know," Rannveig answered, ever discreet, "but they are hungry, so I fed them." If the couple stayed around others could draw what conclusions they would; it was not her role to peg them early, or for anyone else.

Her friends left, and when the couple finished eating she went back over to them. The warrior Sidroc praised her for her cooking, and his wife made a gesture of thanks with her hands. Not a scrap of food was left in their bowls or on the platter.

"This place is a good one," he added, looking at Rannveig.

She paused. They were the same words Dagr had said to her many years ago, the first day he had landed here.

"Can we set our camp nearby?" he asked now.

Rannveig stood before them, looking at their faces.

"I own the hall at the top of this hill," she answered. "It has been empty a long time. You may stay there tonight, and also the Winter, if it suits you."

It took the big warrior a moment to take this in. "I have gold, and will pay you well," he answered. He looked at his wife, all unknowing what was being said, but looking hopefully at them both. His eyes went to Rannveig. "This place is truly a good one," he said to her.

He turned to his wife, spoke in a tongue Rannveig had never heard. The wife's mouth opened in surprise, and she bowed her head to Rannveig in gratitude.

Sidroc turned back to Rannveig, and they talked a while longer. She took the largest key from the collection at her waist and handed it to him. "Come in the morning. I will feed you, and we will talk more," she told them. She sent them on their way up the hill to the house she had been born in.

When they had gone she joined Gudfrid out by the cooking-ring. Tindr was there. She guessed he had seen the strangers but had not wished to show himself. She began to tell him about them. She could not tell Tindr that the big warrior was a Dane. That would mean nothing to him. She gestured instead that he was from afar, shielding her eyes with her hand as if looking for something, taking her other hand and holding it out before her, then moving it a full arm's reach away. This meant far away, not on the island. His wife she was not sure of. She spoke no Norse, and the ruddy gold of her hair and green eyes made her think she was of the fabled lands to the West, where the Danes had met such success in their raiding.

They will need help, Rannveig thought. They cannot run the hall alone. Perhaps Tindr will try going to them. He will still be so close. He can chop their wood and care for their beasts. It will be a start for him. He is too much with me, and one day I will not be here . . .

The first day Tindr went to the hall he travelled with his mother up the short hill. He had seen the warrior face to face at the brew-house the morning after they arrived, and named him Scar. The woman with him, with bright red-golden hair, he thought of like that, Bright Hair. She had smiled at him, looked him in the face and smiled, and had wanted him to come and live with them in Nenna's old house. Now he was here.

He had been inside before, of course, but now he was come to live, and the barrels of grain and chests of goods that had occupied the hall when his mother let it as a ware-house were all cleared away. It was now a swept and empty place, with stacks of new goods Scar and Bright Hair had bought and had carried in. Bright Hair gestured he should choose which alcove he wanted, and he marked it by hanging his bow and quiver above that closest to the forest.

He put his bedding in it, and took his tools out to the stable behind the hall. There was a sturdy workbench there, but the place had held no horses for long years. He raked and swept out the straw dust, making ready. There was still the remains of a pile of firewood outside the hall, and he sorted through it, restacking that which was still sound enough to burn, chucking the rest into the cold kitchen yard cooking-ring. After this he went back into the hall. Scar and Bright Hair were standing amidst barrels of stores, and the potter from the trading road was with them, showing them the cups and plates she had brought them.

As he waited Tindr's eye was caught by the pile of Scar's war-kit. He had seen the bright-hilted seax in its red leather sheath, so different from the knives Gotlanders wore at their hip, which Scar carried across his belly. Now he came close to where sat the long and powerful sword in its scabbard and sword-belt. He squatted next to it. There were strands of beaten gold in the pommel of the hilt, and just under the guard the steel of the blade showed the silvery blue waves of the pattern welding. It was formidable, yet had its own beauty. The weapon-smith made such things, he had seen him at his forge, and sent them on ships far away. It was a tool to kill a man, Tindr knew this; it had no other use. He thought a moment on this, and on the small arrow-heads his Da had taught him to hammer out. He looked now at the two spears, quite different from each other. One was shorter and with a lighter shaft, and a tip not too much longer than those he forged to down boar. The other was long and heavy, like the men of Gotland used when they had need to defend themselves, or to hunt boar. The steel point was incised with ribbing on the socket; the smith had taken care to decorate even this. The face of the round shield was painted in white and black spirals, and the domed iron boss at the centre embossed with small raised circles. He looked at the shield's iron-bound rim, where the strapping protecting the wood had been hacked through. The wood beneath was fresh-looking; the blow from axe or sword which had severed the iron rim was recent.

As he looked on all this Scar came over to him. Tindr pulled a little away from the weapons; he had been careful not to touch them as he looked, but was uncertain if he had got too close. But Scar squatted down next him, an easy look on his face. He pulled his sword from the scabbard and handed it to Tindr. His hand closed about the grip and he turned it with his wrist. Despite its size it was not as heavy as he thought. He turned the blade in his hand, seeing how the waving patterns of the hammered steel danced in the light as he moved it. With a smile on his lips he passed it back to Scar. Tindr now pointed to the shield, and the gash where the wood beneath the rim lay open. He made a little *uh*, and tapped his temple with his finger.

Scar nodded, and took up the shield so that Tindr could put his fingers in the gash. It had been a great blow that had shattered the iron, and as Tindr looked into Scar's face he saw the warrior nod his head in remembrance. Then Scar turned the shield so they looked upon the inside. Tindr saw the doubled handgrip, and above it, carved into the wood, two runes, Sigel and Tyr, drawn one upon the other ᛏ. Tindr knew the story of Tyr, the warrior God who had let his hand be bitten off as a forfeit. He pointed to the rune and brought his hand to his face and made a biting motion. Scar laughed, and nodded, then with serious face pointed to the rune himself, and tapped his own chest. Tindr nodded in return. Scar belonged to the God.

The next days were busy for Tindr, and full of pleasure for him. Bright Hair was generous and smiling, and she spent much time with him, learning his signs, laughing at herself and never him when she did not understand, praising him with a touch at her heart to give him thanks for some task he had done. She went each day down to Nenna's to get ale or just to talk. Sometimes he was there when she came, and saw how Bright Hair listened to his mother. Bright Hair and Scar spoke all the time to each other, but when Bright Hair spoke to Nenna it was hard for her, and he did not know why. Nenna would shake her head and sometimes laugh, then speak again; and he saw Bright Hair's lips move to mimic his mother's mouth.

Scar was busy making tables and benches with Wood Man, his neighbour who sawed planks and gave Tindr the ends to carve deer from. Nenna sent him to his cousin's to buy a cow for Scar, and he led her slowly through the woods to her new home. From folk on the road, his mother, with Tindr at her side, bought hens and geese, which Tindr brought to the hall so they might have eggs, and fowl in their browis, and roast goose at Blót when all killed the beasts that they could not feed over the Winter to come.

He liked sleeping in his new alcove, which was deeper than that at home, and liked that Bright Hair always looked at him and smiled when he neared her. She did not try to rush him, and did not seem impatient if she could not understand his signs. When he laughed she laughed with him, not caring how he sounded. When he was with her he felt almost equal to other men.

The food she made was simple, but good enough, and she made him free of it, not locking anything away,

so that he could help himself if he got hungry, just like at
Nenna's. Bright Hair had beauty, and he knew all thought
so. He had walked with her enough times on the trading road and seen how folk looked at her, men especially.
When Scar was at her side the men looked only at Scar,
not Bright Hair.

He thought of her a great deal, even when he did
not want to. Sometimes their hands touched when they
worked together at something, or when he would take the
bucket from her when she drew water from the well. He
always looked down when this happened, not trusting his
eyes to look at her. One morning when he was bringing
more firewood into the hall, he saw her clad only in her
shift. She was in the room in which she and Scar slept,
and the door was open. She was moving within, and the
shaft of light that came from the window high in the wall
hit her. The thin linen of her shift was bathed in the Sun,
and he could see the outline of her body as she leaned over
the great bed she slept in and tucked up the coverlet. He
saw the shadow of her breast, and the nipple, and the line
of her round hips.

He bit his lip and turned away, not finishing his stacking. He walked quickly out and into the stable. He was
breathing fast and his leggings were tight at the crotch.
He squeezed his eyes shut, wanting to hold the image of
her body within him, wanting to shut it out, fighting the
flooding sensations the Lady had aroused in him so long
ago when she had laid him on his back and straddled him.
He shook his head to try to rid himself of all this. Bright
Hair was Scar's woman, and belonged to him. Scar was a
warrior, had gold, and deserved such a woman.

And he had seen the way they looked at each other, the way Scar looked at her. He did not wish to imagine them together, but he did. At night he would lie in his alcove, knowing the door to the room in which they slept had closed, and think of Bright Hair in the bed. He had never yet stepped inside that room, and did not wish to. It was sacred to her, and what she did there with Scar.

One morning Tindr awoke and knew he should hunt. He milked the cow in the dark, and left the warm pail where Bright Hair would find it. He went to the well and splashed his face and washed his hands in the cold water. He split his long hair and braided it into two braids, to keep it clear of the action of his bow string. At the cooking-ring he chose a charred stick, and drew the hunting runes upon both hands. He never did this without the memory of the Lady of the Forest before his eyes, of how she had taken his hands in hers and kissed them.

It did not take him long to find his deer. He went to a place where She had often times called them, a glade ringed with aspens. When he dragged the deer back to the hall, Bright Hair was in the kitchen yard, and Scar came through the door. When they saw what he had brought, Bright Hair smiled and signed her thanks to him, her hand touching her heart and turning back to Tindr. Scar looked at the single arrow wound and nodded his head at him. Scar saw the runes on his hands, and it was then Tindr learnt that Bright Hair also belonged to the Lady; Scar told him so by his signs, and drawing the Goddess' rune ᛝ in the ashes and pointing to Bright Hair.

The next day he went again. This time he took two stags, both large harts with great racks of antlers. He dropped them both quite close to each other; there must be ready hinds nearby to find them so. He dragged first one and then the other back to the hall; there would be plenty of meat for them, here in the hall, and for his mother.

Scar watched him return with the second hart, and again praised him with his look. Later that day he came to Tindr as he stood feathering new arrows at the stable workbench. Scar held something in his hand, and he passed it to Tindr. It was a silver pin for his mantle, a large circle of metal, cut all about with tiny spirals on its surface so that it flashed. It closed with a long and thick silver pin to slide through the fastening hole and catch on the hook at the other side of the circle. Tindr had never owned so much silver as was in this pin, and in fact it took him a while to accept it. Scar placed it in his hand, then made the gesture of nocking an arrow to a bow, and pointed to Tindr. It was in thanks for his skill as a huntsman, but to Tindr it was more than that. He knew he was somehow made this warrior's man, someone he valued, and wished to reward. He wore it thenceforth, every day it was cool enough to wear a cloak, and did so with pride.

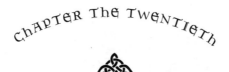
SIGVOR

RANNVEIG had looked without success for a serving woman to go up to the hall and join Tindr. The Dane and his wife were busy morning till night setting up the hall to live in. Alrik the sawyer spent days there, making benches and tables and a bed with Sidroc; and his pretty wife, who called herself Ceridwen, had been sewing alcove curtains and blankets, stuffing featherbeds, making clothes, cooking and cleaning. Rannveig liked her from the start. She came every day down to the brew-house to carry away a small crock of her ale, to ask Rannveig's advice about whom she should buy grain or other necessaries from, and to learn Norse enough so that she might do these things herself.

Tindr had his own many tasks at the hall. He had by now fowl and geese and a cow to care for, as well as his hives to look after, and was hard at work stacking the loads of firewood that Sidroc had ordered delivered up the hill; there was no time to cut his own and let it season and dry before Winter. And now that the stags had come down from the deeper reaches of the forest, Tindr was hunting. This meant hours in the forest, and then the hours spent dressing out the beast. Rannveig had Tindr bring the haunches back here to smoke, so that all would have meat in the coming months, and Gudfrid went up and made pies from the mincings of shoulder meat. Without a skilled cook up at the hall, the newcomers could not make the most of what Tindr brought them, and all they were forced to buy on the trading road, lacking grain and veg-etables of their own.

The best Rannveig could do was Sigvor. She was young, a maid of sixteen or seventeen Summers, and the youngest daughter of four who spun and wove from their parents' large flock of curly-fleeced sheep. Their wool was good, and the thick wadmal fabric the girls wove and then boiled to felt down was considered some of the best on Gotland. Sigvor had got herself mixed up with one of the young sons of the richest fishing family in the area, who sold stock-fish all around the Baltic rim. He was a man who already had a child with another young woman, upland, which did not end in their hand-fast; and though Rannveig knew only a little of this and of Sigvor's affairs, it did not seem from what she had heard in the brew-house to be a promising match for the maid. At any rate, the man in question, Eirik by name, had perished, fishing, at sea. Sigvor had begun to tell folk that he and she would hand-fast, but then he was gone.

Tindr was surprised when Sigvor showed up at the hall. Her older sister, the one that Ragnfast liked to look at, had always come to his cousin's Mid-Summer feast and fire, sometimes bringing the baby of the family with her. The older sister had wed the year that Ragnfast and Estrid kissed, and no longer came to celebrate Mid-Summer with them. Tindr still saw all the sisters on the trading road, in their stall where they stood at their looms or walked about, spinning their wool, but did not expect one of them to come to the hall to live.

He did not have a name for her. Tindr did not name all who he met or came across, thinking of some only as, *this one*, or *that one*. But now that she was come to help Bright Hair he must have a way to name her. She had plump and reddish cheeks, so he chose a double touch at his cheekbones as her name.

She chose as her alcove one on the other side of the hall from his. She swept and laundered and helped Bright Hair chop cabbages and carrots. She did not smile much, and kept her head down as she caught the ash flakes with the birch twigs of her broom. When she stood spinning with her spindle dropping from her hand, her blue eyes looked at something far away. She paid little mind to him, as if he almost were not there, and though Bright Hair showed her how to ask him to do things, she rarely did, asking Bright Hair to tell him.

One morning when he was sitting at table Red Cheeks brought a platter of food and placed it before him. She had already brought the single platter from which Scar and Bright Hair ate, but now brought him one of his own. For other meals she had simply piled food enough for both of them in two or three bowls and laid them on the table. The plate she had made up for him was done with the same care with which she made up that for Scar and Bright Hair, the eggs fried in butter to one side, small loaves of bread next to them, and chunks of baked apples, still steaming, to the other.

He looked up at her as she set it before him, and she smiled at him. Then she sat down on the other side of the table as she always did.

From that day on she looked at him, smiled at him, began to ask him to help her when something was heavy or out of her reach. He saw she was pretty, and very much so when she smiled at him.

One afternoon Red Cheeks stood at the well by the front door, drawing water. It was the larger bucket she was pulling, and when he came around from the stable yard and saw her strain at its weight, he went to help her, just as he did with Bright Hair. He startled her slightly, so intent was she at her task, but she quickly smiled and let him take the handle from him. When he had pulled the bucket all the way up, Red Cheeks laid her hand over his where it closed upon the bail. He almost flinched in his surprise, but she looked at him from under lowered lashes and smiled once more.

She did not hold him thus for more than a moment, but paired with her smile it was enough to know that she liked him. He began thinking of her in a different way. He had carved a little rose from a ball of bees' wax, and given it as gift to Bright Hair; she had remarked over it, and kept it with her at the table that stood by her loom. Now he made another flower, for Red Cheeks.

He hoped to be near her when she might need his help, and now she came to him often to ask. She touched his hand again, touched his arm, smiled under her lashes as she placed his food before him. At night he lay in his alcove and thought of her, so close by, her soft and plump body snuggled under her blanket.

One afternoon when Bright Hair was at the brew-house and Scar away on the trading road, she waved him over as he passed on his way to the stable. She was at the well, and he guessed she wanted to haul the big bucket up for the cook-fire cauldron. But when he got there she had the line for the small pail in her hand. As he neared her she dropped even that, letting the pail rest on the well cover.

She stood there, looking at him, the smile growing on her face. He slowed, uncertain, but with her hand she motioned him closer. He stepped near her, and she lifted her arms and placed them about his neck. She raised her face to him and pulled his body against hers.

Her lips pressed his and did so with firmness. She thrust her hips forward against his, and he felt the soft-ness of her breasts pressing against his chest. His own arms had lifted, and now clasped her about her back. She held herself fast against his body. He was of a sudden trembling with excitement and desire, thrilling to her own desire for him.

Her body was warm and soft in his arms. Her mouth kissed his again. She paused, her chin resting on his chest. He made a sound, a guttural gurgling; he could not help it. She looked up at him, the slightest of frowns on her face. He had reminded her that he was deaf, and could not speak. She stepped back a bit, looked at him once more. He could not read her face other than know that he had done wrong in making any sound.

Two nights later Tindr was at the brew-house when the brother and father of Red Cheeks stopped him. He saw the anger in their faces, and felt it in her brother's clenching hand, closed over his shoulder.

Scar was there and stepped between them, took the brother's hand off him. Tindr wore Scar's big silver pin, knew he was this warrior's man. Because of this he knew he need not fear these two; but he feared what he did not know. They all, with Nenna and Bright Hair, walked up the hill in the dark. Red Cheeks was there, awaiting them.

What happened next was all confused. All were looking at him, him and Red Cheeks, but she herself would not look at him. Her brother was pointing at him, his face pinched in anger. Scar spoke, and Bright Hair spoke to Red Cheeks, and made the tears come into her eyes. Finally Nenna began to sign to him, told him Red Cheeks would bear a babe, asked if he were the father.

He was so stunned he almost howled. They had kissed by the well, nothing more, and when they had done she was no longer smiling at him; her lip was twisted in disgust.

Then the anger turned on Red Cheeks. He feared her brother would hit her then and there, and her father scowled at her.

Scar spoke, looking at him. Scar looked at Nenna, asking her to make the signs for him. His mother stood before him, before them all, and asked him if he wanted Red Cheeks.

His heart was racing. She was pretty, and had kissed him, and she could be kind. She had seemed to want him.

He made the gestures to her, there in front of everyone, clasping his hands together. He would be her man, if
she would be his woman.

It took her a long time to answer, but as she did she
finally looked at him once more. He did not need Nenna
or anyone to tell her that the lifted lip and sneering mouth
meant Nai.

He dropped his shoulders. His heart that had been
pounding felt stopped in his chest. Her father and brother
began to get her things from her alcove. He and Nenna
left then, back to her house, and he spent that night with
her.

Alone in his old alcove he did not sleep. His heart
felt like someone had held a burning coal to it. Everything
had happened so fast; Red Cheeks bringing him his food,
smiling at him, kissing him. Then her folk were angry at
him, had almost come to blows, and she would not have
him after all.

He did not see Red Cheeks again until Winter. During
the time of Winter Feasts he was on the trading road with
Bright Hair and his cousin, and there she was. He could
see that she would have a babe soon. She looked at him
with no expression. Then a man came out of a trading stall
and she turned and went to his side.

He had looked away then, but he had seen the hurt in
Bright Hair's face, hurt she felt for his sake.

$$\times\!\times\!\times\!\times\!\times\!\times\!\times\!\times\!\times\!\times$$

A few weeks later he walked the woods after a fresh
fall of snow. It was not deep, but enough to cover the soil
asleep beneath it. The sky was silver, like the peeling bark

of certain birch trees, and only a glint of Sun shone low overhead. His footsteps slowed; he stopped. There was a fallen tree nearby and he sat down upon the dark trunk, welcoming the solidness underneath him; he had felt almost faint.

He set his elbows on his knees and hung his head. When he lifted it, there She was. The white hind stood before him. She looked at him with raised head, ears unmoving over the deep brown eyes. He had not seen her fully since he had bathed in the forest pool, now years past. Still, there were times when he was out in the trees when he thought he saw a flash of white just out of eye-range.

She would not, he knew, become the Lady of the Forest to him now. She gazed upon him just the same, a reminder of the bond between them. He felt the coolness of her woman's flesh under his hands again, and the warmth beneath that coolness. He felt her palm upon his chest, lying over his beating heart. He saw the beautiful mouth come to his hands and anoint them with her kiss. Here, in her garb as a white hind, she came to remind him of all this, of what she had given him, and how he was given to Her.

The water was come into his eyes, gazing on her. When she bounded away he dropped his head and cried out long and bitter tears.

THE GOLDEN CROSS

The Year 884

WORR, the horse-thegn of Kilton, had sailed for Angle-land the day before. He had taken the serving girl Sparrow with him, whom he would deliver to the convent at Oundle in Lindisse. From thence, before he returned to Kilton, he would journey on to Four Stones, to tell the Lady Ælfwyn of the death of Godwin, the Lord of Kilton; and give to her Ceridwen's letter.

The mistress of Tyrsborg had awakened thinking of these things, that Worr and Sparrow and the merchant ship that bore them were likely past the southern tip of Svear-land now. Turning in her bed, she slipped her hand up on the bare chest of her husband. With his wounded thigh he must lie almost immobile the night long, the leg propped up on cushions to help the swelling. He had slept but lightly; the pain assured that, but he drowsed now. She pulled herself up so her lips could just brush the scar upon his cheek, and left their bed.

Out in the kitchen yard Helga had marshaled the children. Little Eirian and Yrling were already sitting at the table there, spooning skyr and honey into their mouths; as soon as they had wakened Helga had shooed all the young ones out of the hall to leave quiet for the healing of the Dane. The boys Ceric and Hrald stood at the basin of warm water Gunnvor the cook had poured out for them on one end of her work table. Ceridwen could not keep the smile from her face as she saw them; the wonder of having them here was still fresh upon her. As she neared Helga dipped her head to her, and the boys looked up too from where they splashed their faces and hands. They had their tunics off, and as Ceridwen came to them her eye was stopped by a glimmer of gold suspended from her son's neck, hanging above the washing basin.

Her breath caught, and she felt her heart contract. Ceric bore about his neck the golden cross that Gyric had cherished, that given him by Ælfred, King, as token of his love following Gyric's return to Kilton. The cross was from Rome, blessed by the Holy Father himself, and Ælfred had valued it above all his possessions, yet had freely given it to his friend for the succor it might give him. Gyric's eyes had been burnt out by renegade Danes, but he recalled the golden cross well, and the moment the messenger had placed it in his hands he knew what it was. He wore it each day thenceforth. Ceridwen had never seen him without it. Now her son wore it.

She came up to the boys, kissing each in turn. It was a moment before she could speak, though Hrald looked to her expectantly, hoping for news of his father's contin-ued healing. They toweled themselves and pulled on their tunics. Ceric's silver-hilted seax, once also his father's, lay on the table, and he buckled its belt about his waist. His mother found voice.

"The cross you wear," she began to Ceric.

He nodded. "It is father's. The Lady Modwynn gave it me, last year."

She knew it was not likely that Ceric could recall his father wearing it himself; he had been so young at Gyric's death. Now both cross and seax had come into his keeping; his uncle had given him the latter when she and Ceric had left Kilton more than three years earlier to visit Four Stones. She was struck, too, that Ceric no longer called his grandmother that; he was growing up, and at twelve years used the more formal address for Gyric's mother. In three more years he would be given a sword.

"It was a gift from King Ælfred. He is my godfather," Ceric went on, as if his mother were likely to forget that.

Ceridwen could only smile and nod. She turned to Hrald.

"Your father grows stronger by the day," she told him. "I think it will not be long before he can ride again. Then he will take you to Tindr's cousin, Ragnfast, and you will return with horses for each of you."

Tindr came and joined them as they sat. Enough had changed in the last three days that sitting down in the morning sunshine and sharing food took on added meaning. Tindr spent a moment looking about the table before he began. Scar was not there; with his bad wound it would be a while before he could easily walk. Bright Hair sat across from him, tearing bread for the little ones at her side. He followed her eyes down to them. Tindr felt a deep affection for these children; they loved and trusted him, begged that he lift them upon the horses to be led about, helped him gather eggs and feed the beasts, laughed with him and made up new signs only the three of them could understand. He was a part of this place. He looked over at the boys. He had watched Bright Hair hold and kiss them, knew she cherished their coming. They were to be a new part of this place, and he would be part of their lives here. He would matter to them, and them to him.

His thoughts moved on, and his lids dropped a moment over his eyes. He saw again the warrior who had brought these boys. He forced his eyes back to the smiling faces of the little ones.

All partook of what Gunnvor had made, and she too quitted her post at her cook-fire and broke bread with them. She had baked the loaves just this morning, and they were warm enough that the soft butter they spread beneath a crackling crust melted into slick golden drop-lets, so rich that the boys were licking their hands. There was honey too, as much as the boys liked, which there never was enough of at home, and they knew they had Tindr to thank for this. The boys looked shyly at him, sometimes with side-wise eyes, as he sat amongst them. He had already shown the boys how good he was around horses, which mattered to both of them, and they had the promise from Hrald's father that Tindr could teach them the ways of the forest. Now they watched Tindr put down his bread and gesture to Ceric's mother. He pointed to the boys, made a motion as if he were pulling an arrow from a quiver and setting it to the bow, then pointed to his work bench in the stable. She watched with care, nodding the while, then spoke to them.

"Tindr asks if he should make bows for you."

"Yes! Yes," they both said.

She smiled. "Já, já," she corrected, which Hrald, who knew Norse, at once repeated.

Later that day Ceric came to her, alone. Yrling trailed the boys everywhere, but was just now stacking a pile of blocks on the table by Tyrsborg's stone end. He was out from underfoot from Gunnvor's cooking work there, but where she and Helga could keep an eye on him. Hrald had joined him in his building, and Eirian had wriggled in as well, claiming a few for her own.

Ceridwen was standing at her linen loom near the open side door. One look at Ceric's face made her set her shuttle down, tucking it between the taut warp threads. After what Ceric, and all of them, had been through she was alert to his changing moods; it was difficult herself to focus long on any task. In the past she could lose herself in spinning or weaving, but with the little ones scampering about, and now the demands of caring for her husband and making the boys comfortable she was never long at anything. And she was fighting her own memories of Godwin's arrival, and death.

It was of this last that her son wished to speak. He could not do so at first, and after she greeted him with her smile she stood looking at him. Ceric looked down. She knew then to pick out her shuttle from her warp, and began to drive it through the opened strings, her eyes on her work, not him.

"My uncle's . . . grave," he said at last. The inside of his lip had been split when his uncle had knocked his seax out of his hand, and he felt the raised line of the small wound now as he spoke.

She paused, her fingers resting just above the waiting linen.

"I would like to put a cross there," he told her.

She turned to face him. "Of course," she answered. Tindr had made a small wooden cross for Sparrow; he could make one larger.

"Uncle said this was a God-less heathen place," Ceric reported. "There are no priests here, no church."

His hand had gone to his chest. She knew the golden cross lay beneath, under his tunic.

She dropped her voice even lower. "There are no priests, nor any church," she said, all her gentleness in her tone. "Gotland is a heathen place. But not God-less. There are many Gods. The same our people in Angle-land worshipped not long ago. The same my own father and kin worshipped," she ended.

It took him a long time to answer, and she returned to her weaving, waiting.

"Uncle said that you . . . are damned. That you are turned heathen, and will burn in Hell. Like – your new husband."

She let out her breath as softly as she could. "When did he say all these things?"

"On our journeying here. Every day, both when we were riding to Hrald's, and then when we were aboard ship."

So both boys had heard him say such things. Her throat felt like it was closing. "And . . . do you believe what he said?" She waited a moment before she went on.

"This is only your third day here. But you have seen kindness already, from the folk here; and seen the type of hall-moot that the folk hold to make sure of justice when there is trouble." She paused again, turned to look at him, but he again was looking down.

"All the folk here are heathen, all of them," she went on, stressing this last. "Do you think all here will burn in Hell?"

She watched him swallow, saw the green eyes look bravely into hers.

"All of them?" His voice was but a whisper.

She gave a single nod of her head. "I am heathen," she told him. "I was baptised as a child, just as Sidroc was as a man. But I choose, as he does, to worship the old Gods of our folk."

"He is not our folk," Ceric said quickly.

"He is a Dane, yes. But the Gods of the Danes and the Gods of the Saxons and Angles are the very same." She paused again. "We are cousins. The priest Dunnere at Kilton teaches you our history; how we came many years ago and claimed the island from the people of Caesar, who were dying out. My father's folk – and your grandfathers, both of them – came from the same marshy wilds that many of the Danes come from now. That is why our Gods are the same. We are cousins."

"He killed my uncle."

Ceric was staring at her now.

"He did," was all she could say. "But your uncle was trying to steal me from my home, and wanted to kill Sidroc." She felt helpless and almost ill, attempting to beat back a memory that was too fresh to have clouded in her mind. The fear and horror were still alive in her belly.

"And you are heathen," he ended softly.

"Já," she told him, using the Norse. It was her new tongue, that of her new people, those who held the faith she held. He must try to accept that.

Her boy had once again turned his head away from her. She went on, looking at her hands resting upon the warp strings. "Tindr can make a cross; he has skill with wood, which is why he offered to make you a bow. Shall we go and ask him to make a cross for the grave?"

"You ask him. He is your serving man."

She was stung at this, both his words and the sharp tone with which he had of a sudden flung them at her.

"Tindr is far more than a serving man," she corrected, her voice still low. "But I will ask him to make one."

〰〰〰〰〰〰〰〰〰

That night Tindr stood outside looking up at the sky. He often did so, stopping to lift his face to the stars glittering overhead, or to the mellow light of the Moon swimming in the cold dark. Tonight he stared, thinking not of the pinpoints of distant sparks above him, but of what he had seen earlier.

During the day he had gone to a spot on the beach, not far from his mother's house, where he had built a fire three days before. He had carted the dead man's clothing there, along with a quantity of bloodied straw, and set it alight. The warrior's dark clothing was punctured with knife marks and sliced through where his mother and he had cut it from his body. It was saturated with his blood, so much so that when he had gathered it in his arms his tunic had gotten stained. He had helped his mother wash and wrap the man, and now he swallowed back the bile rising in his mouth, recalling the sight of the warrior's broken body. He had wanted no trace of it to remain at the hall. Burning the clothing and straw in one of the cook-fires was unthinkable, and he had chosen a stretch of beach away from the view of any on the trading road.

He had gone back today to clear away the signs of burning. The mound of spent wood was a small one. He kicked it with his foot, shattering it into ashes. His toe dislodged something. It was part of the dead man's black boot, charred, but still recognizable. He looked at it, saw it for what it was, and swiftly buried it further up the tide line, where the pebbles became soil.

He thought of what had happened since the warrior who had worn that boot arrived. Sparrow had left, gone with the second warrior, and the boys were here. His mother had told him these were the sons of Scar and Bright Hair, and had come from afar. The boy with the coppery hair looked like Bright Hair, and looked too like the warrior Scar had killed.

He had watched that warrior twist Bright Hair's arm so that she fell. If Scar had died, he would have shot the warrior to keep her safe, shot him to kill, and would have done the same to the second if he must. As he had watched Scar and the warrior fight he had discovered this, and learning this about himself had changed him. He could kill a man if he had to.

Sparrow sat in the prow of the merchant ship. She liked to sit thus, upon a lashed chest with her pack at her feet, and watch the distant green coasts slide away. The winds were dry and strong and the sail was always filled, billowing out so it was hard to see back to the stern. Worr had made her understand that it would take two or three different ships for them to reach the place Mistress had told her about. She sometimes would lift the hem of her mantle and feel the hard disk sewn there, the gold she would carry to the holy woman Sigewif in return for taking her in. Each time she touched it she felt a tremor of happiness, happiness and a little fear.

Worr treated her as Mistress promised he would. Most nights they landed and slept on shore, and he had a tent for her to sleep in. If they stayed at sea he laced up a little shelter off the gunwale for her to sleep under, and he slept just outside it, so she always felt safe. But on the third day they made land and stopped to pick up a Svear woman and her children. It was the merchant's wife, and she had been almost as glad to see Sparrow as Sparrow was to see her. She spent some time with her husband back near the steering oar, but mostly sat with Sparrow and her three young in the prow, out of the way of the sail and the men behind it. When the ship did not move too much they both could stand and spin; Mistress had given her a thick coil of wool roving to work from to give her something to do. If they could not spin they spoke together, played with the children, and just drowsed in the warmth of the day.

Sparrow and Worr said prayers together each dawn and dusk, asking Jhesu Christus to protect the ship. The merchant's wife cocked her head with interest, and Sparrow tried to tell her about Jhesu, but knew she did not do a good job. Abbess Sigewif would teach her how to better tell others, she knew.

Worr spent time talking to Sparrow each day, and if he spoke slowly she could begin to understand more of what he meant. And she could help Worr, because all on board spoke Norse, and she could ask questions for him and help him understand, and she wanted to help. It was no harder than with Tindr.

She thought of Tindr, of how he had walked into the woods near where she was hiding and left the shoes he had made for her. Inside he had put rabbit skins, as her feet were bare. She had put them on and her feet were no longer cold, nor did they hurt from the roots and rocks of the forest floor. Then he came back and left bread, and a jar of broth. Living amongst the trees she had been so hungry she had eaten green leaves, and they made her sick. She knew then to come back to that place every day. Some days he would set down the food and drink and stay a little way off, waiting for her. But she would not show herself. After this he would leave the food and blow a note or two from his whistle, so she might know it was there.

She had wanted to trust Tindr, but she was afraid he would hurt her. But the Master frightened her most, with his scar and gleaming weapon. He was so like the men who had hurt her over and over onboard the ship, and on land too.

One day Tindr blew his whistle, and she crept through the trees. She waited until she was certain he was gone and then went to the food. She dropped the blanket she had taken from the bed from her shoulders. There was butter and honey too on the bread, and she was pushing it into her mouth when Tindr showed himself. He stepped from behind a tree, with his hands out in front of him. She wanted to turn and run, but the look on his face made her stop. He put his hands together, like a bowl, and just reached them towards her, as if he wanted to give her something, and not take.

He gestured that she should follow him.

Somehow she did. She thought Mistress would beat her, but she did not. And Master never looked at her or touched her. All were kind. Mistress knew about Jhesu Christus and told her many of His stories. And now she had given her gold, so that she might go to a place and pray and live with others who loved Him.

When she was with Abbess Sigewif perhaps she could tell her about Tindr and the rest. Perhaps priests could go there someday and teach them about Jhesu Christus. Until then she would pray for them, and ask Worr to pray for them as well.

Mother and son walked together to the place of burial. Tindr went with them; the cross was large enough that with hammer and block to drive it in all was heavy. Ceric claimed the cross, holding it in his arms across his chest. When Tindr had finished smoothing the wood Ceridwen had drawn the words GODWIN OF KILTON in charcoal on the cross-piece, and then with heated poker burnt in these letters so they would stay.

Ceric had been down to the trading road before, and today his eyes were set forward as they walked. He had not been as far as the great carved figure of Freyr, and as they neared it he saw Tindr nod to it, then look to him as if he would want to as well. Rotting remains of fowl lay suspended in the tines of tall forks behind the figure. It was just like the stories Dunnere told, of the sin and error of the ignorant, trying to worship by leaving animal bodies about. Everyone knew you worshipped God by laying gold and gems on his altars, and by praying and fasting. Here no one fasted nor prayed, not that he could see.

The burial place was littered with round-topped stones lying every which way. Some had runes on them and some were blank or worn off. Off to one side he could see the stone base and heaped charcoal of the burning-place. He knew heathens burned their dead. They thought it made the bodies go to Heaven right away, but it was more likely that they got to the Hell they were going to even faster.

No one else was there. Beyond the place he could see long racks of fish drying in the hot Sun. On the beach were a few old boats with no one around them. The burial place was ugly, with no trees, just stones.

It was easy to see the spot where his uncle lay, the ground was turned over and fresh-looking. The three of them slowed, then stopped, before it. The cross had grown heavy and was gouging into his left shoulder. He thought of his friend Worr digging the grave. He knew Tindr had helped and some strange men too.

He looked down at the disturbed soil. "Where . . . where is the head?" he asked, looking at his mother.

She looked startled. He wished Worr was there with him, and was sorry he had not come when he had had the chance.

Ceridwen scanned the ground, remembering how the body had been passed to Tindr and Worr when they stood inside the grave.

"Here," she said, walking to one end, facing the sea.

Her son nodded, then lowered the end of the cross into the rocky soil. Tindr came and gestured he should steady it as he struck the end of it, but Ceric shook his head. He wanted to hammer it in. Tindr placed the wooden block on the top of the cross, and crouched down to steady the shaft of it. Ceric swung the hammer and pounded on the block. It took a while but he drove it deep enough to hold it.

When he was done he wanted to say a prayer, but did not want to do so before his mother and Tindr. Maybe prayers said in front of heathens went to the Devil instead of to God.

His mother had turned a little away from him, as if to give him leave to kneel or bow his head. But now, free of the cross, he just felt angry. He was angry at his uncle for getting killed, angry that he had seen him try to hurt his mother, angry that his uncle had surprised him with his own violent anger. And he could not forget what his uncle had said about his mother, spat it out to the Dane, "She was my woman before she was yours."

His mother was a widow and could take a new husband, he knew that. But his uncle had a wife, his aunt Edgyth, who was gentle and learned too. Ceric knew what his uncle meant when he called his mother "my woman". It meant they had gone under the covers of a bed together, which was only allowed to those who were wed.

He looked at the stony ground and thought of his uncle's body beneath it, so far from Kilton. He thought of his uncle's soul. Before they had left Angle-land he had made confession and received the Sacrament from Wilgot, the priest at Four Stones; they all had.

He knew his mother was standing just behind him. If she had in fact been under the covers with his uncle, it was a mortal sin. She was heathen and would not seek absolution, so she was doubly damned.

Or maybe his uncle only said that to anger the Dane. Cadmar told him warriors said all sorts of things when facing the enemy, to make them mad and make them careless. These were not lies, Cadmar said, but taunts that were weapons as good as an extra spear. He remembered the Dane saying something back to his uncle that made him yell in return; he could not remember what.

It did not matter anymore. His uncle was dead. He was a great warrior and rich beyond measure, but he had been bested in single combat by the Dane. Now he was buried far from Kilton and Angle-land and any priest to make prayers over his body. When he went home he would tell them he put a cross on his grave, and pounded it in himself.

A few days later, on a morning that drizzled with rain, all sat about the big table within the hall, breaking their fast. Gunnvor had apples in abundance from their upland farm, and she had taken wheaten flour and made a baked apple pudding with some, as the hens were still laying well. There were tangy bowls of the thickened milk, skyr, and of course honey, which Ceric and Hrald could not get enough of. All ranged about the table, all save Tindr; he had done his morning chores but had not yet returned from wherever he had taken himself off to.

The wound to Sidroc's thigh was healing well enough that he could forgo the use of the crutch, though the leg was still stiff and he needed to keep it straight before him as he sat. At times like this, her healing husband next her, Ceridwen felt flooded with content. The goodness of what lay on the table, the nearness of the boys, sitting together and opposite her, and her little ones, sitting between her and Helga, filled her with quiet happiness.

The rain was not heavy and the hall door to the kitchen yard was open. Seated where they were, Ceric and Hrald both saw Tindr return. He had something draped over his shoulder, they could not be certain what it was. He looked through the door, saw them all seated within, and stepped inside. Wreathed about his neck was a string of rabbits, three of them. He had laced them front legs to rear, and now he grinned at those seated as he pulled them off and showed what his snares had produced during the night. Gunnvor clapped her hands, and Ceric and Hrald stood up and went to him. With a smile he pointed to both boys, and made the twining motion with his hand for braiding up the snare. Já, they said and nodded; they wanted to learn how.

Neither boy had done this before. Both lived in great halls with many folk and so had need of much food each day, and a rabbit made one good meal only, and for a small family. Kilton had games-men aplenty, some of whom did nothing but set and check snares; but Ceric had never gone out with them; they were like serving-folk almost, and rabbits were beneath him. When he was older he and his thegns would hunt for deer and boar in Kilton's forests. He had been out after deer once or twice already with Worr, who was good at tracking animals, but found long waiting in a cold and wet woods less exciting than he had hoped. Likewise, no one in the hall at Four Stones set snares; Hrald knew the villagers did so, but he had never trailed along with any of them to learn the craft.

But things were different here at Tyrsborg than at Kilton or Four Stones. As his mother had promised, Ceric had real chores to do each day, and Hrald too; things done by the serving folk at home. They drew water from the well for Gunnvor and her endlessly bubbling pots, and held the heavy ends of wet linens and woollen clothing while Helga wrung the rinse-water from them. They helped Tindr stack firewood and carry charcoal for the braziers, and he set them to chopping kindling as well. With Hrald's father unable to work with Tindr to manage their wood supply, the boys' efforts were needed. They knew they would get horses soon but that they themselves would care for them; there would be no stable-boys to pass the beasts off to after a lathered ride.

They had both asked to stay the year on Gotland. Other than Worr, who was a grown man and the horse-thegn of Kilton, Hrald was the best friend Ceric had ever had. But Worr was gone back to Angle-land, and Hrald was close to his own age. Because Ceric was two years older he often got to be in charge when they did things together, even though Hrald was taller than he. They had wanted to stay to be with the parent they had missed, of course, but also because they would be together. They knew life would be different on this island so far from home.

For one, few paid them any mind. At home they were always watched, always had other men near them. Ceric knew this was because he was a grandson of the great Godwulf, and his uncle was Godwin of Kilton, and there had been a lot of war and his uncle only had one heir, his little brother Edwin. He had never known his grandfather, who had died when Ceric was but a babe, but his Uncle Godwin had been as a second father to him, even more, as his own father had been dead so long. But his parents had given their second son Edwin to Godwin, and Godwin had named the boy his heir.

Ceric would be Edwin's chief pledged man when they both grew up, and because Ceric was four years older he was expected to protect Edwin. So there was always a gaggle of serving men and women and thegns around them, wherever they went.

At Four Stones Hrald was always in the company of Jari when he left the hall yard. He was not allowed to walk or ride out without the big three-fingered warrior, and Hrald understood early that Jari was his body-guard. His Uncle Asberg spent a lot of time with him as well, but he knew Jari was always there to make certain nothing happened to him. When he grew up all of Four Stones and its treasure would be his, and he would have the care of his mother and sisters in his keeping, even Ashild, Hrald's sister, who was older than him and strong for a maid.

Here they could go anywhere by themselves, and no one stopped them. And there were no warriors, not that the boys had seen. Every stall and workshop had a spear or two at hand, standing in a corner by the door, and they guessed the men around knew how to use them. But the boys needed no warriors at their sides to roam around and explore.

They had been down to the trading road with Ceric's mother, and she had spoken to a few of the trades-folk about them, who had nodded back to the boys. The cook Gunnvor had sent them down to the woman who did the brewing to fetch ale for the hall. They understood she was

Tindr's mother; both boys recalled her from the day Ceric's uncle had died. Rannveig had greeted them and shown them off to a group of men who were drinking her ale. The men took the boys in with a glance, listening to what the brewster said about them, which was a little hard even for Hrald to understand. Ceric remembered how some had looked at his seax. He knew it was a good weapon, and had a hilt with silver and gold wire hammered into it. He also had seen enough of the knives the men wore here to know that only he and Sidroc wore a seax. The rest carried the same kind of straight knife that Hrald and the Danes at Four Stones wore. After that no one ever really looked at the boys any different from any of the boys on the trading road.

Hrald's father had promised he would teach them to fight when his leg healed. Hrald had never seen his father fight at Four Stones, only practice his spear-throwing, and both boys saw how good he was. Hrald had seen men fight over land disputes and other things, but never to the death. Ceric had seen the hall of Kilton awash in blood, the Winter day when Danes attacked. Neither boy had spoken to each other about the day they came here, when Hrald's father killed Ceric's uncle. Ceric knew he had to become a skilled warrior, as skilled as his own father was, and try to be as good as his uncle. He wanted to learn from the man who had killed him. Just now he was glad it would not be right away.

Tindr was different. He was not a warrior, but the boys knew he was in a special place at Tyrsborg. He did work like a serving-man, but then Hrald knew his own father, who was a rich and powerful Jarl, did much the same work here. He had built the tables and benches and other things with the help of the sawyer down the road, and worked hard to keep them in firewood.

Tindr worked at many tasks but came and went when he pleased. He wore a big silver pin to close his mantle, one as big as any the boys had seen, and had rings of twisted silver circling his little fingers; no serving man had such treasure. He was clever and made all sorts of things. The smooth spoons they used to eat browis and the creamy skyr were shaped by Tindr from deer antler. He had showed them the ice skates he made from the long and dense front leg bones of the same animal, and they knew he was going to make them skates too. Ceric's mother had told the boys Tindr was the best hunter on the island, and had pointed out with pride all the deer hides to prove it. He even took boar, and wore shoes he had made himself, made of their thick hide and with a boar's tusk for the toggle to close them. The boys spoke of this and thought them the finest trophy a hunter could wish for. The smoke-house at the brewster's was full of deer haunches, all felled by Tindr's arrows. They had watched Tindr at his shooting practice down there, which he did every day, good as he was. They had seen how well he could draw a deer with a piece of charcoal on the planed boards. They were as skilled as the tiny pictures in the books at Kilton, Ceric thought, even though Tindr could not read or even speak, except to grunt.

The next afternoon they went out with him to set snares. They had spent a while watching him make the snares themselves, gripping one end of the dried deer sinew between his teeth as he stripped it with his fingers into fine threads, then braiding these together to make a string so tough neither boy could snap it with their hands.

These, with a small axe and a knife, were all the tools Tindr needed to fill Gunnvor's cooking pot with rabbit meat.

In the woods Tindr's quietness seemed less strange than at Tyrsborg. Ceric thought it was because you tried not to talk when you stalked or hunted. Tindr might lift his hand and stop the boys as they trailed behind him, and gesture to some perching bird or a brightly coloured toad-stool. One dusk he stopped them and Ceric did not know why, until a fox vixen trotted across their path, her two red and white kits tumbling after at her heels. Hrald had been watching Tindr and so saw the fox almost as soon as he did, but Ceric had been looking around on his own and missed the hunter's heightened attention.

On their first day out he led them to a glade open-ing to a large meadow land. The edge of the glade sloped slightly downwards, from tree-line to glade to open field. The boys knew that animals favoured certain pathways in the woods, but everything looked the same to their eyes. They walked along until the deaf man pointed out the slightest of rabbit trails. The grasses were barely bent, and only by looking carefully and at different angles could the boys make out where the furry bodies of passing rabbits had separated the blades the slightest amount. Tindr liked those which were heading downhill, and at the bottom he would build his snare.

They watched him as he stood and looked about him. Some small fir saplings were nearby, and he lopped one down with his axe, then, taking it up in his hands, showed them how supple it was. He struck off the needled branches, and buried the ends of the sapling in a shallow arch over the rabbit run. The sturdier branches, along with any near branches from other trees, he drove in as guiding stakes to keep the rabbits on the track, funneling them closer to where the waiting snare loop hung suspended from the bent-over sapling.

He built one, then found a second run and had the boys do it. They went along like this, finding likely trails, cutting the slender firs or pines, looping the sinew in its double loop, smaller noose and larger catching loop, driving in the guide stakes.

When they went back in the morning three of the six snares they had set held rabbits. Two were dead; they had leapt when they had caught their heads in the sinew loop, and it had closed about their necks. Tindr laid his hand upon their bodies a moment and closed his eyes.

"Is he praying?" Ceric muttered to Hrald. Who would pray to a rabbit, he thought.

Hrald watched the eyelids drop and rise again over Tindr's odd eyes. "Not praying," he ventured. He hoped he was not praying to the rabbit. Hrald liked Tindr and if he prayed to animals that made him like the foolish ones in the Bible that worshipped the golden calf.

"It is like my father's men at Four Stones, those who go and make sacrifices at the statue by the big tree," he finally said. Both boys had wandered down there often enough during the Summer Ceric had spent at Four Stones. The place was always deserted, but once they had seen a dead rooster there, freshly killed, and Hrald had known someone had left it as an Offering. He had seen another man offer there too. It was the custom to thank the animal for yielding up its life. They watched Tindr lace the two rabbits together.

"I think he was . . . thanking the rabbit," Hrald ended.

The third rabbit they had snared was alive. It was sitting, its belly pressed against the trail, front paws extended, the dark beads of its eyes forward. It was trembling as they neared, but other than this ripple of the soft brown coat did not move. Tindr dropped by its side, made sure the boys were watching. He closed both hands about the small creature. They were watching his face, and saw his eyelids lower for a moment. Then he moved one hand to the narrow chest of the rabbit, and they saw his fingers pinch at the heart. Tindr gave a pull at the rabbit's hind legs. It died at once.

The boys saw how quick this was, to hold the hard mass of the heart and quickly separate it from the blood vessels with a tug on the lower body. After they reset the final snare they headed back, a rabbit for each of them. Gunnvor was grinning at what they bore as they entered her kitchen yard, and Yrling and Eirian ran to see. Yrling was jumping up and down.

But they were not done. Tindr showed them how to skin the rabbits, making small cuts at the rear, neck, and paw-tips, and then gently sliding off the furry pelt inside out as if it were a stocking. These he took to his work bench, where he dropped wood-shavings over the flesh side; they needed no scraping. In a few days the pelts were dry and ready to use inside shoes or gloves for cold weather. As they caught more Tindr showed them how to square off the dried pelts and sew them together with a filament of deer sinew to make a large piece of surpassing softness, to line a mantle hood with or even stuff as a pillow. Tindr made needles from the splintered bones of deer, but for this work he used one of the fine steel needles they had seen in Ceric's mother's workbasket. It made a tiny hole in the delicate skins. He kept it safe, stuck in a little scrap of linen nailed above his work bench in the stable.

One morning when they went out to check the snares the boys were surprised to see a squirrel dead in one of the loops. Tindr clapped his hands and grinned, and motioned to the boys that sometimes this happened, as all manner of small beasts used the rabbit tracks. Gunnvor regarded it as a treat, and made a special savoury pie from it, and the boys drew straws for the pelt. Hrald held the longer, and Tindr showed him how to stitch up a little pouch from it, trimming the edges with the fluffy tail, which was softer even than rabbit fur.

Another time, heading back to Tyrsborg from setting snares, they watched Tindr stop at a clump of white birch trees. They knew he cut his arrow-sticks from birches; he had taken them to see the stump of a big tree he and his dead father had felled years before. They had coppiced it by chopping it down and sawing the stump flat, so that a ring of upright birch saplings sprang every year from the trunk, as straight and as perfect as if they had been honed. But this was not an arrow-tree Tindr had stopped at. It looked like an ordinary birch, a little thicker than a man could encircle with both hands.

He squatted down and grunted softly as he looked at it, pointing to a black area of the bark. The boys knelt down next to him to see. It looked like a thickened, raised bit of bark; nothing more. A flat stone lay not far from the tree's roots, and Tindr walked about, gathering others and stacking them about the edges of it. Then he returned to the blackened bark on the birch. With his knife he cut a small piece of it away, and turned it in his hand. It was bright reddish brown within, and crumbled when he rubbed it with fingers and thumb. He set the piece on the stone, and drew from the pouch at his belt his steel fire-striker. In Angle-land flints were plenty, and both Ceric and Hrald could strike out sparks from them. Here on Gotland Tindr used a piece of milky-white quartz, a pretty thing in itself. He struck the quartz against the steel, holding it next to the crumbled bits he had taken from the tree. A spark flew from his striker and flared up, tiny but white-hot, in the reddish brown bits. It caught so quickly it was as if it had fallen on oil-soaked straw. He dropped a few strands of dried lichen upon it. The boys had never seen fire made so quickly nor with so much ease. They picked up bits of the red crumbles and rolled them in their fingers; they were almost moist, but this black-backed growth on the birch bark was best fire-starter one seeking warmth could hope to find.

The boys took turns with their own flints, sharply rapping sparks onto the tiny beds of red stuff, delighting at how it caught and held the spark, feeding it with more lichen and dried leaves. Tindr looked down at them kneeling before the flat rocks and saw their pleasure at what they had learned. They jumped up and looked at the black growth on the birch, looked about them to see if other trees bore it, came back and struck out more small fires, snuffing them out to light yet another. Tindr recalled his Uncle Rapp showing his cousin and him just this same skill, and he saw his younger self in them. His mother had told him these boys must leave when it was warm again. He would give them what wood-craft he could.

I WOULD
FLY AWAY

THE day came when Sidroc felt himself able to ride. The wound to his thigh had healed into a straight red seam, token of the bloody cut dealt by Godwin's seax. The red silk that his shield-maiden had stitched it with had rotted away, leaving only the puncture marks she had made with her needle. The leg was still sore, but he walked without limping. Lifting the leg over the saddle was a challenge, and he grimaced to think how dropping down off it would feel. But having been so confined to Tyrsborg he was restless, and the boys were, he knew, impatient for their promised horses. He and Tindr rode out with the boys to Ragnfast's, Hrald before him on his black stallion, Ceric behind Tindr on the dun mare. Ceric's mother and the little ones sent them off with smiles and waves. The yearling colt whinnied so when he saw his mother vanish along the forest path that Ceridwen winced; Sidroc had turned in his saddle at the colt's call and saw his shield-maiden's brow furrow at the way the colt raced along the paddock fence, calling after the mare.

Ragnfast and Estrid were ready for them. Their young ones crowded about Tindr, and Ceric and Hrald saw how welcome he was at his cousin's. Both boys were suddenly shy, and even Hrald, who understood the speech of Gotland far better than Ceric, said little. But the horses Ragnfast had selected for them to choose from stood waiting, and they went to them eagerly.

Ragnfast had picked out only geldings to show the boys; he had likely mares, and of a good size, but mares could be tricky, and as the boys would only be here until next Spring he wanted them to have the easiest mounts. On the other hand, a mare might come back to him carrying the foal of the good stallion he had sold Sidroc, which would be a gain. He could show the boys mares if asked for one. The dun with her ruddy mottled coat and dark stripe was one of the best he had ever owned, and he always liked seeing her again.

But the boys were happy with the horses Ragnfast had set aside for them. They were black, bay, and dark chestnut, and Sidroc let them choose for themselves. Hrald now rode a bay at home, and he chose one here, and Ceric a black, like onto the black yearling at Tyrsborg. Ragnfast did not ask much for a few month's use of the animals; they would be well cared for, and he was spared the expense of feeding them over the Winter to come. The silver he asked Sidroc for was more for the loan of the saddles and bridles.

Once horsed, the boys felt the island lay ready for them. Tindr took them up and down the coastline, and along such forest tracks as would admit a horse. There were two hills tall enough from which a fair amount of surrounding area could be seen, and they were free to roam wherever they wished. Unlike in Angle-land, there was no risk of Trespass; as long as they trampled no crops nor injured anything, they might ride anywhere.

※※※※※※※※※※

"You did well in bringing that letter from your mother."

Sidroc was within the hall, seated at the thick-boarded table with Hrald by his side. They were alone, and had been talking about the arrows Tindr was teaching the boys to feather.

In the weeks that had passed, this was the first time father had spoken to son about the events of his arrival. Each day had been full, and Hrald was always with Ceric, with Yrling following in their wake. Yrling had latched on to Hrald, and all could see the affection the small brother bore for the older. Just now the little ones were out with Ceric and Tindr, hunting up skogkatt kittens in the stable to give to the grain merchant on the road, who had end-less need of good mousers.

Hrald took this change of subject in stride, and nodded his grave little nod, the pointed chin bobbing quickly. "She told me I should guard it, but must give it up if I felt in danger."

Sidroc paused before he made answer. The thought of either boy being threatened by Kilton was not one he could dwell upon. "I am glad you did not."

He went on to ask the question that he must.

"Your mother, and your sisters . . . how do they fare?"

"Mother is at Oundle a lot, with grandmother, and Abbess Sigewif. I go with her too sometimes. Ashild is

. . . angry. She wanted to come with Ceric and me, and Mother would not let her."

To see me, or because Hrald and Ceric were going, he asked himself; Ashild wanted always to be in the thick of things. She is her father's daughter, he thought, and an image of his Uncle Yrling came into his mind. Strong-willed and impulsive, like Yrling.

"And the little one, Ealhswith?"

"She runs about so fast Burginde cannot catch her. Aunt Eanflad looks after her; Burginde says young legs are needed."

The smile faded from Hrald's face, and he asked a question of his own.

"Will you come back, father?"

It could not be more direct, and Sidroc could do nothing but stare. Hrald's blue eyes were locked upon him.

"I cannot come back," is how he answered. He had given the smallest, but decisive shake of his head. "Four Stones will be yours in a few years. Asberg and Jari will help you run it, as they do now. If Guthrum stays as King there should be peace enough."

None of this mattered to his boy.

"Then I would like to stay with you here, Father."

His answer was swifter than he wished. "You cannot. I spent twelve years winning my lands and treasure. You are the symbol of that in the eyes of the law."

Hrald kept looking at him, his blue eyes wide.

"But it is yours, not mine."

Sidroc looked away for one instant, then back at Hrald.

"You are my son. It is yours by birthright."

He sensed the thought Hrald held: It is what you wanted, not me. And in fact he had always known this first son of his to be less formed for war than for peace. As Ashild was her father's child, Hrald was his mother's.

"But you do not want it now." Hrald's judgement was as simple and bald as this.

"I do. It has cost me much to win, and hold. But I want it for you, for your mother and sisters, for Asberg and Jari and all the men who won it with me."

"But you will not come back?"

There was hope in the piping voice. His son's face was uplifted, looking at him. He held that gaze as he answered.

"I cannot. The Saxon king, Ælfred, will know by now I killed Kilton. The thegn, Worr, has told him, and even given the fairness of the fight, there will be anger over it, both with the King, and at Ceric's burh." He said these things with care, watching his son's face. "If the anger is great, there could be a blood-feud."

"Killing leads to more killing," Hrald answered, looking down a moment. He had heard his mother say it often enough.

Sidroc nodded.

Hrald's clear eyes went to the treasure room door. "The Lady Ceridwen . . . is she your wife?"

"Já," he said at once.

"But . . . mother?" Hrald was biting his lower lip, and now looked down at the planks of the table.

His father let out a slow breath. "The letter you carried – in it, your mother said that she released me. In Angle-land, if a man or woman is gone for five years, the marriage can be dissolved. In two more years your mother will be free to wed again."

Hrald's narrow brow was furrowed.

"Or she may to go to Oundle, and become such as Sigewif, or your grandmother."

The boy seemed to consider this a moment. "But you . . . you will not come back?"

"I cannot, Hrald. I cannot." His father looked away from him now.

Yrling and Eirian's laughing voices could be heard, and in a moment they stood before them, with a grinning Ceric, each holding a squirming kitten. Hrald jumped up and ran to them.

❧❧❧❧❧❧❧❧❧❧❧

They all went to the upland farm to see the goshawks. Eirian rode with her father, and Yrling with Tindr on a horse borrowed from Ragnfast; the dun mare which Ceridwen rode did not take lightly to the drumming of small feet on her withers. With Ceric and Hrald on their black and bay horses they made an impressive troop. Ceridwen, gazing on her daughter sitting before Sidroc, his arm wrapped about her for safety, could not help but travel back many years to when she rode thus with her uncle's thick arm about her. Seeing Eirian's bright smile from her perch told her the girl knew the same gladness she had felt when Cedd had taken her all along their lands on the banks of the Dee.

Ring and Astrid, little son on her hip, greeted them against a background of trees hanging heavy with the flushed cheeks of ripe apples. Ring kept two dogs to aid in the training of the goshawks, and these added their excited baying to the welcome. The boys, faces aglow, headed straight for the hawk-house. Ring spent part of each day, save when the hawks were in their moult, training up the birds within, and with his natural steadiness was well-suited for the patience it demanded. Ceric and Hrald donned gloves, as did Ring and Sidroc, and took each a goshawk upon their hands, grown birds for the boys, and younger for the men. The small brass bells upon the birds' yellow feet tinkled merrily each time they moved. Once in the open air Ring removed in turn the soft leathern hoods the goshawks wore.

They threw the lure out upon the ground, and watched each bird spring in one great motion after it, and then whistled for the bird to return to the gloved hand to snatch a morsel of raw meat. They walked into the grassy meadow beyond the apple groves with the hawks, and Ring sent the dogs running through the tall growth. Starlings feeding from the seed-heads leapt up, and at Ring's signal Hrald thrust the male he held into the air. It streaked from his wrist and had downed a bird in a few mighty wing strokes. They all walked to it, Ceridwen having to restrain the youngest from running. The tinkling bell alerted them to where the goshawk stood, wings outstretched, ripping into its prey. After it had flown back to Hrald's hand the process was repeated, and Ceric's big female stabbed a plump partridge which the dogs had flushed.

"They will take even large ducks, and the biggest hares," Ring told them as they looked upon the pair of great wings oaring their way back to Ceric's arm. The younger birds the men held were not flown, just carried about to acquaint them with hunting with groups of folk about them.

Afterwards Tindr and the boys spent a long while stroking the hawks' streaked breasts and wings, and even legs and talons, to help keep them tame.

"We will have at least three ready for Frankland," Ring assured Sidroc when the goshawks had been returned to their mews. Ring's elder brother Runulv had had great success in carrying the trained birds one at a time to this land of rich noblemen, and could find ready buyers for as many as Sidroc could send.

"I would like to go to Frankland," Hrald piped up. "There are many churches, made of stone there," he remembered from the stories Abbess Sigewif had told him.

"Já," agreed Ring, "and the city of Paris is beyond all others, my brother says. Perhaps one day you will go there yourself."

Hrald smiled a shy smile as if he were considering this thought.

"Why do they not fly away," Ceric wondered aloud as they readied themselves to leave. Their saddle bags had been packed full of juicy apples by Tindr when they were in the field.

It was Sidroc who answered. "Sometimes they do. But most come to accept the hawk-house as their home, with its warmth and protection. Also," he added, gesturing to Ring who cared for them, "here they know they will be fed each day, whether or not they make a strike."

"Like thegns in a hall at peace-time," nodded Ceric.

"I would fly away," said Hrald.

Tindr had taken the boys to a dry stream bed, rich in the white stones shaped like flower stalks and seashells. He had a fine collection of these curious stones, and had helped them in finding their own. Today the boys headed out alone on their horses to find more. The place lay on the other side of the trading road, and inland, and it was a day meant for both a ride and time spent turning over rocks, with a bright but not-too-hot Sun above. The ever-present breeze off the Baltic rippled the grasses near the stable as they saddled their mounts, and after Gunnvor tucked bread and cheese and apples into their saddle bags they were off.

There was no ship at the pier save a fishing boat, though the boys had been told that merchant knorrs sailed in every week during Summer. Such trading was ended this late in the season, but fishermen would go out for as long as the weather held. Still the trading road itself was busy, and the boys walked their horses slowly down the pounded road. Anyone appearing there on horseback was certain to be looked at, as only the rich kept horses, but by now all knew the boys, and nodded and smiled up to them as they passed.

At the end of the road they came upon the tall carved statue of Freyr. They eyed it, wordlessly. There was yet another animal stuck up in the prongs of the tall forks behind it, a goose.

"There is a figure like this," Ceric began, "a day's ride away from the hall of Kilton." He was going to say "on my uncle's lands" but stopped himself in time.

"Is it of Freyr?" Hrald wanted to know.

"Woden, I think. But it is all worm-eaten and falling to pieces."

Hrald could not help but give the carving a quick nod of his head, as he had seen Tindr do, but he had dropped a little behind Ceric before doing so, so he would not see.

Ceric rode ahead. They were now at the place of burial. The wooden cross marking Godwin's grave stood out; all the other markers were low rounded stones. They had walked or ridden past it several times, but always with others. Ceric released his grip on his horse, loosening the reins without really knowing it. The animal slowed. There were two tall upright stones marking the entrance to the burial place, a sort of portal, though there was no fence around it. Ceric's black gelding slowed further, waiting to know which way he should go. Hrald, behind him, slowed too. Ceric reined up before the stone uprights and got off his horse.

Hrald watched him walk to where the wooden cross stood. Hrald had stayed at Tyrsborg with his injured father when Godwin was buried, and again when Ceric had walked away carrying the big cross Tindr had made. Now he watched his friend stand before the cross and stare at it.

Ceric looked at the cross, at the big letters his mother had burnt into it. Rain had stained the new wood, with a few dark streaks, looking almost like tears, running from the letters of his uncle's name. He let his eyes drop to the soil, now settling after having been disturbed. Some broad green blades of grass had begun to push their way up amongst the rocky ground.

His uncle had been dead for almost four weeks. He knew his body was rotting in the binding sheet he had been wrapped in, just under his feet. He knew his body mattered not; it was the soul that mattered. He hoped his uncle was in Heaven.

His father had been dead so long he had little memory of him, just the white linen band wrapping his empty eyes, and his voice. It was a voice unlike his uncle's.

It had been Godwin who had truly raised him, Godwin who had romped and played with him when he was little, Godwin who taught him to sail in the little skiffs at the bottom of the Kilton's steep bluff. When his father and baby sister had died he had gone to live in the treasure room with Godwin and his aunt, to spare him from the fever his mother also raved with. It was Godwin who he was to have served as pledged man. It was Godwin who called him, in quiet moments, Chirp, a name no other used for him. He would not hear it again, he knew.

He fell on his knees. He pressed his hands together at his heart, then lifted the right to bless himself. He wanted to pray for his uncle's soul, and did not know how to.

When Hrald saw Ceric kneel he got off his horse. He walked to him and stood an arms-span off.

Hrald had only met Godwin of Kilton once, when he had brought Ceric to Four Stones. He knew his mother did not like Ceric's uncle, and he did not either. He remembered how his mother had wept as she readied him to make the trip to see his father. Ashild was making trouble because she wanted to go too, but she was a maid and could not. His mother had made him hide her letter in his pack, in a special lining Burginde had sewn, so that it could not be seen even if the pack were emptied out. Even so she made him promise he would give up the letter if Ceric's uncle frightened him.

Ceric loved his uncle, he knew that, and they had both stood there and watched as he fought and died. They had not spoken of this, and Hrald could not see how they could. His father had killed Ceric's uncle, and in front of them. His father did not want to fight; he had said so, but when Godwin of Kilton would not go, his father had told him he was going to kill him, and he did. He had been afraid Ceric would hate his father, or hate him, but somehow he did not.

Ceric was still praying, but Hrald could hear he was sniffling too. He did not know what to do, so he knelt down next to his friend. He crossed himself and began saying the Lord's Prayer, softly, but aloud. Ceric turned his head to him, and then began saying it with him.

When they had done they stood up and walked back to their horses, grazing on the grasses by the upright stones. After they had ridden a while Ceric spoke.

"I will always be your friend, Hrald, if you will always be mine."

CALL ON YOUR GOD

ONE morning Ceridwen watched Sidroc and the boys saddle and bridle their horses. He had been speaking to them as they did so, and she could see the excitement in the boys' eyes. Eirian was standing before her on the outdoor table, so she could more easily measure the hem-length for the new gown she was sewing up. Sidroc walked over to her, leading his horse, as the boys swung up in their saddles.

"Where are you heading," she asked with a smile.

"To see Berse," he said, in the same easy tone he used when something was serious.

It took her a moment to speak. Berse was the weapon-smith.

"Hrald has but ten years," is how she answered him.

Sidroc held his reins in one hand and idly slapped them against the palm of the other. His head turned back towards his son a moment.

"He is with me for this year only. I must teach him what I can."

There was nothing she could say to this. She felt herself swallow, and forced herself to smile.

"To get them . . . swords?"

He let out a short laugh. "Nai. They would only hurt their arms, and pick up bad habits through lack of strength. They can learn much with their knives. I will have Berse make them both shields, sized for their bodies, and spears too."

Eirian now leaned towards her father, spreading her skirt out between clenched fists as if to show it off.

"New," she beamed at him.

He reached over and stroked the bridge of her nose. "And pretty, for a pretty maid," he told her. Yrling popped out of the stable, saw the boys mounted and ready to ride, and began hopping up and down, holding his arms up, wanting to join them.

She laughed. "I will finish Eirian's gown, and take them both for a walk," she said.

She had to catch Yrling up to keep him from running after. He whined out his complaint, and it was Hrald who turned in his saddle and looked back at the child and waved to him. He has every sweetness of his mother, she thought, leading Yrling back.

Once at Berse's forge the weapon-smith did not blink at Sidroc's request. Here was a warrior who wanted to train his boys early, and provide them with the best kit. He looked the boys up and down, then measured their height and the length of their arms with his oiled leathern thong ticked over with measure-marks. Two ash spears and two iron-rimmed shields of linden wood, fitted for the boys, he was glad to provide. He made spears and knives for the men of Gotland, but nearly every sword he hammered out was destined for foreign trade. He had long ago repaired the shattered rim to the Dane's shield, and was happy for more local business now.

A week later Sidroc returned with Ceric and Hrald to pick up Berse's handiwork. They had their first lesson right there, how to mount your horse with your shield slung on your back.

"Tighten your chest strap so it cannot move. If it bumps your horse, he could startle, and run from you."

Both shields were of unpainted wood, with an iron handle inside the central boss for gripping, and a leathern strap to slip the fore-arm through for extra support. They were sized to protect the torso, from shoulder to hip, and thus were noticeably smaller than those for a man. Small as they were, the iron rimming made them heavy.

"You can paint the face of it as you like," Sidroc told them as they rode back to the hall. "You can blacken it with charcoal or pitch, then seal the blackening in with beeswax. You can use powdered limestone to whiten it; or there is a good red paint here, made from copper ore, the same the red-painted houses are brushed with." He was carrying both their new spears and would show them later how to secure them safely to the saddle while riding.

They began as soon as they arrived Tyrsborg, with shield-work, the boys holding their knives as if they were swords, and then their spears. Sidroc got his own black and white painted shield, and Ceric and Hrald flanked him as he moved.

"Fighting starts with the feet," he told them. "Stay light on your feet, knees slightly bent, to more easily swing the shield to ward off blows to the knee and legs, or lift it quickly to block a blow to the head."

He had them face each other, holding no weapon, just shadowing the other's move, watching and guessing which direction the shield would be lifted, and when. He

showed them how to use the shield itself as a weapon, both
to push men over or by catching them unawares with the
rim edge. Mindful of taxing their strength, he had them
put down the heavy rounds and turn their efforts to their
spears. Their thrown spear-work was good, both of them;
they threw with balance and form, though of course not
much strength. Both knew how to find that balance point in
the shaft where one should grip for the longest and surest
throw. Sidroc liked to incise a shallow line there, and tie a
thin strip of leather over it, so he could feel it in an instant,
even in the dark. He brought out his own spears, both the
light Idrisid one and the heavy Norse, to show them.

They took turns hurling their spears at the target
boards on the stable wall. Tindr came back from some
errand as they were doing so, and stopped to watch them.
Knowing how good he was with his bow made Ceric throw
his spear a little harder.

Afterwards they sat together at the outside table. The
target boards nailed up on the stable wall bore many fresh
gouges from their practice.

"You are good spears-men, both of you," Sidroc
praised, at which both boys straightened up a little on
their benches.

"You have watched Asberg well," he told his son.
"Asberg is one of the best with a spear that I have seen. We
fought many battles side by side. I have watched him clear
a path through men three deep." Hrald had in fact begun
to use a spear under his uncle's guidance, and was pleased
to know that his father held him in such esteem.

"And you," Sidroc went on to Ceric, "I think you have
learnt much from the warriors of Kilton."

This was uncertain ground; the chief warrior of Kilton had been of course Godwin, but with the boys staying with them for months he felt they must speak as freely as they could. He had said nothing to Ceric about the duel with Kilton, and did not intend to now. The boy had seen all, had even raised his own hand against his uncle's madness. There was naught to justify nor excuse.

Ceric was looking at him, and nodded. "Worr would practice with me, and Cadmar drills all the men."

At this name Sidroc could not keep from grinning. "The warrior-monk?" He gave a laugh. "He of the strong wrists. I am sure he bests all with a spear."

"Do you know him?" Ceric asked, in surprise.

"I met him at Kilton. I came there twice, the first time you were no bigger than Yrling."

Ceric recalled now being told this by his mother. His only memory was of playing with Ashild; he had none of Sidroc.

"The second time, when I met Cadmar, I came with my King, Guthrum, to celebrate the Peace with your King, Ælfred. There was feasting and gaming."

Ceric recalled this himself, how the Danes had come and sat at table with his Godfather Ælfred, his Uncle Godwin, and his father. The hall had been full of Danes; the Jarl of South Lindisse had been one of them.

Sidroc's own memory flicked back to that stay, but he did not let it linger there. He had come face to face with his shield-maiden at the grove above the burh, and she had given him her kiss. He looked back at her son.

"One night I took silver off of Cadmar at dice. Then he challenged me at arm-wrestling, and won it all back," he ended, with a grin. He paused a moment, the smile still on his face, thinking on all this.

"Never wine before a battle," he thought to tell them then. And no women, he would have added, were the boys just a few years older. "Nothing is worse than fighting with a bad head. Ale, já, of course; or one cup, only, of mead; no more. Save wine and mead for your return, when you show off your battle-gain, and drink to the dead."

In the days and weeks to come the boys practiced with Sidroc nearly every day. He had the boys spar with nothing but their spears in their hands, taught them to block and push, how to quickly drop the point and drive it home on a man's body or leg.

"You will always face warriors more skilled than you, with greater strength and experience. You are young; use your speed to your advantage. Bring your man down, then kill him. A quick thrust to the leg can disable a man, make him lower his shield or weapon, giving you your opening."

He showed them how to fight shield-to-shield, protecting each other as they advanced; and back-to-back as well, to work out of a melee.

"In the heart of any battle, men become panicked and confused. When you are young stay at the edges, where you can work your way to safety. From there you can pick out the weakest opponent, deliver a death blow to those wounded who might still be able to kill one of your brothers with a flung knife or axe. Staying alive is what matters. You are of no use throwing your life away; a dead man cannot kill."

He had them practice throwing their spears standing still, and at a run. He had them trip each other, tumble on the ground and grapple to gain advantage, striking with knees and elbows, pulling at hair or yanking at tunics to down each other. Hrald got his eye blackened, and Ceric a swollen bump on the forehead. Some nights both boys went to sleep with sore arms and shoulders, and neither would admit it.

"Before you head into battle, make sure all your clothing and kit is secure. Tighten your belt, and your weapons-belt. Re-tie your leg wrappings so they hold firmly. If your hair is long, braid it and tuck the braid into your tunic so it is not at hand to be grabbed at."

Sidroc was mindful not to push them to real injury, but mindful too of the passing of the weeks. By the time the cold weather was setting in he began sparring with them, facing them with his own shield and drawn seax or spear, as the boys countered with theirs. He had them both come at him at once, and showed how by staying light in his stance he could pivot his shield and disarm one of them with it while striking with his weapon at the other. He showed them all he thought they could absorb. Most of all, he told them what he knew.

"You can be a good warrior at twenty, and you will have boldness then. But you will not come to your full strength until you are five-and-twenty. If you live, the next ten will be your best fighting years. You will gain in strength, but much more will you gain in cunning. A cunning warrior uses every tool he has mastered to take his advantage over his enemy. Axe, spear, sword, shield, seax; já; but his mind.

"Each man has a style in which he fights. The older you are, the more battles you have seen, the faster you will see that style, know its strength and weakness. You will keep your head when others about you panic and show their fear. You will kill quicker, and cleaner, with less risk to yourself."

Being twenty was a full eight years away for Ceric, and twice Hrald's age. Both knew they would be given swords long before that, and likely have the chance to use them in battle, as Ceric's father and uncle had. But now they heard that these first few years would be those of greatest danger to them. Cadmar had taken his two sons into battle at sixteen and seventeen years of age, and seen them both slaughtered. Ceric knew that, but it was not until this scarred Danish warrior stood before him and suggested that he might not live to see his twenty-fifth year that the danger seemed real.

Sidroc was watching both boys' faces as he said this. Hrald was quiet by nature, and seemed to hang on every word his father spoke. Ceric was more likely to question, or by a slight shake of his coppery-curled head show that he wished not to believe what he had heard. Each boy now looked at him with fastened eyes as he went on. They had finished with their practice and stood by the stable wall, the boys still holding their spears, butt ends resting on the soil.

"Many times battle will swirl around you," he told them. "Men are screaming. You see your brothers be hacked down. Take a breath. Call on your God. Pick the man who catches your eye, make him your target."

Sidroc gazed on them, gravely looking back at him. Both boys would go into their first battle wearing ring-shirts and helmets. He had had no such protection when he started, and only won them later by stripping them off the bodies of the dead. He could see the golden chain around Ceric's neck, the one that held the cross concealed

beneath his tunic. His eye dropped to the silver and gold-
hilted seax at the boy's waist. He and Hrald would step
onto the field with a fine and showy war-kit; one that
would catch the eye of the warriors they faced. He knew
what he must say next.

"If the fighting grows thick around you, and you lose
your nerve, drop your sword. It is better to be held to
ransom than slain through your uncertainty."

He said this in the same flat tone that he gave all his
instruction, without judgment or censure.

Ceric was quick in his rejection. "I would never do
that. That is a great dishonour."

He had pushed his spear shaft a little away from him,
as if thrusting away Sidroc's words.

Sidroc paused before he answered. "I have," he told
the boy.

"I was young, one of my first battles. I had got separated from my kin, could not see them. My hamingja –
my luck-spirit – was frightened. It was leaving me, fleeing,
just as I wanted to. I dropped my sword before the man I
was fighting. He grinned at me, saw I was young. He bent
to pick up my sword; it was a good one. It was then I killed
him with my knife."

He watched the boy's face, knew what he was thinking. "It was not treachery. He made a mistake. I saw it and
turned it to my advantage."

Ceric took a breath, but slowly nodded his assent.

Sidroc stood, looking at the two, their smooth faces
and wide eyes looking back at him. Hrald had a tuft of
brown hair on top of his head that stood up; he had had
it since he was a toddling boy. Ceric was just beginning to
show the sort of frame he would possess as a man, broad

of chest, but not tall. At ten and twelve he was teaching them how to kill. His shield-maiden was right, they were but boys. But he was right as well. He must teach them what he could, now, years before he hoped they would need it.

He could see them, ten years hence, fully armed in their war-kits. Their lands were on the other side of Angle-land from each other; Ceric's far to the West, in the Kingdom of Wessex, and Hrald's in Lindisse, under the Dane-law held by King Guthrum. He could not imagine how, after this year together with him, they could ever meet again. Only war could do that.

He spurred himself and went on.

"You will enter the field with your friends. Once you have fought a few battles with them they will be unto brothers to you. You will see them get hit, go down. You will see them get killed. It will sicken you, or you will feel fury. You must master yourself and not grow reckless. If your anger fuels your fighting, let it loose. But gauge well. Going after the man who killed your friend could mean your own death. Or it could mean the glory of avenging him.

"Later, when you drink to the dead, your brothers who have fallen – be glad for them. They are taken by the shield-maidens to the halls of the Gods, or by your angels to Heaven. Either way you will see them soon."

Both boys swallowed.

"After you fight you will feel the battle-sickness. A taste like metal in the mouth, your belly churning, your mind as if you rode the fastest horse; Odin's Sleipnir himself. You may retch. It is from what you have seen, and done. It will pass. With time it will lessen. But you will always feel it, each time you face death, each time you kill."

"What . . . about berserkrs?" Ceric made bold to ask. "Some men cannot be killed."

It was Sidroc's turn to pause. "Já," he agreed. He had seen this, seen a warrior fight with crazed power: Godwin, as he mowed down men on his way to kill his uncle, Yrling.

And he had fought that way himself; felt the bear-spirit enter his own breast. His shield-maiden had watched one instance of it, the time he fought at sea with Danes, against Danes, to win their way here.

"Some men cannot be killed," he admitted. "If the bear-spirit enters them, they will kill with such ferocity that no man can stop them. A thrown spear or axe is your best chance, but even this they will deflect or dodge."

Now Hrald spoke. "Can you run?" he asked, his voice tremulous.

His father took it with the seriousness it warranted.

"You will know what to do. Even if your hamingja is fearful, your fylgja – your guardian spirit – " he said for Ceric's benefit, "will guide you, tell you whether to run, or whether you must stay and face your Doom."

Later, at dusk, Ceric and Hrald were helping Tindr carry in more firewood. As they stood under the darkening sky by the stacked wood piles, Ceric spoke.

"Hrald, the spirit your father spoke of," he wanted to know, "the guardian one . . . is it like an angel, to us? Does he have one of those, and we don't, because we are Christian?"

"The fylgja," Hrald repeated. His father had told him of all this long ago, told his big sister Ashild too. After his father had vanished he had mentioned his fylgja to Wilgot the priest, telling him he hoped she would take care of his father, wherever he was. Wilgot had clicked his teeth at Hrald, shook his head and told him this was error and belief in magic; Christians had angels to guard them if they were good, and they were not female, but without sex.

Hrald knew that his father was not truly Christian; he had seen him make Offering at the sacrifice pit at Four Stones. He did not know what more to say to Wilgot, so said nothing.

Hrald had taken a long time to answer, and now Ceric spoke for him. "I would rather have an angel, with a sword in his hand, as we do," he declared.

That night when Ceric was in his alcove he thought more of what they had heard that day. Everything about the Dane surprised him. He told them that he had been afraid in battle and had wanted to quit. Then he killed the Saxon who had spared his life. Ceric knew this was what being cunning was. He knew too that Sidroc had used his cunning to help kill his uncle, who was one of the best fighters in Angle-land, weak shield arm or not.

Call on your God, the Dane had told them; when you are panicked in battle, call on your God. He knew one of the runes inside Sidroc's shield was that of the warrior God Tyr. That was the God the Dane called upon.

His hand went to his chest, and the golden cross that his father had worn. It was a gift from the King he had served, and whom he would serve. It was the cross of the God he served, as well.

IS THIS TREASON

MINDFUL that the boys not forget their letters, Ceridwen asked Tindr to build a shallow wooden tray. This she filled with melted beeswax, and so had a wax-tablet for their use. She was grateful for it herself, for it was much easier to scribe the alphabet in wax than the smoothed ashes of the cooking-rings.

Ceric had ever been good at forming letters, and his efforts had won praise both from Dunnere at Kilton and Sigewif at Oundle. Now Hrald, whose practice parchment at Oundle she remembered being blotted with his inky thumbprints, had gained in ability as well, so that only the smaller size of Ceric's letters betrayed his greater skill. She took pride in the fact that both boys wished to read and write with ease; few enough of the folk at Kilton could, and nearly none at Four Stones. Only Wilgot the priest and now Ælfwyn wrote and read there, and unlike Kilton, there were no books. Sidroc she knew could point out his name, or hers, upon a parchment, but signed himself with the single rune Sigel. He knew the runes, but the laws and records of Angle-land were written not in this ancient scribing but in the alphabet of the Saxons. Here in Gotland there was no written speech save that of runes.

The boys took turns writing in the tablet, one holding a sharpened stick as stylus while the other dictated what was to be written. In this way they had practice in their spelling as well. When the wax was filled it was smoothed over with the bottom of a small pan warm from the kitchen yard.

One noon-tide when she had left them to minister to a crying Yrling's skinned knee she returned to hear Ceric reciting a prayer. Hrald's dark head was bent over the tablet, and he was digging away in the golden wax as quickly as he could follow his friend's words. She felt a pang at this; she had not, in good conscience, asked the boys if they said their prayers each morning and night; not when she herself could not join them. They had been away from any Mass or chanted prayer for many weeks. Listening now she heard the ardency of Ceric's voice. When he had stopped Hrald remained bent over his work for a few moments longer, his tongue poking out of the side of his mouth as he studied his work. "Amen," he said, adding this final word as well.

<hr />

Ceridwen and Ceric walked down to the trading road. His boots were worn, and she did not wish to ask Tindr to make him a pair, not with the additional duties which had been thrust on him, so they went to the workshop of the shoe-maker. There was goat hide or cow hide he could offer, the latter in either brown or black. The leather was dressed, and Ceric wished he could have boots of boar hide such as Tindr wore, but chose black cow hide as the next best thing. The shoe-maker drew an outline of his feet, and promised they would be ready in a few days. His old boots, those they were replacing, were brown, and Ceridwen wondered without asking if Ceric now wished for black, as that is what his Uncle Godwin wore.

Outside the stall they passed a family she did not recognize, with three girls, one about Ceric's age. She had long, straight, dark golden hair and deep sea-blue eyes. She was laughing about something with her sisters, and when she lifted her head and saw Ceric, she smiled.

"A pretty maid," Ceridwen noted as they walked on. Ceric paused and then looked back after the maid; he had not noticed her as she had.

"Ashild is prettier," he judged.

His mother gave a little laugh. "Ashild has a beauty for a mother," she answered, but her heart had skipped a happy beat. There was little Ceric could have said to give her as much pleasure as his naming Ashild in this way. Ever since the two had met as toddling babes, she had hoped they would grow to love each other. She remembered them in their first play, stuffing sprigs of thyme into the other's mouth outside the bower house of Kilton. Later he had the full Summer with her and Hrald, when he was nine. And Ceric had spent almost a week at Four Stones before setting sail for Gotland, more than enough time for the two to reacquaint themselves now.

Ceric thought of his mother's words. Ashild's mother was gentle and nice, but tall and thin. Ashild was sturdy, which he liked, and a good rider, and not afraid to get dirty. The Summer he had spent at Four Stones she was always getting scolded for running off at play with Hrald and him. She was hard to scare and did not scream like other maids if you threw a toad at her; she had thrown it right back at him, and it had hit him in the face, which had made her laugh. When he had seen her again before they left to come here she had grown a lot, but he knew he had too.

"About Ashild," his mother thought to add. "Do you know that Sidroc is not her father, as he is Hrald's?"

"Já," he said with a nod, which made his mother smile. When they were alone they sometimes spoke the tongue of Angle-land, or a mixture of the two, and were doing so now, but he had answered her in Norse, which he was working to learn.

"She told me, and Hrald told me too. Her father's name was Yrling, the same as your Yrling, and he was a war-chief." He thought a moment more. "She has a talisman from him, a silver hammer of Thor. She showed it to me."

"And . . . did she tell you how her father died?"

"He was killed."

She took a swift breath, and knew she must go on. "Já. Yrling was killed by your Uncle Godwin."

They were nearly to Rannveig's brew-house now, and he stopped before it.

"Yrling was Sidroc's uncle," she told him. "He watched Godwin do it."

"Why?" was all he asked. "Was it in battle?"

She nodded. "In battle. Yrling was fighting to win the burh at Cirenceaster, Lady Ælfwyn's home. Godwin found him there and killed him, but not for that. He killed him because he thought Yrling had something to do with your father's maiming."

"Did he?"

"Nai. All Yrling had done was accept your father at Four Stones after he had been blinded. You have heard how your uncle sought revenge."

Ceric had, many times. Godwin's vengeance on Hingvar was sung of by the scop at table, and all the thegns knew of it; some of them had even gone with him. He had never known about the death of Ashild's father as well.

"Uncle killed Sidroc's uncle, Yrling," he repeated. "Ashild's father. And then Sidroc killed my uncle."

"Já," she answered, softly. "There were years of enmity between them."

"And Sidroc is Hrald's father," Ceric went on, his voice trailing off. "My friend."

His head jerked. "Ashild . . . does she know this?" He answered himself. "I know she does not." He had turned to her, eyes burning. "She does not know my uncle killed her father."

She waited a moment before she spoke again. "Lady Ælfwyn knows; I told her long ago. And it was I who sent her the silver hammer of Thor. She must feel that telling Ashild will serve no purpose."

The wooden slab bench near the end of the pier was empty, and Ceridwen walked to it now. This was much to take in, and she hoped they could sit together before returning to the hall. Ceric came with her, and sat down. There was no ship tied at the pier, and their eyes went out across the expanse of the Baltic. The light wind caused narrow ripples of white foam to be pushed towards them, like torn and looping threads of linen. A flock of dark sea ducks that bobbed not far out began squawking and flapping their wings, then rose in noisy action, taking flight over their heads.

"Mother," he said at last. "Godwin of Kilton is dead. My place there . . . has it changed?"

Before she could begin to answer he spoke again.

"I know my brother Edwin is heir; you and father gave him to Godwin to be so. I know I will be his pledged man."

She was looking at the profile of his face as he said this.

"But I am four years older than he. Will I not become heir to Kilton now? Edwin is no different than me; we are sons of you and father. Why should I not be heir now?"

Her mouth had gone dry.

Now that Ceric had begun along this path, he followed it.

"Why . . . did you not give me to Godwin and Edgyth, to be their son? I was older and would be fit to fight for Kilton sooner. Instead you gave Edwin, who was just a babe."

She was no longer looking at the line of Ceric's forehead and nose; she was looking out upon the water. The Sun came out from behind a thin scrim of cloud. Its rays were focused on the cresting top of a distant wave, and dazzled her.

He was troubled enough by her silence that he turned to her.

"Is this . . . treason?" he asked. She was forced to look at him, and watch the eyelashes sweep down over his green eyes.

"Nai, nai," she forced herself to say. Her words were almost hoarse, coming as they did from the pit of her belly.

"You are right to question," she said, trying to make strong her voice. "Your father and I could not give you, Ceric; we could not."

He saw tears begin to run from the inner corners of her eyes. She did not lift her hand to wipe them away.

"You were our first-born . . . we could not give you, not for Kilton's sake, nor anyone's."

She was crying freely now, and had lowered her head. He did not understand how he had made her cry so. It was not as if she had given a child to be taken far from her; Edwin was raised just as he had been, at the keep.

"Now that Uncle is dead, would it not be best for me to be heir?"

She was swallowing back her tears, trying to compose herself.

"There was a ceremony," she reminded him, "you were there; I think you might recall it. Dunnere was there to bless Edwin, and bless his becoming Godwin's son.

"Wills have been written," she went on, "both your uncle's and your aunt's, naming Edwin as their son and heir."

"But he is no different than me. Naming him changes nothing. He is the same as me. Their wills name me, the older one, as second."

She had no answer for this. She wiped her cheeks with her hand as he warmed to his own words.

"And I will be ready to fight for Kilton, and for Ælfred, long before Edwin."

"You are eager to return," she asked, when she could speak again.

"Yes," he answered, pointed in his use of the Saxon word. "I want to be with you this year, but Kilton is my home, and my duty."

She tried to smile. "You are young to speak of duty, Ceric. Give yourself more time before it is forced upon you."

"There could be war again, and soon," he returned. Of a sudden he sounded not like a boy of twelve, but eighteen years.

"Who says this?" she asked. It had been no small measure of comfort that peace had held throughout much of Angle-land, with it divided between the King of the Danes, Guthrum, and King Ælfred.

"Cadmar. Worr. And most of all, Uncle. The peace is broken all the time in small ways, by Danes looking to take what they can."

There were skirmishes amongst those Danes who had already settled in the lands of the Angles and Saxons, she knew that; there were always those who grew discontent and wanted more. Nor had those who had been displaced forgotten it.

"Hrald is your best friend, is he not?" she reminded him. "He is a Dane."

"Half," he corrected.

She nodded, went on. "But he will rule a Danish keep, a great one."

"Hrald is different," he conceded. "Others could come, from across the sea."

"Did you hear this from your uncle, as well?"

"All say it." A long moment went by. "Father is dead," he said. "Now Uncle, who should have lived a longer life. And Edwin is little."

"Ceric," she ventured, not knowing quite how to voice her question. "You know that your uncle is dead through his own actions?"

He looked down at the grey-white stone at his feet, and rolled a few pebbles under his sole. Before Worr had left, he had taken Ceric aside. Besides his uncle, Worr was the man he trusted most. One of the things he had told him was that his uncle had died in a fair fight. "You saw it yourself," he had told him. He said something else: It did not matter how great a warrior Godwin was. All warriors will die in battle if they fight long enough.

His mother was still looking at him, and he looked back. For answer he nodded. They stood, and began climbing the hill to Tyrsborg.

That night Ceridwen awakened. The Moon was just past full, and shining in a silver beam through the window high on the wall of the treasure room. She pulled herself up and looked at the pool of light greying the floor boards. She did not know why she had awakened. No dream had troubled her, nor night-bird called. Sidroc shifted next her; he too was awake. Sometimes when she awakened so, she merely turned to him and clung, until she felt she could sleep again. Tonight she looked out into the empty light of the treasure room, and was silent. He would wait, she knew, for her to speak.

"The boys," she asked, her voice a whisper. "What will become of them?"

She could feel him give a slow shake of his head. "Their Fate was cast, long ago. How they work with that Fate will decide the rest."

She gave a small sigh, and he went on.

"Ceric will be second at Kilton, and if his brother dies, first. Hrald will rule Four Stones. That is what they were born to. What more will happen will depend on the Gods – both theirs and ours," he added, with a slight laugh, "and how they can seize the chances that come their way."

A long time passed before she spoke again.

"Ceric asked why he should not be first at Kilton, now his uncle is dead. He is the older, he argued, and will be ready to fight before his brother Edwin."

"And he is right, save for one fact," was how he answered. His voice was low, and held a gentleness he rarely used.

His thoughts dwelt on Ceric, though he said no more.

If he did not know the boy, he would be mindful of something happening to the younger brother, some accident that rendered him unfit or even dead. He could not picture Ceric toppling his young brother into a well, or forcing his horse to bolt. But such things happened often enough in great families that his shield-maiden would know of them.

"There is only one who could make that decision," she went on. "The King himself. Only Ælfred could deem it best that the Lord of Kilton be the one, and not the other."

He would not counter this, despite what he had just been thinking.

"I . . . I do not want Ceric to be chosen as heir," she whispered. There in the dark her thoughts had carried her back years ago, to when threat of Danish attack at Kilton had her asking Modwynn if Ceric would not be safer dressed as any boy, so fearful was she of marking him, through his rich clothing, as the son of the hall, and thus a prize target.

She shook her head to herself. It little mattered to his safety if Ceric was heir, or second in line. To down or capture the lord of any keep was always the goal in battle, and it was the sworn duty of his pledged men to sacrifice their lives to save his. Either way he would be at the centre of any combat.

She asked now what she dreaded asking. "What . . . what if the Peace does not hold?"

"It has held so far; Guthrum is strong in his desire to maintain what he has won, and Ælfred has been skillful in holding what he could." He spoke with care, but with the truth as he saw it.

"It is not in our hands, shield-maiden. Our parts have been played in Angle-land. Our life is here."

She made no response, and he listened to her quiet breathing. Her mind was full of questions he could not answer. He could fix none of this, no matter how much he wanted to ease her heart. He moved his hand from his side. It brushed against the seam of the long scar on his thigh. His finger spent a moment, tracing the length of its raised surface, this scar he would bear until the day of his death.

"Come over here," he murmured, as he turned and pulled her onto his chest.

GAME
GREAT AND SMALL

CERIC and Hrald had been practicing shooting with their new bows. Tindr had drawn a deer upon the target boards hammered to the stable wall, and Sidroc had taken up charcoal and sketched a rough outline of a man's figure. The archers of Angle-land were renowned, and both boys had had small bows and blunted arrows for a few years. Tindr had shown them how a blunt arrowhead could kill a bird or rabbit, just from impact, and with no tearing of the skin. The bows he had made them were almost man-size, and he had forged arrowheads for them as sharp as his own.

Today Sidroc had been watching them as they practised. He had handled the bow himself, but felt no call to it as weapon; the sort of fighting he had always done was face to face and hand to hand, though he had seen firsthand the damage the archers of the fyrd of Ælfred had inflicted on his brothers in some of the larger pitched battles.

"There is much to be said for killing from afar," he noted, when the boys had come and laid their bows and

309

quivers upon the table. He gestured with his head to the quantity of arrows bristling from the boards on which he had drawn the target-man. Ceric had wearied of their practice before Hrald, though he had kept on with it until the younger boy was ready to quit. Shooting well took a kind of inner calmness which Sidroc thought his son might possess, and in abundance. Ceric, at least at this age, found it more difficult to slow his breathing and steady his aim.

"At Kilton our archers killed lots of Danes within the palisade walls, when we were attacked at Twelfth Night," Ceric said, with a boy's simplicity in saying this to a Dane. "Our archers are the best in Wessex," he ended.

"Já," Sidroc nodded. "I have seen their work myself, upon the field at Ethandun." His mind flicked back to that greatest of battles, which led to the Peace between Guthrum and his Danish host, and Ælfred and his. He followed his thoughts in his next words to them.

"Whether you fight with bow, with spear, or sword, if you win the field the dead and dying will lie around you. Kill the dying with your spear, or any thrust through the breast."

He had tapped his own chest here. Ceric and Hrald listened, their eyes going from his chest to his face.

"If . . . if the man is not dying, but wounded . . . ?" his son asked.

Sidroc paused. "You will have to judge. Needless killing is never good. If he is disarmed and disabled, not able to fight, but not in agony from his wound, there are Gods who will reward you for sparing him." He grinned now at them. "Yours is one of them."

He returned his thoughts to the lesson at hand.

"Be wary stripping battle-gain. It is easy to be killed if you are distracted by what you think you have won. Judge quickly, and strip quickly. Swords first; you know they are most valuable. A good helmet is my next choice, and any man with such will also have a good sword, likely pattern-welded. Ring shirt – já, costly indeed, but you will be wearing one already, and they are heavy. They take time to remove. Jewellery next, unless it is gold; strip gold first. Any warrior with gold about his wrists or neck will have a war-kit to match."

Ceric's hand went to his tunic, and the golden cross hanging beneath it. His uncle never went into battle with any show, his ring-tunic blackened, an unworked helmet, a plain scabbard hiding his fine sword. Ceric would do the same. He would wear the golden cross, but keep it well hidden.

Sidroc saw this slight movement, and went on.

"Silver arm-bands and cuffs, of course; and all jewellery has the advantage of being small and light in weight."

He thought a moment longer, recalling his own actions after a battle. These two would have no need to strip a man for clothing and boots, as he had often done when he began. The first few times he fought he scavenged even food from the field; he and Yrling and Toki had had to take whatever they could.

"Do not bother to cut away a man's purse unless you have the gift of time. Men will go into battle with gold around their necks but almost nothing in their belts. I do not know why, but I have seen it myself."

The boys took this all in, wide-eyed, but silent. He was telling them things he had learnt through practice, and through hardship, things that he saw older warriors do. He felt he could do no less, for what Hrald meant to him, and Ceric to his shield-maiden. Both boys would receive hard and long training in arms when their bodies were ready. The more they knew now, the better equipped to bear that training, and the realities of the battle field.

A song bird had been chattering away over their heads, high in one of the spruce trees, and now dipped down near them, almost landing on the end of the table before swooping back to its perch. They all looked at its path before it vanished.

"How many men have you killed," Ceric asked. His green eyes had fallen from the dark boughs of the tree top to Sidroc.

He jolted a little, inside, without showing it. His shield-maiden had once asked him this. Those who had never killed a man always wanted to know how many you had.

"Killed outright – five and fifty," he said. The two sea battles he had fought to win their way to freedom had greatly added to this grim sum.

That was almost the number of thegns at Kilton. Ceric repeated the number in his head. He knew that the last would have been his own uncle, Godwin of Kilton.

⁂

"I do not think I can do it, father," Hrald said to him.

Sidroc was alone with his son in the treasure room next day. He looked at the boy, his question on his face.

"I do not think I can fight. And kill."

He beheld the boy's face, the pointed chin and lifted eyebrows that recalled his mother, the dark hair that recalled he himself. Hrald stood motionless before him, his blue eyes widening as he looked to his father for help.

"I want to be like Tindr, walking the woods and bringing back food for all. I think Tindr could live in the woods. I want that too."

"You cannot be like Tindr, Hrald."

His father gave a single shake of his head, meant for himself. He had shown too much, told too much. He had frighted the boy, when he meant only to make him stronger. "You have but ten years, Hrald," he went on.

"You will not fight for a long time, years." Hrald's eyes were steady, taking this in. "And if the Peace holds, you may not need to fight at all."

He thought what more he could say. He could not tell Hrald that when he went into battle he would be surrounded by his pledged men, Asberg on his right, Jari on his left, as Ceric would be. That was not the way Danes fought. It was every man for himself; even war-chiefs knew this, and took the same chances upon the field as his least follower. The times Danes fought together were rare, and often due to the bond between uncle and nephew and father and son.

"I do not want to kill anyone," is how his boy answered. Hrald saw the look on his father's face, a grave look of wonder. Hrald knew he must speak again lest he begin to cry.

"What you did to Ceric's uncle . . . I could not do that. I could not."

His father took a slow breath. "He would have killed me, if I had not killed him first," he answered. His boy must have seen the justice in that. He kept his tone measured, one of explanation and not defense.

Hrald said nothing.

"If you are threatened, if you are attacked, you must strike out." Here he raised his hand to his head and ran his fingers through his hair. "It is ugly, I know. It was not my wish that you and Ceric saw it. But I want you to know how to fight, to protect yourself, and your mother and sisters."

He could not tell a boy of ten what would have happened to his wife if Kilton had been the victor. Hrald had lowered his eyes, the dark fringe of lashes casting a spiked shadow on his round cheek. He did not answer.

"Is this the doing of Wilgot, and your time at Oundle, with Sigewif?" As little as he thought of him, he did not wish to speak ill of the priest, not when the boy's mother put such store in him. Even less would he speak against the Abbess of Oundle, a woman of capability who ruled her doubled convent with wisdom worthy of her royal blood.

"Have they told you . . . it was wrong to fight?" he hazarded.

Hrald shook his head. "Wilgot blessed us all before we left, and both Ceric's uncle and Worr told us we could be attacked at sea . . . or when we landed."

The boy's eyes glided around the chests and baskets lining the walls of the room. "The treasure at home, the land, all of it," he went on. "It is all from killing men, is it not?" It was a child's question, not the accusation of a man.

"Five and fifty, that is what you told us yesterday."

The boy let his eyes drop once more. "I do not want to kill even one man."

His father too looked about the room; Hrald saw the dark eyes shift as if he looked for something.

"When I was your age I had nothing. My mother was a serving woman who left me with my father. His wife did not like me. Then he went out in his boat and did not come back."

He heard himself say these things, knowing it could mean but little to Hrald. Yet it struck him how alike their boy-hoods had been in this wise. Hrald the elder had sailed off one day, never to return, just as he had vanished by sea, through kid-nap, leaving his own son father-less.

"I went to Angle-land with my uncle, Ashild's father," he went on. "There was no place for me in my homeland, and I worked and fought hard for all I won."

Hrald's blue eyes were unblinkingly set on him. At his age he had no choice. He had a young and reckless uncle who gave him a home, and who would, a few years later, be urging Sidroc to join him in making their way in a new land.

He bethought him that it was killing for plunder that most troubled the boy. And indeed, it was often the killing he had done simply for gain that awakened him in the nights. "What I fought for – silver, treasure, land, horses – you do not need to fight for," he tried. "These things are given you."

He found himself looking up, as if for answers.

"You have only ten years, Hrald. You are a young boy, still. In a few years you will feel differently.

"If someone tries to take what you have from you, you will fight to keep it," he ended.

Just as those you killed tried to keep you from taking what they had, his son thought.

Sidroc did not call the boys to practice that day. Next afternoon when the three of them met Hrald fought with seeming commitment. He knew he had disappointed his father. He also knew his father would not be there at his side when he would be forced to fight his first battle.

seeming commitment. He knew he had disappointed his father. He also knew his father would not be there at his side when he would be forced to fight his first battle.

Tindr brought home a deer. He had left in the dark and not broken his fast with the family. Ceric and Hrald set a look-out for him, perching in the hay loft in the stable, where they could see out a crack between the upright timbers of the wall facing the forest.

The Sun was fully risen when they spotted him. In his dull hunting garb of green and brown he was not easy to see amongst the like-coloured trees. He had brought his take, for he dragged it along behind him in the leathern sling strapped to his waist. The boys scrambled down to meet him as he pulled it along into the kitchen yard.

His bow was on his back and his quiver slung over his shoulder. His hair was braided, the way he always wore it when he hunted. The boys swarmed him and he grinned at them with a small grunt as he released the sling from his waist. Gunnvor was bending over the cook-fire, banking up coals, and she straightened and smiled at him. Yrling broke from the hall door and ran out, Eirian at his heels.

They could see the long and slender legs of the deer, but much of its body was hidden by the flap of leather that covered it. Tindr knelt down and pulled it back. It was a stag with four prongs on each antler. Tindr looked down at the red coat and laid his hands upon the stag's muscled neck. The boys saw this, and also the single puncture between the ribs.

It was larger than the deer the boys had seen at home, and they knew from the racks of antlers about the hall and stable that Tindr had taken greater still. Both of them had dropped on their knees on the other side of the stag's body. Hrald put his hand out, and touched the deer's flank. It was still warm.

Tindr, watching him, nodded gravely at the boy. He lifted his open hands before them, the backs first, and then palms. There were runes drawn in charcoal on both; those on his palms were too smudged to read.

"Will you take us out?" Ceric asked. "To hunt with you?"

He pointed to Hrald and to himself, and made the motion of pulling back a bow string.

"Please," said both boys together, cupping their hands in the bowl shape they knew meant this word.

Tindr looked into the beseeching faces. Their aim was not true enough for them to go after deer. New as they were, they were likely to wound and not to shoot true to heart and lungs. And his taking of these woodland creatures was between him and the Lady. He must be alone to down a deer, and first he must awaken being called to do so. Even then he did not always return dragging his sling. Sometimes he saw the deer, but something stopped him from nocking his arrow, some thought that this stag was better left for another time. Once a great hart stood a long time in his view, and he could not pull back the string. As he lowered his bow he saw a flash of white out of the tail of his eye, and the hart bounded after it. The Lady in the guise of hind had called the hart, just as she as Lady of the Forest had called him.

He shook his head, still looking into the boys' faces. He crossed the clenched fists of his hands at the wrists, while nodding to the stag which lay beneath them. Their faces fell. He pointed now to the small pouch of squirrel fur which Hrald wore at his belt, and turned his head to his workbench, where some of the rabbit pelts they had snared lay drying. Then he made the gesture of fitting an arrow to a bow, and grinned to the boys.

"He will take us shooting, but for rabbits and squirrels," Ceric read.

Hrald looked down at the single wound in the deer's red fur, and remembered the look of the many deer he had seen brought back to Four Stones, pierced with multiple spear points.

"Not until we can shoot as well as he does," he said.

The boys nodded back, and again cupped their hands. Tindr grinned and nodded, pointed to the Sun, then made his sign for tomorrow, his finger turning in a circle.

The Sun had just begun to crack the sky when Tindr met the boys in the kitchen yard. They had laid out their kit the night before, their bows and charged quivers, and had filled their water skins. Gunnvor had packed them bread and strips of dried pig. They were eager to begin their day, but Tindr led them first to a basin of water he poured from a pail. He threw the water upon his face, rubbed his hands over it, and then lifted the water several times, letting it fall through his fingers. He dried his face and pointed to Ceric to go next.

"Why must we wash to go into the woods, where we will just get dirty?" he asked. But Tindr pointed again to the basin, so he did it. The water was so cold it made him gasp. Hrald went next, and both boys were glad for their wool tunics and warm mantles to counter this dousing.

Tindr moved next to the cook-fire, where he drew out a fragment of charcoal. He gestured the boys to him, and took first their left and then their right hand into his, scribing the straight lines of runes upon the backs.

"It is one of the runes he wears, Feoh, for wealth, or cattle," Hrald said, looking down at his left hand, and Ceric's too. He knew from his father that Tindr revered the Goddess Freyja, and he knew it was her rune too, but did not mention that aloud. "And this is Gyfu, gift – he is asking we be given the gift of game."

Neither boy came home with a rabbit nor squirrel that morning, and Hrald lost an arrow in the trees shooting after a big hare. But Ceric spotted deer tracks by a creek whose water had a thin skim of ice on it. Stepping into a clearing they saw a goshawk soar ahead, the wild kin of those at the apple farm. Hrald found some of the black and red tinder bark on a birch tree, and the three of them warmed their hands at a little fire they kindled. The boys came back to Tyrsborg hungry and happy and chilled through and ready to go out again next day. In the weeks that came both boys shot rabbits with blunted arrows, and had unblemished pelts to show for it. Squirrels, scolding them from over their heads, were harder, and both boys let fly arrows that it took a long time to retrieve. When a layer of snow covered the ground they saw a fox hunting mice in it, leaping into it headfirst and coming up with the small morsel in its snow-frosted jaws. The beauty of its red fur caught Ceric's eye, and he raised his bow at it. But Tindr stopped him. You cannot eat fox, he gestured with a grimace. Do not kill what you cannot eat.

CHAPTER THE TWENTY-SIXTH

WINTER

THE days were much shorter now, and Blót, that blood-month of sacrifice had come. In Angleland it was the time of slaughter, when animals which could not be kept over the Winter were butchered. Pigs that had fattened on the nuts and acorns of the woods, sheep too young or too old to survive on Winter fodder with any hardiness, and geese who had grown huge on the rich seed-heads of Summer grasses were rendered up. Their meat was salt-dried, brined, and smoked, and also eaten fresh; it was a month of abundance before Winter's sparseness, not to be relieved until the few feasts at Winter's Nights.

On Gotland all this was true, and more, for alongside the culling and feasting each family, rich or poor, made what Offering they could to their Gods. The taking of life was made sacred by that portion given directly as a thank-offering for the bounty of the year past, and was given too in supplication as folk headed into uncertain Winter and its dangers and hardship.

There was no one day on which Offering was made. Most chose any day of the waxing Moon, as most certain to ensure increase. That was the time when the family of

Tyrsborg made their Offering. Some along the trading road had already done so, coming to the great carved figure of Freyr to kill a beast in the view of his wide painted green eyes. Others had hoisted the bodies of fowl or goat or pig onto an Offering rack at the gable peak of their houses, lifting it close to the Gods as they swept over Midgard's chill and blasted landscape. Up at Tyrsborg the household trooped into the woods to a place that had been chosen their first year to receive the bodies of the seven sows Sidroc had promised as a vow.

"You need not come," Ceridwen was telling Ceric and Hrald as she wrapped Eirian and Yrling in mantles of fur. "You may stay here; we will not be long."

Both boys knew this day was coming, and now had not expected they would be excused from the witnessing of it. Gunnvor had been cooking a special meal for their return; one of the spotted pigs had been killed, its fresh meat enriching both pies and browis.

"I will come," Hrald answered. He had seen the goat his father and Tindr had brought from the goshawk farm, been there when they returned with it yesterday, and had helped Tindr feed and water it in the stable. He knew his father would make the sacrifice and wanted to be with him.

Ceric had determined to stay at the hall until he heard Hrald. He had told him last night he would not go, but had neglected to ask Hrald if he would. Now he did not wish to be left behind, despite the fact that he might be putting himself in danger with God for what he might see. Yet he could not speak to his mother and say Já, he would come. He just went to his alcove and got his mantle and hood.

The Sun was aiming for the highest point in its shallow arc when they set out. Gunnvor and Helga went with them, and Rannveig came up from her brew-house as well. The walk through the trees to the place was not long, the Sun crossing slowly overhead in a dull sky of silver gray. It had rained in the morning, and the bark of some trees was black with wet. A few drops fell from boughs overhead, and the forest had the rich and oaky smell of verdant growth falling into loam. Mosses and ferns were still green, but nearly every tree had lost its leaves, crunching softly underfoot amongst the fir needles on the narrow track.

Tindr had gone ahead with the goat. He had fed it grain mixed with mead, as he ever did with the chosen beast. The creature's head had begun to hang, and it looked unsteady on its feet when Hrald's father lifted his arms and began to cry aloud to the sky.

Hrald had seen his father make Offering at Four Stones, had seen him choose a piglet from the pens and then followed him, unasked, to the Place of Offering. His father was alone, and Hrald could not hear the words he had spoken; he had hidden behind the great tree there to watch. It was when Ceric and his mother had arrived, he remembered that.

Now, watching his father's back as he raised his arms and spoke, he wished to be nearer him. Wilgot forbade him to go to the sacrifice pit, but though his mother knew he sometimes did, she did not chide him. But he knew Abbess Sigewif and the priests at Oundle would count praying there a sin.

Listening to his father praise the Gods and recount the blessings of the year he could not keep himself from going nearer him. One of the things he gave thanks for was his and Ceric's coming, safe and whole, to see them.

As his voice rose and grew louder, Hrald found himself lifting his own arms in echo of his father's gesture.

His father ended his words, and turned to see him, arms uplifted. He looked at him in a way that made him glad he had done so.

He turned then, to where Tindr waited with the goat, and saw Ceric's face. He looked angry and scared both, looking at him like something vile.

But Tindr was holding the goat's head now, and Hrald's father had pulled his bright seax.

It was not the squeal of the goat that made Ceric wince; he had for years seen such beasts be butchered in Kilton's kitchen yard. It was the killing of it in the woods, and for whom it was killed.

On the way back they were all quiet, but Hrald's father had his arm around the waist of Ceric's mother. The boys fell in behind them.

Ceric was angry now he had come. He glared at Hrald when they turned to leave, and would not look at him now as they walked back. They were nearly out of the forest when his mother turned to look back at them. She was smiling when she did, but when she saw Ceric's face her smile faded. She stopped and let the boys catch up to her.

"Dunnere . . . Dunnere would say this is ignorance and sin," Ceric told her. His voice was almost breathless, and he was looking only at her, not at Sidroc. "Do you truly believe your Gods come and eat of this?"

She looked over at Gunnvor and Helga and Tindr, asking them with a tilt of her head to go ahead without them. When they had gone she turned back to her son.

"I do not know, but I know it is left with good intent," she told him. "I know that what is Offered feeds the foxes of the woods, and the birds of the air. And I have seen too, with my own eyes, that the ground on which this blood has fallen is nourished. We are nourishing the Earth with it. What grows there next year will be rich and doubled in bloom; I have seen it. So the Earth is fed by what we Offer, even if the Gods do little but look down and smile upon us."

Her son was shaking his head impatiently at her. She began to feel some little impatience herself.

"Are you so certain about all Dunnere or Wilgot says and does?" she tried him, but gently. "Do you not sometimes wonder if the bread he holds is the body of the Christ?"

Hrald was nodding his head as if to agree with her. Ceric saw this and almost spluttered.

"Dunnere – "

"I know what Dunnere would say," his mother said quietly. "I wish to know what you think."

"There is one true God. Jesus Christ is his Son." He spoke with real defiance. "Believing this makes us different from those who are lost in error."

"Jesus," repeated the Dane. He had been looking on with mild eyes. "Já, I know his Saga. He was a powerful chieftain, and made strong magic. The feeding of many from a few loaves and fishes. The turning of water into wine for all his men, and his host's men, at the hand-fast feast. He knew seiðr, the most powerful of magic, that known to Freyja and Odin. He made a dead man rise and walk again. His Saga-stories are good ones; Wilgot told them."

"It is more than just stories," Ceric countered. He had tempered his tone, but Ceridwen felt it was brave of him to speak so to Sidroc.

The boy watched the Dane consider him, then nod.

"The stories are how we know the Gods," Sidroc told him. "That, and how they answer us when we call on them."

Sidroc posed a question to the boy now. "What kind of God do you seek?"

"Kind of God . . . ?"

"There are many. Gods for war, and for peace, for love and lust, for our beasts and for the hunt, for men, and for women."

Ceric, confused, gave a shake of his head.

"Your God, the Jesus one, is good for peace," the Dane offered.

Ceric nodded; he had heard Him called the Prince of Peace.

They were nearly at Tyrsborg. The wind shifted, bringing to their noses the smell of the pig-meat and barley browis steaming in Gunnvor's large cauldron in the kitchen yard. Pounded fish-paste, sprinkled with Gotland's best salt was there, too, ready to be spread upon hot loaves; and she had made honey cakes as well.

"Peace is good," Sidroc ended, and they headed to the meal that awaited.

"You must write a letter, shield-maiden."

Ceridwen was seated on a bench next Sidroc, snug before the fire blazing in the fire-pit, when he said this. Gunnvor had gone to bed, as had the boys, but Helga stood near her, spinning, and Tindr sat cross-legged on a deer skin at the fire's edge. She was working some nålbinding into stockings, and lowered her work as he went on.

"Like unto the safe-conduct I rode to Kilton with. Put my name on it, written big, and also the name of Ælfred. Runulv will take it with him when he sails for Four Stones with the boys."

She had not wished to think of this yet; Winter was just coming on. But the safest time for Ceric and Hrald to sail would be Runulv's first trip out, as soon as the weather broke in late Spring.

"Já," she said. He was still looking into the fire, thinking of this. She freed one of her thumbs from the looping work and touched his knee. She would not speak to him of her fears for the boys' safety on their voyage home. Less would she now complain of how her heart would ache when they left.

"I am grateful you think of these things," is what she said.

She took a little breath and picked up her work again. "I will go to Sone and have him make parchment for me."

She thought more. "In Spring I will have time enough to gather what I need to mix ink; oak galls are readily found, and apple bark aplenty from the farm."

She looked to Tindr, sitting across from them, carving a deer. "And thanks to Tindr we have many geese. I will have my choice of quills, regardless of how many I spoil."

She glanced at Sidroc, saw he was deep in his own thoughts and had likely not heard. His concern was doubled, she knew; he would fear for the boys, from marauders and from shipwreck, and fear too for the added danger he sent Runulv and his ship and their trading goods into.

Her thoughts moved on. If she had parchment she could write a letter to Ælfwyn, and not depend solely on the boys to tell her how they fared on Gotland; indeed, she wished to say to her friend things the boys never could. She could, if she wished, write again to Modwynn and Edgyth, a letter Ceric would carry . . .

She shook her head at this; it was much to think of. She took too much on her head at once; Sidroc had often told her so.

She lifted her eyes to the tall and spare form of Helga, eyes half closed, dropping her whirling spindle, drawing up the slender thread, pulling out the fluffy roving from over her shoulder to do it again. There was comfort in hand-work, always, in the rhythms of needful goods growing beneath one's fingers. She turned back to her own work.

In the morning she walked down the hill to the shoe-maker. A raw wind blew in from the sea, frosting her breath. Her face felt almost stiff when she opened the door of his workshop, well-wrapped as she was in her fur-lined mantle. She wore her hood trimmed with red fox, and clutched it tight about her head. She threw the hood back as the old man greeted her, rising from his work-bench. Even in the cold the place reeked of the sharp and dark aroma of lye-cleansed animal skins.

"Sone," she told him, as she warmed herself at the brazier on the floor, "I need a hide from you, that I must have before Spring."

"Hides I have many," he said, waving his hand at a stack of them, ready tanned, on a worktable. His fingers looked forever curled from his heavy stitching work, and were stained a smudged browny-black from years of han-dling dyed skins.

"I need a special one, of great fineness. Use a white lamb, not a year old, and scrape the skin so thin that bright daylight may be seen through it."

"Such a hide will cost good silver, and have little strength," he warned her, dealing as he did in tougher stuffs for shoes and boots.

"It needs but little strength," she assured. "It will not be worn, but cut by me into small squares, and used to write upon. As if I drew the runes on stone. But the lamb must be white, or my letters will not show."

He looked at her and nodded, though she was not sure he understood. No matter. By Spring she should have the costly thing in her keeping, on which she would pen words she hoped would guard that which was beyond price.

The celebration of Winter's Nights brought feast after feast to Tyrsborg. The weather was cold but with little snow, which made the summoning of friends easy. Gunnvor and Helga hustled about the cooking fires, both in the kitchen yard and within the hall. Outside, the coals were kept hot and raked heavy over the covered iron baking pans hiding Gunnvor's crusted loaves. Nestled next them were sealed iron pans holding carrots and parsnips slow-roasting in honey and butter. Eggs, carefully saved in cold ashes, were now roasted in these same coals, and once shelled were being popped into hungry mouths. From the cooking frames hung pots of meat broth, steaming away next to those of barley browis, fragrant with dittany and dill and made rich with pig-meat. Fat geese were baked, stuffed with hickory-nut meal, dried grapes, and bread crusts. Pies filled with minced lamb and turnips wore wreaths of whole dried leaves of mint. Haunches of smoked deer meat were shaved thin and savoured with cups of Rannveig's good brown ale. Still-juicy pears and apples were drawn from their cold cellar holes and wrapped in pastry, baked, and drizzled with honey, the fruit bursting with sweet-smelling steam as the crust was broken with a knife. There was golden mead, and also precious wine, swirling dark in the cup, which the mistress of Tyrsborg allowed even the boys a draught, well-watered.

It would be Ceric's and Hrald's only Winter's Nights festival on Gotland, and Ceridwen wished it to be as memorable as they could make it, for all their sakes. Rannveig of course, near and dear as she was to Ceridwen, came to every feast, and at each her ale and mead was celebrated.

It was Rannveig who had taught Ceridwen the rituals of Winter's Nights. These were feasts ruled by female spirits, honoured in the dark of Winter, for Winter is the womb of Spring and birth and increase. It was the mistress of the house who called the gathered guests together, and who then went alone from door to door, sprinkling purifying salt at each threshold, bidding none to open these doors until she declared the feast over. And it was the mistress who called the *dísir*, the female spirits who made themselves free of the household, to join them in their feasting. These were not the spirits of Frigg or Freyja or Sif or any other Goddess, but the female element in all Goddesses, all women, all life.

To other feasts, friends came as they could: neighbour Alrik and his wife and daughter; Ragnfast and Estrid and their brood; the rope-makers Ketil and Tola; Botair, his sons Runulv and Ring, with their wives Gyda and Astrid and little ones.

At one feast at which Runulv and his brother Ring were guests, dice were brought out after the remnants of the food had been cleared away. Deep cups of ale had been drunk during the eating of it, and now sweet mead filled the silver-lipped cow-horn drinking vessels, brought out specially for feasts. The blaze in the fire-pit gave such warmth against the winds howling outside that those who sat closest to it must soon relinquish their seats or fall faint from heat. Every cresset was lit and burning. The cheer and brightness of the hall made all forget the biting cold outside, and length of dark night. Winter's Nights marked the rebirth of the Sun, and each day would now grow longer.

Rannveig sat on the fleece-lined lip of a sleeping alcove, talking with Ragnfast's mother-in-law, Thorvi. Eirian, tiring now, had pulled herself into Rannveig's lap and had nodded off to sleep, despite the noise. Rannveig had pulled her own mantle over the child, whose long legs betrayed her father's height. Her brother Yrling was with the rest of the young ones, led by Ceric and Hrald, at the end of the hall near the front door. They played a game of sticks and beach pebbles, bouncing the pebbles against the stone wall of Tyrsborg's front to see which came closest to the sticks lying on the floorboards.

Ceridwen, her ritual duties complete until the evening's end, sat now with the other young mothers. They took turns passing the youngest babes amongst them, praising their beauty and the strength of the tiny fingers curling around their own. The newest of these was Astrid and Ring's second child, born just last month. Astrid had unpinned the shoulder clasp of her gown and opened her shift, and her new daughter was sucking lustily.

At the table end on the other side of the fire stood the evening's host, Sidroc, throwing dice with Runulv, Ring, and Ragnfast. Fortune seemed to favour all equally this night, and each player's respective piles of silver waxed and waned so that little difference could be seen after long play. They paused in their efforts and took more mead. It was then Sidroc, watching Hrald and Ceric at their own play at the far end of Tyrsborg, spoke to his ship captain.

"Runulv," he began. "In Spring when you sail, you will carry extra cargo."

Runulv was now used to the Dane surprising him with some special treasure to offer in Frankland or Danemark. He cocked his eyebrows, waiting.

"It is the boys, Hrald and Ceric." Sidroc watched Runulv turn his head to where the boys crouched, throwing their pebbles. Ring and Ragnfast looked too, before returning their eyes to their host.

"You must take them to Angle-land."

Runulv had seen the white coast of Angle-land, seen it from afar aboard his merchant ship when he sailed to Frankland. Part of that huge island was now controlled by Danes, famed for pirating at sea.

Sidroc read some of the questions clouding the young man's brow. "After the boys are delivered, you will then sail for Frankland, and trade as you will. But your first and most important cargo will be Hrald and Ceric. They must be delivered to Four Stones in Lindisse.

"You will sail up the coast and land at a place called Saltfleet. I built a pier there, and there will be men day and night to watch it, and collect fees for landing. I will tell Hrald what to say, he speaks both tongues, and you will have a letter too, a safe-conduct, which you should not need. When the men see Hrald that will be enough."

Runulv did not know the word 'letter', and indeed Sidroc had used the Saxon name for it, for there was no word in Norse.

"A letter – it is words, written on hide, like runes painted or carved on wood or stone. It will be in the speech of the Saxons. It will say you have leave of the King of the Saxons to travel to the coast of Angle-land. Also," he added, lowering his voice, "the leave of Sidroc of Lindisse to land. Even those who cannot read this speech will know the look of my name."

The three younger men had been listening with intent. Since the day the Dane had arrived on Gotland he had been the object of conjecture. He wore the knife of the men of Angle-land; those on the trading road had seen Danish warriors who had won them in raids in that far off land. His wife was not a Danish woman, and spoke no Norse, though she had quickly learnt it. After the death of the stranger at Tyrsborg part of the story came out; Sidroc had in fact fought and won land in Angle-land. No one knew the extent of what he had left behind.

Runulv, who had risked his ship and his life over the past four sailing seasons to earn silver for them both, felt he had also earned the right to speak.

"Are you then a Jarl," was what he asked. Ring and Ragnfast were staring at him as he asked this. Their eyes shifted, as his did, to the Dane's face as he replied.

"Jarl of South Lindisse," he said. He had not spoken this title in almost four years. "Hrald will rule in only a few more years."

Runulv's head dropped in surprise. He lifted it as Sidroc went on with his orders.

"From Saltfleet it is a full day's ride to Four Stones. My men will horse you. Your ship will be safe at Saltfleet; you need leave but half your men aboard.

"You will have an escort, but must take the boys yourself to Four Stones. There you will see the Lady Ælfwyn, Hrald's mother. You will take her the gifts we have sent; to her, and to my chief men Asberg and Jari, but are to do no trading.

"You will have an escort back to Saltfleet, and any provision you need. Then you will set sail for Frankland."

Runulv, decisive by nature, took this all in. The boys had come from Angle-land, and to there must be returned. He would face the same dangers he did every outing, shipwreck from storm and predation from pirates. He had been told to do no trading when he landed; nothing must delay his delivery of the boys to the Dane's former keep, and his setting sail for Frankland and the profit that awaited there. He knew without it being said that Sidroc would pay a premium for this task.

"I will want more men," was how he answered. His ship had but eight oars, but a tall and heavy mast that carried a large sail. The young men who signed on with him each trip were not only strong rowers but had been trained to fight; several had been with him from his first voyage for Sidroc. Eight strong backs to row, and him at the steering oar. He was gauging the number of additional men he could wisely carry.

"A crew of twelve," was what he decided. "All oars can be manned and four ready with bow and spear, should we be pursued. With four extra men I can spell those at the oar who tire, as well."

Twelve men would mean nothing if they fell into the sights of a drekar, a dragon-ship of the Danes with its crew of thirty or forty warriors. The four of them standing there knew this. Yet it was all Runulv's stout ship could manage. The Gods had smiled on his every voyage, and he would have to rely on their favour continuing.

Ring, the captain's younger brother, had gone twice for Sidroc, set sail for Dane-mark to trade salt and amber the first and second season Runulv had gone to Frankland. Both voyages had filled his purse with silver. He had been able to hire men to help him clear more land, bought a pair of young oxen, and built up his flocks of sheep to more than two score. The farm he and Astrid worked was owned by the Dane and his wife, and supplied the family of Tyrsborg with grain, vegetables, mutton and fleece, and the apples the place was known for. It was all carried down to them in the large waggon Ring had been able to buy with his trading silver. Astrid had silver brooches at her shoulders and he a big pin on his woollen mantle.

The first time he had been out he had been caught by a storm. He wrestled with the steering oar in the raging sea as his men bailed, frantic against the waves slapping over the sides. It was a near thing that his first trading venture was not his last. He had vowed not to sail again, but following the death of his young wife in childbed had asked to be sent the next season. That time he had smooth sailing, and carried querns shaped of Gotlandic limestone, jars of Tindr's honey, and baskets of amber to Dane-mark. The profit from both trips was such he could not hope to see in five good years of farming.

Then he had wed Astrid. She sat across the fire from him, their toddling boy at her feet, their new daughter at her breast.

"I will go," he said of a sudden. The thought of the gain to be had was enough to overcome his fears, at least that night standing there with Runulv.

The other three turned to him. Ragnfast bred and trained horses and was good at it. Here at this feast he wore a cuff of silver around each wrist, and his wife Estrid had a new pair of shoulder brooches chased with gold. He was of the land, and wanted nothing more. Other than going out with his cousin Tindr as a boy in his Uncle Dagr's fishing boat for the day, he had never sailed, and had no wish to.

Runulv looked at his brother, judging his claim. As boys they had been companions in all, and Runulv would have liked his company on past trips, and for Ring to share the same memory of the greatness of the stone city of Paris. And Ring was stalwart and strong.

It was Sidroc who spoke. "Nai," he told Ring.

They had been drinking mead. It was late, and the fire's warmth, the fellowship and feasting made all such ventures to come look easy. He glanced over to Astrid and the new babe now sleeping on her shoulder. Ring's boy had crawled in his shield-maiden's lap, and she was bouncing him on his chubby legs and singing a little song.

"Nai. Never brothers on the same ship." That was all he said. He must send Hrald and Ceric together; there was no remedy for that. He would not tempt disaster and heartbreak for so many more should Runulv's ship not make the shores of Angle-land.

LEAVE-TAKING

WINTER had been long, as it ever was this far north. The sea raged in wind-swept tempest, then lay deadly calm, locked with thick plates of ice that shoved and creaked upon the water's surface. There had been no cheeses nor eggs gracing Tyrsborg's table for weeks, and even the butter Gunnvor had frozen, well-salted, under the floor boards of one of the outbuildings was nearly gone. It would be more long weeks before the first green shoots of grass could be seen. There were apples, still, with wrinkled skins but some firmness to the flesh, lying hidden in straw; and cabbages, growing limp, and rooty carrots. Only their meat was fresh, for Tindr's bow still brought them deer, at least for another waxing and waning of the Moon; then all the stags would have fled to the deeper reaches of the forest. With the boys he shot also the big blue-grey hares, if they popped up upon a fallen tree trunk or paused on a forest track. Snares could not be laid, for in snow rabbits forsook their pathways and runs and hopped anywhere upon the crusted surface. All such meat was lean, making the little butter left and its welcome fatness a treat. Even Tindr's bees slept, but the jars of honey he had gathered from them sweetened the short days.

Then the snow that had blanketed all began to recede. Rain fell in sheets, softening it to a slushy mess, and the wind that blew did so less bitterly. Each day the Sun rose higher, and stayed longer. Trees showed the swelling buds that promised new leaves, and green sprouts could be seen when dead leaves and snow-crusts were moved with prodding toe. Ceridwen went out and plucked the tiny leaves of birches, boiling up a tangy pale-coloured broth which she drank eagerly and urged upon the rest of Tyrsborg. And Sone the shoe-maker delivered to her the scraped and prepared hide of a white lamb.

She laid it on the great table within the hall and looked at it carefully. She would square it first, saving every odd shaped bit for practice with the ink she would mix. She gauged she could cut six fair-sized pieces of parchment from it, more than enough for letters to Ælfwyn and Modwynn.

More important than the letters was that which Sidroc had asked her to make. She had seen such a document but once, years ago when he had ridden to Kilton with Ælfwyn, bearing in a pouch at his side a parchment of safe-conduct from Ælfred. She had seen it in the treasure room and read it then, and earlier seen Godwin break the waxen seal and unroll it. He had glanced at it with Wulfstan, his chief man, before dropping it there on the table. It was the second day of Sidroc and Ælfwyn's stay. Just the act of Sidroc showing the parchment and naming it a safe-conduct had been enough to delay the actual reading of it.

She lined the lambskin with charcoal run against a narrow piece of planed wood, then took up the sharp bird-shaped shears from her work-basket and snipped through the costly thing. It was not as smooth as the parchment prepared from practised monks, and she tried buffing it with a sheared fleece wrapped about a block of wood; but it would serve. Holding the six sheets gave her a feeling of wealth, almost as if she handled gold, and indeed what she wrote could prove more valuable than even that.

She rode off with Tindr to their upland farm, returning with curved pieces of apple bark lifted from a tree Ring had cut down. She had seen the small round galls she needed on an oak not far into the woods from the hall, the size of walnuts in the shell. Tindr had iron shavings aplenty from his filing and shaping of his arrowheads. When she mixed all these together with water in a small pot and set it to boil Gunnvor watched with interest as the liquid darkened. She strained it through worn linen and let it sit. A drop of the ink looked nearly purple, like the darkest of berries, but it would dry, she hoped, to a near-black.

The parchment needed lines to help keep her lettering level. Without the proper scribe's tools she bethought her of how best to make them, and settled on drawing the sharp point of one of her steel needles across the surface, making the lightest of scratches her inked words would float above. All the time she worked at this she thought of the three letters she would write, and the differing messages they must bear. Her work went on, and the work of the hall went on around her, but each afternoon when the light was at its best she turned her hands and thoughts to this new task.

The first she wished to write was that most needful, the safe-conduct, a letter she hoped would never need to be read. She had a store of long goose-quills she had gathered from the stable, and with Gunnvor's sharpest knife made her five cuts to admit and hold the ink, ready in a tiny pot. She lit three cressets and set them all about her on the table; it was yet too cold to leave open the hall doors, and she wanted as much light as she could make to guide her.

She beat her memory to recall the wording. She had heard many documents of the King and high churchmen read aloud, and did her best to mirror their language.

> I Runulv of Gotland travel as protector to Ceric of Kilton, godson of ÆLFRED KING OF WESSEX and Hrald son of SIDROC OF LINDISSE, to deliver these same into the care of Lady Ælfwyn of Four Stones. None are to hinder nor harm this party, in their coming or going, under penalty from ÆLFRED and GUTHRUM KING OF ANGLIA.

She read it aloud to Sidroc. He listened with eyes lifted to the dimness of their peaked roof.

"That is fine," he praised. He looked upon her work, his finger going first to his own name, and then to Ælfred's. "This will serve well," he told her.

It would only serve if it had a chance of being read, he knew. If a war-ship filled with his brothers bore down on Runulv, waving a piece of white lambskin at them would provoke nothing but hooting laughter. If however, he was stopped by a patrol of either Ælfred's or Guthrum's forces, it might keep them from being seized, even if those aboard could not read it themselves.

"You will teach Runulv how to say every part of it, as if he could read it himself," he thought aloud now. She saw the wisdom in this and nodded her head.

"Show me which part is my name," Runulv asked next day. He had listened to Ceridwen read it aloud twice, and was still wondering over the small circles and curved lines that said so much.

His eyes narrowed at the cluster of letters she pointed to. "Do you see how the first letter looks like the rune Rad?" she answered. It was one of the few likenesses she could make to her rounded script and the mostly straight symbols of the runes.

He began to repeat the letter after her, following her finger as it moved across the cream-coloured parchment.

"These are the most important words, the names of Ælfred, King of Wessex, and Guthrum, King of the Danes of Anglia. All men in Angle-land will know their names."

"And those at sea?" Runulv asked, and then answered himself. "If we are challenged at sea we will act as we must."

As Spring came on, the wild-flowers which were one of the glories of the island burst into bloom. The splashes of reds, blues and yellows amongst the vivid greens of meadow growth always brought to Ceridwen's mind her precious weaving, the carpet Sidroc had taken from the Idrisid ship for her. The mild air was full of flying insects hovering above these flowers, Tindr's thirsty bees amongst them. The lakes and streams, unlocked from ice, brimmed with fish. The hens warmed themselves in the sunshine and began to lay again, and there was grass enough for the cow that her milk grew richer, rich enough for good butter to be drawn from it. Soon peas and early greens could be savoured, and fresh herbs enliven Tyrsborg's meals once again. The young pear and plum trees Ceridwen and Tindr had planted before the front door their first year had blossoms, and the hard grape vine buds were swelling.

Yet Spring meant the boys must leave with Runulv, as soon as he deemed the weather safe. There could be no fixed date for this, and Ceridwen would look at the calendar she had drawn of the wheel of the year on the wall of the treasure room, and point out to herself where they were today, with no knowledge of which day she must say fare-well to Ceric. And her grief was nearly doubled, for Hrald had stolen her heart with his sweet and winsome ways. She had always loved the boy as Ælfwyn's son, but living with him these many months had endeared him to her in a way she did not know could happen with a child not her own. Indeed, Hrald felt partly her own, through the love she bore for his mother, and that she bore for his father. She was bound to Hrald for his own sake, and for theirs.

The boys, freed from the confinement of the long Winter, ranged about on their horses, wandered the woods with each other or with Tindr, even tried swimming in the still-frigid sea. They kept on in their work in the wax-tablet, as Ceridwen was mindful they not seem to have slipped too far in their skills. Tindr stood with them many hours before the shooting target on the stable, guiding their wrists and steadying their stance as they aimed at the charcoal deer drawn there. And Sidroc worked almost every day with them, flinging spears at the second target, that of a man.

Each boy had grown some, he could see that. He thought Hrald would surely be as tall as he; his mother was tall, and he need look at the boy's face to remind himself how young he really was. He had thought over Winter's Nights it might be best to go to Berse and have short swords made up for the boys after all; they had progressed so much in their skill. But the giving of a sword marked a threshold over which no boy could retreat. He had asked much of them, shown them much, told them more. He would not lay that which they could not handle on their young heads. He hoped, awakening in the dark, that with Hrald he had not already done so.

"In the treasure room at home," he told him one evening when they were alone, "there is the black chest." Hrald had nodded, recalling it. His father had many times shown him the prizes within, a trove of worked steel, all carefully wrapped in fleece to save the blades from rust. "Our finest swords are there; you will have your pick of them. Asberg will help you choose."

They were the swords of dead men, Hrald knew this; those swords of the Saxons his father had killed, and those killed by his men who had given them to his father in tribute. Some he knew were swords of Danes who had died as well, picked up from the field of battle. If they had no kin the sword was always forfeit to the war-chief who led them.

Yrling's sword was not amongst them. Sidroc had watched Godwin of Kilton kill his uncle, then stoop over his dying body and tear the silver hammer of Thor from his neck. Lifting his head he had seen Sidroc, and sprang with face contorted in fury after him. Neither could stay to collect the sword still in Yrling's bloodied grasp. It was a great regret of his he had not got it. When his shield-maiden had recounted to him Kilton's return and the showing of booty, he knew Kilton had not got it either, and took some comfort in that.

⁂

Sidroc thought carefully of what trading goods would be sent to Frankland. Barring the rarities of silk or spices, goshawks could always be counted upon to bring the greatest return.

This year he would send but one hunting bird to Frankland, whereas in the last two he had sent two. The mews at Ring's had produced several chicks, but only three birds were trained up enough to sell to the noblemen Runulv would seek out. And of these, Sidroc had determined to send two to Four Stones.

"The silver female, and the grey male, both as gifts," he told Runulv, when they met to discuss what treasure he would carry. "Ring is readying them now. The big female to Asberg, the male to Jari. They will be able to raise up their own, if luck is with them."

Runulv took a breath. This was rich treasure to send as gifts, but the birds were Sidroc's to give.

"The brown female you will sell in Frankland," he was saying now. Runulv had seen her; she was a fine bird, lightning fast in the air, and he was glad to know he would have something fit to offer to Charles, the King of the Franks, or to his chief men.

For other treasure-worthy items, Sidroc turned to the trading road. Berse the weapon-smith came to his aid, being able to hammer out two swords and three knives, all pattern-welded, he could take. The hilts and pommels were plain, and Sidroc took them to the silver-worker Tume, who beat in strands of silver wire. He had amber, as always, both beaded necklaces and small ornaments of it, and knew it would once again fetch a good price.

When the snow had fully melted, Sidroc rode along muddy tracks to Thorfast, the fashioner of stone far in the East of Gotland. He took Tindr and Hrald and Ceric with him, so the boys saw the furthest and rockiest reaches of the island, where it narrowed to a thin neck of land before opening again to its wild wind-swept end. He ordered five stone querns from the man, destined to grind some woman's grain in another land. He had the boys with him when he bargained for the white salt crystals grown by Asfrid, the woman on the trading road, and the several times he dealt with Berse over the making of the treasure which was his blades. All these things would make the voyage to Frankland. He had vowed to teach them the ways of trading, and did so by having them watch and listen. And he gamed with the boys, teaching them every trick he knew when playing dice, especially that of knowing when to stop, "Which may take you some loss of silver to truly know," he told them one night, when they played together with Runulv and Ring.

To his wife Sidroc gave the task of choosing fitting gifts for the women of Four Stones. Ceridwen did not need to think long on this, sending Ælfwyn ten large fleeces of the long-woolled Gotland sheep, a chest of fragrant beeswax tapers, and two jars of Tindr's honey, knowing she would delight in all of it. For Burginde and Ælfwyn's daughters and sisters she chose an amber necklace each, and each different from the other; some with round beads, some with long narrow ones, some with amber of gold hue, some almost green.

Anything she might send was but a token, for nothing would give Ælfwyn the joy of seeing Hrald safe and home again. Thinking on this Ceridwen felt her heart contract with her coming loss.

As she lingered over the necklaces she had chosen, she bethought her how alike the houses of Kilton and Four Stones had become. Each had lost its Lord – warriors of great renown – and had now only young sons rule in their stead. At Four Stones it was Hrald, and at Kilton, Edwin, and after him, Ceric. They ruled by consent of their lost fathers' faithful men, and with the approval of their corresponding Kings. She knew Ceric was eager to return, and sensed that Hrald was not. Yet eager or no, their Fate was cast.

There were tempests of rain and high winds, and skies split with the arced flashes of lightning. Runulv brought his ship to the wooden pier near Rannveig's brew-house and he and Sidroc began its lading. The captain gathered his men and they all came to Tyrsborg for a feast. Their high spirits and jesting wore well on their fresh and open faces. They were good archers and spears-men all, and better sailors. After long Winter they were eager for adventure, and counted themselves fortunate to have been chosen again to sail for the Dane upon Runulv's stout ship. Ceric and Hrald mixed easily amongst them in that natural fellowship of the young. Ceridwen looked on the two, showing but little shyness as they shared some laughing talk with the men, and saw Tindr look upon them too.

Tindr knew they were leaving within a few days, as soon as the weather cleared, and would sail far. They had been part of his life in the woods, and the life of the hall, for three seasons, and were passing back into that more akin to these other young men. They must become warriors like Scar and the two that had come after Bright Hair, or Scar would not have given them warriors' weapons and spent so much time training them up. He had taught them how to track, how to snare rabbits, had made them bows and quivers and shown them how to make arrows and shoot them well. He had liked showing them these things, and knew he would miss them, especially Long Legs, who watched him carefully, and had learnt the signs he used to make himself known.

Two days later the sea rolled on a steady stream of low swells. The wind was cold, but the sky was blue and endless above. Runulv and Sidroc began their final lading. The goshawks in their woven cages had been brought by oxcart to Tyrsborg, and now these cages were lashed aboard, and blankets of heavy wadmal secured over them, to keep the birds dry and warm. And as the goshawks would take no meat save that which was fresh-killed, or they had snatched from the air or meadow themselves, Ring had netted a score of starlings, live, to take along, so that the great birds would feed during the voyage. These were in their own wicker cage, laced with small branches from which the smaller birds cheeped.

Runulv had the safe-passage, sewn in a linen pouch and then rolled in leather, in his small chest by the stern. With them were two more letters, one for Hrald to give to his mother, and the second for Ceric to deliver to his grandmother, both filled with thanks for the boys' presence, and wishes for the good of all at their respective halls.

The household walked down together to see them off. Gunnvor had already filled their food bags, and now she and Helga stood wiping their eyes with their apron ends. Eirian and Yrling were at their skirts, just beginning to understand the boys were going away, and beginning too to worry over the sorrow on their mother's face. "Fare-well, little brother, fare-well, little sister," Hrald told them, as both boys bent down to touch the children's heads.

Tindr gave them each a parting gift of ten arrows, feathered and tipped, to add to that store already packed in their quivers. Each boy hugged him, then used Tindr's way of saying thanks, a touch to the heart, with the hand turning outward to he you were grateful to. Rannveig came from her brew-house, summoning Runulv's crew, as she ever did, to come and carry off a cask of ale as her parting-gift. She gave each boy in turn a quick embrace, fighting her own coming tears as she watched Ceridw-en's lips quiver. She turned from the boys to give her an embrace, willing her be strong.

The boys lay down their packs and shields. They came first to the other's parent. Hrald threw his arms around Ceridwen, and she clutched him to her, kissing his face and head. "I thank you for everything, Lady Ceridwen," he told her. "I will not forget this time with you, and Tindr, and Ceric."

He was on the verge of saying, "And I would stay with you if I could," but she was crying, and he knew this truth would likely make him cry as well. He drew back enough from her embrace to be able to kiss her cheek. She had that smell of warm roses which she always bore on feasts and other special days.

Ceric went to Sidroc. "I thank you for the gift of arms," he said, as he stood before him, "and for what you have shown us."

He made no move to embrace him, and Sidroc too held back. "You are a good friend to Hrald," the Dane told him, "and I thank you for that. It will be my wish that you two will always be so."

"Of course we will be friends," Ceric was quick to answer. "My mother has asked me that I go to see Hrald at Four Stones when I can, now that I am older."

This surprised Sidroc. "I am glad for that. And there is no need for you, now in peace-time, to take ship to do so. The ride across the Kingdoms would be one worthy of a good rider like you."

Ceric did not expect this praise, and his cheek coloured slightly.

Sidroc placed his hand on the boy's shoulder. Hrald was coming to him, and Ceric turned to his mother.

Mother and son spent a moment looking at each other.

"Fare-well, mother," Ceric said. His eyes had back flicked to Sidroc who stood behind her, and now returned to her. "I will never see you again."

Her hand flew to her mouth. "Ah, Ceric, do not say that – do not," she faltered. She could not speak more; her tears stifled her.

"Your life is here," he answered, but there was some water come into his own eyes now. "That is what you told Uncle."

"But you are my life as well," she said, when her throat opened enough for words. She had taken up his hand and was now kissing it.

She tried to smile. "I cannot return to Kilton, and you must. You are of Kilton, it is your Fate." She held his hand in her own, and pressed it as she went on.

"I was never of Kilton. But out of love for your father I bore you, that Kilton might live and thrive. We gave your brother for the same end." She wiped her eyes with her free hand. "Please do not hate me for not being able to give more."

"I do not hate you, mother," he said, in a low voice. "But if you were with me you could convince the others to name me Uncle's heir."

She lifted her head at this, as if in surprise. He felt her hand stiffen where it held his. She let go that hand.

"That is for Ælfred to decide, only him," she answered, but with gentleness. She nodded slightly, considering what he had said. In truth, the King was Ceric's godfather; he might indeed abrogate the will of a dead man for the seeming good of Kilton.

Her own green eyes were looking into his, as she studied every part of his young face, impressing it into memory.

"My wish for you is that you will be your own man. Not your father's son, nor your uncle's nephew – but your own truest self."

Hrald's face was buried in his father's tunic. He was stifling tears; his father's arms, wrapped about him, felt the heave of his boy's chest. Sidroc looked down at Hrald's brown head, and the tuft of hair that stood up at the crown. He smoothed that tuft as he looked over at Runulv's waiting ship. He had had no last fare-well with his own father, and felt now the mercy in that. To have had Hrald with him for these many months, and to lose him anew was a pain unlike any he had known. His losses had always been tempered with hope, or had been balanced with some gain. The only gain he saw in losing Hrald was that Four Stones would one day have a worthy leader in him, and at this moment, his boy clinging to him, that did not seem enough.

Finally Hrald broke from him enough to look up.

"I will do my best to keep your treasure for you until you return," his boy told him.

He had no words to answer this, and found himself lifting his eyes to the broad blue sky above their heads.

He must speak, and found himself saying that which he had before. "Your mother – your sisters – when you are older they will be in your keeping. Four Stones will be yours. Honour Guthrum our King, and the Peace with Ælfred, and all should go well."

He caught sight of Ceric's coppery hair, bringing to mind that boy's uncle. He paused a moment before he spoke the next. "You will not be made to answer for my act," he assured his son. "All should go well."

And if all does not go well? Hrald ached to ask.

Runulv gave a whistle from aboard ship. The mast had been lifted and the men eager to raise sail and be off.

Sidroc held his son by the shoulders, an arms-length away. He swallowed to master his voice, and saw Hrald swallow too as he looked up at him.

"Fare you well, Hrald. Remember what I have taught you. I would like to think I will see you in Asgard, in Freyja's jeweled hall where I hope to be called. But you, I think, will dwell in the Heaven of Wilgot and your mother."

So that was it. His father did not expect to ever see him again.

Ceric was coming over. Hrald glanced at him and back to his father. "Fare-well, father," he said, then pulled away to join Ceric.

The boys climbed aboard and stood together at the rail while the ship heaved away. After a short while they parted. Ceric went to the prow, looking forward, ahead across the waters to their goal. Hrald walked to where Runulv stood, steering oar in hand, in the stern. He stayed there looking back, waving still at the cluster of folk, until he saw the tall figure of his father turn and leave.

※※※※※※※※※※

The tears Ceridwen wept that day felt wrung from the depths of her heart. The sight of the boys' empty sleeping alcoves brought a fresh wave of grief, and Helga stripped the bedding out of them, tears streaking her own face, so that no one need see them and be reminded of those who had so lately slept there.

It was a strained and silent day for all. Eirian and Yrling wandered mournfully about, asking when Ceric and Hrald would return. Sleep did not come for Ceridwen that night, and when she turned Sidroc's arm wrapped about her.

"He told me he would never see me again," she whispered in the dark.

He felt a spark of anger against the boy at this. It was likely true, but Ceric would only say such a thing to pain her. He did not tell her that his son had said something equally wounding, that he expected him to return to Four Stones. As hard as they had been to hear, he knew Hrald's words were meant as a wish.

Four-and-forty days passed before Runulv's red and white woven sail was spotted in the distance. He was welcomed at Rannveig's, as he ever was, though after his first words to Sidroc and Ceridwen – All is well – called out when he was still at his steering oar, little else mattered. Seas had been heavy, and they had laid in on the Svear shore for two days until the skies cleared, camping on a deserted beach. Thanks to their early start they had made the voyage past Dane-mark and to Lindisse unchallenged, and found Saltfleet as Sidroc had described it. He had spent but one night at Four Stones before returning to the ship.

It took four days from there to reach Frankland, for the winds were contrary, but once there the passage down the Seine was swift. The Gods had been with them, and the fat King of the Franks had been at Paris; Runulv had no need to travel deeper inland. As he had hoped Charles claimed the brown goshawk for himself, and Runulv sold one of the swords and two of the knives to the King's own companions; the other blades to a trader in Paris. The amber, querns, and salt found buyers in the many stalls that lined the narrow streets. Runulv emptied a bag of silver before them, handfuls of coins rolling, and plucked at a tiny pouch amidst the silver. "For the goshawk," he smiled, pulling out three pieces of gold.

"One is yours," Sidroc told him, "and half the silver, for delivering Hrald and Ceric as you did."

Runulv's men, cups in hand, let out a cheer. He paid them from his own share, and like their captain, they would be rewarded for the extra time and danger they had faced.

"I have things for you, from Four Stones," Runulv said, after sweeping his portion of silver back into the bag. A movement of his head indicated he meant both of them.

He asked one of his men to join him, leaving the others at the brew-house. They stopped first at his ship. He and Sidroc went aboard and carried off a small but heavy iron-handled chest. The third man joined them, reappearing with three leathern packs piled in his arms. Ceridwen saw the smallest of the packs was dyed green. It was creased with age, but the scrolling designs she had worked into it as a maid were still visible.

"My packs," she said. Within must be her clothing, her pear-wood comb, the scant jewels she had taken to Four Stones.

"The Lady had kept them safe for you, and bid me return them now," Runulv said.

These things seemed as lost to her as the years that had passed, and seeing them again gave her a queer feeling of mixed happiness and startle. The green-dyed pack and her comb were her oldest possessions. Within might even be her father's seax with its chipped blade, older and dearer still.

Runulv and Sidroc carried the iron-bound chest between them, the man with her bags trailing behind. They walked up to Tyrsborg, Ceridwen at Runulv's side. Away from the brew-house she was able to ask about their sons, and of Ælfwyn.

"The boys did well, and are both good sailors. From that Lady I have a – a letter," Runulv told her, again using the Saxon word. "It is in my shoulder-bag." He was grinning now at them. "The feast she gave us was a great one," he went on, "and Asberg and Jari did not stop remarking on the goshawks, carrying them about amidst the other men."

Once in the hall he and Sidroc lifted the chest upon the great table, and her packs were set there as well. Runulv drew from his shoulder-bag a waxed linen tube, which he placed in Ceridwen's hand.

"I will see you later," Sidroc told him, for the opening of letter and chest would be private unto themselves.

When they were alone Ceridwen snipped open the tube. She had felt something loose within, and now a bronze key came clattering out. She unfurled the parchment and read aloud.

MY DEAREST CERIDWEN

Nothing could give more joy than to behold Hrald and Ceric safe before me. They have grown so that they are children no longer, but ever our beloved sons. I thank you both for the kindness of your gifts of fine sheepskin, and envy your weavers to have such stuff to work into goods. The tapers of beeswax are generous beyond expectation and half I shall take to Oundle to grace the holy altar. The amber beads already adorn the necks of Burginde, my sisters, and daughters, and they are well pleased with such beauty. Hrald and Ceric have told me of the huntsman who keeps bees so well, and this gift of his honey will add sweetness to our days ahead.

The chest holds something which Hrald begged I send. I could not refuse him, when it is his to give.

I pray God that you and yours remain safe and well. Knowing we have shared our sons like this strengthens our bonds of love. Ceric will return overland under escort to Kilton, and has vowed to return to Four Stones as he can. More than one female here wept upon seeing him.

YOUR LOVING ÆLFWYN

She brushed the tears from her eyes as she lowered the letter. She knew Ælfwyn meant Ashild in the last line, and could not keep a small smile from her lips. If Sidroc understood as well, he did not show it. She picked up the bronze key.

"It must be for you," she told him, "Hrald sent it."

He slid the key into the lock and turned. They heard the latch lift within the dark wood panel. He pushed open the lid.

A sheep-skin, fleece down, lay on top. He lifted it.

Within was his ring-shirt, each steel ring gleaming. In one corner, wrapped in another piece of fleece to keep it from rust, lay his helmet. He had left both with his horse at the foot of the bluff near Saltfleet, four years ago. He had not expected to see them again.

She knew them too for what they were. She recalled the incising on the nose-guard of the helmet, and the spiraling tracing along its curves.

He said nothing, and she could not read his face. He understood why Hrald had not sent his red and black painted shield as well. His boy had told him it lay every night on the oak table, marking the place where the Jarl of Four Stones used to sit.

He lifted the helmet in his hands, turned it as he looked. He laid it back within the chest.

"Your boy said you would not meet again," he began. "Mine told me he would wait for my return."

Later that day he hoisted the chest into the treasure room. When he was alone he again lifted the lid and parted the white fleece hiding the treasure within. He looked to his sword, hanging in its scabbard from a peg on the wall, within ready reach. He never had need to wear it, but had kept it polished. Now the rest of his war-kit had been returned, sent by a son who awaited him.

EIRIK

SIGVOR stood in the doorway of the house, her spindle dropping from her hand. Her boy of four Summers was romping, alone, by the edges of the vegetable rows. The older children had gone off, with their father, to his mother's farm for the day. She wished to stay behind, with her older boy, and her younger, coming two, who had trailed in his brother's wake but now set himself down in the grass under the spreading boughs of the linden tree.

She wound up her finished thread and pulled anew from the mass of wool roving she had tucked over one shoulder. The house was far from the next farm, and even farther from the trading road and her parent's farm on which she had been raised. All her sisters lived closer in, and she missed the days working with them in the trading stall where they sold their finished woollen cloth.

Her mother-in-law did not like her, and the sentiment was shared. She had urged Toste to go off and visit, and leave her in peace so she might get some spinning done. She had made hand-fast with him four years ago and gotten his four children into the bargain. The eldest was the same age as she, a girl so homely that Sigvor doubted any man would try for her. Sigvor and her sisters were known for their prettiness. But she had come to Toste carrying another man's child, and now had another, with him.

The ox cart bearing Toste and his brood had vanished down the dusty clay road, and had not been gone long when she took up her position in the open doorway of the house. As skilled a spinner as she was she had no need to look at her work, and she let her eyes roam. A figure appeared, walking in the middle of the road, from the direction the ox cart had gone. She straightened up. Few came this way, and she wondered at the sight. It was a man, and as he neared she thought his gait familiar. He was still far from her, but her fingers slowed.

He left the road and began walking across the grasses, his eyes fixed on her. Her slowing fingers stopped. Her spindle hit the planks of the floor, and she brushed the roving from her shoulder and let it lie by her feet. She took a step out of the doorway, closer to the approaching man.

He was just before her now, a young man whose golden hair brushed the collar of his blue tunic.

"Eirik," she said. Sigvor had a natural high colour, but all of it had fled from her face. If a ghost had appeared before her she could have been no paler.

He was looking at her, and at the doorway she stood in, and at the house itself, as if gauging what his response would be. While he stood there considering her she awakened from her shock. She took a bound towards him, as if to fling herself into his arms.

He pulled back, freezing her in her action.

"Eirik," she said again. "You are not dead." Her voice was just above a whisper.

He smiled at that. "Nai. My boat was taken by Danes." He looked about him for a moment before he went on.

"They set me to the oar in their war-ship. When I had proved myself I gained their trust. I raided with them a year, then they let me go my way."

He told the story as briefly and as tersely as this, like a man who had recounted it many times already and was sick of hearing it himself.

Sigvor was shaking her head at all this, as if she could not believe his presence. She raised her hand to touch him, but he drew back once more.

"Why . . . why did you not come home then?" she asked. Her older boy had come around from the garden and looked at them before scampering away once more

He gave a short laugh. "I meant to. I got as far as Skania in Svear-land, and found I liked it." There was a carelessness in his tone that chilled her, yet reassured her that it was truly Eirik.

"What were you doing there?" She did not wish to cry before him; he hated tears. She bit her lip to try to keep herself from breaking down before him.

He did not reply at once. When he did he was looking once again at the house, and not at her. "Fishing, and some raiding, when the take was easy."

He had been raiding. Sigvor did not know what to say to that, but she hardly knew how to answer anything Eirik said, or the fact that he was alive and before her now. She spent some time just looking at him before she went on.

"You have been gone so long . . . we all thought you dead. Other boats came back and said a storm was gathering, that surely you had gotten caught in it."

"Nai. Just the Danes."

"When did you come back?" she asked now.

"A week or two ago," he said. He looked over to the small boy sitting under the tree.

She winced. "All this time, and you have not come to see me?"

"They told me you had wed," he remarked.

"Já, but that boy is yours," she told him, pointing at the child who ran the length of the bean rows.

He glanced at the toddling boy who sat watching them, pulling stalks of grass in his chubby fist. "They look the same to me," he told her.

"The older boy is yours; anyone will tell you. I was big by the time Toste wed me." She had not meant to allow her hurt come out as anger, but it had.

There was the merest shrug of his shoulders. "And Toste, of all men," he taunted. "My stiff-necked old cousin. Why him, of anyone?"

She looked about her, flustered. "He was settled, owned a house, this farm . . . and he would have me . . . " She knew she made it sound as if she had been desperate, yet bargaining for the best deal; and she had been.

"But I never wanted him," she ended.

"It matters not; you made hand-fast with him. You could not have waited," he returned, not a question, but an accusation.

"How could I? We thought you dead. I would bear your child soon. I went to your parents, who sneered at me." She was near tears now, and risked stepping near to him once again. "Please let me touch you, Eirik."

"I do not think that is smart," he answered.

"Yet you are here. You must have wanted to see me," she pleaded. He made no answer, and she clung to his silence. "You did, did you not? You learnt that Toste would go to his mother's today. You waited until you saw him leave. Because you wanted to see me. Is this not true?"

"I only came to say good-bye."

"Where . . . where are you going?"

"Gotland is a small island. I will go back to Svear-land, and make my way there."

"Take me with you!" she cried.

He gave a snort. "You are Toste's wife. You have made your decision."

"It was never mine to make. I hate Toste!" She had never thought of it just like this, but the moment she said it it was true. The remembrance of Toste climbing aboard her, pawing at her with his roughened hands, rose in her gullet and sickened her. "I want you, and only you. Take me with you!"

He paused a moment before he answered her. "You are burdened with brats. I must travel quickly when I go."

Sigvor had never found happiness in her first son. Eirik's parents' rejection of her made her hate the child in her womb. This boy had caused her to make an unhappy match with a man she did not care for. She looked to the second boy, whom she had had with Toste. She had some tenderness for him, even given her disdain for his father. Já, she thought, if I must give you up too, I will do so.

"I will leave them behind," she declared. "You need take only me."

Eirik considered this. "You are harder than I thought." He smiled at her then. "You must want me."

"I love you, Eirik. Please take me from here. We can go to Skania; our lives will be what we used to dream about before the Danes caught you."

"Our memories differ," he answered. He shifted on one foot, as if he was weary of their talk.

Sigvor paused, looked about her for answers. "If I can bring you gold, will you take me?"

"Gold? Where would you find such?"

"It does not matter. A friend, who will give it me."

"Bring me the gold, and we will talk about it."

Her answer was firm. "Nai. Tell me you will take me away, and when we are ready to leave, I will give the gold to you then."

He studied her face. Her hands were closed into fists at her sides like a demanding child. She was still very pretty, and he was not unmoved by that fact.

"When will he be back?" was what he said, inclining his head down the road.

"Not until near dusk," she answered.

He looked past her into the dimness of the house to the sleeping alcoves, and jerked his head.

"Then . . . "

He took her by the wrist and moved into the house. She closed the door behind them, closing it too on her boys. She tried to lead him to one of the alcoves the children slept in. But no, he looked about, spotted it, and pushed her into the alcove she shared with her husband. She felt shame at this, letting him take her in her marriage-bed, but her need for the reassurance of his touch was greater than her shame.

※※※※※※※※※※※

Four days later Sigvor, through a series of lies, found a way to come to the trading road alone. It was a long walk;

she had started just after daybreak, and it was nearly mid-morning when she stopped at the stall in which she had once worked. Only her older sister Sigrid was there now; her other sisters were at their husbands' farms. Sigrid had, years past, wed a man with even more sheep than her parents, and had now taken over the sale of the woollen wadmal that she and her sisters made at home and brought to her.

Sigrid was glad to see her, gave her ale and brought her a basin of sea water in which Sigvor bathed her sore feet. When Sigvor had rested she told her sister she wished to go to the end of the road and see the brewster, whom she remembered with fondness. She smoothed her hair under her head-wrap, shook the dust from the hem of her gown, and set off.

Sigvor did not stop at Rannveig's. She walked straight up the steep hill to the hall Tyrsborg at the top. As she neared she kept to one side of the pounded road, so she might see, without being seen herself, if any folk be out in front of the hall, or at the well.

No one was there, and the broad oak front door was closed. She would need luck to stay with her to avoid being seen in the kitchen yard, which she now must enter. It was empty. And there, framed in an arch of sunlight in the doorway to the stable, stood he who she sought.

Tindr stood at his workbench, half-turned from the open stable door. When Sigvor walked in, her shadow fell upon the horse carved of wood he was smoothing, a toy for Yrling. He saw the shadow was a woman's and turned with a smile. It was not the mistress of Tyrsborg who stood there, and his lips parted in surprise.

Red Cheeks. He had glimpsed her a few times over the last four years on the trading road, but she had never looked at him. She had been with her husband and child, and one year he saw there were two little ones with her. Now she stood before him, alone, and back at Tyrsborg.

Despite the change on his face Sigvor made herself smile at him. She neared him, and he stepped back slightly, forcing him into deeper shadow. She had planned in her mind how she would tell Tindr what she needed from him, and now she must do it.

"I need," she said, stretching out her hand and bringing it to her chest, "a piece of gold."

She thought that gesture meant Want, not Need, but Tindr often used one and the same sign for similar feelings. For the gold she had ready a whole coin of silver, which she opened in her hand, then touched, shook her head Nai, and brought the gold-coloured fabric of her sash to. "Gold, not silver. I need gold. One piece. Please." She had racked her brains recalling how Tindr gestured this, the cupping of his hands together, and did it for him now.

He looked at her, shaking his head slightly, watching her hands and lips.

She repeated it all, the reaching, the coin that was not quite right, the yellow-gold of her sash touching the coin. The cupped hands, begging. Tears were coming into her eyes, at her helplessness to express her need, and her frustration that he could not hear her. All knew he had many pieces of gold somewhere. She asked for only one.

"It is no good to you," she told him, as her tears ran. "It will be everything to me. One piece. Of gold. Please." She went through the signs again.

Tindr looked at the coin, the gold-coloured sash. He understood, and nodded. She had hurt him badly once, but now she needed help. He did not know why she wanted gold, nor why she cried to him about it, but it was clear her need was great. The gold coins from the sale of the great narwhale horn lay in a small pottery jar under the floorboards of his alcove in his mother's house. He and his mother had put them there together, and she had told him over and again they were his. He would give her one.

She saw he understood, saw he agreed. She clasped her hands together. "Tomorrow morning, in the cove beyond the fish drying racks. Bring it to me then." She did not know how to sign this, and looked about her. Tindr's workbench was covered with fine sawdust. She drew the Sun with its rays with her finger, then a half Moon. Then the Sun, rising from the wavy lines of water. "In the morning." She drew a fish, on a stick, then pointed with her hand to where the great racks of salted stock-fish were hung to dry. The coin again, in her palm.

He nodded, smoothed the sawdust, drew an outline of the wooden figure of Freyr, and just past this a quick lattice work of lines for the fish racks.

"Já, já," she nodded. "That cove. In the morning." She felt of a sudden wonderfully free, and on the edge of great happiness. She wanted almost to kiss him.

He saw the tears dry on her face, and the gladness in her eyes. The promise of a piece of metal did this for her. He would be there in the morning, with the gold for her.

Ceridwen was walking up the hill with Eirian and Yrling, and her serving woman Helga. Yrling had run ahead a little to see what their neighbour Alrik was working on in his croft; he always had planks of wood he was sawing or smoothing, and little waste-blocks he gave to the boy. Eirian was walking between her mother and Helga, with a hand clutching at both their skirts, and was singing a nonsense song as she swung the fabric back and forth in her fists. Both women were laughing.

A woman hurried down towards them, coming from Tyrsborg. She was short and plump, with yellow curling hair streaming out from under her linen head wrap. She had lowered her face as soon as she spotted the approaching women. Helga did not recognize her, but Ceridwen knew her at once. As the woman neared, Ceridwen opened her mouth to voice her greeting. Sigvor kept her face resolutely down, and Ceridwen did not speak after all.

After Sigvor left him, Tindr turned back to his work, but after a few minutes set down the horse figurine. He was troubled enough by seeing Sigvor to want to get the coin now and have it ready, so he would not have to think of it later. He brushed the sawdust from his hands and began to cross the kitchen yard. As he did he saw Bright Hair and Helper come back, with the little ones. Bright Hair looked at him in a way that made him slow. Her green eyes were wide, and her mouth looked worried. She left Helper and came to him.

Ceridwen rarely saw Sigvor, and was not happy that she had been here at Tyrsborg. There was only one person she would wish to see, and she feared for him. As she stood before Tindr she touched her eye, then lifted both hands to her cheeks to name Sigvor. Then she turned and gestured down the hill.

Tindr nodded. He had lowered his eyelids over his blue-white eyes. She did not know what had brought Sigvor to see him, but pausing before Tindr she reminded herself that he was a man with a right to his own life. She had at times to check her protectiveness towards him, just as she urged Rannveig to worry less about her son's future. In the past when Tindr needed help, he had come to her and Sidroc, just as he had gone to his mother for advice. Looking at his lowered lashes, she wished to leave it go at that, sorry she had even let him know she had seen Sigvor.

Tindr went on his way down to his mother's. He passed through the empty brew-house and found Rannveig, where she was almost sure to be, standing in her open brewing shed. She was crumbling dried barley and looked up and smiled as Tindr waved to her. He passed Gudfrid where she sat crouched by the ash-covered baking pans, checking her loaves for doneness. The door of his house was open and he walked through it.

His gold was buried in a little pottery jar set into the soil under the floorboards of his old alcove. He folded the deerskin which lay upon those boards, giving it a pat; it was that from the great hart he had taken, his first, in the company of his Uncle Rapp and cousin Ragnfast. The boards fit closely together but the tip of his knife slid between them was enough. The jar was not sealed, just had a wood stopper. His fingers reached in and closed around one coin. It was a pretty thing, and on rare occasions he had seen men or women wearing jewellery, necklaces or arm rings, of the stuff, which were even prettier. But many folk died for gold, he knew.

As he was spreading his deer skin over the boards his eye fell on the little bone whistle on a thong of leather hanging above his bed. It was just like that which hung about his neck now, inside his tunic, but the one on the wall was the last bone whistle that Dagr had carved for him. When he was little his father made him whistles from the leg bones of sheep. Tindr oftentimes broke or lost them, so his Da had made him many. When Tindr began to hunt deer, he asked his Da to use the deer leg bones. One day Tindr wanted to make his own. He had chipped the mouthpiece of this one, and used it for his model as he fashioned a new one. He remembered going to Da afterwards, and blowing it for him to make sure it sounded, and his Da ruffling his hair and smiling, Já. But he kept this last one Da had made. It was a precious thing, far more precious than the gold in his hand.

THE COVE

TOSTE was hacking at weeds in the cabbage beds with his oldest daughter when his neighbour reined up in front of the house. Krok was rich and owned a horse. Toste put down his hoe and went to greet him.

"You were down to the trading road yesterday," Krok observed, leaning slightly over the pommel of his saddle.

Toste's face clouded with confusion. "Nai. I was out moving my sheep with my boys."

"Ah," returned Krok. "Well, I saw your wife there; I was at Rannveig's and watched her walk past."

Toste did not move for a moment. Sigvor had told him she wished to see her sister who lived further upcountry. She had said nothing about going to the town.

His daughter straightened up in the row and stretched her back, and looked over to where her father stood visiting with his friend before bending once more over her work.

"Já," Toste lied, looking back at Krok. "I forgot she was going. Where did you see her walking?"

"Heading up the hill behind the brew-house. The hall of the Dane."

Toste went back to his work, pondering over this. Sigvor had acted strangely the night he returned from visiting his mother. She was oddly happy; he thought then the day alone had in fact done her good. She had been sweet to him, and snuggled up to him in bed. Even though he was tired he acted on it, and she had responded with welcome eagerness. In the morning he thought he should try to give her more time to herself, if this was the result.

He had heard from his mother that his cousin Eirik was returned, as if from the dead. A trader had put him ashore, and he had been at his parent's house for several days now. His mother had clucked and shook her head as she repeated this to Toste. She disliked the boy's wild and spendthrift ways, pinning it all on the unfortunate marriage of her sister to a man whose own family had luck in fishing but little else commendable about them.

When Toste had arrived home, he had already decided he would not tell Sigvor that Eirik was back. If he was here to stay she must find out sometime, but he would not be the one to tell her. Few in the family believed Sigvor when she came to Eirik's mother and father and told them she was carrying his babe. His boat had then been gone for more than two months, and here she was, claiming that Eirik had made hand-fast with her, had promised her that as soon as he had returned he would take her to his home and tell his parents about his choice. They had stared at her. Eirik already had a son with another woman, one he had refused to wed, and it had cost them some silver to end her complaint, giving her enough to dower her to another man. Sigvor would not get a single coin from them. They had no knowledge that Eirik was seeing her, and her babe might be anyone's.

Standing before them she seemed almost to consider herself their son's widow, as if they should take her in. Yet Eirik had never mentioned her.

Toste knew all this, because Eirik's father had come to him a few days later. Toste's wife had been dead over a year. He was lonely, and his two daughters needed a woman in the house. Sigvor was pretty and handy and her people well-regarded. Eirik's father felt badly for the girl, suspected that she was telling the truth about the babe, if not the fact that Eirik had made hand-fast with her. Would not Toste wed her? It would be an end to all their trouble.

It was a mistake, from the start. Sigvor disdained his daughters, was indifferent to his sons, and showed little warmth to her own child. She regretted being far from her family, and was left angry that they had urged her to accept Toste. He had tried to be kind to her, but oftentimes lost his temper. She was joyless in the marriage-bed, and made him feel she submitted to him, nothing more.

What had she been doing at the hall of the Dane, he wondered, as he sliced the hoe blade into the dry soil. He had found out, after their hand-fast, that Sigvor had tried to ensnare that simpleton, Tindr. He lived at the hall. Would she have gone to see him?

He thought over the past few days. She had seemed distracted. On two of the days he had been gone long hours, busy tending to their sheep, and going to the iron-smith. His daughter had mentioned that her step-mother had walked down the road and was gone a good while, but had returned with an apron full of strawberries from the meadow. Had she gone to meet Eirik there?

He had come to the end of the cabbage row. He looked over to where his daughter knelt, carefully separating bindweed from the throat of a young cabbage. She was not a pretty girl, he knew, but she was good. He rested his hoe against a fence post, and slapping his hands free of dirt, went into the house.

His young wife was there, kneeling in front of their alcove. Under the box bed were two shallow chests, and she had pulled one out and was looking through it. It was the chest in which she stored her better clothing, those things reserved for feasts and visiting. She turned when he walked in, and he saw the startle on her face. Their little boy was playing in the alcove he shared with his older brother. Her older son out with his own boys, walking the sheep to another pasture.

He did not ask what she was doing. There was no reason for her to be looking at her fine gown and fancy shawls; there were no near feasts. He walked out again, without a word.

Later when she was out of the house he went to the places where he kept his silver. There was a jar behind a loose board in the wall by their alcove, in which small amounts of coins and hack metal were kept, and a crock laid in the soil under a tight-fitting floorboard. The crock was set with a wooden stopper sealed with wax. It had not been disturbed. But the jar, which he had not cause to look into for a while, held far less than what he had recalled.

⋙⋙⋙⋙⋙

That night Sigvor told Toste she would go to the trading road in the morning. She had completed a bolt of wadmal, and would take it to her sister Sigrid to sell in the stall. Toste knew she had finished the cloth; it had been hanging to dry out beyond the medlar trees.

"Wait a day, and we will go together," he told her.

Sigvor's answer was swift, and given with a small recoil of her head. "Nai, nai, it must be tomorrow; Sigrid is waiting for it."

Toste did not even ask how Sigvor might know that. He simply nodded his head.

It was still dark when he felt her leave the bed. He feigned a yawn, and turned where he lay, eyes lowered but not shut, towards her where she stood, pulling on her shift and gown in the dark.

Sigvor put her shoes on as quietly as she could. Her thumping heart sounded in her ears so loudly she feared that Toste would hear it, wake, and speak to her. She had made up many lies in the past days, but did not think herself up to another, not as shaky as she felt.

The alcove next theirs was where her two boys slept. Her packs were in there with them, where she had hidden them last night. She parted the woollen curtains. She could just make out the dark forms of her boys where they huddled together in sleep. She felt a pang looking at them. Could she not take them with her? The elder was Eirik's own boy; surely he would come to love him. And the younger – she had real affection for him; he was even-tempered and always smiling. But how would she get them to the cove? She would have to wake them silently. The elder could walk, but the little one she would have to carry, and she had her packs. And she must hurry; she could never carry him and them too. Then she imagined Eirik's scowl if she turned up at the cove with them. If he refused to take them she could not leave them alone on the beach, and he would leave her behind too. She bit her lip as all this swirled in her mind. Finally she bent to kiss each small brow. The older boy's hand lifted as if to brush away her touch. She took her packs from the foot of their bed and pulled their curtains shut.

She crept to the door, slid the bar. The grey light of coming day fell on the floor of the house as she opened the door. Then she slipped out.

Toste had watched her go from the slit in the alcove curtains. He sat up. The moment she stepped out of that door with her bundles she had left him, and abandoned her children, too. He was stunned that she could do so. Sigvor could pout and be petulant, but he thought her at core a decent woman, and she was a hard worker as well. Now she had deceived him, and likely with the same man who had first gotten her with child, a child he himself was now raising. He felt, with rising certainty, it must be his cousin Eirik, the ne'er-do-well so lately returned. Sitting there he felt his blood rising in his body, thrumming in his neck veins. His shock grew to rage.

He pulled on his leggings and shoes and yanked a tunic over his head. In the corner of the house, nearest the front door, his spear stood waiting. He had it in his hand and was out the door after her.

Sigvor was making, with as much speed as she could muster, her way down the road heading to the sea. He wanted to trail her silently until he caught them together, and kept to the shadows of the trees lining the road. She did not look back, not even once.

Sigvor left the dusty road and took a path skirting meadowland. It led to the sea, just past where Eirik's family hung their catch to dry. Toste felt his grip tightening on his spear shaft as he realised this. There was little doubt now she ran off to meet his cousin. He forced himself to take a deep breath, to loosen his clenched hand. There was no way they could remain on Gotland; he would hunt them down and kill Eirik and drag his wife back home, and have the right of the law on his side in doing so. They knew this and had chosen the sea to escape.

He had to slow, as the path held few hiding places. Yet it was just like Sigvor, in her stubbornness, to refuse to turn and even look to find if she were being pursued. When she made up her mind she could see nothing else.

The Baltic was before him now, lying grey and flat. The wind was light, as it almost ever is so early, but the birds were chirping and darting in the growing sunlight. The meadow ended in a line of trees and clumping shrubs. He let Sigvor make her way through them. Beyond that was the white limestone pebbles of the beach.

Tindr had made his way along the empty trading road. He passed the great wooden statue of Freyr, and gave him a nod. He went down to the shoreline and walked on the beach, skirting the place of burial. The long fish drying racks, half full of salty slabs of white herring and cod, lay beyond this. The ground rose a bit as he entered the next cove. He saw a small fishing boat, not beached, but in shallow water. A man waited on the beach, alone. Tindr went up to the shelter of some hazel shrubs. When he regained sight of the man he was no longer alone.

Sigvor's heart leapt when she reached the sea. She had been walking as quickly as she could, and her arms ached from holding her packs. She was breathless and frightened, and no small part of her fear was that when she got to the cove Eirik would not be there after all. But no, there he was, a boat behind him, pacing as he awaited her. Despite her breathlessness she forced herself to run to him these last few steps, feeling the sharp stones of the beach through the soles of her shoes. She dropped her bundles at his feet and threw herself into his arms.

"Where is the gold?" was the first thing he said.

She clung about his neck. "It is coming," she answered. Tears were smarting her eyes at his greeting. She remembered afresh that all depended on Tindr. "It will be here soon."

She turned a moment to scan the beach.

"Who is bringing it to you?" Eirik demanded. "And what did you do to deserve gold?"

He might as well have slapped her. "Eirik," she cried, "I love you, only you. Do not doubt me!"

She had tightened her grip upon him. Her back was to the sea, his to the line of shrubs and trees. As she looked over his shoulder her husband stepped forward, his spear held aloft and ready. He took a lunging step as he let it fly at Eirik's back.

At the first sight of Toste Sigvor's mouth opened. No scream came forth. Her eyes went from Toste's contorted face, then to the raised spear. She held Eirik tightly in her arms, and twisting her body, tried to spin him out of its path.

She caught the brunt of the thrust. It struck her sideways through her ribs, into her lungs and heart. As she toppled over with the man she loved she felt a crushing blow, nothing more.

Toste's empty hand hung in the air, as if he could recall the thrown spear. He had killed his wife. Eirik lay beneath her, struggling. Toste's spear had penetrated her body and entered the chest of his cousin. It was not a fatal wound, but he had pinned them together. Sigvor's head was cast back, her wide blue eyes open. The blood from her wound spread over her bosom, drenching the top of her gown and Eirik's chest. Eirik was making a gasping sound as he flailed, trying to push Sigvor's body off him. He heaved himself away from her, eyes starting in his head.

Fueled by his rage, Toste was at his side in an instant, his drawn knife in his hand. His teeth were gritted in fury. It was his mind, not his throat, that was screaming: You are the cause of her death. You die too. A single plunge of his fist buried the blade in Eirik's chest.

Toste dropped on his knees by the carnage. Eirik's chest had jolted with the blow, and his blood now pooled over his tunic.

Toste had said nothing all this time, but now became aware of someone screaming. It was a howl, not dog-like, but almost not human. Someone had run up to his side. He turned his head.

Rannveig's son was there, Tindr. Why had he been there, had he been walking on the beach? Yet Sigvor had likely been to see him, the day she lied and went to the trading road. Was this simpleton part of it?

Tindr stood there, looking down at the bodies, and howling. No, thought Toste, as his thoughts raced ahead; if he were guilty of anything he would not have shown himself to me.

Toste rose. He knew his hands were shaking. Tindr stepped back away from him, but Toste opened his palms; he had no other weapon than the two now lodging in the bodies of the dead.

For one wild instant he asked himself if he could name Tindr as the murderer. It would be his word against Tindr's. He knew Sigvor had tried to get Tindr as her husband, before rejecting him. Now Tindr was back to kill her as she ran away with yet another man. But no, Tindr did not use a spear. If he were to kill folk, it would be the same way he took game. And his mother was one of the most respected women on the coast; to accuse Tindr would almost be like accusing her.

Toste could not rein in his thoughts, and knew he must. He had killed his wife, and his cousin. A man could kill another without punishment if it was clear his wife was being stolen. Eirik was his own kin and not well liked; he need not fear reprisal from his own people. But Sigvor – her people loved her, and they had standing amongst folk. He could be outlawed.

He trembled the more, considering this. The breeze had picked up and he felt as cold as if snow lay on the ground. A decree of outlaw was a living death. He would be forced to forfeit his farm, and his children, and to leave Gotland. He would lose everything. Any aiding or abetting him were subject to being outlawed themselves. He had always been an upright man. Now he had killed a wastrel who had seduced his wife. He had meant to do so; Eirik deserved it. But he had wanted only to frighten Sigvor. He would give her a birching like the spoiled child she was, and that would be the end of it. But he had killed her too, and first.

If Tindr had watched, he would have seen this, and seen too that he had been aiming for Eirik's back. It was Sigvor who spun him out of the path of his spear.

He saw now that Tindr was his only hope. Rannveig could speak to her son, learn the true tale. If Tindr's accounting agreed with his, he might be free to go on with his life.

The Sun had fully risen from the water. The baldness of what his weapons had done grew more ghastly in the harsh light. Tindr stood there, panting almost, unable to take his eyes from what lay before them. Then Tindr pointed at Toste, arm outstretched, a hard, direct accusation. He grunted, and turned his pointing finger along the beach, past the drying racks and towards the trading road.

Toste nodded. If he ran now from Tindr, he would only prove his guilt, and look the worse for him. Keeping his hands open before him, he took his place alongside Tindr as they turned to go.

A few folk were stirring on the trading road, rolling up their awnings, settling down to work. Toste knew they would make straight for Rannveig's brew-house, and they did. The awnings were rolled down closed as they entered, and the space was dim. Tindr had pulled his whistle from his tunic, not wanting to leave Toste alone while he found his mother, but by chance Rannveig was there, carrying in cups and stacking them on the back table.

One look at her son's white face told her something terrible had happened, and that Tindr had seen it.

She went to his side, touched his hand.

"What?" she said, tapping her temple, her voice already quivering.

Toste was once again trembling as he watched.

Tindr lifted his fingers to his face, touched his cheeks.

Rannveig drew breath. "Sigvor," she said.

Tindr made a stabbing or hurling motion. Then he pointed at Toste by his side.

Rannveig stifled her gasp with her hands.

"Sigvor is dead," she repeated. She looked to Toste. Her words were very low. "You killed her."

Toste buried his face in his hands.

Rannveig turned her head from him. She looked her son in the eyes, nodded slowly, telling him she believed him.

Watching this, Toste's shoulders began to shake, but he raised his head and looked to her. "I meant to kill Eirik, only Eirik, never Sigvor," he cried.

Rannveig took breath, tried to gather herself. She made a small gesture with her hands, that Toste should stop in what he was telling her. She drew a second breath. She went to the awnings and rolled them quickly up, one after the next. Daylight was needed in such cases, and plenty of it. She gestured to both men that they sit. Toste slumped down at a table, and lowered his head, his hands coming up around the back of his neck as if to ward off blows. Tindr sat at another table, staring at him.

She vanished out the door, returning with two cups of hot broth, and set them before them. Gudfrid followed her in from the kitchen yard, and Tindr watched as she gave her orders, gesturing up the hill, and down the trading road.

The first to arrive were Sidroc and Ceridwen, their concern clear on their brows. They had been at table when Gudfrid had hustled around through the kitchen yard door to summon them. They did not know why Tindr had not been about the hall that morning; it was Summer and he was not hunting. But Tindr sometimes vanished without telling them, and they felt no concern. Now Rannveig's eyes darted to them as they entered. Tindr stood up, facing them.

Scar was the person Tindr most wanted to see. His mother was here to speak for him, and now with Scar here he took hope. Bright Hair gave him a little smile, worried as her face was, and her hands rose gently in Tindr's direction, as if to send comfort. He swallowed and nodded his thanks to her. His eyes fastened on Scar, as the warrior looked from his mother to him. Scar held his eyes, nodded at him. Tindr was his man, and by that nod he acknowledged their bond.

Rannveig stood before her friends. She knew that all that was said this morning might matter, and chose her words with care.

"This is Toste, Sigvor's husband," she said, opening her hand to the man seated before them. "Sigvor is dead. She was found with Eirik, the father of her first born."

Ceridwen spoke first, though in her shock she could hardly form the words. "Her old sweetheart?" she asked.

"Já."

Sidroc looked to the man, then back to Tindr. His hand rose to his head and he ran his fingers through his dark hair. "What part did Tindr play in this?" he asked.

"I do not know yet," his mother told him. "He saw it happen. I have sent for her parents, and Eirik's as well. And Botair, Ketil, and Berse. I do not think either of them should tell until the others are here."

Sidroc nodded. "The first telling is the truest," he agreed.

The four of them waited as the others arrived, striding from their various homes or workshops, bringing others with them. Toste looked as if he could not hold his head up, sprawling on the top of the table for support. Tindr sat down again at his table, and as the chief men and women of the place filed in, watched them give hushed greeting to the others before staring at Toste's lowered head.

Sigvor's parents came in, with her older sister Sigrid, the two women already weeping from the little Gudfrid had been able to tell them. With eyes glaring at Toste, her father demanded the story as soon as he strode in. Rannveig was quick with her answer; nothing would be said until all closely connected were gathered. The parents of the dead man were last to come, living at a place far removed. His mother was wringing her hands, but his father's face was set.

Twenty or more people were now ranged before the two men, Tindr and Toste. Berse, the weapon-smith, had been speaking with Botair and Sidroc, with Rannveig listening in. Now Berse stood up and addressed all.

"This is a dark day for us. Blood has been shed, and lives ended. Toste will tell his story, and then Tindr. The telling will be hard, the listening more so. But we are a peaceful people. No weapons are to be drawn."

Berse paused a moment, looking to Sidroc and Botair, who had placed themselves nearest the two who were to speak. Berse himself, working all day hammering steel, was a formidable man, and would be in the centre of the room should any need to be restrained. All the men sitting there, and most of the women, had knives at their waists. All knew the sanctity of any place in which the truth was to be told, that it must not be sullied with violence.

Toste arose and told his story, his fingers steepled on the planks of the table top. He began with the day he had gone to visit his mother, told of hearing of his cousin's return, and how he had begun to suspect Sigvor was seeing Eirik and planning her escape. He told of the lie he had learnt about, when his neighbour Krok had seen Sigvor in town heading up the hill to Tyrsborg. It was here that heads turned first to Sidroc, then to Tindr. Tindr's eyes widened, but as Toste went on the others stopped looking at him.

He came to the difficult part, watching his wife slip out of the house with her belongings, trailing her to the beach. Seeing her there in Eirik's arms. Toste's voice had risen in pitch as he told this, and the noises coming from those sitting before him grew, an undercurrent of gasps, barely spoken oaths, and grunts and snorts of startle.

"Já, I meant to kill Eirik, I did," Toste was saying, his voice shuddering. "But Sigvor – Sigvor turned him out of the way! I did not mean Sigvor to die . . . "

There was a tumult of shouts and cries. Sigvor's father was standing, straining forward towards Toste. "Where is she?" he barked. "Where is my daughter?"

Toste was sobbing now, and Sigvor's mother and sister wailed, watching him. Eirik's parents too were standing, calling out their question, and Berse gestured to them they must still themselves.

"When I saw what I had done, I killed Eirik with my knife. He was the reason Sigvor died!"

Eirik's parents sat down, his mother with her hands covering her face, his father white-knuckled as he listened.

Berse looked to Rannveig. "What did Tindr see?" he asked her.

She rose and came to stand at her son's side. With a few gestures of hands and head she asked him to act out what had happened. He began in a way that surprised all. Touching his cheeks to represent Sigvor, he then repeated how she had asked him for a coin. His hand went to his belt, and he held between his fingers the bright gold piece for all to see. Toste straightened up at this, they all did. It seemed to prove his tale, that Sigvor had plotted to leave him, and was not above asking a man for gold so she could do so.

Eirik's father lowered his face then. It was all too like his troublesome youngest, to have demanded gold from a woman he was stealing away. The tears were running from his wife's eyes as he sat there, but what he felt was the shame Eirik, even in death, had laid on his family.

Ceridwen, watching Tindr, found herself rising to her feet. She could not add much to the telling, but wished Tindr to see her stand in his support. Her husband's eyebrows lifted as she stood, but she looked to Berse, who nodded to her.

"I saw Sigvor on her way back from Tyrsborg, the morning she came to Tindr," she told them. She hardly knew what to say next. "I was surprised to see her there; she did not part happily from our hall. I know she saw me, but she did not lift her head so I could greet her."

Heads nodded; folk shifted on their benches. All knew Sigvor had left Tyrsborg hastily, years ago, after falsely accusing Tindr of having gotten her with Eirik's child. Rannveig's anger over the girl's behaviour back then had been just.

"Have him tell of the murder," Sigvor's father called out, staring at Tindr.

Toste answered him, his voice catching. "It was not murder. She turned him away . . . "

Berse ordered all to silence, and Rannveig had Tindr go on. He still held the coin in his hand, that which he had never had a chance to give Sigvor, and now set it down. He moved with his mother before the table he had sat at, and touched his eye. He wrapped his arms about Rannveig, so that she was looking out at the crowd. Rannveig had heard enough to know Sigvor had spotted her husband and had pushed Eirik out of the path of the thrown spear, and she turned Tindr away. They parted, and Tindr grunted, nodding his head, touching his mother's side to show where the spear had entered.

Fresh cries came from the folk before Tindr; he saw their gaping mouths and the tears on the cheeks of the women. It was terrible for him, worse than when Purple Neck fell from the rock. Red Cheeks had been killed before his eyes, and by the man pledged to protect her. Then the same man had, with savage violence, driven a knife through the other man's heart. He knew women were precious and men would kill for them. Tindr had watched Scar kill a man with equal ferocity. But the man Scar had severed the throat of was a warrior who had wanted to hurt Bright Hair, and was then trying to kill Scar. Tindr himself had nocked an arrow at the strange warrior's back, ready to let it fly if he must. He remembered how he had felt, standing behind the warrior, not feeling his own breath, nor even the beating of his heart.

He scanned the faces before him, all looking back at his own face. He could not tell what blame he bore in all this. When Purple Neck had died, it took his cousin and Da and Nenna a long time to make him understand he was not the reason Purple Neck had tried to climb, and died doing so.

His mother signed to him he should sit now, and he returned to the table. She had given his hand a little squeeze when she left him, and as he sat he saw Scar look at him, and open his hands flat before him: Good.

"And she lies there, on the beach?" Sigvor's father was shouting. Her mother now joined him. "Where are my grandsons?" she called to Toste.

Toste had not even time to give thought to his farm. His children would have risen and found neither parent there. His daughters would have fed and clothed the boys, but all would be wondering where they were. The spectre of them looking for him, of Sigvor's two crying for her, rose in his eyes.

His mother-in-law was standing, shaking her fist at him. "Sigvor's boys will not spend another night under your roof, the man who killed their mother."

Toste found himself dumbly nodding back to her, já. She would take Sigvor's sons, it was only right.

He was light-headed; there had been no mention of outlawing, no oaths of vengeance sworn by Sigvor's father. He would be made to pay the dowry she had brought with her; he would do that without complaint. He would go back to the farm, and be no worse off than he had been after the mother of his own children had died. He grasped onto this thought, then felt the hollow falseness of it. He would never be the same. He had killed two people. No woman would wed him now. His plain older daughter would never wed, and his sons would bear the shame of their father's act. He and his daughter would grow old, living together but alone in his farmhouse. He lowered his head into his hands again, and sobbed.

Berse called out for quiet. He looked to Sidroc and Botair. "We must now, those of us who choose to, go with Toste and Tindr to the cove."

No one spoke. Some of the men had begun to rise, and some women too. Sigrid, Sigvor's sister, had her arms about her mother to keep her there, but the older woman broke free. Sigrid rose herself, biting her lip ruefully. Sigvor's father held his hand up to stop his wife. "Nai," she answered, before he could speak. She was not crying now, and her voice was as hard as the steel which had pierced her daughter. "No one will stop me from looking on my dead girl's face."

Sidroc looked to his own wife. He had learnt early that giving her orders rarely worked, but he would do so now if she rose to follow him. She had seen slaughter, much of it, but never here on Gotland. The night-mare which had often carried her away in their early days here had left her. He did not want the sight of the slain lovers to call the dark mare back again.

He need not fear. Her eyes were trained on Rannveig. Ceridwen saw in Rannveig's face her unwillingness to let Tindr go alone, then saw her look to Sidroc. Tindr would not be alone.

Sidroc motioned Tindr to his side. He watched his wife rise and go to Rannveig, sit down next her with her arm about the older woman's shoulder. Ceridwen lifted her face, and he nodded to her as he went out the door. They set off, Toste between Berse and Sidroc, and Tindr beside Sidroc.

The party of ten or twelve made their way down the trading road. Their numbers quickly swelled as others joined them, those who had heard little or nothing of what had happened that dawn. They looked up from their work with questioning eyes at the cluster of grim faces passing before them, and many found themselves rising to follow in their wake. They joined at the rear, speaking in hushed voices to those who had been at the brew-house. Berse stopped at the grain-sellers, told him to ready his ox cart and follow them to the cove.

In the brew-house only women were left. Ceridwen yearned to take Rannveig out into the herb garden, and wished to be there herself, under the sky and amidst the scented flowers. But the way her friend sat there made her know that Rannveig could not or would not leave; she would await the return of the others here, in her brew-house, the room around which her life and the lives of so many of the local folk revolved.

One of the women sitting there was the salt seller Asfrid, seated near Eirik's mother, who was softly crying into a corner of her head-wrap. Asfrid would have liked to go sit with Rannveig and the wife of the Dane, both of whom she liked. But Eirik's family were nearly all fisher-folk, and her best customers, so she stayed near to the weeping woman. And she felt pity for the woman, who had lost her son twice, so to speak, once when his boat had not returned, and now at the hands of another man. Eirik was no good, but a mother's love endured.

Gudfrid moved amongst them with a tray of ale. The day was warming, and with all the words that had been spoken and tears shed ale was welcome. As they sipped the women scarcely spoke. Rannveig was silently berating herself once more for ever bringing Sigvor to Tyrsborg. The woman had attempted to take advantage of her son's sweet nature, and had hurt him badly. She had hastily left the hall with no apology when all had given her a chance at a good home and stable life. Now she had dragged Toste down, caused the man to lose his senses and cover himself in her blood. And she had left her two boys behind her, all for the love of a good-looking scoundrel.

Rannveig felt, as well, the cruelty of Fate. When Tindr had taken the golden piece from his belt to show what Sigvor had asked him for her heart had turned in her breast. It was true she had told her son from the start that the gold earned from the sale of Dagr's rare narwhale horn was his. But she had told him then, and he had understood, that it was for his wife and him, and their coming babes. She did not have the resolve to go through those gestures again, stressing that he wait until his hand-fast before spending any of it. Tindr had been single so long that such a day was not to be looked to.

Yet Rannveig knew within herself a glimmer of gratitude to the dead woman. She had rejected Tindr. She shuddered to think what would have happened if Sigvor and Tindr had made hand-fast, and then Eirik returned as he did. It was unthinkable that Tindr would kill as Toste had, but the wound to her boy would have been great if she had run off as she had planned to do.

Those who had gone to the cove neared the place. They saw the boat first, listing slightly in the receding tide. Eirik's father, shaking his head to himself, knew it at once to be the second vessel of his oldest son, stolen by Eirik. They stepped upon the white limestone of the beach. As soon as the yellow of Sigvor's skirt could be seen, Tindr hung back. Toste too was unwilling to go closer, but pinioned as he was between Berse and Sidroc he was forced to approach. Even so he stopped several feet short of the slain pair. They let him be.

Toste's spear lay at a low angle from Sigvor's body, firmly lodged in her ribcage. The wind was fresh and the hem of her gown was fluttering slightly over the tops of her dark shoes. The tips of her yellow hair were likewise stirring in the breeze, in a ghostly mockery of life. One of her cheeks rested on the stones of the beach, where she had fallen. Eirik's arms were flung out on either side of him, his back still arched from the action of his head lifting as Toste had neared him with his knife. It was buried, almost to the hilt, in his chest.

Sidroc went up to the bodies, passing a small pile of leathern packs. He had never seen the man before, but the woman he had known slightly a few years past. Sigvor had lived under his roof for a month, had brought him food, gathered eggs, swept the floor. He recalled her voice. She had walked the Earth some twenty years, and was now a bloodied corpse. His warrior-mind skipped through these facts, selecting those things needful to the task before him.

He scanned the length of the bodies, then squatted down. With deep wounds to the vital organs they had quickly bled dry, and the blood had soaked the clothing of their upper bodies and stained the white rock on which they lay. Little pools of it lay cupped in shallow stones around them, and begun to thicken in the warmth. The meaty smell of it was intense, lightened only by the slight salt tang of the steady sea breeze.

Despite the blood he could see the first wound Eirik had received, under the right breast, when the spear had run Sigvor through and pierced his chest. Toste had been very close when he had hurled his spear.

Berse came up to his side. Sidroc knew the weapon-smith could fight, and had in his youth gone raiding. The look on Berse's face told him long years had passed since he had looked on bodies such as these. Sidroc pointed out the place where the spear had caught them both, pinning them briefly together. Berse nodded and swallowed.

Botair and the others had slowed as they neared, but now that Sidroc and Berse stepped away, they came in twos and threes and looked down on the dead. Sigvor's mother was sobbing in her husband's arms, Sigrid on the other side of her, tears running from her face, but look they did. Some did not come close at all, but lingered back where Tindr stood, staring out at the sea. None stood by Toste. There were large clouds swimming in the blue sky, and the Sun vanished for long moments behind them, casting them in a shade that was almost cool.

When all who had wished to neared the bodies, Berse asked the key question of the day. "Do any of you, looking on this, and having heard what you have heard, call for the outlawing of Toste?"

The man named had kept his head resolutely down. He raised it now, looking not at those who had formed a loose circle about him, but solely at Berse.

None answered. Even Sigvor's kin kept silent, save for the weeping of her mother and sister. The girl had shamed herself, but without Tindr's showing that the spear was truly meant for Eirik, they would have pressed for outlawing.

Berse glanced about them, scanned their faces. The last he looked at were Botair and Sidroc. The two joined him a moment, their voices so low that none could discern what they said. Then Berse faced them all and gave the decree.

"This woman's death was accidental. The killing of this man was just retribution for the stealing of Toste's wife."

Berse looked at Sigvor's father as he said this last. The weapon-smith thought the grieving father would have been justified in killing Eirik himself, for the shame he had brought Sigvor to.

Eyes turned to Toste. He was swaying where he stood, and looked as if he would swoon. He bowed his head before all.

There was little left to say. Toste was free. Botair would go now, with Sigvor's father and Toste, to his farm, to fetch Sigvor's young boys; her mother had been speaking the truth when she had said they would not spend a single night under the same roof with Toste.

Before they left Sidroc walked to Sigvor's parents. They had looked stricken when they had first heard the news, and now had seen that which had changed them, and forever. He had killed enough men and watched their faces as he did so to be able to say something to them, and he did.

"This wound," he began, glancing an instant to what was behind them. "She felt little, just the power of the thrust. As if she had been punched."

They nodded their heads at him, wanting to believe she had not suffered. Her mother mouthed the words after him, *As if she had been punched*, considering them, taking them in. In coming years when she would awaken haunted by the look of horror on Sigvor's face, she would remember the big Dane's words, and draw comfort from them.

Tindr still stood, his back to the beach and what it bore, looking out at the sea. A shadow fell upon the bleached white of the rock he stood upon. He turned to see Scar there. The warrior raised his hand to his ear, then touched the scar on his face. A little smile cracked his lips. He placed the tips of his fingers together, for the steep roof of Tyrsborg: Tindr and Scar go home now.

Tindr nodded, and breathed out a deep breath, one he felt he had been holding for hours.

After they left the grain-seller's ox cart appeared at the edge of the shrubs. His good wife had set two dark woollen blankets within, so that the dead lovers might be decently covered.

They were not burnt together. Sigvor's body was claimed by her parents, and consigned to the flames at the place of burial later that day. Her ashes were buried on the family farm, not far from the tree the girls used to swing from when they were small.

Eirik's body was carried to the home of his people. There his father and brothers set it in a tiny skiff charged with oil-soaked kindling. They towed it out next morning at dawn. When it was beyond the forces of the incoming tide they flung a lighted torch into it. His mother, watching from shore, saw the fierce blaze flare up like a fallen star, then be blotted out in the cold water.

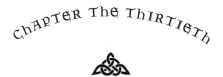

THE SÁMI

The Year 886 Late Summer

T INDR stood at his workbench in Tyrsborg's stable, re-feathering arrows. Yrling came running in to him, jumping with excitement, eyes shining.

"Look, look," he said, touching his eye. His small hands now rose to the top of his head, spreading out like antlers. "Deer, deer!" He pointed down the hill, as if to Nenna's house, or to the pier.

He grabbed Tindr by one hand. Tindr set down his arrow and followed the boy along the side of Tyrsborg until they stood by the front door. Tindr saw Scar and Bright Hair already there, standing near the well, looking down the hill.

Yrling jumped up again, his hands making antlers, then pointed down to where an odd waggon made its way to them.

Tindr stood, transfixed. It was neither oxen nor horses that pulled the waggon. Over the heads of the beasts that bore it rose long and broad antlers of great

397

sweep. He took a step forward. He could scarce believe it. These were deer, and they were harnessed and pulling the waggon up the hill.

A rider rode alongside the waggon, on a horse. Tindr looked to those within the waggon. Fur Man was there, he who had come almost every year since Tindr had lived at Tyrsborg. Fur Man wore nothing but the hides of animals, and brought piles of furs for Scar to trade for. He liked honey and Tindr had been given a seal-skin and other hides in return for jars of it. But in other years Fur Man had come with the man on the horse, with his furs in an oxcart.

His eyes went from Fur Man to another man, driving the deer, then saw a boy seated there too, in the back of the waggon. Both were dressed, as Fur Man was, in the skins of beasts.

The deer were closer now, and Tindr took yet another step forward. They were like no other deer he had ever seen. They were not red, and their heads were big and blocky, akin to that of a horse. They were brown and white, with longer white fur about the neck, and thick legs that flared to feet larger than a horse's, covered over with tufts of white fur. And they were big-boned, with broad shoulders and deep chests. Yet they were deer. They were beasts of the forests, yet utterly tame. Tindr could not move his eyes from them.

"So it is true," Sidroc was saying to his wife.

She was shaking her head in wonderment. They had been awaiting the arrival of Osku and Gautvid, and now they were come, and come with the special deer of the far North that Gautvid had told them of. The Gotlander's ship had just landed them there at the pier, and after the beasts had been harnessed and the waggon loaded, they made for Tyrsborg, their first stop.

Gautvid was a Gotlander, a cousin of Tindr's cousin Ragnfast the horse-breeder; and Osku's trading partner. It was Gautvid who sailed his broad-beamed ship to the northern reaches of the Baltic Sea, where the Sámi folk lived. Gautvid called them Skridfinn, Striding Finns, for the Sámi roamed great distances to hunt and fish. But Osku had his own name for his folk, Sámi, and that is what Ceridwen and Sidroc called him.

Osku the Sámi had not come to Tyrsborg last Fall. Gautvid came to the trading road alone, and with few furs. He said little about why the Sámi trader did not cross from the northernmost limits of the Baltic that year. Thus Sidroc was doubly glad to see both Gautvid and Sámi, and to note the size of the waggon Osku's deer pulled.

Yrling had been joined by Eirian, and both had run down to greet the waggon, and were standing by the side of the road with Alrik's children, who looked on open-mouthed. As it neared Tyrsborg Ceridwen heard the clicking of the wheels on the hard and stony ground, and saw that more folk than Osku sat in the waggon. Tindr was standing, stock-still, awaiting it, and like Tindr it was the deer that her eyes fastened upon. Their heads were broad and strong-muzzled, the coats as thick and bristled as a wolf's, with cream-coloured bellies, and grey and brown backs.

They wore no bits in their mouths, and the harness they were hooked to was of the simplest design. They tossed their heads as they pulled the waggon up the packed clay road, the many-pronged antlers shaking in the still and warm afternoon air. Somewhere there were bells

tied to them, for she heard a merry tinkle as they moved.
Now she looked beyond the beasts themselves to the folk
who sat within the waggon they drew.

Osku was easy to mark; he sat upright next to the
driver, and with his loose white-yellow hair resting on his
shoulders and tunic of tanned animal skins looked as he
ever had the years he had come to Tyrsborg. But he had
always come alone, with Gautvid. Now he had his own
kind with him, for the waggon was driven by a young
Sámi man, dressed in skins as was Osku, and behind them
perched a Sámi boy of ten or twelve Summers. The driver
was of slight build, with two long white-yellow braids
coming down from under his skin cap and falling almost
to his waist. The young boy too had the same light hair,
short and loose about his face. They must be Osku's sons,
and even from the distance she could see how pleased the
younger was, with eyes wide open and a smile stretching
across his mouth.

Gautvid smiled down from his saddle at those before
the front door. He was ten or more years older than his
cousin Ragnfast, a small and wiry man, brown haired,
and well-suited to the hardships he endured on his forays
North to bring its costly furs to the trading folk of Gotland. He did not speak yet, for there were customs which
must be followed with trading, and with the Sámi folk.

He and the waggon were close enough now for Ceridwen and Sidroc to hear the snorting breath of the big deer
as they neared. The waggon came to the top of the hill and
turned in. Ceridwen marvelled silently at their beauty, and
their seeming strength. Even more to wonder at was their
tameness, though Gautvid, who had travelled for years in
the lands of the Sámi, had told of the great herds the folk

kept there, how they trained them to pull their sledges in Winter and waggons in Summer, and even penned the she-deer after they had weaned their young and milked them and so made cheese.

"Ren deer, we call them," Gautvid had once told them. "The Skridfinn have their own name for them, but the use of an animal's name is a sacred thing, and they do not often do it, for fear of bad luck. But if you saw a team of ren deer pulling one of their sledges over snow, you might think they flew. They are as fast and sure-footed on ice as a skogkatt up a tree."

The waggon had now stopped, and the young driver sat with quiet hands as the deer tossed their heads a final time. Ceridwen could not see the driver well as Osku was next him, but was close enough to see the black fringe of lashes that framed the dark and lustrous eye of the ren deer nearest her.

Sidroc now moved forward to greet the trader. Osku stepped down from the waggon, and turned to face him. Sidroc opened his hands and spoke.

"I welcome you, Osku," he said, and inclined his head to his guest.

"I am welcomed by you," answered Osku, returning the nod. He pressed his own hands together at his chest. "May our trading leave both of us happy and prosperous."

Osku did not know much of the Norse tongue when he had first travelled to the hall, but each visit had shown him with a greater command. What he did not know, Gautvid could tell him, for he was versed in the speech of the Sámi. Yet as Sidroc had often said, trading needs no speech. All merchants knew a good sale could be made without words. But if the trader was to be one's guest, it was more pleasant for all to be able to share a few words in common.

The mistress of Tyrsborg now came forward and dipped her skirts to the Sámi. Osku smiled upon her, and lifted his hand in greeting.

Tindr now came nearer himself, and Ceridwen could not help but see how struck he was at the Sámi's return. Tindr had always looked long at the man, perhaps because Osku wore only the hides of animals. Osku's light brown tunic was of napped animal skin, as were his leggings, and his close-fitting cap. The only bits of cloth about him were the lines and dashes of bright blue and red wool thread that had been worked into the neck-opening of his tunic, and circled the sleeves at the wrists and ran up to his shoulders. His cap was also worked over with such designs, and Gautvid had told her that each Sámi man, woman, and child had a pattern unique to themselves in the thread-work that adorned the cap that sat upon their heads. The head, centre of thought, was sacred, and deserving of such attention and hand-work.

Tindr wore wool and linen clothes, like all on Got-land; and deer hide tunics in Winter. But he made his own boots, cut and sewn by him from the tough hides of the boar he had killed in the forests. He had made his first pair when he took his first boar, his mother Rannveig had told her. Ceridwen thought he did this to return the strength and vigour of the beast back into the forest in which it had run, lived, and died. When he trod the forest floor with his boots some part of the animal's vital energy flowed back into it. Like Osku Tindr left the fur upon his boots. Dressed all in skins as he was Osku seemed almost as much animal as man, and Tindr had responded to this with looks of awe.

Now here was the Sámi arrived in a waggon pulled by animals which should have been wild, yet were not. It seemed a form of magic to her, and she not could imagine how Tindr looked upon it. He came close to the ren deer, but did not touch them, even though they stood as quietly as halted oxen. He just stood, taking it in with his blue-white eyes.

Osku turned his head to the waggon, waved his hand at the boy who had sat behind him. The lad came forth, dressed as was Osku, all in skins. His cap was worked in red and blue thread of squares that interlocked. He smiled, showing strong white teeth.

"Ulmmá, my son," Osku said, and put his hand on the boy's shoulder. The young man who was driver now jumped down from his seat and came around to them. He stopped a little behind Osku and Ulmmá, and Ceridwen looked at him.

It was not a man at all. The driver was a maiden, of perhaps eighteen Summers, she thought; maybe more. She was so slender as to have little womanliness in her form; or the loose fitting skin tunic and tight leggings she wore hid it well. Her tunic was longer than that of Osku and the boy, and bore more of the bright thread-work in red and blue, and her cap was covered in the same wools closely stitched in circling designs. From under that close-fitting cap fell her whitish braids, not thick but wondrously long, for even braided they did indeed fall to her narrow waist. After moving nearer to them she stood perfectly still; her face unmoving, eyes trained on Osku's back.

Even up close a quick glance might have fooled one accustomed to more womanly dress into believing that a young man stood before them. It was the fullness of her lips that checked this; that and the fineness of the skin on her throat, white skin through which thin blue veins faintly shone. She had an odd and fey beauty, and there was no woman Ceridwen had seen she could compare her to. As she stood staring at her she glanced her way. She was indeed like no other woman, and now she saw why. She had a face like a deer, not those she drove, but those in the forest behind the hall. The face was narrow and fine-boned, with cheekbones so high and sharply-angled as to make the eyes appear slightly aslant. Those eyes as she looked back at her were a clear and unclouded blue.

She was much struck by her, and could only think: If Freyja comes as a white hind this is how she would appear.

The woman glanced away, forcing her own gaze to shift, and she saw Tindr, just to her right and near the ren deer's head, staring at her too.

Tindr had lifted his hands in the air, almost as if they reached toward her. He saw she was a woman, and saw too that she looked like a deer. It was not the face of the Lady who had come to him, but the high cheekbones and planes of her visage were doe-like. This, and her near-white hair, brought his Lady to his mind. He had some-times imagined that if she donned clothing she would wear the skins of the animals she ruled over, loved, and protected.

Osku half-turned to the girl, and said, "Šeará. My daughter."

Šeará, Ceridwen repeated inwardly. Her name sounded like the hiss of wind soughing through trees, or the sigh the waves make as they are sucked back across the rocks to the ever-hungry sea.

Tindr saw Fur Man gesture to the woman and then speak. He saw Bright Hair and Scar speak to her, nod their heads in greeting. The woman watched them speak, and cocked her head without replying.

She is like me, Tindr thought; she cannot hear. He had been holding his breath as if he neared a wild beast in the woods. Now he took a silent intake of air.

She did not smile as did her young brother, but only nodded at Sidroc and Ceridwen in turn. Tindr stood unmoving looking at her, and her head turned. She held his glance a moment.

Ceridwen was watching them both, knowing she should make some gesture of welcome to her, to them all; but was caught and held by the Sámi woman's striking face and still form.

Gautvid spoke and broke the spell. "It is good to see Tyrsborg again," he said, and swung down from his horse.

Tyrsborg had been a source of wealth to Gautvid, from the first Winter when Sidroc had surprised his wife with the bundles of furs he had bought from Gautvid to keep her warm, and then through the last three trading seasons but one when Gautvid had brought Osku himself to meet and trade with them. "I hope you had fair trading last year in what I sold you."

Sidroc took his arm in greeting and grinned back. "Only fair," he teased.

"Then perhaps you have no desire to see Osku's cargo," Gautvid teased back.

Sidroc laughed. He had been such a good customer that Gautvid always came to Tyrsborg first, so that Sidroc might have first pick. "I will take a look," he answered, still grinning.

Ceridwen opened her hands to all in a gesture of welcome. "You will be the guests of Tyrsborg for this night," she invited.

Her thoughts had already gone ahead, gauging if Gunnvor could feed all of them. She baked every second day, and had done so this morning, so that there was bread aplenty; and the browis she was already at work on could readily be doubled. Helga could go down to the trading road and meet a returning fishing boat and buy several fat herring or cod.

"The ren deer," Sidroc said, looking to the beasts. "We have a second paddock; they are welcome to it."

Osku was looking to Gautvid, who spoke back to him in the Sámi tongue. Osku responded, and Gautvid nodded at Sidroc.

Šeará went to the ren deer's head, Tindr close behind. Ceridwen heard her make a sound to the deer – not the clucking noise made to horses or oxen, this was almost a sung call – and the deer ambled onward, with her resting her hand on the neck strap of one of them. They wore the simplest of bridles, a headstall and cheek piece only.

Tindr saw her lips part, and the flutter at her throat. He saw too how the deer responded, following at her call. She was not deaf.

The others led the way into the grassy space near the stable, the deer walking after. Gunnvor had set up ale and buttered bread on the table by Tyrsborg's back stone wall, and now seeing how many they numbered, turned to bring out more cups, and a jug of honey-water too. Osku and Gautvid went to the back of the waggon and began to untie the leathern cords over-strapping the bundles there, Sidroc at their sides.

The Sámi woman began the task of unfastening the harness on the ren deer she had led. Tindr stood but an arm's length from her, leaning towards her in his readiness to help. He made a low grunt, which made her turn her eyes to him. He shook his head, brow troubled, as if he were sorry. He cupped his hands together and extended them towards her: Please. Then he pointed to the second ren, and made a gesture like unbuckling. She said something then; he saw her lips move again. Tindr's blue-white eyes fastened on her face, and her own darker blue eyes looked back at him. He shook his head. She spoke again. She saw the struggle on his brow as he grunted back in return.

Šeará paused. Then she stuck out her tongue, and touched it a moment with her finger. She closed her mouth and opened it again, gesturing with her hand that he do so too. Perhaps he could not speak because his tongue had been cut out. He opened his mouth, his tongue lolling. She saw his brow furrow as he looked at her.

He was almost desperate to speak, and yet feared making the braying call which answered for his speech. He forced his mouth closed.

Then he placed his hands one over each ear. He shook his head rapidly: Nai. I cannot hear. His hand went to the neck of his tunic, and he pulled out the little bone whistle lying there. He blew softly into it, showing how he summoned folk.

Šeará, watching all this, nodded. She did not speak again, but just stood looking at Tindr. Now he made a little bow towards her. He touched his right hand lightly to his right ear, then touched his chest. This is my name and my sign, he was telling her. He repeated the movements.

She looked at him, but shook her head. She touched her finger tips to the corners of her eyes, then pointed to him. I will know you by your eyes, she was telling him.

No one had ever given him a sign other than that which he had given himself, that for his deafness. He smiled then, and nodded to her.

He kept looking at her, and then took both his hands, fingers splayed, and lifted them a moment to his temples as if they were antlers. Deer. Then he pointed to her. I will call you Deer.

Something like a smile bowed the Sámi woman's lips, and she nodded back.

Tindr once again cupped his hands, then pointed to the ren: Please. Šeará nodded back, gesturing that he could help with the second harness. Together they freed the big deer from their slight trappings. Tindr's face as he handled the ren showed his delight, and he looked from the animal's driver back to it, and to the Sámi woman again. He led the way to the second paddock, passing the first where Tyrsborg's three horses lifted their heads, pointed ears twitching, to look at the new beasts walking before them.

Young Ulmmá was hanging on the paddock fence, staring at the horses, Yrling dangling from a lower rung. Ceridwen, watching from the table, wondered if their horses seemed as wondrous to Ulmmá as his ren did to them.

Once all had slaked their thirst the trading began. The contents of Osku's deer-drawn waggon did not disappoint. The Sámi opened bundle after bundle of glossy round beaver pelts, large waterproof hides of ringed seals, long narrow pelts of otters and martins, and the dense-furred skins of surpassing softness of the brown creature called mink. There were four pelts of fox in their Winter whiteness, and seeing them Sidroc knew would try for all of these. Brought out last of all was the Sámi's pride, the pelts of three great brown bears. These Osku handled with special care, unrolling them and laying them out on a tanned hide-skin one by one so that they might be admired each in turn. Sidroc wanted at least one of them.

He knew from Gautvid that the bear held a place of highest honour to the Sámi. It vanished into its den before snow blanketed the ground and lay in death-like sleep for months before being re-born in the Spring. Bear cubs emerged with it, born to a mother who seemed dead. This alone was strong magic, and made the Sámi revere this strange creature. The eating of bear was always a sacred meal, and some years Sámi only lived through harsh Winters by being able to partake of its fatty meat and rich marrow of its bones, which would feed a family for weeks.

Yet the bear was the animal most akin to folk themselves. Like men, bears stood up on their hind legs. They could sit on the ground as men did, and their paw prints looked like that of men. Like men they were clever. Gautvid said that skinned, even the body of a bear looked like that of a man. He said the claws and teeth of bears were always saved by the Sámi, and never sold or traded, and in fact Osku had never offered any such. Now the skins of three brown bears were laid before them, and Sidroc must decide how many he would trade for, and what price he was willing to give.

His task was made harder by news that had come in late Spring. Paris, the stone city on an island in the great river Seine of Frankland, had been a ready buyer of the

furs Runulv had carried for him, but this year Runulv
had not made it that far. A fleet of Danes in their fast and
narrow war-ships had sailed up the Seine, and asked leave
to pass by the fortified city. This was denied. The Danes
laid siege, and after long and bloody battles overran and
sacked the island city. Charles, the King of the Franks, was
not at Paris, and was slow in sending any aid to his people
stranded there.

Runulv told the tale of his ship, of how when he first
landed on the coast of Frankland he had been warned of
the marauding Danes. He dare not approach the mouth of
the Seine and sail to Paris; there was little left. He learnt
that Charles was far inland, a journey that would take
Runulv and his men away from the safety of their ship. All
Runulv could do was turn back. He stopped at the lesser
trading places along the coast of Frankland, and then at
Aros in Dane-mark, and sold what he could, but carried
back almost half of the furs rather than let them go for
too little silver. Likewise, denied the chance of showing
them to the noblemen surrounding Charles, he had found
none willing or able to meet his price for the two trained
goshawks he carried.

As Sidroc had listened last Spring to the returning
Runulv's tale of the sack of Paris, his first and fleeting
thought had been, Would I were there. This was followed
in an instant by a smothered oath. Paris was the source
of his riches. Her noblemen and King had filled a chest
buried under the treasure room with Frankish silver and
even gold. Now his brothers had come and ruined it,
robbed his best trading partners of their wealth.

He had unsold furs and hawks, and lacked the silver
they should have brought him. He did not know if Runulv

could return to Paris and its rich markets next year, or ever. Yet the beauty of the furs spread before him now made his mind up. Without risk there could be no reward. He would take from even that which he held in reserve to buy more. If he could not return to Frankland he would seek other ports to send Runulv to. One of the things Sidroc prized was a broad silver arm-cuff of great value, bought last year from his profits. He would give it up without regret if need be. He would have enough.

It was time to bring out their own goods. Osku did not trade for silver, but for goods. In the past he had wanted bags of grain, caskets of salt, lengths of cloth, balls of wool thread, and Tindr's sweet and pure honey. Sidroc had learnt two more things in recent years, that Osku valued the good steel blades made here on Gotland. The other was that the Sámi people liked ornaments of silver. Osku did not wear such things, nor, perhaps, did the women of the Sámi, as his daughter had none. The way Osku had handled the little things he had claimed from Tyrsborg the last time he had been here made Sidroc think they would be left as Offerings to his Gods.

Together Sidroc and Tindr went to the stable and pulled out the hand-cart, heaped high with bags of barley cut from the upland farm. Tindr fetched two crocks of honey from one of the kitchen store houses and placed it on the table where the ale cups sat. And Ceridwen and Helga carried out folded lengths of red, blue, and green wadmal, the heavy woollen cloth they had spent months weaving. Sidroc vanished into the hall and returned with a wooden box. This he sat on the table, and drew out five well-hammered knife blades, two small and three large. From the bottom of the box he lifted a linen bag, and set three pieces of sparkling silver on the wood table-top. The first was one of the big domed box brooches the wealthy women of Gotland favoured, its silver sides worked in an open weave, almost like a basket. The second was the larger half of a belt-buckle, the work of Angle-land Sidroc thought, incised with golden wire and bearing a small red garnet. The third was nothing more than a bunch of tiny silver keys Sidroc had asked the silver-smith to make up. The keys were too small and too soft to be used for any lock, but they shimmered in the sunlight, and strung together as they were on a linked silver chain made a jingling noise, like unto small bells, when shaken.

Osku's face had been immobile as they brought these things out to him, just as Sidroc had tried not to betray excitement at the furs he had cast before him. Ulmmá, with Yrling at his heels, was still over by the paddocks, but Šeará stood a few paces away from her father, watching with an unmoving face at all brought before them. Only when Osku began handling the goods did he allow his interest to show. He plunged his hand into a barley-bag that Sidroc opened for him, and with a sweep of his hand showed us that he wanted the entire cart-load. He took two lengths of green wadmal, two of blue, and three of red, and set them at one end of the table. His face broke into a smile when he lifted the wooden top from Tindr's honey crock, recalling well the goodness that lay within. He dipped his finger in and brought it to his mouth, and smiled as he had the first time he had traded for it. His daughter looked at him, the question in her eyes, but he did not motion her forward to test it herself. He went on to the knife blades, selecting four of the five, and set them aside. The silver ornaments pleased him very much, and he held each in his hand, turning it about and studying it. The little bunch of keys he held and shook several times, laughing aloud with the jingling they made. He claimed all three ornaments, and lay them with the rest of the goods he desired.

Then began the work of bargaining. Sidroc chose those furs he wanted, three of beaver, many of otter, a number of the soft mink, and two of the great brown bear skins. He chose only two of four white fox pelts, which would have surprised his wife if she did not know he aimed for all four. In their bargaining the two men moved the piles, took or added things, offered others. Gautvid and Ceridwen sat down and watched them, but Šeará remained standing, even though Ceridwen gestured her to sit. Tindr too remained standing, looking sometimes at Sidroc and Osku as they bargained, and other times darting a glance at the Sámi woman who stood across from him.

After a long while and much moving of goods Sidroc had only three of the white fox pelts, and had let go of the second bear skin he had taken. Osku had surrendered one of the knife blades he wanted, as well as the green lengths of woollen wadmal. Neither man seemed happy. Sidroc stood over the goods, some on the table, some on the ground, some piled on the handcart with all the barley Osku asked for. He ran his hand through his hair, then looked up at the sky.

"Apples," he said aloud, and made off to the outbuilding in which they were laid up. He brought a barrel out, rolling its round iron-bound heft toward his guest. Osku had seen them before; his eyes lit. Sidroc took one from the barrel and offered it. The Sámi's teeth crunched through the red skin and into the juicy flesh. He ate it all, even the core. As he licked the juices from his hand Sidroc took the fourth fox and laid it upon his pile. Osku nodded and grinned.

The trading concluded, the bartered goods were now collected, those Sidroc had won to the treasure room, and those Osku claimed lashed into the back of his waggon, waiting by the stable wall.

With such fair weather the meal was taken out of doors. As they gathered to sit, Šeará stood apart. Cerid-wen gestured with her hands, come and sit, but she gave a small shake of her head.

"It is not the custom that Skridfinn women eat with the men," Gautvid explained.

Ceridwen showed her surprise on her face; Osku had taken meals with them in the past, always with her and Gunnvor and Helga there as well. But she knew different folk had ways unlike her own.

She looked to Gunnvor, who rose with her. Gunnvor took up the bowl that had been set for the woman, and filled it with browis. Ceridwen took another and lay a portion of the fish, a loaf, and a smear of butter upon it. They carried this to the kitchen work-table, and Gunnvor brought her work stool. Ceridwen opened her hands to Šeará, gesturing her, come. She did, and seated herself with a nod of her head and the smallest of smiles.

Tindr had been watching this. He had hoped to sit by Deer, and had lingered himself, waiting to see which place she would be called to by Bright Hair, so he might place himself at her side. Now she was at the work-table, alone. He watched her lower her head over her food, the slender white hands unmoving at either side of her bowl. She had been given one of the deer-antler spoons he had fashioned, and he watched her pick it up and look at it, running her fingers along its smoothness. After a moment she dipped her spoon and began to eat.

"Their chief Goddess is a woman, and lives under the floorboards of every well-kept house," Gautvid was saying. "It is the women who speak to her. But men and women eat apart."

There was ale on the table, and Ceridwen rose as lady of the hall and filled a pottery cup for Šeará. She placed it in her hand, wondering if she had before tasted it; she had taken nothing earlier in welcome. She smiled at the woman, prompting her with a gesture to lift the cup. Šeará took a sip, the narrow nose wrinkling. After a moment her face relaxed, and she made another small smile.

On an earlier visit Gautvid had told them that the only drink the Sámi had was that of the rich ren deer milk, well-watered; and another of the washings of the cheese the women made by pouring the milk into a ren-hide bag and letting it form hard and chewy curds. By shaking the curds with water they made a second drink. Both were sustaining and had nourishment, but neither had the power ale or mead possessed, to make men forget their cares.

After the food had been cleared from the large table Šeará rose. Tindr watched her walk to the waggon, and pull a hide bag from it. He stood as she swung it down; it was fairly heavy. He went to her, and took it from her hands. Those at the table saw them head for the paddock where the ren deer browsed.

Ceridwen looked after them, then at Osku, whose sharp blue eyes also followed. She felt some concern; if the Sámi women were not to eat with men, perchance

Tindr was giving unknown offense in being so close to Osku's daughter. Osku had always seemed well-disposed towards Tindr, but now the man's daughter was with him. Tindr had not touched her, but they walked shoulder to shoulder together, and he had scarcely stopped looking at her since she had climbed down from her waggon board. But the man only nodded after her, neither telling young Ulmmá to help his sister, nor calling out to her.

Tindr handed her the bag, slipped the latch on the paddock gate, and followed her in. Her deer came to her, noses forward, thick necks extended at the sight of the bag she held. She took handfuls of grey-green moss from the bag and scattered them over the short grasses of the paddock. The great racks of antlers lowered at once, muzzles following from clump to clump. Tindr had the chance to truly look at the beasts, studying the large nostrils, heavily furred ears, and solid legs. He bent down and peered beneath one. It was male, but when he looked, saw the deer's stones were gone; it had been gelded like a horse. He looked beneath the other, and looked again. He straightened up, pointed to the animal, and made a milking gesture with his hands.

Šeará nodded her head. It was female, despite the sweeping rack of antlers it sported.

He raised his hands in wonder, and smiled at her. She smiled back. She looked at the female ren deer, and made the same milking motion Tindr had. She made a gesture like drinking, then as if shaking something in a container; he thought it might mean making butter or cheese. She drank their milk, she was telling him, and made these things to eat. She looked down at her leathern leggings and touched them, then laid her hand upon the thick leg of the deer. Her leggings were made from the very hide of the ren deer's legs. The deer still had its head lowered, and she bent to touch the broad brow of its head. Then she pointed to the boots she wore. This thick brown hide from the beast's face made up her furred boots.

She pointed then to Tindr's own boots, the fur still on them like hers, but of such different hide.

He nodded and turned his ankle so she saw the tusk that served as toggle. He lifted his fingers to his mouth, in flaring imitation of the boar's great teeth. She looked at the tusk on one boot, and then the other. She knew boar, and knew their danger. She nodded at him gravely, her lips pursing for a moment.

Tindr could not move his eyes from her. They were alike; he saw that. Deer wore the skins of the beasts she counted on for food and for travel, just as he counted on the red stags and boar of the greenwood to feed and clothe him.

He kept looking at her. He knew she spoke, had seen her sing to her beasts. But unlike all others, she did not speak to him when she faced him. She watched his signs to her, and repeated them back, and made signs of her own. Her lips were sometimes gently parted, but did not move in speech.

He looked at those lips, full and soft-looking in her narrow face, and looked too at the deep blue of the eyes above those lips.

She looked back, unabashed, meeting his gaze. At last she let her eyes drop once more to Tindr's boots.

She pointed to them, then looked at him, her question on her brow. He cocked his head. She made a motion as if she flung a spear.

He shook his head, then crossed his fists at the wrist. She watched, understood. He drew an invisible arrow to a phantom bow, opened his string fingers.

She nodded. A bowman. Her people hunted mostly by trapping, that and the spear and net. They hunted for furs, and to add to their food stores, but their ren deer gave them almost all they needed to live.

I will show you, tomorrow, Tindr was telling her now. His hands went to his temples, flaring like antlers, then pointing at her as he smiled. He touched his eye. He pointed to the lowering Sun, then drew an arc in the sky. Tomorrow I will show you.

As she stood watching him her head turned sharply. He looked too. Fur Man was standing near the table he had risen from, calling. She picked up the hide bag and he let them out of the paddock.

Osku could not sleep in a house he had not built himself; to do so was to invite evil spirts to enter his soul as he slept. When he had before passed the night at Tyrsborg he had pitched a tent, and he did so again. Ulmmá and Šeará joined him in raising it, past the spruce trees, on the grassy swath near the pathway into the forest. Tindr had wished to help, but the slightest shake of Šeará's head stayed him, and the three Sámi had the tent up before Tindr had finished milking the cows and penning the fowl.

When they had done, the Sámi family stood before Sidroc and Ceridwen, bowing their heads and pressing their hands together in thanks for the meal. Gautvid walked them to their tent, and stood speaking with Osku. Eirian and Yrling had scampered after them, wanting to spend the night in the tent, and a smiling Ceridwen had to retrieve them and send them to their own beds. The Sámi joined his children in the tent, and Gautvid returned.

To celebrate the trades that had been made Ceridwen had brought out mead, and poured out cups for her household and guest; Osku did not take strong drink. Tindr, his chores done, sat with them a while.

"Osku will barter on the trading road for salt tomorrow," Gautvid was telling his hosts. "Then he would like to travel North, to a rich farmer who I know will be a ready buyer for his smaller skins. I can take him swiftly by ship, and we will be back after one night. He asks if he might leave his children and ren deer in your keeping while we are gone. The sea voyage was long and not easy on his ren; he needs them strong for when we cross the island to trade on the West."

Gautvid turned his cup in his hand as he asked this, looking first at Ceridwen and then at Sidroc. Ceridwen's eyes flicked to Tindr. His own were fastened on the outline of the tent, growing less distinct in the deepening owl-light of dusk.

Sidroc gave a slight movement of his shoulders. They had never been denied shelter on their travels on Gotland, and had welcomed all asking it of them. Still less would he refuse a man who had been the source of so much richness as Osku had been. Yet he could not ignore the way Tindr regarded the Sámi woman. He did not want trouble, not with Osku, and not for Tindr's sake. He looked at his shield-maiden; she ran the hall, and the choice and judgement would be hers.

"They are most welcome," she told Gautvid. "I am sure the voyage was not easy for any of them," she went on, turning away from the rising memory of her own time aboard ship.

She looked at Tindr, wishing she could somehow tell him then and there that Šeará would be with them a short time. As if he read her desire he turned to her. She could do nothing but smile and gesture her offer of more mead; his cup was empty. But he rose and bid them good-night. She watched him walk not into the hall but out into the darkening trees, skirting the path near where the Sámi tent stood pitched.

"Osku – " Sidroc now asked Gautvid, "why has he brought his young with him?"

The trader's eyes went from Sidroc's face to the tent, and returned. "There has been some trouble at home," Gautvid explained. "Trouble around the girl, which made it best for Osku to bring them." After a pause he added, "A man has died because of her."

Sidroc's eyes widened the smallest bit. "Two men fought for her?"

Ceridwen dropped her eyes at this, so swiftly that Gautvid saw it. You as well, thought Gautvid. A man has died because of you. His eyes returned to Sidroc's face. The expression there had not changed.

"Nai," returned Gautvid, answering his question. "That is not the way of the Skridfinn. From what I could learn, she refused one who had long sought her. After this he was found dead, in a way that could only mean he killed himself." He shifted slightly on the bench. "There is great shame in this, as his spirit will be unquiet. The shame fell on the girl."

"Is this why Osku did not come last year?" Sidroc asked.

"Já, it all happened just before I came for him. The turmoil was such that he could not leave."

"What will happen to her?" Ceridwen asked.

"The girl? I do not know. Perhaps now none of the men will want her. If she will be haunted by the dead man's spirit, it would be ill luck. It was all the worse, as the man took his life in Osku's house. The desecration was such that the house must be burnt. Osku laid the fire."

"He burnt his own house," Sidroc repeated. Fire, the greatest and most feared of destroyers, took Osku's home, and by his own hand.

They had heard earlier this evening that the chief Goddess of the Sámi lived under the floor of that house; what had it meant to drive her out as they had done by setting it to the torch?

"The children, do they have a mother – does Osku have a wife," Ceridwen wanted to know.

"Já, I have seen her. But she is in charge of the household rites; cared for the three Goddesses living in the house. She says she hears them shrieking, angry that their home had been defiled."

"They have built another," Sidroc said.

"Já, another. But the Skridfinn live in tribes of ten; ten men and their families, a small timber house to each. Osku as richest is their chief. Now – " he did not go on, and did not need to. The man and woman he sat with could well imagine the loss of face Osku had suffered.

CHAPTER THE THIRTY-FIRST

THE
MEMORY STONE

TINDR left the table that night and walked towards the trees. He took care not to pass too close to the tent where Fur Man and Deer and the boy were sleeping, lest his shadow be cast by the half-Moon on the hide face of the tent, and cause startle.

He did not know where he was going; he only knew he could not sleep yet. This day had not been like any other. He had seen deer unlike those here in his woods, tamed deer with massive antlers who pulled a waggon, beasts come from the woodlands to live with and help folk. He had touched them, alive and trusting. The woman who drove them – he stopped on the track he went along.

Deer – she was young; when he realized she was a woman he had thought her Fur Man's daughter. Now he wondered if she could be his wife.

He shook his head. He could not think this. He had thought her deaf, as well, and she was not. But she could not or would not speak to Scar and Bright Hair.

He went along the track. There was just Moon enough to light his way. Over his head an owl rose from a bough, spreading its round-tipped wings and gliding up the path in front of him.

He kept on, a long way into the forest, until he found himself near the pool where the Lady had come to him. He did not often return there. The remembrance of the sorrow of waking without Her had become greater than the joy he had known with Her. Tonight he knew he wanted to gaze into the pool again, even if it brought him sadness.

He found the turning and walked in. The little light made the thick green moss where he had lain look black, and the water in the pool bore only the slightest of glimmers from the Moon above. He sat down on the moss, arms clasped about his knees, looking at the angled lines of light moving slowly in the dark water.

He thought of Deer. She lived with her animals as fully as he did; more so. She drank their milk, ate their flesh, wore their hides. They carried her goods. She was of them, and they of her.

She did not move her lips when she spoke to him, did not speak aloud. She used signs alone. And she had given him a new name, touching her eyes to mean him. Tindr knew he had odd eyes, lighter than any others; he had seen them reflected in still waters, and saw them every week when he looked into his mother's disk of polished silver to shave himself. That was what mattered to Deer, his bright eyes, not his deafness.

He touched his forehead to his knees, clasping himself tighter. Fur Man always stayed only one night. In the morning he would take Deer away.

He jumped up then, unable to think about this. The Moon was sliding down the night sky. Before he left he moved to the edge of the pool and looked in. His likeness stood there, wavering on the dark surface, a man alone.

⁂

Šeará awakened in the hide tent; she knew she had not been asleep long, and did not even know if she had truly slept. The Moon had dropped in the sky. Its beams pierced the openings of the tent in sharp lines, and shown faintly through those parts of the hide which had been scraped thin. She lay looking up at the ridge of the tent, and tried to calm herself. She felt fearful, though she lay safe between her father and brother. Both were breathing deeply and she knew they slept.

She pushed the wolf skin off her and stood. She picked up her tunic and leggings and boots and lifted the flap of the tent. The air was cool on her bare skin, lifting the fine hairs on her arms. She let the tent flap drop silently behind her and pulled her clothing on.

Even setting as it was the Moon gave good light to the openness before her. She looked at the house the tall man and his wife lived in. It was much the larger than any she had ever seen, save for those buildings she had glimpsed on the shore when they had landed. She knew these folk were rich by the numbers of goods they used to barter for her father's furs.

She turned her head to the darkness of the forest, its trees thick and tall. But she walked forward, toward the pen where her ren waited. She passed the sleeping horses, dark shapes standing alongside the fence. Her ren were brighter, their white chests and throats nearly glowing in the little light. She found the latch and lifted it, let herself in.

She went to where they stood, standing almost back to back to each other. She stood with them as they dozed, not touching them, just standing next their silent forms. This is strange to you, she thought, this green island. Just as my home is now strange to me.

A night bird called out, a soft whistling, one she had never heard. It too was strange to her. It made her lift her head and look up into the darkness of the spruce trees.

Many birds were singing the day Ággi came to claim her. She had told her parents she would not have him, she would not go. Ággi was the son of the chieftain of the next village, and she the chieftain's daughter in her own. It was right, it was Fated, that she become his woman, and yet she could not do it. She had seen Ággi many times in her life, had been told since she was little she would be his wife. She did not think much on it; all women wed, every one, save those lame or deformed. But as she grew older and saw Ággi she grew wary of him. He could look in a way that frightened her, seeming to speak to spirits, hear voices no one else could hear. His eyes would roll, and his face twist like the shaman's as he was about to fall down on the ground to have his dreams. He could be calm and kind and then angry and fierce, his shoulders hunched, his eyes dark, fists clenched at his sides. Did not his parents see this, did not hers, she asked. Ággi had shaman-blood in him, they said, that is all. Do not fear a man meant to be your husband. He is a chief's son and all will be well.

She was to have gone to him last year. Together she and her mother sewed the special bridal tunic, of pure white ren deer hide, so rare that only the daughter of a chieftain could be so arrayed. With every stitch she made, pulling the strong sinew through the soft hide, she felt she sewed herself into her burial shroud.

Ággi and his people came to her village at Mid-Summer. The feasting would last three days, and on the third she would be given to Ággi and go with him to his own village. That first night after the feast she met Ággi alone and told him that she would not be his. He had been so angry that he had struck her across the face. She wondered if she would ever stop tasting the blood in her mouth; she had never been struck before, never. He left her in the same fury in which he had struck her, but not before looking stricken himself. She ran to her house, crying in fear and in hurt. Her parents were angry, not at Ággi but at her. In the morning all was in an uproar, and he and his people left.

Two days later, on the day she should have left her village for his, Ággi returned to her house. No one was there. He went in the women's door in the back. Then he killed himself with his knife, a hack through his wrist.

The shock when they found him was great, the floorboards soaked with blood, the dark blankness of his eyes, open and staring at the ceiling. They sent word to Ággi's people. They called the shaman, who lived apart with his family. All the families of her father's village, and that too of Ággi's father, supported the shaman, contributing to his maintenance and that of his family with gifts of meat and fish. The shaman came with his birch drum, and entered their house, alone. They heard his yowl, long and low. Ággi's body was carried out and taken by his people to his own village.

The matter of the house itself was grave. The shaman beat his drum, went into a trance and made his decree. Her father could remove half of their belongings from the house, and no more. The other half, along with the house itself, must be burnt, as a sacrifice to cleanse the violence which had occurred there. All faces turned to her; it was on her head. As her father fired their house she saw the tears streaking his cheeks. Her mother wailed, and Ulmmá hung back, eyes glistening as their home smoldered and went up in flames. Her father had left the costly white ren tunic to burn, the most tainted thing that lay within.

They built another house further away. They had to clear many trees, a large effort, and one they did with bowed heads. All of this caused great shame to Osku and his family.

Now a year had passed, and more. No one would walk over the scorched soil which had held their lost home; it was become an evil place. She was not shunned in her village, but neither was she at home there anymore. Her mother was growing older. "If you had wed Ággi you would have a child by now," she had said to her, and shook her head. "Ulmmá is young. I may not live to see his child."

It was then her father told her he would take them with him on his trading trip. She wished to go, and Ulmmá wanted nothing more.

Now she was here, she did not know what to think. She knew these folk spoke another tongue; the trader Gautvid whose ship they boarded had been coming to their village for years. Folk here lived in big houses, kept cattle and sheep and horses. They did not use the number of ren they herded to proclaim their wealth; they owned no ren. Ren could not live here; without their moss from the northernmost forests they would starve. Her father had brought two of his best to pull the trader's waggon, so they could visit as many rich people as he could, replenishing their goods. She and Ulmmá had spent days gathering bags of ren moss for the trip. Other than the trader with the ship these were the first strange folk she had met. They seemed kind; the wife and old woman had brought her food and smiled at her. They did not know she was the cause of a man's death.

Wolf Eyes . . . . She had to pause a moment. He was unlike the others, and unlike other men. She thought of how she had named him thus, looking into his blue-white eyes. Wolves were the great enemy of her ren, picking off the wobbly young, running hale deer to exhaustion. This man . . . his eyes were that of a wolf. Yet he had looked at the ren with wonder, and laid his hands upon them like they were a holy thing.

He moved slowly, looked with care. She saw he liked to look at her. He could not hear, but that did not matter; she could not speak the tongue of his people. He looked a few years older than her, and could not be the son of the young wife and the tall man with the scar. Perhaps he was kin.

As she stood there next her sleeping ren she saw something move from the tail of her eye. She turned fully to face it. Wolf Eyes was there, walking, as she had, to see her ren. He saw her, stopped, then raised his hand to her as if asking if he could enter. She nodded her permission, waiting as he walked to her. Her ren scarcely moved at his approach. She was there, and they knew they were safe. Wolf Eyes saw this, she knew, and the smile he wore on his lips and in his animal eyes showed it.

He stood without gesturing, just looking at her and the deer she stood beside.

He wanted to tell her that her deer were beautiful. He wanted to tell her that she was beautiful. He had no signs for this. If he extended his hands out in front of him, palms upward, it meant, This is good, or You may do something. He had no signs, no gestures for this woman in her ren skins.

Šeará returned his gaze, looking back at him with care. He had hair the hue of the honey her father traded for, dark honey, but with lighter streaks in it where the Sun had touched it. His brows were straight and full, and his nose and mouth had a beauty she had not often seen in a man. And his eyes; no one would forget such eyes as he kept fastened on her. They alone made him different.

The ren nearest her shifted where it stood, bumping her slightly at the wither-point. She smiled then, looking back at the strong head crowned with antlers. She stepped aside, laid her hand on the ren's side just behind the leg; on its heart. She moved her hand gently up and down over it, as if she could feel the great heart within beat. Then she took the same hand and pressed it to the ground they stood upon.

The Earth has a ren deer heart, she was showing him. The beating heart of the Earth is that of a ren.

She repeated it, placing her hand over the deer's heart, then pressing it to the soil.

He understood, nodded to her. His Goddess took the form of a deer; it made sense that the Earth itself would have her heart.

Seeing the smile grow across his face made her own smile spread. She nodded back.

He stepped closer to her. He wanted so to touch her, but dared not.

He shook his head suddenly, made a small *uh*. Do you go in the morning, he must know.

He lifted his hands to make antlers at his head, pointed to her, then stretched out his hand towards where the ship lay moored at the bottom of the hill. He made the sign for the sea, his hand waving up and down, and pointed at the remains of the Moon.

She watched, shook her head. She had heard her father speaking to Gautvid, knew he wished to leave her and Ulmmá for one night. She gestured this, pointing to the Moon, making a circle with her pointing finger. It would rise and set one more night before she must leave.

His face showed the gladness he felt. The best he could do was to thank her, by touching his heart and turning his hand out to her. She watched, and understood.

Then one of the horses whinnied, making her ren move. The Moon was nearly set. Šeará made an arc in the sky with her finger, and together she and Tindr left the paddock, he to the hall, she to her tent.

Osku and Gautvid walked down to Asfrid the salt seller's early. Tindr went with them, pulling his small hand-drawn wain. They returned with two lead-lined casks of salt, which went into Gautvid's high-wheeled waggon. Then Gautvid and Osku took ship, leaving with the morning tide. They had selected pelts of marten and otter to carry to the farmer up the coast, packing them into hide-covered baskets. Household and guests had broken their fast together, and those remaining went about their day. Ulmmá was at once taken up with Yrling and Eirian, as they pulled him into the stable to help collect eggs from hens and geese, and watch the thick-furred skogkatts clamber up the posts after mice rustling in the hay piled in the loft.

Tindr had been up at dawn. Now with morning chores done, he looked to Šeará. The early coolness had worn off. It would be a fine day and he was eager to be off in it. She had gone to where Gunnvor stood over her basin, washing up the cups and platters they had used, and shown her willingness to help, indeed it was the Sámi way to do so. The cook had smiled at her, letting her dry and stack the crockery. Tindr stood across the kitchen yard from them, waiting. When Šeará stepped away from the big work table he gestured. She went to him, a small smile on her own lips. She was ready for a walk in the woods, having tied a shallow birch drinking cup to her sash, and also a short knife. Tindr saw the handle was of antler.

The first place they went was to the smaller of the kitchen outbuildings. The door was still opened and she followed him within. Ranks of wooden shelves met her eyes, crowded with crocks and pots, small wooden boxes and baskets of wicker work. Tindr took a crock from a shelf of many of them. He lifted the wooded lid, dipped his finger in. It was honey.

He had watched Deer take some at the table, dribbling a small spoonful over the bread she held in her white hand. She had taken so little of it; he wanted her to have more.

She knew what it was, knew it was costly and rare, for her father had been bringing it back to her village for the past few years. Last year when he did not come here there had been no honey, none for her family, nor to trade with others. Here was jar after jar of it.

Wolf Eyes brought his finger to her lips, touched the honey to them. It was the first time he had touched her, his finger lightly on her lips. Then he took his hand away. Her pink tongue slipped out, licking at the sweetness. It made Wolf Eyes smile at her. He made the smallest sound, and with his hand offered that she dip her own finger in, and eat of it. She did, coating her finger with the thick and sticky goodness. She placed it in her mouth, a flood of sweetness.

⚕⚕⚕⚕⚕⚕⚕⚕⚕⚕⚕

The mistress of Tyrsborg saw Tindr and Šeará enter the path into the forest together. She stood a moment, looking after them, until the flash of the light coloured skins the Sámi woman wore was lost in the trees. She put down the linen-charged shuttle she had just taken up.

When she reached the brew-house she found Rannveig in her larger brewing shed. The older woman saw from her friend's furrowed brow that something was amiss. She had been mixing dried herbs to flavour her ale, and now shook her hands free of the fine particles.

"Osku is with us," Ceridwen told her, without any other greeting.

"Já, I saw Gautvid's ship yesterday, and the tame deer that pulled the big waggon. I thought Tindr would be down here by now, to tell me of them."

"The Sámi you saw driving the deer – she is a maiden. Osku's daughter." Ceridwen returned. "Tindr is much taken with her."

Rannveig's eyebrows rose. She had all but lost hope that any woman here on Gotland would choose her son.

A hundred questions began flooding her mind. Ceridwen answered the first one.

"She is strange," Ceridwen began, "but beautiful. Her hair is almost white, and she dresses as does her father, in the skins of deer. She wears leggings, like a man, and a tunic longer than her father and brother. Her name is a lovely one, Šeará."

"How strange?" Rannveig asked. She did not want her boy mixed up with a sorceress, or one mad. Then she shook her head at herself. "Tindr is strange," she reminded them both aloud.

Ceridwen tried to answer her question. "When I first saw her, I thought her the skogsrå. She looks like a deer."

Rannveig caught her breath a moment. "Then no wonder Tindr likes her."

"They have gone into the woods together," her friend told her. "I came as soon as I saw them leave."

Rannveig's mouth opened. "What are their customs?" she asked.

"I do not know. But Gautvid told us last night that Šeará may be in disgrace. She refused to wed the man she was pledged to. He returned to her home and killed himself there, defiling it so that it must be burnt. Gautvid thinks perhaps no man will wed her; she has the taint of the dead man's blood upon her. But none of this seems her true fault."

Rannveig searched Ceridwen's face. She had spent hours in the Sámi maiden's company, and had instincts about folk that Rannveig trusted. "Is she good?"

"Já, I think she is. At least I cannot help but like her. She has an inner quiet about her, like Tindr himself."

"And they are in the woods now, alone and together," recounted Rannveig.

Her friend nodded. "She is not a child; she has eighteen, twenty Summers, perhaps."

Rannveig wore her worry on her brow. "We do not know their customs . . . We do not know if Tindr would be considered by Osku as fit for his daughter. Or if he is giving great offense by being alone with the maid." Her hands had risen to her face as she said these things.

Ceridwen could answer none of these concerns, and waited for Rannveig to speak again.

"And you say he is much taken with her?"

"He has scarcely lifted his eyes from her, or from her ren deer, those that come to her as if they were oxen." She did not wish to raise false hope in so dear a friend, but must also say the next. "And Šeará – she has looked at Tindr. Her eye is not bold, but I believe she knows the regard he holds her in.

"She is already signing to him, making herself known. She speaks no Norse, and so they are almost equals. Even if Tindr heard she could not speak to him."

"Do you think then . . . Osku would consent . . . ?"

A flush of gladness came over Ceridwen at this. "I am so happy to hear you wish this for him," she said. No mother was more devoted to her son than Rannveig to Tindr, and Ceridwen knew she wanted a love match for him, not just a woman who knew that Tindr had wealth.

"Tindr's gold means nothing to Šeará, indeed, she or Osku do not even know he has such treasure," she pointed out.

Rannveig's eyes had moved to the empty pier. "When will Gautvid's ship return?" she asked now.

⚭⚭⚭⚭⚭⚭⚭⚭⚭

Tindr led Deer up the path through his woods. The trees and shrubs were still fully clothed in their greenery; only those who looked with care would see the slightly browning rims on the pointed ash leaves, or crisping edges of the curling ferns, warning that Fall was soon to come. The coolness of the morning and night air foretold it, but the warmth when the Sun was fully overhead was nearly that of high Summer.

Seará saw the half-ring of white birches before Wolf Eyes left the path for them. The six trees rose straight up behind a curtain of shrubbery. She caught a glimpse of something else, just rising above her sight line. A rack of deer antlers, resting atop a great standing stone.

A push through some hazels and then they were before it. Wolf Eyes stepped aside so she might see the place fully.

A huge stone of light grey rock stood upright. It was far taller than she. At its top was set a much smaller, flatter stone, and on this lay the double rack of antlers. They were not ren horn, she saw. Perhaps they were of the big deer with the red coats; the spread of the antlers was great.

Her eyes dropped to the large stone itself. Its surface was covered with ranks and files of small drawings of animals, beginning at the base and extending half-way up the stone. She took a step closer, saw the drawings had been scratched into the stone itself with a sharp point. There were deer after deer, each crowned with antlers, a huge herd of them; and mixed in with them, boar with flaring tusks.

She turned to Wolf Eyes, found herself taking a step back to his side. It was a holy place, but not taboo for her to see it; she felt he would not have brought her to harm her.

Tindr saw the uncertainty in Deer's face, saw how her lip nearly trembled. He gave a smile, nodding his head once at her. Then he extended his arms out, strong bow-arm straight, string-arm cocked at his eye, phantom arrow resting against phantom bow. He aimed for the many figures crowding his memory stone, opened his fingers, and let fly the arrow. These are the beasts the Lady has sent to me. This is how I feed myself, my people. This is where I give thanks for the lives I have taken, that we might live.

She lifted her head in recognition, eyes looking upward to the patch of blue sky above them. She looked back at Wolf Eyes, her wonder in her face. He was a great hunter.

She turned back to the stone. She let her eyes drop to the grass that grew around its base, and saw the very first etching there, a hart with huge antlers. A boy's first kill, and he had taken a forest giant. The Deer-Spirit loved him to have given him thus. Her eyes travelled up the ranks of deer and boar. She thought of each beast, of the skill it had taken to down them, of the reverence the hunter had shown in recording them here.

She found her hands lifting gently at her sides, palms up, beholding this. She heard a soft drumming in her head. It was that of the beating hearts of these beasts, and she knew she must make joik for them. The melody came to her in chanting rhythm, giving form to each beast in song.

Tindr watched Deer stand before his stone, saw her arms lift, her eyelids drop a moment over her dark blue eyes and then open. She was praying, he knew, speaking to the spirits of his deer and boar, or perhaps to the Lady herself.

Now her mouth opened, her lips moved in full throated song. He watched her eyes trace the lines of beasts he had drawn, and how she sang for each and every one.

He came closer to her, within her line of view. Her lips were bowed in the slightest of smiles as she sang, and as he smiled at her her own smile deepened. He risked lifting his hand to her throat. She moved not, let him place his fingers over the small knob there so he might feel the song she sang through his fingertips.

Šeará did not know where this joik came from; she had shaped joik for folk and animals and trees but never for a holy place where deer and boar were recalled. She would never sing this joik again, but she had made it. She had no choice but to make it; it had been summoned from her. And the holy place had heard it, and Wolf Eyes had heard it too, felt her song fluttering in her throat.

She came to the last drawing, that of a deer, the last he had killed. Perhaps its flesh was in the food she had already eaten with him. She lifted her head higher. She finished her joik. Her mouth closed, and after a moment Wolf Eyes let fall his hand from her throat.

She dropped to her knees. She must pray, here and now. She raised her arms, elbows bent at right angles, and bowed her head rapidly to the Earth her knees were pressed upon. Ren did not live on this green island, but the heart of the Earth was a ren heart. Perhaps that heart was also the heart of these beasts.

When she straightened up she saw Wolf Eyes was on his knees at her side.

Tears were in her eyes at the wonder of it, at his prowess as a hunter, at this holy place he had made. And the joik she had shaped had taken something out of her heart, something dark. Even kneeling on the ground she felt light.

He looked troubled at her tears, and she smiled at him. He used the same gentle hand to touch one that welled at her eye. She watched as he brought his fingertip to his mouth, tasting this drop of sea that she wept.

She smiled now, fully, and took her hand and pressed it to the Earth. Ren deer heart. He nodded back at her. Then she looked to his stone, pressed the Earth again. And these beasts too.

He nodded. These beasts too.

She took his hand and placed it on the pale leather of her legging, placed it on the napped hide of her tunic. Then she pressed his hand to the Earth.

She let go his hand, pressed her own over her heart. Then she placed her hand over his heart.

She felt of a sudden his chest trembling under her palm. His wolf eyes were staring into hers as she pressed her hand back on the Earth. We are part of it, this beating heart of our Earth.

She was leaning forward towards him, hand still upon the Earth.

He moved his arm around her, pulled her to his own heart. Their knees and thighs touched. Their arms wrapped about each other's backs as they pressed their hearts together.

Tindr felt her slight form in his arms, the narrowness of her waist, the small breasts pressed against his chest, the strength in her slender thighs. Her yellow-white braids fell down her back; he felt them against his wrists. Her chin was on his shoulder. He could feel her ribs expand as she drew breath, and feel as well her arms wrapping his own back, moving with his breathing.

He did not want this moment to end. All he wanted was here in his arms.

But she pulled away now, with urgency on her face. She must feel his heart against hers, skin to skin.

Her hand went to her leathern cap, covered with the bright thread work. She pulled it off, and he saw the top of her head for the first time. She untied the sash at her waist. Her hands went to the hem of her tunic, and in one gesture she pulled it over her head and dropped it on the grass they knelt on.

He caught his breath. Her skin was paler than milk, and her nipples looked like budded roses. An odour arose from her; she smelt of the spice of pine needles and female musk and something too of that bright smell before rain.

He lowered his forehead a moment on her bare shoulder, just to breathe her smell, know it fully.

His own hands went to his tunic, and he pulled it off, and the tiny whistle hanging there. He pressed his chest against hers, flesh against flesh, heart to heart. His own was pounding so he felt it one with hers. Her warmth spread over him. His hands reached up her naked back to the nape of her neck. He felt her own small hands slide into his hair and grasp the roots of it, their cheeks pressed together as they breathed as one.

Lady, give me her, he was crying within him.

The heat inside him grew so that he felt aflame. He made a sound, like one almost of pain. She pulled her face away so she might see him. He placed his hands at her waist. There were laces there, at the top of her ren skin leggings. His fingers went to them and began to pull them loose. She was trembling under his hands, and she felt him quiver as well. Her hands went to his own leggings, found the toggle, freed him. He turned to the furred boots she wore, and he drew them from her feet. She slipped the boar tusk fastener from his own, and pulled them off. He stripped off her leggings, seeing the tuft of yellow curls where her slender thighs met. She pulled at his own, and together they took them off.

Still on their knees they looked at each other, not touching, their naked bodies straining towards the other.

He paused a moment, uncertain if he should lie back, as the Lady had bid him do, so she might straddle him. The long-ago image of the man and woman in the hay field flashed before him, she on her back and he moving above her. Stags reared up behind the doe, as did all beasts he had seen in this sacred act.

Deer too paused, waiting. He looked at her face, her eyes. She looked happy, and frightened too; she had not done this before. She was not the Lady, he knew. Her flesh was warm, without the under touch of coolness the Lady's had borne. He took her in his arms and laid her on her back.

He pressed his legs between hers, pulling her knees apart. Her blue eyes were wide as she gazed into his. She lifted her head and looked down the length of their bodies at his prick, hard and craving. He lowered his face to hers, brought his mouth to her mouth. He tasted the sweetness of the honey she had eaten at the corner of her lip. No honey had ever been as sweet.

He began to kiss her, her mouth, her face. His few days' growth of beard surprised her; it was light, and stiffer than it looked. A man had never touched her face with his own before. She kissed him back, her lips lingering on his, her mouth seeking his chin and brow.

He brought his hips to hers. She shifted beneath him as he sought the deep warmth of her hollow. She arched her back, raised herself to meet him. He pressed hard to open her and saw her flinch in pain. He stopped, looking down into her eyes, but she smiled up at him, biting her lower lip. He went on, until he had gained the ease of her body.

She did not take her eyes off of his, did not close them against him and what was happening. He moved within her. He felt the magnificence of his body, and the beauty of hers. She was a woman, not a Goddess, and she was come to him, and was giving herself to him.

Šeará had her arms about him, holding him at the waist. He had lowered his animal eyes, and gave a thrust deeper than the rest. Beyond his closed eyes he saw deer, leaping through dark woods, yet bathed in the most brilliant of light. A cry came from his lips, and his body quaked above her.

He brought his head to her shoulder, let his brow rest there a moment, then lifted his head and kissed her mouth. Her hands stroked through his hair, and once more they were heart to heart. They lay a while like this, the warmth of their bodies dissolving all that had come before that moment they had first seen each other. All began anew.

He pulled slowly back from her, and saw her flinch the slightest bit. He placed his hand over the tuft of golden curls he had just moved from, and with his lips touched her belly. When he looked at her face she was smiling at him. He lay on his back and pulled her over and across his chest, her cheek against his heart.

For an instant he thought he slept. Then his eyes were wide open, and his hands clenched about Deer so that she started.

Fur Man would come tomorrow and take Deer away. He had never felt as panicked as he did at this moment. He would not let that happen. Deer was his woman, she had given herself to him, and he to her. He would fight to keep her.

He was almost panting, and he knew sounds were coming from his throat. Deer hung about his neck, trying to calm him, but he saw the fear she too felt.

He must find Scar; Scar would help him. Scar would speak with Fur Man and tell him Deer must stay here.

He tried to tell Deer this, touching his cheek to indicate the scar of he who could help.

They dressed. Deer once more dropped on her knees before his memory stone, once more raised her arms and bent her head to the Earth they had lain upon.

Then they were off. As they moved through the forest many things tumbled in his mind. If Fur Man would not give him Deer, he would run off with her. He knew places no one would find, caves and hidden shelters. He would feed them with his bow. He would leave Scar and Bright

Hair and even his Nenna if it meant keeping Deer at his side.

※※※※※※※※※

Sidroc had just turned his horse into the paddock at Tyrsborg. He had ridden to see Ring at the upland farm, and as he fastened the gate behind his stallion he looked to the second paddock where the ren deer stood. His bridle was in his hand, and his eye fell on the simple halter the deer wore. This morning he had watched Osku's boy Ulmmá ride one of the ren around the paddock, and then laughed with Eirian and Yrling as the boy had lifted each of them in turn before him on the ren's back. The children had whooped in pleasure, the deer steady and placid under their delighted calls.

Now as he turned to the stable he saw Tindr and Šeará step from the dimness of the forest path. The hurried way in which they walked, and the set of Tindr's face made him stop and await them. As they neared his eye scanned them, and he took a long and slow breath.

He did not need Tindr to tell him what had already occurred. He could read it in the way he had her hand tightly clasped in his own. They walked hip to hip, arms extended straight down between them, as if he feared letting even a hand-span come between him and the Sámi girl.

He had had her on her back, that was clear. Osku had left his daughter with him, and now she stood before him, clinging to Tindr, who had claimed her. He looked up at the sky and ran his hand through his hair.

Tindr did not let a moment pass. He stopped before him, lifted the hand which held Šeará's to his chest, pounding on it as he grunted out his distress. Sidroc nodded, raised his hands to signal calm.

He looked at the two, the girl standing slightly behind Tindr's shoulder. There was hope in her face, but real fear in Tindr's. He wished Rannveig was there, and Gautvid and even Osku too, so they could settle this now. As it was he asked the question he could. He laid the bridle on the fence rail, and clasped one of his hands in the other, the sign for hand-fast.

The girl did not know the gesture, but Tindr grunted, nodding his head, já, já. Hand-fast. This is my wife. All Sidroc could do was nod back.

A CHIEFTAIN'S
DAUGHTER

TINDR and Šeará spent that night in a round tent they built in a forest glade, not far from Tyrsborg. Tindr brought axes from his workbench, and together they cut saplings for uprights, fixing them above a bed of fir boughs Šeará chipped from trees. With Ceridwen they collected enough deer hides from the hall to serve as ground cloths and covering, lacing the hides together with thongs cut of more hide.

They took their small bridal supper at the table where they had eaten the night before, but this time Šeará sat next Tindr. Ulmmá listened with questioning face as his sister spoke to him in the lilting speech of the Sámi. The boy seemed to understand, and when all cups were raised and smiles wreathed the faces of those around him, he too smiled.

Another woman sat there with the household of Tyrsborg, Rannveig. She had brought a jar of mead with her, and as she watched the Sámi woman take her first sip of it, she hoped that the new day would bring them to a feast unclouded by uncertainty. They could salute the young couple tonight, bless and wish them well, but on the morrow Šeará's father would return. She knew from watching Tindr's face, changing in turn from happiness to worry, that this was never far from his thoughts.

Ceridwen too worked hard to show the joy she truly wished to feel. Gunnvor had made honey cakes, and seeing the pleasure with which the new couple ate them together gave her hope. Her twinned children were clamouring with excitement, thinking that the ren would stay here at Tyrsborg too, and nothing she could tell them would disavow their belief.

None went far from Tyrsborg next day. Tindr and Šeará walked back hand in hand from their forest shelter, slowly this time. As they entered the kitchen yard Ceridwen saw them and went to embrace each in turn. They looked as if they had known but little sleep, and she did not think it was due only to the joys of each other's bodies.

All knew when Gautvid's ship sailed in; Yrling had been set to watch for it from the crack in the stable loft wall, where he could peer far out to sea. Rannveig, watching from her brew-house, saw it too.

Sidroc stood outside the front door to greet them; the others awaited by the table in the kitchen yard, which held ale to greet the returning traders. It was still early in the day, and as Osku and Gautvid carried nothing with them Sidroc could read that they intended to be off again as soon as they could load the ship.

Gautvid grinned at him. "Fair sailing?" Sidroc asked, to which both men nodded.

"And good trading," added Gautvid, as he came up nearest his host.

Osku, as the older man, trailed a little behind on the steep hill. Sidroc took this chance to speak.

"Ah – Gautvid," he began. "I will need your help. While you were gone, Tindr and Osku's daughter – "

Gautvid's head jerked back.

"Já," affirmed Sidroc. "They have hand-fasted, and as you will see nothing will pry them apart."

He did not have time to say more, for they were crossing the grassy sward along the hall's long side. There, arrayed in a half-circle near the table, waited every member of the household, even the youngest. In the middle stood Tindr, and next him Šeará. They were not touching, but the look on their faces made her father slow and look at all standing before him.

Osku's eyes shifted to Sidroc. He took a breath and began, slowly, and with care.

"Osku, we have been partners in trade these several years. We have dealt honestly and honorably with each other. You have seen my man Tindr, many times."

Sidroc was watching the Sámi's face, making certain he understood, looking often to Gautvid who stood at Osku's side. Osku nodded as if he followed, and Sidroc went on.

"Today Tindr asks that your daughter may be his wife. He cannot speak for himself and so I speak for him, just as his mother Rannveig will speak for him."

Osku's mouth dropped open, and he turned to Gautvid. Gautvid repeated what Sidroc had said.

"Tinder is the finest hunter on Gotland," Sidroc went on. "No other man is as true with bow and arrow as is Tindr, all will tell you this. You have stepped inside our hall and seen the deer skins there, and eaten of his kill as well. He takes as well the mighty boar. Your daughter will always be fed."

Gautvid added a few words here, raising his hand to the hall, gesturing an arrow being set to a bow.

Sidroc could not read the Sámi's face, other than his surprise. He saw the man look to his daughter, to Tindr, and back to her.

Tindr, looking at both men, could only wish he knew what Scar was saying. He glanced at his mother, who with a stay of her hand tried to reassure him.

All Sidroc could do was go on. "He does not get drunk. He does not squander his silver in gaming. He is a hard worker." He was running out of things to say to convince the man of Tindr's merit. "His bees make the sweet honey that you favour."

"And he is the cousin of my cousin," Gautvid thought to add, for which Sidroc was grateful.

"His mother Rannveig owns the brew-house at the pier." Sidroc finished. "She is respected by all. She will speak next for her son."

Rannveig had waited long years to bargain for a wife for her son. Now she must speak to a man who she was not certain could understand her, and might not value those qualities which marked Tindr above other men. Sidroc had already said that which most fathers would wish to hear. As a woman she spoke now those things which the girl's mother would want to know, should she be here before her.

She took a step forward and looked at the Sámi. The mass of keys at her waist jingled as she did, catching the man's ear and eye. He liked how she sounded.

"Tindr has no other woman," she told him. "He has waited for your daughter for a long time. He is kind, and will treat her with gentleness. And I will love her as my own daughter."

Her eyes went to Gautvid, bidding him add that which in the man's own tongue would make clear what she promised.

Gautvid turned his head to speak to Osku, but the Sámi's eyes were fixed on his daughter.

"Come here, Šeará," he told her, in their own tongue.

She left Tindr's side and went to stand before her father.

He looked at her, as slight and slender as a birch-wand. But she had shown that her will was strong as iron, one which had caused much grief to two villages. He heaved a sigh, recalling it all. He could not look back at what had happened; like them all he must look forward.

"Do you want this man?" he asked.

"I do want him, father. And Wolf Eyes wants me."

A smile flickered at the corners of his mouth at her words. "Wolf Eyes. I thought the same when I saw him. He has another name. It is Tindr."

She tried the name. "Tindr," she repeated. She liked the sound. But he could not hear her speak it. She would go on naming him as she had the first time she saw him, and touching her eyes to mean him. She wished to know him by his striking eyes, and not his deafness.

"His Gods are not your Gods," he cautioned. He looked about a moment. "Your Gods may not follow you here."

She had thought of this; perhaps her Gods would not wish to come and live with her here. "His Gods will be my Gods," she answered.

She and Wolf Eyes would build a house in the forest, one of wood, and when it was done she would ask the Goddess Máttaráhkká to come and dwell beneath the floor boards. Perhaps the Goddess would not wish to come, but she would invite her just the same.

Father nodded at daughter. He had heard enough. He gestured her to return to Tindr's side.

Osku now spoke to all, and in Norse. "She is a chieftain's daughter," he warned.

He looked to Gautvid, and Osku seemed to struggle for his next words. They spoke.

"What does he offer for her," Gautvid asked, turning from Osku to Tindr.

All looked to Rannveig, waiting for her to sign to her son. But she herself spoke.

"Gold," she said, with no hesitation. "He offers gold."

She had a thick coin of it ready in her palm, and all the rest of the gold coins she had won from the sale of Dagr's narwhale horn in a little pouch hanging amidst the keys at her sash. She would give all of it if need be to win this woman for her son.

She pressed the coin into her son's hand, pointed to Šeará, then to Osku. She made the gesture for payment, something being passed from hand to hand.

Tindr held the gold up between thumb and forefinger. He moved to Fur Man, placed the coin in his hand. When he had done so he dipped his head before the man, cupping his hands together, Please.

The Sámi's face was unmoving. Tindr looked back at Deer, watching him.

Osku considered him, considered the gold. It would make right his losses when he fired his house. He would have enough to bury rich Offerings on the old site, so that Máttaráhkká would stop shrieking.

He spoke again to Gautvid, and at length.

"You will not take her from this place; you will live here so he might see his daughter each year when he brings his furs, so he may make sure she is well supplied," Gautvid dictated.

Rannveig did not need to ask Tindr about this. "They will live here, in a house such as your daughter chooses," she assured the man. She looked at the two young people. "She will have all she wishes," she added.

After Osku heard Gautvid's version of this, he closed his fingers around the gold resting in his palm. He again spoke now for himself, haltingly, but clearly enough.

"Then Osku accepts this gold for his daughter," he announced.

Tindr was still before him, and saw the man's face crease in a grin. He turned to see the others raise their arms in joy. Osku extended his arms to embrace him.

Šeará turned to Rannveig. The older woman opened her arms to her. "My daughter," she said. Šeará could not know the words, but the kiss Rannveig bestowed on her was clear.

Osku was moving to the waggon where waited his furs. He pulled out a bear skin, and passed its bulk into the hands of Tindr and Šeará.

"For your bed," he told them. "You will sleep as well as bears do in their den."

That night a feast was held at the brew-house that the trading road had never seen. Gunnvor and Helga joined with Gudfrid to cook for all. Fresh fish were baked with green herbs, and salt fish was pounded and boiled with dried peas made plump by soaking. Haunches of deer meat, brined and then smoked, were carried from where they had been hanging. Deep bowls of apple sauce graced every table. Geese were roasted, and eggs beaten into puddings scented with mint and lavender. Gunnvor turned out honey cakes by the score. Rannveig opened cask after cask of her good ale, and wore a smile on her face that few had ever seen. At one point she stepped through the curtains from brew-house to the store room, and thought she saw Dagr in his green fishing tunic, turning to fetch more cups for thirsty revelers. She put her hand on her heart and spoke his name.

In the middle of this sat Tindr, with Šeará at his side, flanked by her father and brother. Ceridwen and Sidroc sat with Gautvid and the children on the other side of the table, along with Ring and Astrid and Ragnfast and Estrid, come from their farms. Rannveig was everywhere at once, receiving the good wishes of the townsfolk, coming to sit down when she could.

Before it grew dark the hand-fast couple was sent away, up the hill to their round tent, waiting snug for them. They stopped at the paddock that held the ren, and Šeará went to them and clasped her arms about their furred necks. Tomorrow her father and brother would be off, with Gautvid, heading overland in the waggon. They would be back in a week or so, but after that she would not see her father for a year, and the ren, ever.

Of all she was leaving the ren would be hardest for her to lose. All women must leave their families and villages and go live apart in their husband's new home, and this she knew. But wherever she went she would find ren at her new home. If her parents owned many they would give her her favourites to take with her. This green island had no ren, and this would be the last she saw of them, unless one day she and Wolf Eyes could sail North to visit the wind-swept steppes and birch forests of her homeland.

Tindr watched her make her fare-wells to the deer. Tears were running from her eyes, but she tried to smile. When she turned to him he took her hand and placed it over her heart, then over his own. Then with her he bent over and pressed her hand to the Earth she and the ren stood on. These beasts. And you. And me.

Late that night Sidroc and Ceridwen walked up the hill together, back to Tyrsborg. Helga had gone ahead with the sleepy children, and Gunnvor was enjoying a well-deserved rest, sitting with her feet up with her sister Gudfrid, down at Rannveig's.

The breeze off the sea had picked up, reminding them that despite the warmth of the day, Fall winds would soon shake the leaves from the trees. Ceridwen pulled her mantle about her more closely.

"Years ago, on one awful night, you told me Tindr would not find his wife in a hall," she remembered aloud.

"And you were right," she went on. "Šeará is not a woman of any hall. Nai, she is akin to a woodland creature, like Tindr herself. The man she loves. The man she wants."

Sidroc stretched his arm out around his shield-maiden's waist. "I did not know then how his tale would end," he agreed, "only that the Gods were saving a special woman to be his."

They neared their front door, over which he had carved his bind-rune during their first days there.

"Just as Freyja saved you to be mine," he went on. He smiled down at her.

"You wear your red gown," he observed next. "That which you wore our first night here. I have sat next to you all through the feast, watching you in it, wanting to take it off you. In a moment we will walk into the treasure room, and I need wait no longer."

Tindr walked alone in the woods. The first snow had yet to fall, but the leafy trees were now bare against the deep green of dark pines and firs. He had taken many stags this season, and the smokehouse at his mother's was full of their haunches. He was not hunting today; his bow and quiver hung at home, untouched. He had awakened and kissed Deer as she lay curled next him under the furred skin her father had given them. Then he made his way into the trees, called into the woods just the same.

He walked slowly, for the pleasure of seeing his woods revealed to his sharp eyes. Rivulets of water still ran; no frost had yet locked them into ice. Ferns lay limp but still showed the curling openwork of their leaves, and the green mosses and yellow lichens lent vivid splashes of colour to a brown landscape.

He thought of Deer, and the tender warmth of her body as he had arisen. He and Deer had built a small house of wood planks on stone, built it with the help of Scar and Ragnfast and Bright Hair. It was a fine house, filled with the hides of stags he had taken, and down cushions Bright Hair and Nenna had made them.

He went each day to Scar's hall and cared for the beasts there, and filled its kitchen yard stores with meat just as he did for Nenna, and for Deer and himself. Most days Deer came with him to the hall. The little ones crowded round her, and she had sewn them each a set of hide leggings and tunic as she wore. He saw how they laughed and spoke to her, and how they made her laugh.

Bright Hair and Nenna spoke to her too every day, and now Deer spoke back to them.

One other thing had changed. All signed for him now using the name Deer had given him. He was no longer known by a touch at the ear, to mean his deafness. When others gestured to him about himself they pointed to their eyes, the way Deer did. She tried to tell him his eyes were those of a certain and powerful beast. It did not live on the island, and Bright Hair had understood Deer. Bright Hair knew this beast, and made a drawing of it for him to see. It was like a dog, but with a thick furred coat. Deer had renamed him.

He thought of these good things as he walked. The weak Sun was rising higher in the sky, and he would turn back soon. Deer had been sleepy these past few days, and might still be under the skin Fur Man had given them.

He thought of the sweetness of her sleeping, how he had looked at her in the dim light of dawn. His heart had swelled within his chest, she so filled it. He wondered what more could make him happier, or more complete.

He came to a place he knew, a great fallen tree trunk, its loosened bark covered with lichen. Beads of dew sparkled in a forgotten spider web hanging from one end of the trunk. He recalled why he knew it: The white hind had shown herself here, one Winter day, the Lady in her guise as a deer. He sat down upon the trunk, as he had then.

He lowered his eyes to the forest floor, and drew breath in the coolness of the moist air. As he raised his eyes he saw a flash of white. It was Her, the white hind. She stepped before him from out of a clump of hazels, turned and looked his way. But this time she had a white fawn at her side.

Here ends the tale of Tindr.

THE WHEEL OF THE YEAR

Candlemas – 2 February

St Gregory's Day – 12 March

St Cuthbert's Day – The Spring Equinox, about 21 March

High Summer or Mid-Summer Day – 24 June

Sts Peter and Paul – 29 June

Hlafmesse (Lammas) – 1 August

St Mary's Day – 15 August

St Matthews' Day – The Fall Equinox,
about 21 September

All Saints – 1 November

The month of Blót – November; the time of Offering

Martinmas (St Martin's) – 11 November

Winter's Nights – the Norse end of the year rituals,
ruled by women, marked by feasting and ceremony

ANGLO-SAXON PLACE NAMES,

WITH MODERN EQUIVALENTS

Æscesdun = Ashdown

Æthelinga = Athelney

Basingas = Basing

Caeginesham = Keynsham

Cippenham = Chippenham

Cirenceaster = Cirencester

Defenas = Devon

Englafeld = Englefield

Ethandun = Edington

Exanceaster = Exeter

Glastunburh = Glastonbury

Hamtunscir = Hampshire

Hreopedun = Repton

Jorvik (Danish name for Eoforwic) = York

Legaceaster = Chester

Limenemutha = Lymington in Hampshire

Lindisse = Lindsey

Lundenwic = London

Meredune = Marton

Sceaftesburh = Shaftesbury

Snotingaham = Nottingham

Sumorsaet = Somerset

Swanawic = Swanage

Wedmor = Wedmore

Witanceaster (where the Witan, the King's
advisors, met) = Winchester

Frankland = France

Haithabu = Hedeby

Land of the Svear = Sweden

Aros = Aarhus, Denmark

GLOSSARY OF TERMS

brewster: the female form of brewer (and, interestingly enough, the female form of baker is baxter . . . so many common names are rooted in professions and trades . . .)

browis: a cereal-based stew, often made with fowl or pork.

chaff: the husks of grain after being separated from the usable kernel.

cooper: a maker of casks and barrels.

cresset: stone, bronze, or iron lamp fitted with a wick that burnt oil.

dísir: female household spirits, celebrated at Winter's Nights feasts.

ealdorman: a nobleman with jurisdiction over given lands; the rank was generally appointed by the King and not necessarily inherited from generation to generation. The modern derivative *alderman* in no way conveys the esteem and power of the Anglo-Saxon term.

fulltrúi: the Norse deity patron that one felt called to dedicate oneself to.

fylgja: a Norse guardian spirit, always female, unique to each family.

hackle: the splitting and combing of fibres of flax or hemp with opposing brush-like tools.

hamingja: the Norse "luck-spirit" which each person is born with.

joik: (also, yoik) A chant-like Sámi song, evoking the essence and spirituality of a person, animal, or landscape element, and unique to each recipient.

Máttaráhkká: The Sámi mother Goddess, creator of human bodies, who lives under the floor boards of Sámi dwellings. She is the mother of Sáráhkká, patron of female fetuses, menstruating women, and those in childbirth, whose domain was under the hearth fire; Juksáhká, guardian of male fetuses; and Uksáhkká, patron of children. These last two Goddesses lived by a door.

nålbinding: a form of early knitting or crochet, using one's thumb and threaded needle to form interlocking loops.

rauk: the striking sea – and wind-formed limestone towers on the coast of Gotland; the one on the cover of Book Four, *The Hall of Tyr* is at Fårö, Gotland.

seax: the angle-bladed dagger which gave its name to the Saxons; all freemen carried one.

scop: ("shope") a poet, saga-teller, or bard, responsible not only for entertainment but seen as a collective cultural historian. A talented scop would be greatly valued by his lord and receive land, gold and silver jewellery, costly clothing and other riches as his reward.

skep: a bee hive formed of coils of plaited straw, built up into a conical shape.

skirrets: a sweet root vegetable similar to carrots, but cream-coloured, and having several fingers on each plant.

skogkatt: "forest cat"; the ancestor of the modern Norwegian Forest Cat, known for its large size, climbing ability, and thick and water-shedding coat.

skogsrå: "Lady of the Forest"; a womanly wood spirit who protected woodland animals, and yet guided hunters she favoured.

strakes: overlapping wooden planks, running horizontally, making up a ship's hull.

thegn: ("thane") a freeborn warrior-retainer of a lord; thegns were housed, fed and armed in exchange for complete fidelity to their sworn lord. Booty won in battle by a thegn was generally offered to their lord, and in return the lord was expected to bestow handsome gifts of arms, horses, arm-rings, and so on to his best champions.

wadmal: the Norse name for the coarse and durable woven woollen fabric that was a chief export in the Viking age.

verjuice: "green juice"; an acidic juice from unripe grapes or crabapples, much used as we would vinegar.

wither: the highest point at the top of the shoulder of a horse or deer, marked by a projecting knob.

withy: a willow or willow wand; withy-man: a figure woven from such wands.

wool-wax: (also wool-oil, wool-fat) All earlier names for lanolin. Lanolin was extracted from sheep's wool by boiling washed wool in water. When the pan was left to cool, a milky white grease would be floating on top – the sheep's waterproofing. The globules were further refined by squeezing them through linen cloths. Lanolin was invaluable as a simple remedy for chapped and roughened skin. Blended with powdered or crushed herbs, it served as a medicinal salve.

ACKNOWLEDGMENTS

Great thanks to my wonderful First Readers for *Tindr*: Carol Bray, C.C., Breila Cicero, Suzanne Dixon-Sheppard (head wrangler), Kellie Jordan, Jennifer Joyce, Kim Komaromy, Nancy Langford, "Flashlight Barb" Martins, Favira Rahman, Violet Reynolds, Ellen Rudd, and Jennifer Stetson. Your feedback and encouragement made this a richer book, and I am indeed grateful for your continuing loyalty to my work.

To Kimberly Gerber Spina, my California Goddess of Abundance, giver of Light and every needful form of sustenance: You are the bow string to my arrow, and have made strong my wrist.

FREE CIRCLE OF CERIDWEN COOKERY BOOK(LET)

You've read the books – now enjoy the food! Your free Circle of Ceridwen Cookery Book(let) is waiting for you at octavia.net.

Ten easy, delicious, and authentic recipes from the Saga, including Barley Browis, Roast Fowl, Baked Apples, Oat Griddle Cakes, Lavender – scented Pudding, and of course – Honey Cakes. Charmingly illustrated with medieval woodcuts and packed with fascinating facts about Anglo-Saxon and Viking cookery. Free when you join the Circle, my mailing list. Be the first to know of new novels, have the opportunity to become a First Reader, and more. Get your Cookery Book(let) now and get cooking!

ABOUT THE AUTHOR

Octavia Randolph has long been fascinated with the development, dominance, and decline of the Anglo-Saxon peoples. The path of her research has included disciplines as varied as the study of Anglo-Saxon and Norse runes, and learning to spin with a drop spindle. Her interests have led to extensive on-site research in England, Denmark, Sweden, and Gotland. In addition to the Circle Saga, she is the author of the novella *The Tale of Melkorka*, taken from the Icelandic Sagas; the novella *Ride*, a retelling of the story of Lady Godiva, first published in Narrative Magazine; and *Light, Descending*, a biographical novel about the great John Ruskin. She has been awarded Artistic Fellowships at the Ingmar Bergman Estate on Fårö, Sweden; MacDowell Colony; Ledig House International; and Byrdcliffe.

She answers all fan mail and loves to stay in touch with her readers. Join her mailing list and read more on Anglo-Saxon and Viking life at www.octavia.net.

Made in the USA
Middletown, DE
28 October 2024

63372936R00286